Escape

Haven Series: Book One

Tracy Myhre

NBD
PRESS

First Edition

Published 2024

Tracy Myhre, author.
NBD Press
Suite 146
3080 - 11666 Steveston Hwy
Richmond, British Columbia
V7A 5J3
Canada

Title: Escape

ISBN: 978-1-7380623-0-0 (Paperback)
ISBN: 978-1 -7380623-1-7 (Ebook)

Editing by The Open Book Editor
Cover Design by Dissect Designs
Book Formatting by The Open Book Editor
Book Description by Sheppard Edits

To Julia, my number one fan and cheerleader.

The one who listened to my stories, acted them out, and encouraged me to write.

Love you...

CONTENTS

Author's Note

This story takes place in Spokane, Washington and across Idaho. For the sake of the story, I have altered some details of the landscape and taken a few liberties with an actual town. Thank you in advance for understanding an author's creative license.

Maps

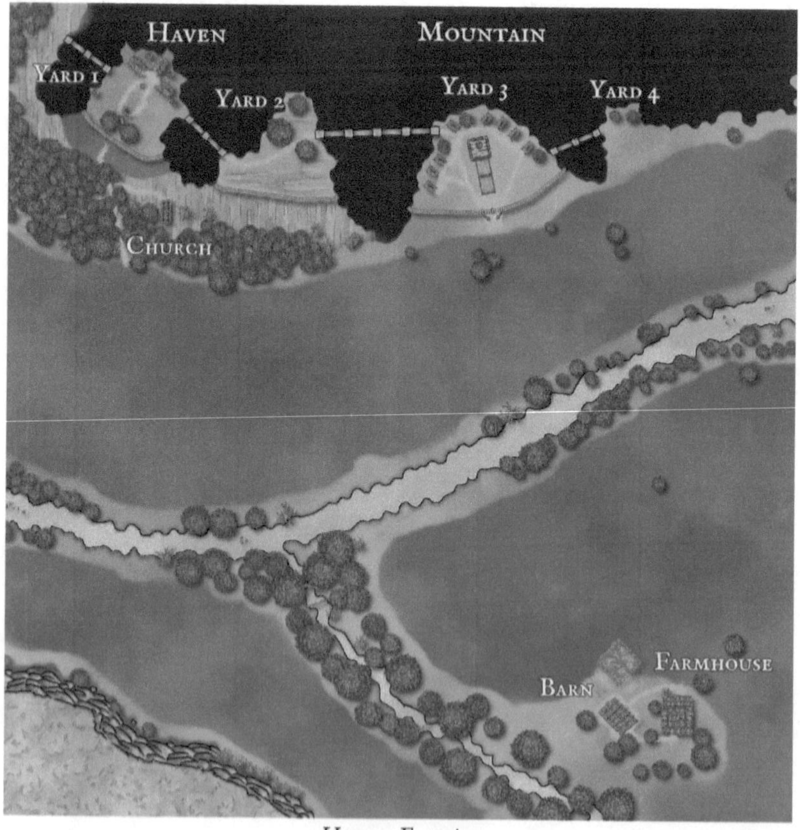

Haven: Exterior

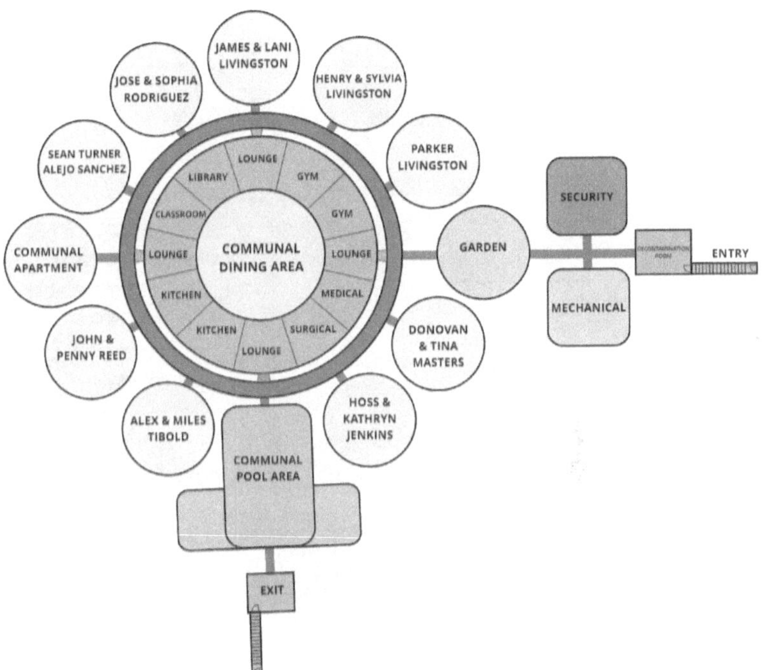

Haven: Interior

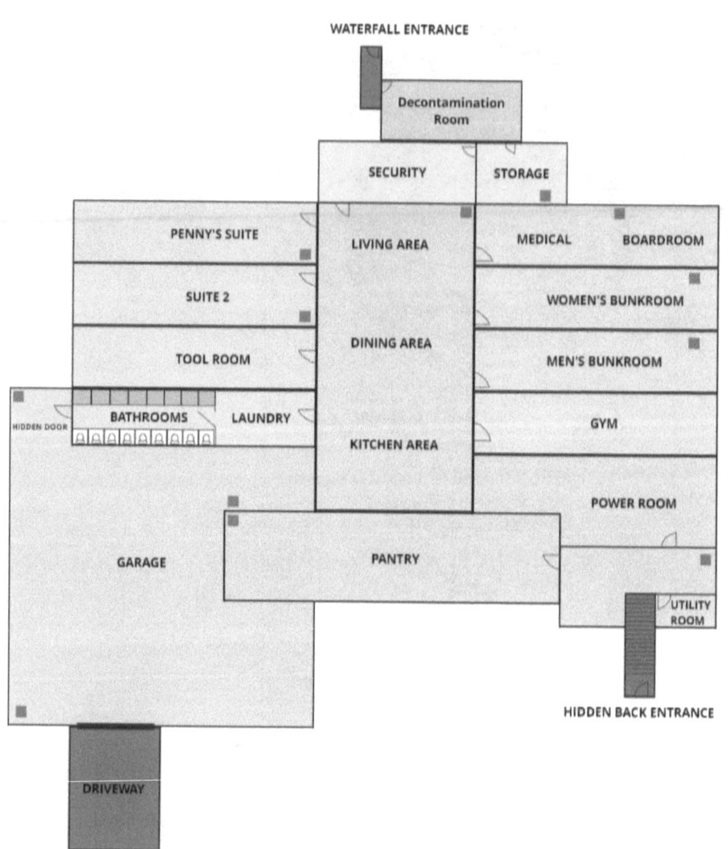

Reed: Interior

FAMILY TREES

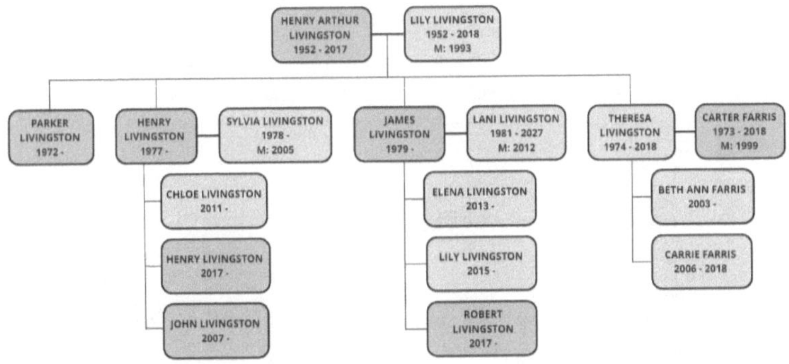

Livingston Family

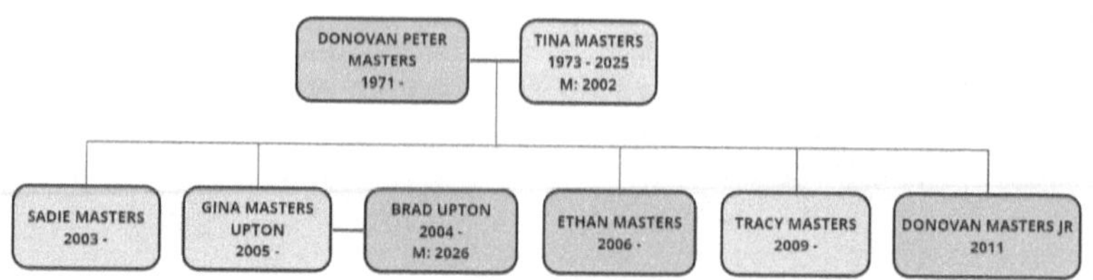

Masters Family

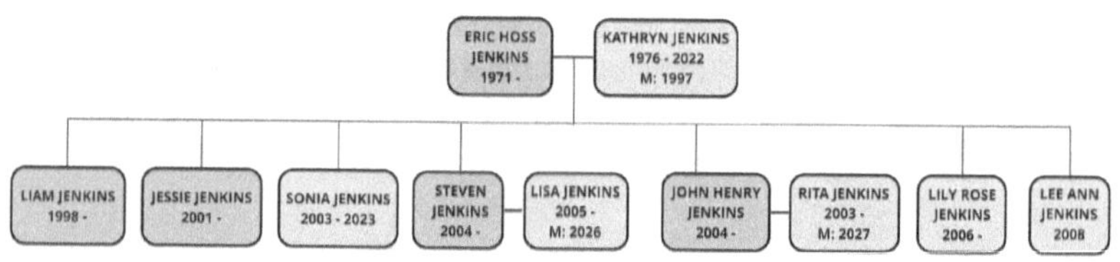

Jenkins Family

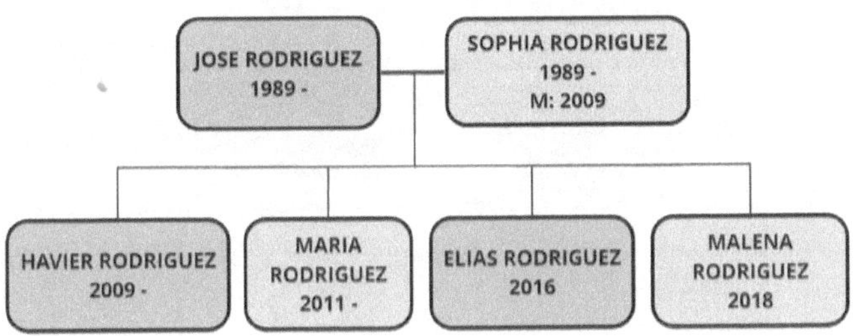

Rodriguez Family

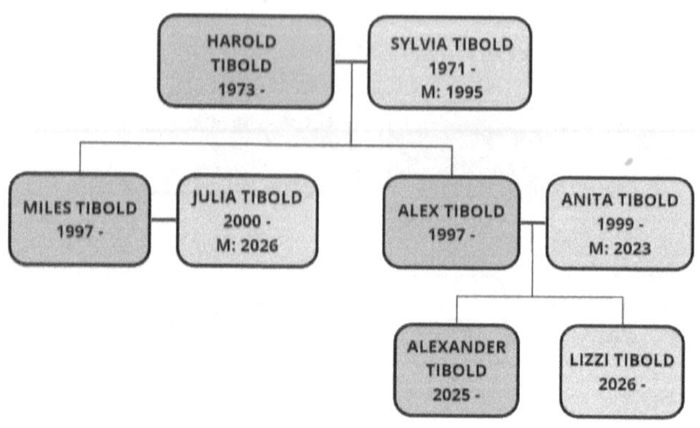

Tibold Family

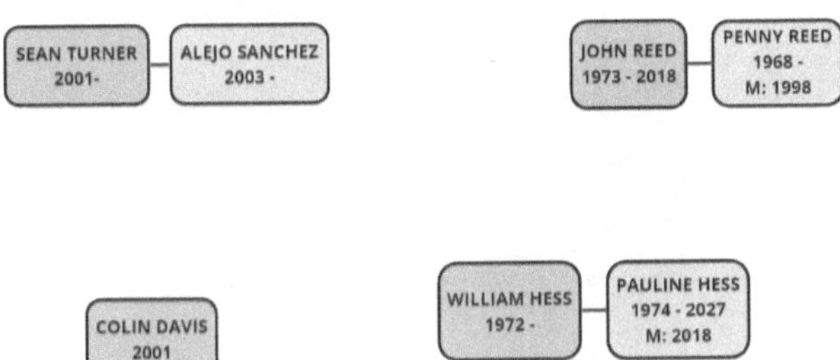

Reed, Hess, Turner & Davis Families

[1] **Haven:**

A place of safety: Refuge.

A place offering favorable opportunities or conditions.

---

1. *Merriam-Webster.com Dictionary*, s.v. "haven," accessed March 8, 2024, https://www.merriam-webster.com/dictionary/haven.

CHAPTER 1
May 20, 2027

Beth hustles down the street, her heart pounding erratically, and her cross-body bag clenched between white knuckles. Her hooded coat flaps wildly in the biting wind, threatening to sweep her away. *How could I be so stupid?* The words echo in her mind, intensifying the knot of anxiety tightening in her chest.

Because you think you know everything.

The repugnant voice taunts Beth, amplifying her self-doubt to unbearable levels. She has to get to the diner, see something familiar, and sever the haunting vision she knows will follow. This is bad. She quickens her pace, passing a corner store, then a gas station. Each step echoes with the rapid drumbeat of her racing heart.

Her memory sucks her back in.

No...

Her dad's spicy aftershave floats into the back of their car. His deep, unintelligible words are directed at her mother in the front as he drives. The headlights of oncoming cars illuminate them, then taper off in waves.

No...

Beth swats her sister's head, then laughs as Carrie pierces her with an ineffectual death stare. Her sister bares her teeth and wails.

No...

Light fluctuates. Her father's frame twists in the driver's seat, his hands gripping the wheel tightly. His extended finger shoots anger and disappointment her way, causing her stomach to churn.

A familiar ringtone yanks her out of the memory. In her haste to answer, she stumbles. *Thank God!* Determined not to break stride, she reads *Haven* on the display of her cell. They never let her birthday go but, this time, they get a pass. She swipes the screen.

"Hello!" Her voice trembles with the residue of fear, but the connection to the caller on the other end provides a glimmer of relief amid the storm of her emotions.

"How you doing, Chickie?" Not keen on starting the conversation with a greeting, Parker gets straight to the point. The familiar moniker gives her the space to refocus.

"Fine." *I miss you.*

Her uncle took up the daunting task of raising her; then, a teenage girl with "issues." He wasn't prepared, but like a dutiful Marine, he jumped in anyway. He assigned her a nickname because that's what Marines do: Little Chickie. Cute but accurate. He towers above her five-foot-five frame so, to him, she is little. "Now I'm worried," he says.

Beth can feel her determination faltering, but she rallies. "Don't be. I'll get through this day like any other."

Every year, on this day, her adopted badass motherfucker (BAMF) dads, as she dubs them, worry about her. In the past, she tolerated the hovering and multiple phone calls, but this year is different. Except for Jose, they are all up at the farm they call Haven.

"Is it just any other day, though?" he asks.

It's never a perfect day for her. She'd hoped this year would be different.

The word *Parker's* in white, flourished handwriting scrawled across a red awning catches her eye up ahead. Her uncle's diner. Working as a dishwasher limits her spending, but she earns enough to keep herself fed and clothed. It's taken her a while to get to this point in her life, so she doesn't complain about a repetitive job where the voices disappear, and she can, too. *One more block.*

"Went up to sis's grave this morning," Parker says, "said some words." She doesn't respond. "Maybe you should take the day off if you're feeling nervous?"

Beth stops mid-step. Her pulse quickens. A single word reverberates through her mind like that of a siren: Run. Her feet obey. On the road, facing her, an ambulance approaches. Picking up speed, she declares, a little too loudly and proudly, "Doc says do one thing that scares me, so I'm walking to work!"

"You left the apartment?" He sounds panicked. "Where's Alejo?"

She ignored Alejo's call earlier. Her family and friends drive her to work or walk short distances with her, ensuring she's never alone between her safe zones. Until today. Beth senses her uncle shifting from panic to hysteria, or perhaps she's projecting her own fears. "I didn't ask. I'm branching out."

She wants to do things her way. Moving out changed her life, but it isn't enough. Beth is missing something; she can feel it in her bones, even if she can't put a finger on what *it* is.

The ambulance creeps closer. *Please, don't go off.*

Beth understands Parker enough to know he's rubbing his head and kicking himself for heading to Haven without her. She wishes he could forgive himself. She was fifteen when she tried to end her life. It wasn't his fault; it was hers.

He struggles to sound assured when he says, "Glad to hear you're moving forward, then."

The ambulance passes. Beth's fear amplifies, and she breaks into a sprint, her breaths coming in panicked gasps.

"Hoss says next you'll be jumping out of airplanes and shit."

Beth leaps through the diner's door with her heart pounding in her chest. The shrill ding of a bell goes off, jolting her further. The comforting scent of leather mixes with the dark aroma of brewing coffee to envelop her as she stumbles in, straightens herself, and crosses a charming, colorful, modern diner. On the wall above the kitchen hatch, a sign glows. Her uncle's favorite words glow in red neon: *Time to rock 'n' roll.* She shoots down the length of the chrome counter, waves to Sophia, who's setting up for the day, and hustles toward the kitchen.

With an apron strapped around her waist, Sophia flashes a kind-hearted smile and waves in return. Beth's good at hiding her inner turmoil; plenty of practice.

"You at the diner?" Parker asks.

"Yeah." Beth moves through the creaking kitchen swing door and does the same routine with Sophia's husband, Jose, as she passes by. He was a culinary specialist in the Navy. A year after his exit, he became one of Parker's partners in the diner and the chief cook.

"Just called to say happy birthday. You okay?" Parker asks, the question laced with concern.

They ignore her pleas to forget her birthday every year, so she endures it with gritted teeth. "Yup, thanks."

Beth covers her mouth, concealing labored breaths, and steps into a tiny office with a heavy desk and a beat-up filing cabinet. The kitchen noise abruptly diminishes as she closes the door. She deposits her bag and plunks down on an uncomfortable, cold, metal chair, then concentrates on slowing her breathing. The tension leaves Beth as a sense of accomplishment rushes through her. *I'm safe.*

"Heard Colin's coming up Monday. Things change between you two?"

Ever the overzealous friend, Alejo signed her up for tango lessons without asking. Sneaky devil. The studio paired her with Colin, who was experienced but patient with her. Alejo had a good idea for once, but she keeps that thought to herself or she'll never hear the end of it. Dancing opened her up and silenced the negative thoughts in her head. This spurred her on to dance more and more, and in doing so, she gained experience and a superb partner. "Still friends, Uncle."

She never thought about dating; at least, not until Colin asked for one. For nine years, she's struggled to overcome her fears, take control of her life, and rediscover the person she lost in the accident. After moving out a year ago and getting a job, dating seems like the next logical step, but after meeting Colin, she's not so sure.

Parker raises his voice and says, "No kidding! Cause for celebration, then!"

Static pierces Beth's ear. She yanks the phone away as a distressed voice comes through. "Hell no, girl! You and Colin?!"

Beth hits the speaker and places the phone on the desk. Her uncle's best friend and brother-in-arms, Eric, dislikes Colin for mysterious reasons. Everyone calls Eric by his nickname, Hoss. Once her BAMF dads found out about Colin through Alejo, they showed up at the dance studio one mortifying night and grilled him. Hoss remains the only holdout on that front.

She dispels that notion quickly and says, "No!"

In the background, Parker bursts into laughter. She rises from her chair and scrutinizes her reflection in the wall mirror. Her anxiety eases as a smile returns to her lips.

Hoss joins in the merriment, struggling to contain himself. "Je-sus, Parker, my heart can't take it." In the very next breath, he hurls a question at her. "When you gonna get a boyfriend?"

Does the man never stop to breathe? When he delivers this kind of query, she fires off one of her own to unbalance him, and she's learned something juicy. "When are you going to ask her out?" Hoss has a crush on Penny but hesitates to make a move out of respect for her deceased husband. Beth corrals her long, damp brown hair into a messy bun with a clip. *No one cares what I look like.*

His soft chuckling comes through the phone line, a warm and comforting sound. "Touché, girl. Happy birthday by the by. Glad you're finally comin' up."

Doubt creeps in, and her smile drops in the mirror. "I don't know if I can."

"Stop lookin' for the rain, girl. You deserve to be happy. If you don't come up, I'm comin' down and kidnappin' you myself."

She rolls her eyes, unable to suppress a grin at his suggestion.

"I'm done. Hold your knickers," Hoss says to someone in the background before returning his attention to her. "Will wants on."

"Hey, Chickie. How you holding up?" There is a tenderness in William's soft-spoken tone.

"I should ask you that." He recently lost his wife, Pauline, to cancer, and their decision to spend her last year at Haven was a bittersweet one. Watching her waste away must have been heart-wrenching.

"Well, I'm glad I had the time I had. Good deflect." He knew her too well.

"I'm improving. I took the call this time, didn't I?"

William's hearty laughter comes through. "Yeah, that's a plus. Hey, listen. I know it's going to be tough coming up here, but this is something you need to do. It's time."

"Is it?" Beth values his opinion above the others. Maybe he's right.

"The last time you were here wasn't so good. We need to change that."

Her family's funeral day is a painful memory that still haunts her. While everyone else attended that day, William took Beth inside Haven as she'd had a panic attack.

"We have a new gate and walls. Wait till you see the atrium. We're actually keeping plants alive." William says, interrupting her thoughts.

Her lips curve up. "I don't believe you." The crops failed last year, but that didn't deter them from planning afresh.

"Come up and see for yourself," he says, daring her to take the leap.

She sees through the ruse, but curiosity nags at her. What they were building was inspiring, even if they didn't end up using Haven for its originally intended purpose. If she could just conquer her anxiety and do one thing...

"Besides," he continues, "I haven't seen you in a year. You like torturing an old man? I'm dying here without you."

She grins. "You're not dying, but I'll come up."

CHAPTER 2

Under the clang of a bell, Ryker ambles in with slumped shoulders. He scowls at the offending object and scans the diner for an empty booth against the far wall. No luck. He counts six booths, four tables, and seven stools. The jukebox, below neon signs, is playing a melancholy tune about a lost love. It's modern enough, yet still has that fifties vibe.

Ryker's nervous, having his back to the door. *Man up, Kensington, you're being paranoid.* There's a mirror, so he adapts, crosses the diner, and wanders up to a counter stool close to the kitchen hatch. He's not sure who's staring back at him in the reflection and rubs a day's worth of stubble. He considers himself fit enough to be in public and loosens the knot on his tie. Last he checked, he is six feet tall, and from what his brother told him, he has his father's dark features. *It's been twelve years, Mal. Where are you?*

Two weeks and eight interviews, but still no job. Not even a nibble. This shouldn't surprise him. Other than farming, Ryker's served since he was old enough to enlist. Everything feels off today. Perhaps he needs to shift tactics or... He peers around and sniffs his underarms. *Nope, smells fine.*

After his three o'clock interview, Ryker wandered up Sprague and perused the tiny mom-and-pop shops, needing a change of scenery. The striking red awning of the diner piqued his interest, so he thought he'd check it out. Besides, Ryker was hungry.

Two men jeer at a passing server from a nearby booth as a Hispanic waitress waits on patrons behind the counter. Some booths clear out. She waves them out as she taps a computer screen and calls through the kitchen hatch. "Beth, hon, you're up!"

Ryker takes in the older woman as she hauls up plates from the serving counter, deposits them in front of two suits at the other end, and laughs at their jokes. *Efficient. Attentive, motherly.* On her return, she beams at the cook through the hatch. Ryker notes her wedding ring, respects the mad passion that crackles in the air between them, and sighs.

Ryker thirsts for the same. Love. Something he'd like to resolve, single to...not single. He's served so long, he's never had a decent relationship, and swore when he got out, he'd search for someone. He'd have to find a woman to date first, though.

The waitress scoops up the coffeepot, establishes eye contact, and rattles it. Elvis's voice fills the room. Ryker shoots a tired smile in response. The problem is, he doesn't know what he wants. He can't rely on his past flings as a guide. They were a means to an end. The sex was entertaining, but he wants—

A sudden bang goes off to his right. Ryker's head snaps sharply toward the kitchen door, his shoulders tense and hands clench, ready for anything. His mouth goes dry, heat rushes into Ryker's face, and his heart pounds in his ears as the noise in the diner fades.

Wow!

A curvy, younger woman in a rubber apron wanders out, her brown hair disheveled, face sweaty, with an empty bucket between her gloved hands. Ryker fixates on this beauty with downcast eyes as she moves behind the counter, seemingly blind to him or anyone else. She hauls her bucket along on autopilot, clears soiled dishes, switches buckets, and moves to the next table. He notices his mouth is open, clamps it shut, and swallows, but his embarrassment isn't enough to overcome his desire to watch her move through the diner.

She focuses on her task and clears plates of a recently vacated booth on one knee, her leg extended into the aisle. Ryker tilts his head, letting his eyes drift down that lovely leg. To his surprise, butterflies fly up the back of her calf in beautiful hues. Transformation. *Definitely a leg man.*

Two men in an adjacent booth try to catch her eye, but she ignores them. *Of course, who wouldn't hound a woman like her? She's gorgeous.* Elvis belts out another line about love.

A rich voice breaks through Ryker's focus. "What's your pleasure today, hon?"

Her.

Ryker swivels his head forward to find the same waitress from before. As she pours his coffee into a mug, he takes the chance to glance at her name badge: *Sophia.* "Apple pie...with ice cream, please...ma'am." He washes his face with a hand. *Christ! I'm surprised I could put two words together.*

Grinning from ear to ear, Sophia winks. "Coming right up."

Ryker's fingers slide into the handle of the coffee mug. His gaze moves back to the woman in the gloves. He marvels at the light wisps of hair that caress her rosy cheeks and the way she rubs her lips together when tucking dirty dishes into her bucket. *Wonder if there's a ring under those gloves. If there isn't, there should be.*

One man in the booth curses at her. Her facial muscles tense. Ryker's focus shifts. He places the mug down, swings out, and plants both feet firmly.

She hoists her awkward burden and angles to flee. The same man seizes her arm. The bucket crashes. All eyes turn.

In one fluid motion, Ryker launches forward, forces the guy's hand off her, and curves the man's pinkie in the air. Pain registers in the man's twitchy eyes as desperate moans escape his squirming lips.

"Beth!"

Beth. Sweet and wholesome images run through his mind, but her tattoo says spicy, and he likes spicy. The kitchen door swings on its hinges, and Ryker tracks the steps of the approaching cook. From his wide stance and unblinking stare, it's clear he's seen what happened and is backing Ryker up. It feels right, having a man at his back. "You should pay up and leave," Ryker says in a low, menacing tone.

The men throw bills and scurry out. *Good riddance.*

Ryker straightens up as soon as the threat is gone, pivots, and surveys his surroundings with heightened vigilance. Sophia positions herself protectively behind Beth, her concern clear. Ryker gives Beth a once-over and notices the way she holds her arm at the elbow, her eyes downcast. He reaches out, a gentle touch of his fingers to her shoulder. "Hey. You okay?" Up close, he appreciates her pretty freckles and notes the rapid pulse in her neck. *Wonder what color her eyes are?*

Beth responds with a nod, but Ryker feels it's a lie. He notes the scar over her left temple. *There's a story there.* Sensing Beth's distress, the cook gently massages her arms and encourages her to take a break. *Not family, but close.* With gratitude in his eyes, the cook turns to Ryker and extends his hand. "Jose. Thanks for having her back."

Ryker hesitates, then faces him. "Anytime. Ryker." He reaches out to grip Jose's hand.

Jose gestures at the waitress. "This is my wife, Sophia."

Ryker's smile deepens as he shakes her hand and scrambles to think of a way to get Beth to talk to him. *Apple pie?* "Beth, do you like ice cream?" He notes the bewildered glance Jose and Sophia exchange and the fact that the jukebox is between songs.

Beth's eyes come up.

Christ! Everything ceases to exist, except her. Stupefied, Ryker's lost in olive-green eyes; the tension and irritation from earlier dissipates, replaced with a different tightness; one he hasn't felt in a long time. He wants more of it. Ryker struggles to remain steadfast, wanting to reach out and touch her again. He needs to rein these feelings in.

I'm in trouble.

Chapter 3

Holy crap!

Beth freezes; her lips part. The anger she was repressing dissipates, replaced with... She's not sure what the feeling is. She expected... She's not sure what she expected. The man in front of her is, well, hot as fucking hell comes to mind. He towers over her in a white, starched, button-down dress shirt, the first two buttons undone. His dark chest hair matches the five o'clock shadow covering his clenched jaw.

There's a strong desire in her to be closer to him, but she resists. Beth formulates quickly that behind his rugged, dark looks, he's a bad boy, but the suit feels out of place. Whatever is happening, Beth finds him alluring. The man's brown eyes scour Beth's curvy frame, causing her to blush. He looks like the type that doesn't miss much. He dealt with those men quickly.

"Will you have pie and ice cream with me? My treat."

Beth's brain stumbles. "No. I mean...I'm good. I—" *Jesus, get a hold of yourself.*

Jose interrupts. "Coming right up!"

Traitor! Her anxious eyes bore into Jose's back as he returns to the kitchen. The echo of his soft laughter fills the air. Her attractive rescuer hides a smirk by rubbing his nose. *I'm in trouble.*

She drops to her knees to gather the broken plates...and her thoughts. *I can't have pie with a total stranger. A delicious-looking stranger, but still.* Beth smooths her grimy apron with her gloved hands. *God, I'm a wreck!*

He and Sophia bend down to help. Beth tries not to notice how strong his hands are or the fragrant essence of his spicy cologne. *Stop liking it.* They pick up the same plate. She unhands it quickly, letting him have the win. He makes eye contact and, for a sweet moment, he lets loose a smile that she'd kill to see more of. *Stop looking!*

Beth reaches for the bucket, but Sophia swiftly plucks it up and out of her reach. Beth meets Sophia's unapologetic gaze. She gestures toward the closest booth. "Sit, hon, Jose'll bring the pie out."

As Beth rises, alarm spreads across her face, pleading with Sophia not to leave her.

Bucket secure on her hip, Sophia holds her hand out. "I'll take your apron."

Beth hesitates. *Is this happening? I can't...* "I'm not finished in the back, but if you're sure." She can't believe those words came out of her crazy mouth. Her fingers think differently, untying the apron before handing it over.

"I'm sure, hon. Gloves?"

Beth tears them off, lays them across the bucket, slides into the booth, and smooths her hair. Her face flushes with heat as he takes a seat across from her, his eyes focused intently on her hands. He throws her another alluring smile, which draws her to his mouth and scrambles her brain. *God, what was his name again?* "You have quick reflexes...Ryker." His name on her lips sounds unfamiliar but appealing. *Bet his kisses are... Stop!*

He leans in and cologne floods her senses as he whispers, "My hidden super-power... Beth."

His husky voice invokes a warm blush, and she stifles a moan. The heat in his eyes compels her legs to tighten. Good grief. Parts of her are dancing. Ryker's eyes stay with her like she's the only one in the diner when Jose returns and lays two wedges of pie with perfect scoops of vanilla ice cream.

Beth doesn't know where to look under such scrutiny. The love in Colin's eyes pains her, but the hunger in Ryker's stare elicits impure thoughts. Things she wants to do but has never done. She likes it, desires it even. She shouldn't.

Jose places spoons on the table and a steaming mug of coffee in front of Ryker. "So, what do you do for work?"

To her disappointment, Ryker cuts their connection to look up at Jose. *Here it comes.* She drags a spoon across the table. Her head dips, and she attempts to take an avid interest in her pie.

"Jose!" Sophia yells from the kitchen door. "Leave them!"

Beth shaves a generous portion of ice cream and transfers the icy treat to her mouth.

Jose turns and says, *"Voy, mi vida."*

Ryker steals a glance at Beth during the exchange, then peers up again at Jose. "I'm a Marine."

Oh, crap. She almost says it out loud as the chilly ice cream forces her mouth to pop open. Her BAMF dads would love it if she went out with a Marine. It explains his air of confidence and how he dealt with those men so efficiently.

"No shit!" Jose animates and points at himself. "Navy. Beth's uncle and I own this place. Active?"

She steals a shy peek and slides a spoonful of pie in to hide her growing smile.

"I got out last month. Trying to lock down employment." He glances back at Beth, and on cue, she blushes.

"What kind?" Jose continues.

Ryker tugs on his collar. "Been in the service so long, I'm just applying to see what sticks."

Beth loves the way he glances over to check up on her as he speaks to Jose. Observant, like all the men in her life are. She admires the suit and tie but thinks he's uncomfortable by the way he tugs on his collar. *Definitely not an officer.*

"If a job doesn't stick, swing by, and we'll see if we can help you out," Jose says, offering a genuine smile.

Ryker's eyebrows lift. "Thanks."

He's not used to unsolicited support from a stranger, even a military brother. Interesting.

Jose turns his attention to Beth and points two fingers from his eyes to hers. "Eat slow, don't snarf it down like you usually do, Chickie."

Busted.

He walks away whistling.

She gulps slowly. Nervous glances and grins begin as they dig into their pie, letting the silence grow between them. Beth's never felt this nervous before. Like a bee stirred up in a jar. *Is it hot in here?* She clamps her hands on her fidgeting legs and wills herself to relax. Beth appreciates the offer but she's not sure what to say to a handsome stranger. This is the disadvantage of not having a life: she has nothing to say.

They tumble over each other's words: Ryker, "I," and Beth, "You."

He shoots a nervous smile her way. "Sorry? You first."

"You from here?"

"Originally from Missoula. Living with my sis here 'til I land a job."

Beth's eyebrows draw together while recalling the last time she laid eyes on her sister. Carrie's big saucer eyes pleaded with her. Beth rubs her temple scar to shake the memory away.

Ryker tilts his head, trapping her in his stare. "You okay?"

She does an about-face, grins, and nods. *I don't deserve this.*

He washes the pie down with a healthy swallow of caffeine, raises an eye at the mug, and focuses back on Beth. "Raised on a farm. You?"

"City. All my uncles are Marines." Her face lights up. "They bought a farm." She's not sure why that slipped out, but she decides he's trustworthy enough.

He pushes the empty plate aside and spreads his arm across the back of the seat, giving her his absolute attention. "Yeah? Near here?"

"Idaho. North of Swindon, on the river."

"Remote. Which river?"

"Canyon. You know the area?"

"A little. Is it off the highway?"

"Yes. We either take the logging road north off Highway 90 or the Coil Trail from the south on foot."

"What compelled them to wanna buy a farm?" he asks with an air of repulsion.

Beth's curious to know why but doesn't want to pry. She pushes her empty plate forward, leans both arms on the table, and gives him the answer she's permitted to give. "They bought it for their retirement. They like to keep busy."

"That's demanding work. You need labor to run a farm."

She sits up straight. "My cousins and I are supporting them this year." She calls them that. They're not blood relatives but are close enough to be her family.

"Yeah?" He purses his lips into a smirk.

"We're traveling up there soon." *Maybe.* "Kinda like a family reunion."

"I'm new to Spokane." He raises his chin. "What do you do for fun?"

"Tango lessons." Her eyes swell as she bites her lower lip. *Did I just blurt that out?*

He zeros in on her mouth. "Wow, that's unique." Desirous eyes glide up to hers. "You have the legs for it. Love the tattoo, by the way."

Oh, gosh! She feels her cheeks redden before she can dip her head down. *I'm going to die now.*

"I'm a little rusty at this, but, ah, I was wondering, would you go on a date with me?"

I wish. She speaks into the table. "I don't date."

"Boyfriend?"

Colin comes to the forefront as Beth shifts. "No."

"Then why don't you date?"

I don't deserve one. "You ask a lot of questions." A stray hair escapes from behind her ear.

She follows Ryker's hand sliding across the table, but he backpedals and reaches up to scratch his head. *Was he going to touch me?* A thrill runs through her at the thought. What would it feel like if he touched her?

"The only way to learn what I'm up against...and how I'm going to get around it."

If he knew, he wouldn't want to date me.

Jose picks up their plates, and Beth and Ryker break eye contact. She poises to stand, but Jose blocks her with a gentle hand on her shoulder. "Sit. I'll wash up." He turns to Ryker. "Pie's on the house."

"Thanks, I can pay, though."

A friendly smile plays across Jose's face. "Nonsense, it's Beth's birthday today." And just like that, he drops the bomb before leaving again with a skip in his step. *No.* Beth's lips tighten, and her eyes close in defeat. *Please don't say it, please don't—*

"Happy Birthday."

She shifts and sighs.

"Don't like people knowing it's your birthday?"

"I don't like celebrating it."

He opens his mouth, closes it, then pouts. "I'm kinda sad you don't wanna date."

Without hesitation, she states, "I never said I didn't want to. I just don't."

"So, there's hope, then?" His lips curve upward, savoring some kind of victory.

Beth tucks her chin in, not able to hide a shy smile. If he bottled up that smirk, she'd be the first in line to buy it. But there's no hope. A piece of her wants to grant his wish, but in the end, he'll be better off without her.

She sneaks a peek. Something devilish sparkles in those brown depths. *Why does it feel like I've opened a can of worms?*

***

County Correctional Facility in Coeur d'Alene, Idaho.

"It's set?" The cold metal table shifts as Kaden's bulk lands unceremoniously. Black-ink rose vines, decorated with skulls, encircle his forearms. Gideon has seen enough of his friend to know the ink coils up each arm and past Kaden's shoulders to encompass his neck. So much beauty in his tattoos that once you're entranced, you're trapped between the thorns, unable to escape. Just like with women.

Gideon rubs his itchy beard as he sits idle and emotionless on a piece of prime real estate in a room of few tables, biding his time. Prisoners perch on a nearby tabletop, sizing Gideon up. The putrid stench of so many bodies cramped in the cell block bothers him, but he won't be here for long.

Gideon has grown the beard deliberately. First, it covers his pock-marked skin; second, it gives an impression he's not affable. Every advantage in this dismal place is useful.

"Yup." His eyes cut to Kaden, who appears relaxed, but his jaw muscles twitch, giving him away. He was a small-time thief when Gideon met him. Their mutual hatred for women and unquenchable desires anchored their relationship, while robbing banks became their shared passion. Kaden hates being isolated and wants out of this hellhole as much as he does. Kaden's not family, but he's loyal. Their crime spree lasted quite a while, but their luck ran dry, and now, they're awaiting a transfer back to Spokane to face charges of robbery in the first degree.

"How are they getting us out?"

Kaden's referring to Gideon's younger brother, Greg, and older brother Hunter. The pigs charged them both for being in the getaway car on that last heist, but the government couldn't pin anything else on them, so his brothers did their time and got out. The difference between armed robbery and just plain robbery is time, and the law will want Gideon to serve a lot of it. "Knowing my brothers, with lots of firepower."

Wendall's going to owe him for getting Hunter caught. That's what his older brother wanted. Wendall thinks he's smarter than all of them put together. *Maybe he is, maybe he isn't.* He's serving life imprisonment for first-degree murder up at Doleridge Maximum Security Prison. Not a simple place to vacate, so there he rots, much to Gideon's disappointment. He can't collect if Wendall's in prison.

CHAPTER 4

Looking stately and outright gorgeous in his designer jeans and T-shirt, Brad grasps the top of the door as Beth and Colin walk into his and Gina's apartment. He's a fashion model by trade and, despite his good looks, he's a generous man who loves Beth's best friend with a burning passion.

In a long-sleeved knit sweater and jeans, Gina walks up beside Brad, wearing a warm expression. "About time you two showed up." She steps into Beth's open arms. "Happy Birthday!"

Five inches shorter, Beth fits perfectly into Gina's embrace and, after crushing her friend's ribs, glares at her through Gina's long brunette hair, captivated by her gilded-brown eyes. Beth shoots a quick frown at her, telling Gina she could do without the teasing. Her friends would love nothing more than for Beth to find happiness with Colin. After all, what's not to like? He is clean-cut, has an impressive jawline, golden-blond hair, and a ton of confidence. *He knows they think of him as boyfriend material.* Plus, Colin's career as a heavy-duty equipment mechanic is solid, he keeps in tip-top shape with dancing and his other love, yoga.

He holds back a satisfied expression as he passes a bottle of wine into Brad's care. He leans in and kisses Gina's cheek while Beth hugs Brad shyly.

Colin asked her out on a date several times, and each time, she refused. She wasn't ready. Might never be. But Alejo caught wind of this and talked her into agreeing to go out with Colin once. More like ganged up on her, but Beth knows Alejo meant well.

Charting unknown waters scares her, but the date began well when he recommended a restaurant around the corner. They talked and laughed, and she admits the date was relaxing until the moment she'd dreaded materialized. The kiss. It mortified Beth to admit her innocence on the subject. He said it honored him to be her first. The kiss was pleasant, but awkward as hell on her part, although Colin must have enjoyed it enough because he'd asked for a second. Instead, Beth withdrew and relegated him to friend territory. *Nothing like crushing someone's dreams.* Beth had felt horrible, but she wasn't ready. His disappointment had been unmistakable, but with a terse nod, he'd respected her request to be friends.

That was a few weeks ago.

In that brief span of time, Colin has established himself as a good friend on the surface. Underneath, though, it is clear he still hopes she will change her mind, like her friends do. At Alejo's last dinner party, Sean let it slip they were heading to the farm. Colin picked up on it, much to her disappointment, and asked about the trip. She tried to steer the conversation away, but Alejo wouldn't let her. He suggested Colin come up with them, leaving her with one more reason she had to go.

Beth walks into the living room to a jubilant chorus of "surprise" as everyone jumps out from behind the furniture. Alejo had said they wouldn't make a big deal about it. Liar.

Alejo flicks his dark, blond-tipped hair as he slinks forward, rocking a pair of dark jeans with a pink frilly top, and squeezes her with an eager hug. "Open my present now!" He shoves a card into her hands, claps, and jumps up and down. "I can't stand it."

Beth leans back to regard his change of hair color. When they met, his shoulder-length black hair was purple-tipped. It was the day she moved into her new apartment. Her BAMF dads were forcing her leather couch into the elevator when Alejo strolled into the lobby, a handbag perched on his forearm, wearing a stylish pantsuit and yellow slingbacks, with a firm grip on his chai latte. They stopped their assault on her couch to gawk. Alejo, not hiding the fact he liked the attention, boldly turned to Hoss, who was closest. "Honey, you are hot, like bear-man hot. Which one of you wants to make my dreams come true?"

The men stared in uncomfortable silence, which brought a smile to Beth's lips.

Hoss, however, took it in stride. "That depends on what you got to offer."

Alejo's confident eyes slid to her, and she could have sworn he purred with excitement. "My coffee will knock your clothes off, hon." His brows lifted. "You in?"

And just like that, everyone visibly relaxed, and Hoss piped in, "Sure. Our Beth here's movin' in." He shoved her forward as an offering, and after the men got the couch upstairs and accepted coffee, they fled. From that day forward, Alejo wormed his way into her life, and they've become good friends.

Beth blinks the memory away. "Blond? Sean finally convinced you. I love it."

Alejo smiles, batting his eyes at the compliment. His half-Hispanic partner, Sean, dressed in a cozy flannel shirt, hugs an infatuated Alejo from behind. "You better open the card or he'll be hard to live with." As a forester by trade, flannel is Sean's go-to. He may root for the other team, but Beth loves his smooth, sensuous voice and the nice way his shirt hugs his chest.

She unfolds the flap of the envelope. Alejo, unable to contain his glee, shouts. "It's a couple's day at the spa for you and me!"

Alejo loves his spa days, especially when Beth's involved. Sometimes, he's like a scatterbrained child... Okay, most of the time, but that's what she likes about him. They just clicked from the start. She beams at him. "Awesome! Thank you, A."

"What did Colin get you?" Sean teases.

Colin slides his arm around her shoulders. "Dinner at Chez Robert."

Beth's smile tapers. She's still trying to close this particular Pandora's box. But the thought brings up Ryker's playful smile and a healthy dose of heat to her cheeks.

Hoss's son, John Henry, steps forward, hugging his petite, demure wife to his side. "Took Rita there for her birthday." He leans into Beth. "You'll love the snails."

Rita rolls her eyes. "Oh, stop, it was really romantic."

Beth chances a look at Colin. He stares back like a lovesick puppy.

Of course it is.

***

"I'm confused. You're not cousins?" Colin directs the question at Gina, who is on the couch, resting against her husband.

Colin's so new that he's not up on all the inner workings of her friends. He also thinks he's in with the group because her dads approved him, but he hasn't passed muster with her other "cousins" yet, or her uncle.

Remnants of birthday cake litter the coffee table among half-empty wine glasses. Gina's apartment exudes a cozy atmosphere; warm colors and lots of plants. Colorful birthday balloons decorate the walls along with other bright decorations.

Beth stares at the back of Colin's head, lounging at her feet, as he converses with everyone seated around them. He's chosen the floor instead of a chair to be closer to her, but Beth says nothing. It's something she needs to address, but not tonight. Gina catches her suppressing a smile. She probably thinks it's for Colin, but she'd be wrong. A certain Marine has taken over Beth's thoughts, sending tingles up her spine.

Gina points between herself and John Henry. "Our dads, Hoss and Donovan, served with Beth's uncle Parker. We grew up together in California."

That was before Beth knew them. They lived in base housing at Camp Pendleton.

John Henry clarifies. "There's eleven of us. We call ourselves cousins, but we're not."

"That's like an entire football team!" Colin says with incredulity.

Everyone smirks or grins in their own way, remembering the running joke about that same observation. They always had enough players to play football at Donovan's barbecues.

"When they retired, our families moved back to Spokane." Sharing a warm-hearted smile, Gina reaches for Beth's hand across the couches. "That's when we adopted Beth into the fold."

In her twelfth year, at one of those barbecues, Beth and her sister, Carrie, met Sadie, Gina, and Hoss's daughter, Sonia. Thick as thieves, their families dubbed them the five musketeers from then on. But Beth's world turned upside down when she lost her sister and Sonia vanished from their lives in a horrific apartment fire.

John Henry says to Colin, "My brothers, Jessie and Steven, serve with the 101st Airborne, so they can't make it this time."

"Are they off base?" Beth asks. She used to have a schoolgirl crush on Jessie.

"At Ramstein? Not right now. Dad said they're on leave for a week, partying in Ibiza."

"Off the coast of Spain," Brad says. "It's beautiful. I did a two-day photo shoot there. Ibiza's a wild ride at night with loud music, hangovers, and hookups. How's Lisa feel about that?"

"That's Steven's new wife," Beth whispers to Colin. Beth isn't close with Lisa, but she makes Steven happy, which is all that counts. At their wedding the year before, Beth allowed herself to dream about being in love. She believed it was a good sign; pushed her into moving out, at least.

"He sends her some incredible pics." John Henry glances at his wife. "Rita, we should go there."

"If the men are just as hot as the women, I'm in," Rita replies with enthusiasm. A brief burst of laughter makes the rounds.

"I hear Liam's on leave, too," Gina says, hiding a smirk with a sip of her wineglass.

John Henry returns the smug smile. "He's on the way to the farm as we speak."

Sounds like there's something afoot here and only John Henry and Gina are in on it. Beth opens her mouth to ask, but Gina places her wineglass on the end table and says, "We're picking Sadie up at the bus station on Saturday."

An idea forms in Beth's mind. Could it be that Liam has woken to the fact that he needs to make a move on Sadie? He'll have to go through Donovan, but good for Liam.

Reclined with Sean, Alejo interjects flirtatiously, "Ooh, how terrible for Sadie?"

Colin glances up at Beth with a frown of confusion. "If I'm going to meet all these people, I'll need a pen and paper to keep them straight."

Brad offers a knowing smile. "Memorize them. They'll grill you on day two."

"Colin, Liam has it bad for Sadie. She's Gina's older sister." Beth turns and squeezes Gina's hand. "Do you think Liam will ask your dad for permission this time?" They've been dancing around each other for years. Gina shrugs. Beth thought Sadie had given up on Liam a long time ago, but perhaps Beth's missed something recently.

John Henry catches Colin's eye. "My bro's afraid of their dad."

Rita gives him a gentle slap. "Hey, he'll come around."

Gina cranes her neck to look up at her husband. "Hope he catches Dad in a good mood 'cause it was a year before Bradley got permission."

Beth respected Brad for sticking it out when Donovan pushed back on letting Gina date him. Donovan was testing Brad, of course; said any man who wants to be with Gina should be prepared to walk through fire.

Brad pouts. "I still have the scars."

"Oh, come on, Donovan's a pussycat." Beth's words drip with sarcasm. Laughter erupts around her.

***

Gina enters her galley kitchen, hip to the counter, and waits. Dishes clank as Brad stacks plates in the cupboard from the dishwasher. Sometimes, she can't believe this man loves her and pinches herself.

Two years ago, with her mother's death still fresh, Gina wandered over to the park bench her mother frequented during the early stages of her cancer. It was a place of solitude, overlooking an expansive pond. As she sat there, raw and used up, a little gray, trembling, unleashed Lhasa Apso came prancing up to Gina. She immediately collected the poor thing and tucked him into the front of her jacket to warm his tiny body up. This relieved, handsome man followed and thanked her for saving his mom's dog.

Brad interrupts her thoughts and rubs her forearm. "Yes, lovebug." His eyes dip to her frown, then to the negative pregnancy test in her hand. He draws her in gently and plants a kiss on her forehead. "I love you."

"I love you, too." She melts into his chest, taking comfort in the softness of his cable-knit sweater and the sweet scent of his aftershave.

"It's going to take some time."

"I know...but I was hoping."

He lifts her pouty chin. Her heart skips when he looks at her this way.

"The expression on your father's face will be epic, honey." He flashes a satisfied grin. "Also, he won't like it when I call him grandpa."

Her eyes widen at the prospect. "Definitely not. He'll have a coronary." She's sure her dad will secretly love it. He'll be a fantastic grandpa.

"I'm certainly loving the practice part. Speaking of..." To her delight, he gives her that come-hither look, lifts her up into his arms without warning, shoves the dishwasher door closed with his foot, shoulders the light switch, and carries her out.

Me, too.

36

Chapter 5

The bell above the door chimes. Dressed in a suit, Ryker steps in, clutching a tie. Two interviews today; one looked promising. Security. Not like the military, but he'll take anything right now. He wants that date but needs the cash flow first to do it right. The aroma of food leads him to the counter, and he finds he's suddenly hungry for roast beef. Sophia is waiting on customers there and deposits dirty dishes in the bucket underneath.

The jukebox plays a soft, loving tune that reverberates off the white-tiled walls. Voices mix as people come and go, and servers glide around tables, dishing out food. The sounds of regular people doing ordinary things, unafraid and comfortable. It'll take him a while to adjust to this passive lifestyle, but if his nightmare last night is any sign, he might just be going in the right direction. In the past, they always began and ended on the day he lost his military brothers Elvis and K-Man, but last night, it ended on a high note, with Beth.

Sure, Beth turned him down yesterday, but then she gave him hope, and he's no quitter. So, in a good mood for once, and when he found himself near the diner, he hoped for another opportunity to talk to her. He approaches the bar, wanting to be close to the kitchen.

Sophia gazes at him. "What's your pleasure tonight?" Her voice sounds bubbly.

Seeing her.

Ryker rests his lean frame on a bar stool and lays his tie in a crumpled pile on the counter. "Coffee. Black, please. Is that beef I smell?"

"Yep, tonight's special. You feel like roast beef, mashed taters, and green beans, hon?"

His sister said she'd be home late tonight. "Okay, I'm in."

She taps a screen on the back counter, her finger poises to strike the screen again, and her eyes come back to him. "Comes with your choice of apple or cherry pie."

One side of his mouth rises, and his eyes flick to the kitchen door and back to Sophia. "Apple's my favorite now."

"Coming up." Sophia turns to the kitchen hatch. Jose makes eye contact and blows her a kiss. Ryker grins. *These two need a room.* He admires what they have and hopes he'll find something like that someday. Jose raises his chin at him, and Ryker returns a halfhearted nod.

The kitchen door squeaks and swings. Beth, her face flush, steps out in uniform and apron, carrying an empty bucket. *She gets prettier and prettier.* Ryker's eyes follow her as she dodges servers and walks down the counter to replace the dirty dish bucket below him, still oblivious to everyone around her. He straightens when she goes down on her knees in front of him. His mind goes into overdrive as he leans in. *A little domination could be fun.*

Olive-green eyes peek up. His heart jumps, but it's not the only body part he has jumping for joy. *Yup. I'm in.*

She does a double take and smooths her uniform as she rises to her feet, a hint of a grin on her face. "Ryker."

That stroked him in the right place. "Beth." Ryker zeros in on those pretty lips and enjoys the red tinge as she blushes and averts her eyes. She does an about-face and weaves her way back to the kitchen. This obsession is new. He's never had this overpowering need for someone before and enjoys watching those hips sway. He could be an ass man. Ryker catches Sophia following their exchange with amusement before she returns to her customers. He'll need allies in this endeavor.

The bell rings. Ryker jumps.

Sophia reaches out to steady him. "Hon, you okay?" She beams a smiling gaze past him, not catching his curt nod.

"Sophia!"

She opens her arms with a wide grin. "Hey, my little munchkins!"

Three excited kids jump up on the barstools to Ryker's right, and Sophia grabs them, planting kisses on each forehead. "Can we have ice cream?!"

"I don't know. Dad?" Sophia asks, gazing past the children.

A barrel-chested, older man comes up behind them, glances at Ryker, then gently choke holds two of the younger ones before saying in their ears, "Okay, quiet down. You're giving the customers heart attacks." He looks at Sophia. "Beth here?"

Ryker's optimism drops. *Husband?* He re-examines the kids and determines none of them is young enough for Beth to be their mother. *Boyfriend?* The older child, a girl, stares at Ryker in awe. Her resemblance to Beth baffles him. Caught gawking, the girl's smitten eyes slide to the floor, and Ryker smiles inwardly.

Sophia calls out, "Beth, your uncle's here."

Ryker releases the air from his lungs, only to suck it back in when Beth steps out.

***

Heat rises in Beth's cheeks when her gaze connects with Ryker's. He grants her a smile she's growing to like a hell of a lot. She returns the sentiment with weak knees. *Crap, he's hot.* She's kicking herself for saying no. Her head still says it's for the best, but her heart...

"Beth!" Elena hops off a stool, meets her halfway down the counter, and says, "Happy Birthday!" Uncle James follows behind her. He served as a dentist with the First Battalion down at Pendleton. They moved to Spokane this year to be near the family and help Parker with the farm.

As Beth hugs her fourteen-year-old cousin, she catches Ryker's eye again. He flashes that handsome smile, and she can't help but blush. Why does she keep searching for him? They've only met once, but she has this incredible urge to walk over and say hi; to sit and chat with him. *What is wrong with me?* Elena pulls out of the hug, and Beth steps back to admire her blue dress with white bows and patent dress shoes. She's surprised because Elena's a tomboy through and through. "You look amazing. You should wear dresses more often."

Elena beams up at her. "You think so?" For reasons unknown, Beth can do no wrong in her cousin's eyes and such compliments tickle her pink. Beth suspects she's tired of being a girl and wants to be a woman.

"Of course it's okay when Beth compliments you, but dear old Dad can't?" James asks, interrupting them.

Elena rolls her eyes.

Beth beams up at Uncle James as he says, "Yeah, we cornered her, whipped it on before she could say no." He bends down and whispers in Elena's ear, "And I felt your eyes roll up like a shutter in your head, Missy."

Elena's cheeks turn red, so she gazes in Ryker's direction and crosses her arms. "Dad!"

This pulls Beth's eyes to Ryker. His heated stare pierces her, bringing on a familiar rush of blood to her nether regions. *Is that one of those panty-melting looks they always write about in books?* The need to do something naughty is almost overpowering.

"Yeah, yeah." James brushes his daughter off and turns to Beth. "Knew you wouldn't answer the phone yesterday, like always, so I waited a day. Happy Birthday."

"Thanks, but you could have waited till I saw you up at—"

"Hell froze over? You're coming?" He's mocking her.

Beth's eyes slide to Elena. "I feel your pain."

"You know, we have bets on what year you'll show, right?" He yanks her in for a tight hug.

"Have you lost yet?" Beth asks, loving the comforting scent of his familiar cologne.

"Nope."

"Good," she says, winking at Elena.

***

After the dinner rush recedes, Beth comes out, bucket in hand, and glances down the counter in Ryker's direction. He likes that she checked. "Stuck on you" by Elvis starts up in the background. *Do they play anything else?* He tracks her as she veers toward the diner and clears tables till her bucket is full. He loves the way she concentrates with an odd flick of her tongue and the fleeting glances his way, thinking he doesn't notice her. His heart skips a beat, and a thrill courses through him like a schoolboy with his first crush. Ryker does and wants that date; needs it now that he's talked to her. All he desires is to hear a yes roll off that velvety pink tongue of hers.

Dishes collide, bringing his eyes back to Sophia on the other side of the counter. She's clearing his plate into the bucket underneath.

"Need anything else, hon?"

"Nope. I'm good."

"You here for the food or Beth?"

She doesn't mince words, and he likes that. He grins like he's been caught with his hand in the cookie jar. "Am I that transparent?"

"What's your intention toward my girl?" Sophia seems suddenly serious.

"To get to know her." More like, he wants to worship her, but he figures that's going a little too far.

"She's not the kind of girl you toy with and she's got a lot of muscle keeping her safe, so no funny business. You understand that, and we'll get along fine."

"Yes, ma'am. I assure you, I do not intend to toy with Beth."

Sophia eyes him with a critical stare for a moment. "Well, here's your chance. I'll bring out two slices, but you owe me for the heat I'm going to take."

Inside, he laughs. An ingenious plan, if it works. Big on the if.

Sophia busies herself with a cloth, wiping in wide circles over the counter down to the end. Beth steps in front of Ryker once more. His thoughts stray into naughty territory when their eyes meet. She hauls up a full bucket of dishes and says, "Hey."

"Hey, can I talk to you for a sec?"

Beth hefts the bucket to the back counter. She turns back, straightens, and glances over at Sophia, who is dishing out the pie.

"Wondering if you thought about my offer?"

"What offer?"

Is she for real? Her lips twist, hiding a smile desperate to surface. *Yeah, she's fucking with me.* The sound of a *hmm* vibrates his throat. She averts her eyes and sucks on her bottom lip. Parts of him stir. *Damn, she doesn't know what that does to me.*

Elvis sings about chasing and kissing. Ryker agrees, wanting those lips on his.

Sophia drops two slices of apple pie on the counter between them, cutting the mood. Disappointment registers on Beth's face, showing him that she's no dummy. His heart seizes. Their ploy didn't work.

"Beth's officially off now. Eat with Ryker."

"Sophia!" Beth warns.

He's losing her.

"Ah, no arguing. Have some fun." Sophia winks at Ryker, then heads to the kitchen without a backward glance.

Beth's lips purse together. She gazes at him from across the counter. He hangs on that look, afraid to breathe. She doesn't enjoy being pushed. *Fuck, I forgot.* "I said nothing."

She turns her back to him, her fingers still latching on to her bucket.

He backs down. "It's all good. You don't have to eat with me." *Please stay.*

Her shoulders slump, head dips. She twists to Ryker. Those sharp, green eyes pierce him. Ryker feels the sting but hopes his face doesn't betray his sincerity. He really wants to know why she fights what's obviously happening between them.

"I'll be right back."

Ryker releases a deep breath. He'll take the win. *Stay calm, Kensington.*

She takes off with purpose, hauling that bucket like she's on a mission. *Watch out, here she comes! And she's armed.*

CHAPTER 6

The kitchen door groans as it swings. Jose and Sophia step back from each other like teenagers caught kissing in the dark. Any other time, Beth would think it cute. She wends her way across to the dishwashing station and unloads her bucket with a crash, careful not to break any more plates than she must to make her point. She leans over the metal sink and stares into the drain.

Why does everyone have to interfere? It was a big deal when she announced she was moving out of Parker's house. They were all shocked, hesitant even, but everyone helped her move, and no one interfered. It was time, and she's proved it. In the last year, she's met new friends, learned to tango, and even trained with Hoss.

She made other decisions after the move, too. Some, they wouldn't like, if they knew.

Jose's disembodied voice asks. "Beth, are you alright?"

"I will be when everyone stops pushing me to where they think I need to be."

"We love you. We'd never steer you wrong, Chickie."

They mean well, but it's time they stood back and let Chickie fly on her own. Beth doesn't want to sound ungrateful, so she claws back unkind words and takes a few long breaths. He's waiting. She glances at the clock; not much time left. Better get out there before Gina comes to pick her up. A hand touches her shoulder. She shirks away. "I have dishes to do and a man waiting for me to eat and no time—"

"We'll clean up. Go eat."

He can be so tender sometimes. Without looking Jose in the eye, she takes her apron off, hangs it, and removes her gloves before laying them on the dish rack. She faces the kitchen door, breathes, and tries to keep it together because tears of frustration are beginning to surface. She forces them back, puts on her best face, and moves through.

On the diner side, she comes to a standstill. The hinges squeak as the kitchen door sways behind her. Ryker removes the hand from under his chin and straightens so his tie ends hang loosely around his shoulders. Having shed his jacket and rolled up his shirt sleeves, he greets her with hope in his eyes and another broad smile. She likes how his crew cut is maturing into wavy, dark locks, and his thriving beard makes his rounded jawline more attractive. Parts of her tingle. Her eyes dip, feeling embarrassed for gawking, and she saunters down the length of the counter.

"You want to eat at a booth?"

Still trying to clamp down her emotions, she says, "Sure."

Ryker picks up the two plates and gestures at the counter. "You bring the coffee." A moment later, they slide into a booth across from each other. "What's the secret to this coffee?"

Alejo comes to mind. He has a childish nature, but he's always serious about two things: his coffee, and his thriving business. She wonders what Ryker thinks about the LGTBQIA2S+ community.

When she doesn't answer, he fires off another question. "Have you thought about my offer?"

"You're like a dog with a bone."

Ryker leans back, crosses his arms, and displays her favorite part of him so far. She tries not to notice the biceps or the edge of a tattoo, which is also dying to reveal itself. "More like a handsome guy with an offer for a beautiful woman."

Beautiful? Beth digs into the pie to avoid letting her mouth fall open. *Not in this uniform.*

"You having a better day today?"

She glances up. Ryker hasn't moved to eat, and the concern on his face compels her to respond. *Should I be honest?* How much can she say to someone who doesn't understand the pain she suffers daily? Her struggle to overpower thoughts that want to tear down everything she's built to stay alive. To accept that it's okay to exist in a world without the family she put in the ground. Beth thought she was doing well. Her life was going in the right direction until yesterday.

They stare for what seems like a long time before Beth sighs and says, "No."

Ryker grins sadly, like he understands what she means, reaches into his pocket, and slides a velvet jewelry box across the table at her. "Perhaps this will make you say yes to that question."

She stares at the box like it's a bomb and grips her forearms. Why can't everyone understand her need to forget her birthday?

"I saw it and thought of you."

He thought about me? A small burst of excitement passes through Beth. *What made him think of me?* Unable to help herself, Beth slides her fingers over the soft surface of the velvet and drags the box to her side of the table. *You don't even know me.* She pops the lid open. *Oh, Ryker.* She glances across the table at him in shock.

His satisfied grin pokes at the tension she has been feeling since coming out here. Beth looks down on a necklace of colorful, interwoven butterflies, and tiny spasms of excitement melt her heart. *Carrie.*

Frustrated tears spill forth. Beth tries to hide them and swipes her sniffling nose. Ryker slides out from his seat, and she turns away to wipe her cheek. She startles when Ryker's hand covers hers over the box. *Gosh, he moves fast.*

"This isn't a birthday present. I know you hate that, so this is just an I-thought-of-you present, okay?"

Despite her tears, she laughs. The heat of his rough hand distracts her and warms her insides. Needing to take a step back to regain control of herself, Beth slides her hand out from underneath his, regretting it instantly. "Thank you. Sorry, I'm a mess."

"Don't be. I didn't mean to make you sad. If it's the necklace, I'll—"

"No, it's not you." Stray tears fall, and she reaches—

Ryker's hand darts across the space between them, his knuckles stroke Beth's jaw, and his thumb skims across her cheek, swiping her tears away. She closes her eyes momentarily, enjoying his touch. *I don't deserve this...*

"What's wrong? Can I help?"

She wishes he could. *I wish my life had turned out differently.* "I'm tired of everyone pushing me."

"I'll stop asking."

"No! Don't." Surprised at her words, Beth kicks herself mentally. *What am I doing?* She can't reconcile it, but this feels right somehow. She looks at the necklace again. He doesn't know her, but the butterflies... "Can I tell you a secret?"

He inches closer, the powerful scent of male enveloping her as he wipes away more escaping tears. "Of course."

"My uncles think my tattoo is about my transformation, but it's an homage to my sister. She loved butterflies."

He dons a look of joyful surprise. "That's a beautiful gesture. What happened to her?"

Beth shakes her head. "Now that I've told you a secret, you owe me one, but tell me when I see you next time."

"Okay, but first," he says in a low sensuous tone, "I'm asking for that date."

She forces a laugh. "I'm counting on it."

His one-sided grin appears. "So, um...you want to go out on a date?"

"No." They laugh together.

"One day, you're going to say yes."

If you only knew how much I wanted to say it. "Yeah, one day," she lies.

"Let me help you put it on." Ryker slides her hair aside as Beth turns. His deft hands brush along the skin of her neck, causing shivers down her spine. He raises the necklace over her head and encircles her with his arms. Cold metal lands on her chest; goosebumps rise as the chain drags along her skin, the scent of him enticing her. He latches it in place.

Composed again, Beth rotates to face him, brushing her knee against his outer thigh, and runs her fingers over the smooth surface of the pendant. "What do you think?"

"I think…" Ryker's eyes dip to her lips, sending her heart into overdrive, then crawl back up. "Did I improve your day?"

"Yes."

He puts his arm on the back of the booth and cups his chin. The heat in his eyes drives her to glance around nervously. She's not sure why he's looking at her like this, but it makes her veins burn and prompts her to bite her lips.

The bell rings. Ryker startles.

PTSD? She sympathizes. *Something they have in common.* Beth uses the distraction to wipe her face.

Gina ambles in and cranks her neck to their booth. Brad follows her close behind and raises his eyebrows when he spots Ryker with her. *Crap!* They came early. Beth twists back to her pie. *Time to wrap this up.*

Gina walks up to their table with a sheepish grin. "Beth, you didn't tell me you had a date."

Beth turns once more and slides her knee along Ryker's thigh again. "It's not a date. Ryker's new to the neighborhood."

Gina raises her eyebrows. "Right." She extends her hand to Ryker. "I'm Gina. This is my husband, Brad."

"Nice to meet you."

Gina's eyebrows draw together. "Are you okay?"

Feeling self-conscious, Beth smooths her clothes. "Yeah, fine."

Ryker's familiar scent surrounds her as he leans back. "I just asked her for a date."

Oh, crap! No, no, no.

His eyes slide to her with a teasing, mouthwatering grin she'd like to... She glances up at her friend, willing those thoughts to stop.

Gina is staring back with a you-go-girl attitude.

This girl isn't *going* anywhere.

"She's not said yes yet, but it's only my second rusty attempt," Ryker says with a flirtatious gaze directed at her. Beth can't look away.

"My best friend's a hard nut to crack," Gina says. "It might take some time."

"Don't worry, I'm waiting her out."

A distinct sizzle arcs between them, the force of which causes Beth to swallow.

Gina's words break the spell. "Well, I'm not one to interrupt an obvious date, so I'll talk to you later?"

"It's not a... We're finished."

Ryker stifles a grin, and Beth zeros in on his lips. *God, if his eyes can do that to me, imagine what his... No, no, stop!*

"Nice necklace," Brad says.

Shit, I'm never going to hear the end of this.

Ryker pulls his broad shoulders back. "I just gave it to her."

"Really. A birthday present?" Gina asks.

"Gina!" Beth narrows her eyes, and they stare at each other for some time as an invisible war wages between them. *The teasing needs to end.*

Gina tries to look innocent when she says, "Yes?"

Ryker takes this as his cue. "I have to be on my way. Give us a couple of minutes and she'll be all yours."

Beth thinks it sounds like he is going to say for now at the end. Or is she just hoping he will? *Stop wishing.* Sometimes, she tires of this voice that thwarts her at every turn.

"Sure, take your time. We'll go visit in the back. Nice meeting you." Gina winks at Beth before she and Brad walk toward the kitchen.

"Likewise." Ryker turns his attention to Beth. "I won't hold you up. Just wanted to see you. Ask my question."

Leaning back, Ryker regards her with gentle eyes and curls a strand of stray hair over her ear while stroking her sensitive skin. He sighs, licks his lips, then slides out and offers his hand. Beth finds the strength in his warm fingers as she accepts. She's not sure why—whether it is the necklace or the gentle way he soothes her with a touch of his hand—but she doesn't want their time together to end and tightens her hold on him. He rewards her with a warm gaze, causing her to flush.

He stands, waiting, looking unsure. She doesn't know what to do, either; this is all new to her. It would be inappropriate to kiss him, but she has the urge to. *You can't.* Beth cranes her neck, then falters. "Thank you for the butterflies."

He leans in.

She swallows.

His eyes dip to her lips and back up as he says in a husky whisper, "You're welcome."

***

Colin's in awe; Brad hits more strikes bowling than anyone he knows. *Someone must have genetically implanted clovers up the man's ass.* For weeks now, Brad has shown him very little he isn't good at. He travels the world with ease, is the poster child for tons of men's products, owns his apartment, and adores the catch of a woman he married. For gosh sakes, the man cooks and cleans! What kind of man cleans? If Colin were a woman, he'd marry Brad, too.

Gina arrives at their table with drinks and snacks as Brad swings his ball again. Colin watches it sail down the middle of the lane. *Clunk!* Ten pins tumble in a mishmash of white. Another strike. *Horseshoes, maybe?* Brad pumps his fist on the way back to the table.

"Good one, baby!" Gina slaps Brad's hand on the way to peruse the balls waiting in the return tray.

Colin's jealous. If Brad could rub some of that off on him, he'd be grateful. He glances at Beth. She's quieter than usual tonight. She was warming up to him yesterday, when he held her hand and lounged at her feet at the birthday party. Today, not so much. He regards the empty seat beside Beth across from him. She's distancing herself again. No one is upset about it, which surprises him. Colin scoots across to sit next to her and places his arm across the back of her seat. "What's up?"

The smile Beth presents him doesn't reach her eyes. "Nothing. Why?"

The sound of Gina's gutter ball draws him to have a look. "You seem preoccupied."

"Hmm... Well, I'm enjoying these two lovebirds."

With his hand on Gina's ass, Brad snickers in their direction. "A little more to the right, honey. It's a sure win."

A strike with one ball left? Fat chance!

Gina swings, lets the ten pounder tumble out of her hands, and with a thud, it rolls right into the gutter. She lashes out and slaps her husband amid his laughter at her expense. Their love is clear, though, when Brad corrals a reluctant Gina into his arms and pulls her in for a smoldering kiss. Colin loves the way she melts, then molds to his body, giving as much as she gets. They fit together like peanut butter and jam. Sweet and sticky. Colin's eyes swing to Beth. He wishes he fit with Beth. The irresistible pull to bring her in and lay a hot one on those luscious lips compels him to rein that urge in. He has to bide his time. She'll freak if he pushes her.

Once Brad lets his wife's lips go, Gina says, "Beth, your turn."

Beth jumps up like someone stuck her with a pin, grabs a bowling ball, and approaches the lane to toss it. Masking her relief as enthusiasm doesn't make Colin happy. Instead of sticky and sweet, he gets hot and cold.

Gina plunks down in Beth's seat.

"What's up with Beth tonight?" Colin asks, not able to let it go.

Beth knocks down nine of the pins, turns, and grabs the next ball.

Gina turns on a radiant smile. "She's fine."

"Something's off."

Beth knocks the last pin down, claps, and raises her hands in victory.

When Gina's smile falters, Colin's alarm bells go off. "What's wrong with Beth, Gina?"

"Nothing."

Nothing, my ass!

***

"You didn't need to walk me to my door." Beth senses Colin's suspicious eyes on her as they walk down the hallway to her apartment. He lives on the same floor but in the opposite direction.

"I know, but I wanted to."

Beth yanks a set of keys from her pocket and inserts one into the lock. She hopes this is quick because it's not lost on her that they were in this position a few weeks back and it was a total disaster.

"Beth?"

Spoke too soon. Her key stops turning midway in the lock. "Yeah." She faces him with what she hopes is a pleasant smile.

"You've been avoiding me all night."

"No, I haven't." She has been. All night, her thoughts have been straying to Ryker, thinking things she shouldn't about a man she will never date. They've been intruding at inopportune times, like when a man in the bowling lane next to them started a game with his children. When he and Beth had reached for the same ball, his touch had reminded her of Ryker's, rough and warm.

"You know you have. What's going on? Talk to me."

She throws out a confused face. "I'm not sure what you want me to say."

"You were quiet tonight. Why?"

That'll teach you to let him in.

"It's all over your face. I'm not leaving till you talk to me." He steps closer.

Her eyes narrow. Now he's pushing. "Colin, good night."

He leans in. "Don't blow me off. I'm different from everyone else."

You'll never... Mean thoughts surface, but she doesn't want to hurt him and stays silent.

"I asked Gina, but she's covering for you."

Gina kept Ryker to herself. Relief flows through Beth, then anger. *What is this? The inquisition?* "There's nothing going on!" Beth turns her back on Colin, but he steps closer. The hint of mint on his breath besieges her. She twists the key until the lock clicks, then grabs the door handle.

"I'm not leaving."

Unable to contain her frustration, she whirls on him, forcing him to step back. "Colin! I'm fine, but I won't be if you keep pushing me! Now go home."

His frown is unmistakable, but he's crossed the line and concedes by trudging down the hall in a huff.

CHAPTER 7
May 22

The bell rings. Ryker glances up, vexed at forgetting that hellish thing dogging him from above again. He pushes through the prickly feeling, saunters in, and gets a whiff of maple syrup and bacon as a server bogged down with plates walks by. The early morning light in the diner streams across patrons near the windows, enjoying their breakfasts. The jukebox is noticeably silent.

He traded his suit and tie for an olive Henley T-shirt, olive-green cargo pants with a dark brown belt, and lace-up brown suede work boots. He hopes his relaxed attire makes a better impression on Beth than the suit did. The squealing kitchen door catches his attention, but he's disappointed to see Sophia holding a coffeepot and a stack of pancakes. She serves it to a man at the counter. Her face softens upon seeing him. "Ryker, what can I get you?"

In the kitchen, Jose waves and lends his ear to the hatch, wiping his hands on a towel.

Ryker smiles in anticipation and heads to an empty seat at the counter. Despite his discomfort with the door behind him, he decides it's worth the risk to move closer. "Is Beth here?"

Sophia's smile drops a notch. "She's off for a few weeks, hon."

Damn it, should have asked about that. "Right, the farm. She mentioned going but didn't say when."

A look of realization crosses Sophia's face. "Coffee?"

He nods, and she pours sympathy into his mug.

A nearby customer asks for a cup of joe. She apologizes, sprints over, and pours the man's coffee. A few weeks is a lifetime for Ryker. Beth's not just affecting his dreams but every waking moment now. How will he survive without seeing her for so long? He should focus on planning their date. It has to be perfect, not to his specifications, but to hers.

Sophia works her way back to Ryker, pouring refills along the way. "You taking a break today, or did you get an offer?" she asks, looking at his clothes.

He needs people who know Beth to pull this off. "No offer."

"Sorry, hon." She hands him a menu, but he waves it away.

"Can I ask you something?"

"Shoot."

"Beth's turned me down for a date. I'm trying to figure out how to change her mind." He brings the steaming mug to his lips and takes in the delicious aroma of a dark roast, then holds the mug back to have a look. "This is good."

"We have it specially made by someone." Still holding the coffeepot, she leans against the counter with a satisfied smile. "Don't know about you, hon, but that wasn't a question."

He grins into his mug and contemplates as he lowers it. "What does she like and not like?"

Sophia stows the coffee pot back in its cradle. "Well, you can guess by the tattoo that she loves butterflies. That was a nice gift you gave her, by the way."

The memory of Beth's tender expression the moment she opened the velvet box warms him. He nailed it for sure. That she's been parading his gift also puffs up his pride. She isn't afraid to show it off.

"She's a homebody, so if you get a date with her, keep it close. She likes to walk, instead of taking a car."

"That's good, 'cause I don't own a car yet."

Sophia grins. "She has a fixation on strawberries, loves dancing, and when she's stressed, chocolate chip cookies work best."

He files the info away for future reference. "What else does she like?"

Her smile grows. "Well, she definitely likes you."

That catches his attention. He tilts his head. "How do you know that?"

"You mentioned the farm."

He's not sure what that means.

"Listen, Beth holds things close to the vest. The farm is one of those things. It took her some time to inform her friends, but she wasted no time telling you, so I'm certain."

What is so important about this farm that she keeps it a secret? The mystery intrigues him. Her trust shocks him a bit. He doesn't know what he did to garner that, but it fuels him in his quest.

The bell rings, and he jolts out of his skin. If he could strangle that—

Sophia gazes past him. "Duty calls." She walks away to greet the new customers.

Yes, it does. Finding his younger siblings became his top priority after he was discharged, leading him back to the only place he'd ever called home, his stepfather's farm. Elias acted proud of Ryker when he'd returned, and didn't hold back at showing distaste for his other "worthless" kids—his words. He certainly didn't seem to care where Ryker's older siblings, Mal and Krystal, were.

After Ryker was born, his mom had three more children with the same man. During his visit, Ryker found out one was enrolled at an East Coast university, far away from Elias, and the baby of the family enlisted last year. So that just left Libby.

He found her in Spokane, taking cosmetology courses at the community college. Libby could have gone to a local college in Missoula, but her move here showed him there was no love lost between her and her father. Ryker loves her ambition and confidence, something his mother lacked while he was growing up. Libby was five when their mother died.

He regretted leaving his younger step-siblings to fend for themselves against his stepfather, but he and his two older siblings had no choice. Elias was hard and unforgiving. He cared about two things: the farm and the military. The latter had given Ryker a way out.

Libby had noticed the change in him last night. Once she'd extracted the reason for the silly grin on his face, she teased him mercilessly. He didn't mind, though. Felt good to do something normal; it's been a long time. And once again, butterflies had dominated his dreams last night and chased the nightmares away.

Sophia stashes menus behind the counter and arranges a coffee mug and saucer.

"Go slow with Beth. She hides from life," Jose says from the kitchen hatch, extracting Ryker from his musings.

"Why?"

Jose holds a hand up. "Her story to tell, but I can tell you that she's just existing right now, not living. She's missing out."

Sophia picks up the coffeepot. "If she lets you in, you'll get sweet and giving, but it's Beth who needs the sweet and giving, hon." She winks. "Goes without saying, but don't give up."

For people he's only known for a few days, he's grateful that they think highly enough of him to encourage his pursuit of Beth. He doesn't want to misplace their trust. They're good people. "Don't plan to. How do I get through?"

Sophia stops to think. "When she gets back, show her what she's missing."

***

"Ford can't touch Chevy's superiority!" Donovan laughs while challenging Hoss.

Their long-standing argument echoes around the underground garage they buried long ago in Yard Three. The powerful odor of grease and oil mixes with the fresh mountain air drifting down the driveway. Parker's at a workbench against the side wall, tinkering with the electronics of a ham radio he's had for untold eons.

These two are opposite in more than their looks. Donovan is tall and lean, while Hoss is shorter but stocky. After they served, Hoss dropped his clean-shaven baboon face for a full red-tinged beard. On the contrary, Donovan prefers the shaved look and doesn't deviate from his disciplined nature. They argue but, in the end, they come together, and somehow, their friendship has endured through all that life has thrown their way.

"Tell me, how many times have you had that thing in the shop?" Hoss asks.

"Hmm…" Okay, he has Donovan there. If Parker were a betting man, he'd say Hoss is pointing at Donovan's Chevy Silverado. That truck was, at one time, a great deal, but it's on its last legs. Hoss's Bronco is older, but he restored it a while back with some extra mods. Parker's surprised every time Donovan makes the trek up and arrives with all his truck parts intact. The road to Haven is rough, as is evident from the heavily shocked trucks in the garage behind him. Yet, without fail, the Silverado has always managed to arrive, year after year. Parker's lips raise.

"She doesn't need a shop. She has me," Donovan says, defending his baby.

A loud rumble bounces around the walls of the garage. Parker places a worn and familiar screwdriver down, swivels in the shop chair, and faces the open metal garage doors to their underground dungeon. The blast doors look like they come from some futuristic sci-fi movie. It was quite a show, back then, watching the workers slide them into place.

Hoss and Donovan have their heads in the engine of a farm tractor, surrounded by wheeled chests and various lifts. The Silverado is on one of those lifts.

A jacked-up F-150 truck drives down the driveway and into the garage, music blaring, and easily backs up in line next to Hoss's prized possession—a first-generation matte black Ford Bronco Wagon. With every new arrival, Parker's one step closer to his goal of running the place at half capacity. It brings him joy that the men organized for their children to lend a hand this weekend.

The music cuts off sharply, as does the engine. Liam, a Navy Corpsman, jumps down, looking self-assured and walking with a slight swagger in his step like his father. Liam inherited his height from his mother's side, along with the golden-blond hair sprouting from his shaved scalp. His mother sure was a looker.

Hoss suffered when his wife died. Parker was there when he broke the news to his kids. Poor Liam was serving somewhere in the Atlantic when he was told. It was a long night for everyone.

Hoss and Donovan place their tools down, rub their hands on shoulder rags, and walk toward Liam's truck. Even though Hoss is shorter than his son, he snatches Liam up as he exits in a hug. The family calls their group hugs the "Jenkins sandwiches." Parker chokes up a bit. He doesn't want to detract from his relationship with his niece—he loves Beth with all his heart—but when the guys are close to their families, he regrets not having one of his own.

Thinking of Beth brings up a painful memory...and guilt. The last time Beth was here at Haven, she was a teenager. He brought her up for their family's funeral... Forced her to come. It was a mistake and definitely the reason she continues to keep away from the farm. He didn't understand the trauma he'd caused. By the time they'd arrived, her teenage body was squeezed into the back seat in the fetal position, and she remained in the truck, despite everyone's attempts to persuade her to get out. William was the only one who recognized the issue and proved able to drag her away from the three urns beside her. *I was such an idiot.*

"Yo, Parker!" Hoss calls out.

Flushing out that tormenting reflection, Parker approaches and extends his hand to Liam. "How was the drive?"

"A couple of downed trees. Nothing a chainsaw couldn't fix."

"Thought there might be some of those," Parker says. A wind storm laid siege to the valley the night before. They gauged the damage to the logging road by the mess cleaned up earlier that morning around the front gate. "Weather people forecasted more of the same tonight, so it's time to sharpen the blades for tomorrow."

"I'll call Brad to bring his saw. Sean'll have one for sure in his truck," Liam says and turns to his father. "Thought you'd be in your bunk by now."

Hoss's favorite spot was the "bunk" he'd created across the river, overlooking the valley with a full view of the farmhouse and the open fields they'd been plowing for the last few weeks. With a sniper rifle strapped to his back and dressed in one of his many ghillie suits, he likes to traipse through the underbrush to keep his skills sharp. He knows the valley they've collectively nicknamed "the playground" like the back of his hand.

Hoss grins and slaps Liam. "Was goin' to head up but thought I'd wait for you. Scout with me later?"

"Yeah, sure. Alex and Miles show?"

Liam's best friend, Alex, and his twin brother owned one of the ten apartments here in Haven. They were also Marines from the unit Liam served with.

"Showed a couple of days ago with their families," Hoss says, and points toward the compound.

"Excellent. I brought those extra tools you needed and more fencing. They're in the back. Where you want them?"

"We'll get them. Go on up and see Alex." Hoss gives his son another hug before following Donovan to the back of Liam's truck.

"I'll walk with you," Parker says, walking up the ramp alongside Liam. Parker breathes in the clean forest air under the shadow of the mountain they buried Haven next to. At the top of the driveway, he asks, "Heard you made a stop before the trip?" Hoss had told Parker his son was picking up a ring at the jewelry store before coming up this weekend.

Liam's smirk answers that, but he adds, "That I did."

"'Bout time you found the courage. You going to ask Donovan's permission before she arrives?" Donovan has a strict policy where his girls are concerned. No one takes his daughters out before being approved. It is archaic but it's his friend's way. Understandably, Sadie isn't too fond of the practice. The two often butt heads during her teenage years.

"No. I'm going to wait for her to show first. I have a lot to make up for."

That he does. Liam might be jumping the gun a bit. He's avoided Sadie in the past, so this plan could backfire on him, but Parker keeps that thought to himself. Donovan's oldest daughter is no dummy and is strong, like her mother was.

"Since we have all the boys here, we should pull out the good stuff tonight and celebrate," Parker says, overlooking the mature forest in front of him.

Liam pats Parker on the back. "Sounds good." He walks toward a metal door embedded in the mountain wall, punches a code into the keypad, and enters.

Parker is lost in thought as the door clicks shut. Eventually, a man will propose to Beth. He's not sure how he feels about that. Donovan speaks highly of Colin, but Parker hasn't had the chance to meet him. If Colin can arrange for Beth to join them this weekend, Parker might warm up to him. But Beth holds Colin at arm's length by the sounds of it. Parker's proud she's moving in the right direction with her life, but she still holds back, waiting for the other shoe to drop. His hope right now is that she continues to move forward, but PTSD is a slippery slope he is all too familiar with.

CHAPTER 8

Noon

Framed by Alejo's wet dream of a kitchen and sitting on a leather counter stool, her phone held aloft, Beth listens to her voicemail. She leans on a sleek white island surrounded by dark gray cupboards and stares at black-lined geometric shapes on the back wall above a counter, where a stainless espresso machine sits. Circle lighting hangs overhead as she thumbs the edge of a black induction stove top. Sometimes she dreams this is her kitchen. On her salary, it isn't possible, but it costs nothing to dream, right?

Alejo's ass juts out as he rummages through the open freezer drawer.

Sophia's teasing voice drifts into Alejo and Sean's apartment. "He showed up this morning looking for you. Give him a chance. Love you, hon. See you up there."

The freezer drawer slams closed. Eyes narrowed, Alejo puts his palms on the counter and leans forward. "Who's she talking about?"

Beth drops her cell into her brown leather purse on the counter. He'll hound her till she gives. "Someone asked me for a date."

"Uh, huh? And?"

"I said no."

Alejo gasps, his manicured hands flying to his face. "Are you insane?" He straightens on a thought. "Was he ugly, old, or just gross?"

"Hot, older than me, and not in the least bit gross." Far from gross.

Ryker came to the diner to see her? This tugs at her closed heart, causing her fingers to seek the necklace. *Here it comes.* She braces for Alejo's wrath, which comes out like a whine.

"Beth! You say yes when a hot man asks. There should be no question." Visibly shaking the calm in, Alejo pours and hands her the best coffee she's ever had. "Okay, this is salvageable."

"I already said no twice, A." Is that regret in her voice? Beth raises the mug to her lips, taking what little comfort it gives her.

"Twice!" Not deterred, he dips his chin and glances over red-rimmed glasses at her. "He's not leaving because you said no. You'll say yes when we get back."

That was a little too confident. The sweetness of Alejo's coffee awakens her taste buds. "Not sure I'm ready to go to Haven."

His eyebrows raise. When Alejo gets agitated, his hands move around like he's conducting a symphony. "What? No, no! If I have to go—" He points at her "—then you're definitely going. Haven is Sean's gig, not mine."

Beth tenses up. The room spins. She closes her eyes and brushes her fingers over her temple scar. Warm hands curl around hers, halting her circling motions. Alejo says, "Long drive in a car's hard for you, I get that. But that's what drugs are for."

Beth opens her eyes. Alejo's sympathy is on full display. She dismisses his words and moves to break their connection.

"You need to work on being happy—" He waves his hands over her, and his head moves like a bobble-head doll. "—and break down these zones you've got going on. Don't you see?"

The only thing she sees is her sister's empty seat. "Haven't been there since my parents..."

He enters her space and fusses with her hair. "Honey, we'll make fresh memories. Go finish packing. Sean and I have to pick up some last-minute items. We'll come get you when Colin arrives. Take a nap, read, or find some vibrating love."

She scoffs.

"Whatever it takes to get you in the mood to push through the day, babe. Promise me."

Beth frowns and picks up her purse. She vacates the chair and walks a few steps before returning to hug Alejo. "I promise." She snatches the mug.

"That's my girl."

Everything will be better later...right?

***

2:15 p.m.

Gideon's prison security bus travels down the I-90, escorted by two marked sheriff's vehicles, one in front, one in the rear, lights flashing. The other cars on the road give them a wide berth as they pass a sign that reads *Entering Spokane County.*

Shouldn't be long now, he thinks.

Kaden and Gideon are chained to two separate seats but both move with the sway of the bus. Gideon scratches his sore wrist where the cold handcuffs rub. Patiently, he's bracing for what's coming. He was told to expect a pickup. They're moving at a steady clip, though, so he's not sure how to interpret that. Up front, two guards, buckled in a double jump seat, sway in time with them. Further on, the driver. Gideon's also aware that two more guards are sitting behind the steel cage at the back near the emergency exit. Another prisoner, Dugal, is sitting in a seat in the last row. Pretty much keeps to himself. He's up on charges of rape in the first degree.

Gideon glances outside and locks eyes with his brother. Greg gazes up from the passenger side of Hunter's beat-up truck, driving at an equal pace beside their ride. Not jaded like the rest of them, Greg is the youngest. He's seen lots of shit, but his three brothers have guarded him well. Their grandmother didn't get too much of a swing at Greg. He follows and he's loyal, which is all that matters. Family is family, after all.

Gideon slaps his knee. Making eye contact with Kaden across the way, the same thought passes between them. Kaden braces.

***

Beth dozes on a ratty, torn, well-used leather couch, one hand over the book that is lying across her stomach. The cover, a shirtless man cradling a woman in his arms, slowly rises in time with Beth's steady breathing. Deep in sleep, Beth shifts between snores to face the inside of the couch, the book crushed and forgotten.

In contrast to Alejo's apartment, Beth has incompatible thrift store-style furniture. The lamps don't match and neither do the coffee tables. A gray patterned carpet covers the scuffed hardwood floor. Above the couch is a piece of metal art: butterflies in flight. To the right of the butterflies, a window frames the apartment buildings across the street. Power lines plummet between the buildings.

Under the window is a cabinet covered with delicate crocheted doilies, birthday cards, and picture frames. Familiar faces peek from behind glass. Parker, her adopted dads, and all their teenage kids with Beth on camping trips. One stands out, larger than the rest. Two excited little girls smile for the camera in front of a *Molbak's Butterfly Garden* sign; between them, a butterfly perches in one of their hands. A flawed, sad, purple butterfly stuffy that's seen better days lounges among the frames.

Old tile counters and simple cupboards made of oak with serviceable black handles show the kitchen is far from designer, and the tiled island boasts no bar stools. All of Beth's appliances are white, and the electrical stove displays a digital clock with a military time of fourteen thirty. The display sputters, blinks, and blanks out. A normally ignored hum dies. Flashes light up the kitchen amid popping sounds.

A shower of sparks flies off the power lines outside Beth's window. A blinding flash forces the darkness to flee momentarily as the room shakes. *Ssshblamm!* Something slams into the wall, causing the ceiling to belch dust. The windows blast inwards. Shards spray. The cabinet under the window pitches forward with a crash. Multiple fissures slash their way through the living room wall like a high-magnitude earthquake, unsettling the metal butterflies. Outside, the electric power poles cascade down out of the frame. The apartment building breaks up across the street. The ceiling plummets and shrouds the couch, entombing Beth. Dust floats across the apartment as the absence of sound creates an eerie moment of silence.

Chapter 9

"What's up?" Parker rushes into Haven's security room, drawing in sharp breaths after the steep climb.

The subtle odor of gun oil hangs in the air along with burned gunpowder. The familiar scent doesn't ease his anxiety as it usually does, brought on by William frantically announcing "Warning: red" through the speaker system in the compound. They are words Parker didn't want to hear; they mean a hostile attack is in progress.

William Hess stands grounded in front of a multitude of screens displaying tiny pieces of the outside world: goats pace around a pen, earth-churned farm fields in the afternoon sunlight, lush forest, and a shaded stone-steepled church, to name a few. Not seeing anything amiss, his friend's silence draws Parker's eyes to the big-screen TV on the back wall. Ticker tape races across the bottom of the screen while a 24/7 news channel plays on mute. What's on that screen takes Parker aback: a chaotic aerial satellite view of New York he hasn't seen since 9/11, but this is different. The destruction isn't confined to a few city blocks.

"It's happening, Parker."

He gazes at his friend's stiff linebacker shoulders. "What's happening?" Parker doesn't need to turn around to know Donovan and Hoss are both entering through the nondescript door behind him. Their breaths come in quick succession, too, albeit slower and shallower than his own.

"You called?" Hoss asks.

William turns to them, the shock plain to see on his face. "The US is under attack."

Impossible. They'd never get through our military defenses.

"What?" Donovan slides past Parker for a better look at the screen. Ever the sergeant, Donovan is used to taking control of their small band of brothers. He is a man of action but too hotheaded, which is why Parker is their chosen leader. Donovan fumbles around the desk for the remote and presses the mute button.

On the TV screen, the nervous, disheveled small-town journalist, dressed in a T-shirt and leather jacket and looking like he's just got off a plane, says, "We lost connection with our big sister stations in New York, New Orleans, Tampa, and Washington, DC at five thirty, eastern time. We're getting reports that short-range missiles were fired from military installations stateside. It appears we are bombing ourselves." The man isn't reading from a teleprompter but he is trying to sound like he is. Parker detects fear, too. "Is it a computer glitch gone wrong or cyber warfare from our enemies? The East Coast is reeling from a simultaneous antimatter missile attack. We're also hearing of massive casualties from New York all the way down the coast to Miami." The screen displays a satellite feed of the eastern states dotted with dark circles, indicating large craters where there should be none.

Parker hates to agree with the reporter, but he knows antimatter missiles create dark craters like that. The military acronym used is Aunties. Once they found an efficient and cost-effective way to produce and contain the antimatter three years ago, the United States, along with Russia, Korea, and China, began stockpiling them. The technology is still in its infancy, but it makes for powerful weapons. One tiny nanogram is enough to erase anything it touches made of matter.

The loss of so many lives, snuffed out upon impact, pains him. *They didn't have a chance. And why Aunties and not nukes?*

In an instant, Parker considers innumerable questions. Should they be thankful? Surely, Spokane is too small to have been targeted? If Beth is seeing what he is, she will know what to do. She has no choice. He hopes the military is still intact. With Washington damaged and possibly without government control, the nukes the US has could fall into the wrong hands. They could survive here, but there are things they haven't purchased yet. Things they'll have to do without now.

"There's been no sign of a press release coming from the White House as to what is happening. While we wait for President Huxley—" The journalist cups an ear, going silent while listening into his earpiece.

Why hasn't the president responded? *Damn Democrats, always sitting on their hands instead of taking action.* It is ludicrous to think his country would bomb itself. There must be another explanation.

The journalist continues, "It's not just the East Coast. They're saying it's widespread. The West Coast has suffered similar bombings... Reports of various missiles and long-range missiles launched, going... Where? Unknown at this time. Perhaps our president is retaliating." He cups his ear again, but this time, the level of anxiety coming off him is palpable. He stares, at a loss for words, then blinks. "It's not just major cities. Our bases... They're bombing our bases...nationwide."

Who's "they"?

The reporter shifts in his chair, searches around the studio, then looks into the camera, clears his throat, and in a shaky voice says, "If you're just tuning in to the satellite feed, the US is under attack. We lost our connection to—"

Donovan cuts the sound; the sharpness of it stabs Parker's heart. Fairchild Air Force Base is west of Spokane. *Beth.* Their family—Parker's brothers, Jose, Donovan's daughters, and Hoss's sons—are in the thick of it. If the antimatter didn't reach them, the shock wave would have done massive damage to the town. "We need to mobilize and rescue our family," Parker says with conviction.

William turns to face them and, with equal conviction, says, "No."

Guilt consumes Parker. Beth could be trapped or injured. He should have insisted she come with him this time. "We'll drive back into town and grab everyone before it gets too bad. Shouldn't be more than a couple of hours."

"No!" William repeats the word, sounding like a gavel slamming into a block of wood.

Alex and Miles amble in from topside, with Liam bringing up the rear. "What's going on, Dad?" he asks Hoss. "Our phones lit up. The boys and I need to get back to base."

William intercepts Hoss's reply. "CONUS is under attack from an unknown source. Bases across the continental United States no longer exist, Liam. You aren't going anywhere. We need to stick to our plan to combat this."

Screw the plan! Parker hadn't planned for the shit to hit the fan while they were all at Haven without their kids. Any attacks were supposed to happen while he was in town and able to rescue Beth and keep her safe.

"What?" Liam's eyes widen at the TV screen. "Holy shit! Sadie?! She's on a bus."

"William's right," Donovan says with an edgy calm. "It kills me to say it, but we need to stick to the plan." He gazes at Liam. "Sadie's bus is still two hours from Spokane, which means she's nowhere near the base or a major city."

"Beth's in Spokane! She's alone and won't make it through this. I need to go get her." Parker walks toward the racks of weapons and military-grade trunks lining the floors and walls. He'll have to grab supplies for the truck and chainsaw his way out to the main road. William cuts him off. "William, get out of my way! You know it's true. She'll never survive." Parker pushes against William, but he doesn't budge. *Why is he doing this? He loves her as much as I do. He's wasting time.*

Hoss frowns. "Parker, if we go off half cocked, we'll be no good to anyone. This is why we have the plan. We need to be here when they arrive."

Of course he'd say that. His sons are in Ibiza, well out of reach of those missiles.

Donovan nods. "The kids have their plan, and we have ours, Parker."

He can't believe his friend isn't on board with two daughters out there. Gina lives closest to the base, and Sadie may be out of danger for now, but she still has a long road to get to Idaho without weapons, food, or water.

"Liam, you boys pack up. We roll out in an hour for Reed," Donovan says in a commanding tone.

Liam tips his head, and the twins follow him out.

"Beth's not alone," William says. "Between Jose and her friends, she'll survive. She's tougher than you think."

Parker's past talking. He pulls a punch, only to be tackled from behind by Donovan and Hoss.

"Let me go!" Parker breaks when William yanks him in for a tight, brotherly hug. Parker's anger dissipates with one last attempt to turn his friends. "She needs me!"

"No, Parker," William whispers, "we all need you."

Chapter 10

What the fuck was that? Gideon hangs from his chains, trying not to think about the excruciating pain in his hands and feet as he waits for rescue. In a fog, he stretches his neck and gazes down at a moaning Kaden lying on his back, blood oozing from his nose. The bus flipped. That much he's garnered from the blacktop, visible through the shattered window beyond Kaden, behind the metal mesh enclosure. "You good, Kaden?"

"Never been fucking better," he says, as blood trickles from his mouth.

The bus shakes. A blast of air brushes Gideon's exposed skin bringing with it the foul odor of burned gas. *Something exploded?*

Up front, the two guards shake glittering glass off themselves. "Fuck me, Bill. What the hell happened?"

"You okay?" the other guard asks the driver.

The driver brushes himself off. "Yeah, let's call it in and check on the others." He reaches up, pushes out the emergency hatch on the driver's side, and uses the seat to climb out. The other guard follows suit. Bill looks at the guard at the back before heading up and asks, "You good back there?"

Asshole acts like there aren't three humans between them. Rage boils inside Gideon.

The guard in the back calls out, "Yeah, meet you outside."

What is this? A fucking social call? The back emergency door hinges creak open and close with a final click. Pain sears through Gideon's wrists. *Fuck!* "Hey, you can't leave us!" Gideon shakes his chains in anger at a significant cost to himself. "I'm hanging here!"

Bill's eyes land on him. "Greaves, don't get your panties in a bunch and shut the fuck up." An arm reaches down from the driver's escape hatch to help Bill climb out as if there wasn't any problem.

Goddamned pig!

Shards of glass tinkle as Kaden sits up sluggishly below Gideon. "I'll take the strain off, Gideon. Give me a sec."

"Oh, shit! Threat at ten and two o'clock!" a guard bellows as metal groans and pops under scattering pairs of boots from above. The faint noise of people screaming in panic elevates.

My brothers.

Boots make contact with the pavement around the bus. "Dispatch! Prison transport down. Under fire. Requesting backup!"

Clunk! Plink! Beams of light pierce the shell of the bus amid sounds of discharging weapons. The men cower and swear out loud.

"Fuck me!" Gideon can't believe it. This isn't the way he wants to go. He wants to die with a gun in his hands.

After what seems like forever, a moment of silence prevails. As his heart races, Gideon's eyes lock on what lies below. Kaden is still lying there, no worse for wear and a little ticked. Their eyes connect, and Kaden nods, letting him know he's alright before he stands. He stretches his hands skyward, toward Gideon; the chains grow taut, preventing Kaden from getting closer. Frustration at having to wait grinds on Gideon's nerves as tears force their way out. The pain in his ankles becomes unbearable. *All I want is to get out of these mother fucking—*

"Gideon, we clear in there?" Hunter shouts from outside.

Air escapes Gideon's lips as the pain sears, threatening his resolve. *About fucking time.* "Yeah! Can't feel my fingers. Fucking hurry!"

Bang! A gunshot rings out opposite his brother's position. Footsteps crush the ground and circle outside. "All clear, Hunter," Greg calls out. Gideon's spirits rise. He misses his little brother.

Metal chimes. Hunter says something unintelligible, but Gideon hears his name used and the word shit. Boots connect to the metal shell of the bus and echo inside as someone climbs up to the emergency hatch at the front of the bus.

"Gideon, Greg's coming in!" Hunter's filtered, low voice says.

"How'd you pull this off?" Gideon asks, distracting himself from his torment.

Greg jumps down. Relief washes over Gideon. Keys jingle in Greg's hands as he attempts to locate the right one to free them. Kaden fidgets below, attuned to Greg's movements.

"I didn't. Everyone in one piece?" Hunter replies.

Gideon picks up on his brother's monotone voice. He hasn't seen Hunter since the robbery but he knows this attitude well. *Still thinks he's better than us.* "Looks that way. What do you mean?"

"You wouldn't believe me if I told you."

Gideon's hackles rise. Keys slam to the ground, and the cage door screeches open. Greg steps into the prisoner area, reaches into his back pocket, and pulls out bolt cutters.

"What's wrong with the keys?" he asks Greg, annoyed at having to wait a second longer than necessary.

His younger brother gazes at the bolt cutters. "This is faster."

Gideon nods at Kaden. "Him first." He twists his head and gazes skyward. "What's the plan?"

Kaden's chains clank to the ground. In an instant, Kaden lifts Gideon. He sucks in a breath as the pain slices sharp. Greg positions the bolt cutters.

"Plan's changed," Hunter says.

Gideon's irritation brews under the surface. *Changed?* He hates it when Hunter uses vague words. Kaden helps Gideon stand, who ignores the sting in his wrists and ankles and stretches to pull his brother Greg in for a hug. "Let's go."

Kaden steps to the front. "I'll find the first aid kit."

Someone coughs. Three sets of eyes peer back. Dugal, chains off, taps a paper clip on his knee. His scraggly, shoulder-length dark hair is too long for Gideon's taste. He prefers his head and face shaved, but to each their own. Not wasting time, Gideon heads for the front. "You with us? Or you on your own?"

Dugal jumps down and follows. "If there's no pussy, I'm out."

Gideon emerges from the hatch. "Holy fuck!" In the distance, a mushroom cloud hovers. *A nuke? Radiation?* Plumes of black smoke rise from Spokane's direction. The tallest buildings still standing appear fractured, and the trees, divested of their leaves, reach out to the sky, broken and twisted.

On the highway, amid horrific screams, vehicles lie scattered, like carelessly thrown toys. In the center, what used to be a tanker truck lies on its side, smoldering. *The explosion earlier.* A few upstanding citizens are attempting to rescue people from burning vehicles but their efforts are fruitless.

This is bad.

Greg climbs down to an alert Hunter, his deadpan face scanning around and back. His familiar jagged scars traverse a face the girls in school used to like once upon a time. Not now. He was born with a broken and twisted spoon, like the rest of them, but Gideon can't remember the last time Hunter smiled and dismisses the thought. Hunter slides his stony eyes up at him.

Resolute, Gideon understands the plan has changed. "We need to get Wendall out."

Hunter responds with an expression of dread and reluctance. He doesn't need words. *Suck it up, brother. Family is family.* He's not leaving Wendall to rot without paying his debt.

Kaden and Dugal climb out and stand beside Gideon, both men wearing the same expression of shock.

"How you want to play it?" Kaden asks. Ever the yes-man, Kaden goes with whatever Gideon says. Life is simpler with Kaden.

The original plan was to lie low up at the farm while they waited for the heat to dissipate after their escape. But it would seem luck is on their side; the law has other things to worry about now. *Could be room to play here.* Gullible, scared people will be ripe for the picking. And vulnerable women... He lingers on the thought. "Let's do what we do best. Rob people. Pussy's on the table, Dugal."

Dugal ties his hair back. "Let's go get some snatch, then."

Gideon scowls. "No roughing them up. We'll need 'em."

Dugal nods but doesn't reply.

Gideon jumps down, spots Bill propped against the bus tire, bleeding out but alive, and stills. *Fucker.* "Give me a weapon."

Hunter doesn't comply. "Leave him. He can't harm us."

"Give me a fucking...weapon!" Under Gideon's stare, Hunter caves, serves him a handgun, and turns away. *Never could stomach it.* Gideon strolls to the man staring death in the face and aims. "I don't wear panties, and no one tells me to shut the fuck up."

The blast of a gun echoes, and Gideon's satisfied grin follows.

CHAPTER 11

Doleridge Max Penitentiary lies before Gideon in the waning sunset, an ominous sight to behold. The dark frame of the building stands in sharp contrast to the backdrop of the eerie, red, glowing sky. Dark billowing smoke rises from the air force base in the distance. He covers his face with a bandanna and gazes at his bandaged hands, the pain ever present in his wrists. Out here, in the boonies, the wind blows acrid smoke unhindered, bringing with it the essence of freedom.

"You sure you want to do this?" Hunter asks as Kaden stands on guard nearby.

It was never a question of whether Gideon wanted to do this. Growing up, his family exposed him to fear, which made him immune to it. The devastation they passed on their way here cemented his resolve, and he knows the window of opportunity is wide open. Gideon has to break his brother out before it closes on them. "He's our blood, and I ain't leaving Wendall to die in there. You saw what we're up against."

With distaste written on his face, Hunter turns away from Gideon. Ever since Gideon can remember, Hunter's personality clashed with Wendall's, repelling each other like two magnets with the same polarity. Hunter regards their family as a prison and Wendall is the warden. *Can't choose your family.*

They had five, soon to be six, people, so they hijacked an SUV and a beat-up truck after leaving the prison bus. Took a while to find ones that started, which he found disconcerting. Gideon stashed the vehicles a half mile down the road and walked, leaving Dugal and Greg to guard them. Gideon second-guessed his judgment of allowing Dugal to ride along with them when the man opted out of the rescue and to stay with the vehicles. He didn't trust that the vehicles would be there when they came back, so he told Greg to stay behind. His brother didn't take it well, but Gideon always protected him from the brunt of things, so Greg had no choice. It's their way.

Their predicament became clearer on the drive to the prison. Damaged vehicles and lost people clogged the highway, so Gideon diverted them into downtown Spokane. They narrowly survived a collapsing building, which sent even more debris and dust skyward, and masses of injured people overran Deaconess Hospital. It wasn't safe there anymore. They had weapons, but not enough ammunition.

The curveball Gideon was not prepared for was the crashed jetliner that exploded as they passed, sending thousands of fragmented pieces into the nearby fields north of the Spokane airport runway.

The air here at the prison is cooling down, but the gravity of their plight makes his skin tingle, raising his goosebumps. Gideon focuses back on the task at hand. "We go in, find him, and extract his ass." Gideon hands Kaden a switchblade. "You feel threatened, this'll do the trick. Conserve the ammo."

Before his arrest, Gideon had visited his brother frequently, so he knows security is tight, but the sight before them gives him hope of extraction. *Could it be this easy?* Whatever hit the base has shaken the foundation of the prison walls, toppling the tall guard towers on the south side. Between the rubble of the towers and the penitentiary, life and death play out amid gunfire in the open fields; the prisoners and guards are fighting each other for control or survival. Unsuspecting inmates who must have been in the yard when everything went down writhe in pain, entangled in a mangled mesh of barbed steel wire. Men in orange jumpsuits spill out of a crack in the prison's north wall like ants fleeing the nest. Wendall was in the north cell block, last Gideon knew. He hopes his brother is still inside. Wherever his brother is, they'll find him. Time to collect.

***

"He's not coming. Saving his own skin," Wendall says, perched on the lower bunk of his shared cell. He should really consider it a compliment that no one wants to break him out. Wendall scrutinizes the hairline cracks that snake down his cell walls. He's not claustrophobic, but in this case, the walls are actually closing in on him. The cold fluorescent light bulb in the ceiling went dark after the building shook, and it has stayed that way, which means the backup generator hasn't come online. His cell door didn't budge when he tried it, so he is lying low, waiting for the inevitable. He is as sure as the sun rises that someone with a score will come knocking. He is a shot caller in these parts, but not in the other cell blocks. Ironic, that his enemies would be his salvation. Only time will tell which one will have the nerve to open that cell door.

"He'll come," Sonny says, his confident voice ringing off the dreary gray walls. Wendall's short, stocky cellmate wants to settle a score. Newly minted, he is in for the same crime as Wendall and more. Sonny robbed and killed a couple walking their dog at night. He talked a good talk about raping the woman, but there were never any charges brought against him for that. His bravado backfired, and Sonny ended up on the wrong side of the shower room. The man owes Wendall for literally saving his ass. In truth, Wendall had a grievance to settle and used the opportunity to take the other inmate down a peg; the same man Sonny hopes is going to come through their door.

Prison-issue shoes dash and scrape the polished floors outside their cell; the sound of men escaping. Gunfire, amid shouts and screams, echoes off the walls inconsistently. Moans compel him to walk to the plexiglass window and peer out, but he remains glued to the bunk, staring at the floor.

The cool metal of the shiv in his right hand bolsters his confidence in the stark space he occupies. The improvised knife didn't take long to make once he'd acquired the items he needed. Hiding it from the guards was a challenge.

Once his cell door swings open, he's prepared to come out fighting. There's no way he's rotting in this hellhole.

Wendall loosens his collar and inhales rank air. Sweat trickles down between his shoulder blades as the heat rises. This is not the way he wanted to go. Those words remind him of his brother. Gideon had said it over the years, particularly when a few robberies went south on them, but they always made it out in the end.

Growing up, there were days when Wendall had thought his grandparents would kill him, but as it turned out, they enjoyed torturing him and his brothers too much to let them die. All the boys suffered under their verbal and physical abuse, and it only brought the four of them closer. They each had their own grievances against each other, as brothers do, but on the subject of their grandparents, they agreed. Stick together, keep yourself scarce, avoid contact, and stay out of the line of fire as much as possible.

Hunter is supposed to be liberating Gideon today. Hunter visited a couple of days ago and spoke in code; the walls have ears here. He and Greg had a plan to intercept the prison transport bus, but Wendall's unsure how Hunter's going to pull it off. They planned to hide out at the family farm in a remote area of Idaho. He wonders if the boys succeeded. If Wendall can get clear of this place, he'll follow. *If...*

The voices die down. Before Wendall can get to his feet, the door clicks and slides open with a metallic twang. Pungent air floods the room, smoke stings his eyes, and a breeze caresses his face. His head swivels to Pee-Wee, named for his pasty complexion, red lips, and a face like plastic surgery gone wrong, darkening his doorstep. Sonny was right; it's the same inmate Wendall took down a peg, and all two hundred pounds of Pee-Wee's cocky, antsy muscle is looking for the newbie. He is unarmed, but with the size of his hands, he doesn't need a weapon.

"Greaves, I ain't got no beef with you. Where's the little shit?"

Well, ain't that a relief.

Wendall rises to his full height of six feet. It is subtle, but the man outside flinches. People respect strength. Wendall isn't interested in fighting Pee-Wee, either, but he doesn't like how the man is blocking his way out.

"On the bed," Wendall says, crossing to his side of the threshold. He leans his hand on the door frame and slaps his concealed shiv against the cold inner cement wall. "Move aside." He might not be looking for a fight, but sometimes, it comes looking for you.

The man calculates for a split second. "You got beef with me?"

"No, but we can change that."

Pee-Wee takes that into consideration, then gives Wendall a wide berth. *Maybe I won't need it after all.* Wendall hits the corridor unarmed and invites the man to go in.

Pee-Wee's menacing voice says, "Get down out of that bed, you little pissant!" His shoes scuff the floor as he rushes into the room.

Wendall takes in his surroundings. Stress cracks slice their way up the cement walls. He gazes up to see sky greeting him where there should be none. Pee-Wee yelps out in pain. Shoes squeak and dance on the polished floors behind Wendall. He's clueless as to what happened outside this bleak place, but inside is a different story. Something powerful rocked the old prison.

Gurgles and choking resound in the background, mixed with moans and screams in the day room below. The roof appears to have partially caved in after the initial shock, and it took no quarter as it fell into the room below because orange and blue uniforms lie trapped under large chunks of it...along with splashes of red. Perhaps he is the lucky one.

Wendall gazes back to find Sonny, who is wearing only his underwear, wiping the shiv on Pee-Wee's clothes and stepping over his kill, pleased as punch. Sonny's ploy of stuffing his clothes with the sheets to appear like he was in the top bunk worked. He swings the handle of the shiv toward Wendall, who shakes his head. "Keep it. Collect your clothes off the dummy."

"Wendall!"

Some profound things in life make an impression on a young mind, like the aroma of your mother's floral-scented hair, the sight of your sadistic grandfather folding his belt in half, and the sound of your brother's annoyed voice hollering across a field of corn. Recognizing the strained voice as Gideon's, Wendall gazes down upon his armed brothers waiting below and a man with tattooed arms. *Kaden.* His brother's unwavering partner in crime.

Wendall is proud, almost. What love might be like if he possessed that emotion? The sight injects new life into his limbs as he approaches the stairs. He's impressed but suppresses this reaction. "'Bout time you showed up!" His tone is serious.

"Yeah, yeah, get down here!" Gideon eyes the exits and doorways around him, no doubt looking for threats; as close to an act of love as this family is capable.

"Not without Cain," Wendall says as he descends into the pit of hell. A place he wants to see in his rearview soon. "You injured?" Someone has bandaged Gideon's wrists.

Gideon ignores the question. "You don't understand. We need to vacate fast."

He doesn't have time to argue. "Spit it out. Why?" Wendall scans the far wall for the door he needs. They're numbered. Hunter hands him a rifle. The silence fills the space between them, and a cool vibe of resentment radiates off Hunter. Wendall will wade through the minefield of his brother's temperament later, when he has time.

Gideon exchanges a look with Hunter. "A missile has been fired, and the city has been leveled. Electrical grid is down, planes are coming out of the sky... We got bigger fish to fry than your vendetta with Cain."

D615. Cain's door is closed. "There's no vendetta. I'm breaking him out." Wendall sprints around the perimeter, careful to avoid the bloodstains on the floor. Reaching D615, Wendall shows his face in the rectangular window before he slides the bolt on the door.

Fueled by high energy, a lean, redheaded man springs forth from his cell with equally nasty shivs in both hands, ready to battle his way out. "You got a plan?"

Cain is all action and few words. Military, through and through. Perfect for the predicament they find themselves in, and Wendall owes him. *Not anymore. Debt paid.*

"You ready to kick this place to the curb?" Wendall asks.

Cain eyes the men armed to the teeth around him before concealing the shivs. "Where's my toy?"

Upon Wendall's approving nod, Gideon passes a handgun to Cain, who promptly ejects the mag, checks the ammo, slams the mag back in, and chambers a round in one smooth motion. "Let's kill our way out, then. How much ammo you got?"

Sonny joins them, the shiv steady in his red-stained fingers, ready for anything.

Wendall holds his hands up. "Hold on, let me think."

"Wendall, we have to go!"

This is why Gideon doesn't lead. He's compulsive and brash. Not a thinker like Wendall. A missile means they've been attacked. The base makes sense. He's not sure what Gideon means by Spokane being leveled. "Have any other cities been affected?"

"Don't know. There were no police or emergency vehicles on the road. Just us."

With the city in shambles, anarchy will reign and their food supply will dry up in a matter of days. Why attack only this base? There has to be more to this, but what?

The farm is definitely still their best destination. They'll lie low for a while, then he'll head out to find answers. They'll need to find and rob some stores along the way; Sonny, Cain, and he can't wander around in orange jumpsuits for too long. "How much food do you have at the farm, Hunter?"

"Six months' supply for the four of us."

Hmm, his brother isn't keen on having more come along for the ride. Regardless, if they hide out at the farm, the food there won't last. They'll need a show of force to steal supplies.

Wendall surveys the other cells. *Useful bodies trapped behind each door that will otherwise die here.* Plus, they'd owe him. "How many vehicles do you have?"

CHAPTER 12

Fuck. Mal leans against the cold cement wall near the steel door, in the dark, waiting for rescue, ironically from an enemy. It certainly won't be the guards. They'd let the prisoners rot for sure. The shuffle of feet died down a while ago, which meant Mal's chance of escape was circling the drain quickly.

It ticked him off. If there was wind in this godforsaken prison, it stank. It's the mantra Mal lives by. He goes where the wind takes him and it never fails him. The one time he didn't was after he committed his crime, when the wind told him to run after the bloodlust cleared, but did he listen? Ultimately, he knew he'd end up behind bars again. It was just a matter of time. He vowed to never go against his natural instinct again. It's the only thing left in this world he trusts.

"How are we going to get out of here?" Mal's scrawny cellmate paces the length of their cage, forcing Mal back to their present dilemma. His cellmate uses his appearance as a scared little punk at will, but underneath, he is a ruthless motherfucker when he has the advantage. He is also stupid, which confounds Mal.

Whatever hit the building shook the cell walls. Dust rained down and settled all within what seemed like seconds. Felt like an earthquake, but it didn't ring true and made Mal nervous. Rumbling and cracking echoed throughout the prison, but their walls remained intact, except for the jagged fissures zigzagging down the walls. And as long as the walls remained intact, they were safe, but trapped.

The cell door bolt slides out. *Showtime.* Mal focuses on the T-shirt, wound tight between his hands, and gazes at the faint outline of his sister's name tattooed on his skin. The shirt was the only weapon he had within reach, but it would have to do. The door swings open, and a flashlight casts a beam on his cellmate, who raises his arms. No one enters. The smug look on his cellmate's face shows Mal their rescuer isn't just anybody but a somebody. To whom does he owe the pleasure?

"If you work for me, I can get you out."

Wendall.

Why did he pick this cell? Mal loosens his hold on the T-shirt, drapes it over his shoulders, and changes his demeanor to a nonchalant attitude. No way can he win a physical fight with this conniving bastard, and Wendall wouldn't open a cell door without backup.

His cell mate laughs. "For you? I work for no one."

A muzzle blast bounces around the enclosed space, piercing Mal's ears as his cellmate's body shoots backward, trailing a mist of red, and slams, with an audible crack, against the metal toilet on the far wall. It will be hours before Mal will be able to hear right again, he knows.

Wendall enters, points a gun, and asks in a warped, low voice, "What'll it be, Kensington?"

The wind has changed... He is fucked.

***

Gideon grabs a nearby tree. Heavy breathing and moaning reverberate through the chilly night air, punctuated by the snapping of the underbrush as the men they have liberated traipse through the trees. They escaped the prison, not finding any resistance. The light of day is replaced with a blackness he remembers from growing up on the farm. It was a hindrance to their escape, not having any light pollution, but they stayed together somehow.

"Gideon, keep walking," Wendall commands. His older brother's vision in the dark was always superior to the rest of the boys growing up. The air moves in the wake of his brother passing him. Gideon follows in silence. Behind them, the occasional gunshot still echoes out, but not as much as when they arrived. What is of greater concern is the gunfire he can hear ahead of them, and the closer they get, the louder it sounds.

Up ahead, the flickering lights of the trucks guide them. *Why are they doing that?*

The sound of men screaming and moaning sharpens. They aren't the only group that has been drawn to the headlights. *Shit!*

"Greg!" Hunter calls out.

The light drives confidence in their footsteps. The air is filled with the sharp crack of shooting as they race onto the road, finding themselves amid a frenzied battle of men in vibrant orange garments. Gideon leaps over bodies as a prisoner jumps into the driver's seat. Gideon aims, shoots, and yanks the body out.

Out of nowhere, a redheaded man hurls himself into the throng, swinging a knife and firing a handgun at will. *Cain.* The sea of men parts faster than a whore's legs and runs from him in fear. Cain carves a man from ear to ear with cold accuracy, apparently without fear of the bullets flying around. *He's crazy.*

The frenzied mob retreats. Wendall steps in front of Gideon, firing into the backs of the fleeing men, dropping bodies.

"Gideon!"

His head snaps at the sound of Hunter's panicked voice. He never panics. Gideon spots the boots of an unmoving body on the ground. *Greg!* He races toward the back of the truck in a cold sweat.

Hunter grabs Greg's shoulders. "Lift him!"

Gideon catches on and hoists his brother onto the tailgate. With so little light, Gideon can't gauge his brother's injuries. He's still alive though, as Greg has a death grip on Hunter's arm, and his terrified eyes search Gideon out.

Wendall forces his way between Hunter and Gideon. "Greg, stay with us. You did good, brother."

Relief flits across Greg's pained face. His lips move, but no sound slips through. Liquid trickles out instead.

Wendall hikes to the passenger side of the truck. "Drag him into the bed, Gideon. Hunter, you drive!"

Hunter leaves to jump into the driver's seat. Gideon climbs onto the bed, drags Greg's body into the back of the truck, and lays his brother's head in his lap. Men scramble in, slamming the tailgate as the truck jolts into motion. Cain catapults into the bed, weapons held firmly in his capable hands.

What is happening? Losing control confuses Gideon. Greg reaches up, smearing wetness across Gideon's bushy beard. He cups his brother's head and bends as his words filter into Greg's ears. "Don't speak, little brother. I'm proud of you. We'll be at the farm in no time." It is a lie. Gideon blinks back tears, glad it's dark out so the others don't see his weakness.

Greg attempts to speak, but blood gurgles from his mouth, spilling down his cheeks. Too much. The writing is on the wall. The memory of his grandmother writhing in agony on the floor under the kitchen light clouds his vision. Blood flowed from her mouth this way, too. He shakes it off. Gideon wonders what his brother wants to say so badly. Does he know he's dying?

Greg's body goes rigid, and Gideon pulls back as blood sprays into the air, dousing everyone. He slams on the back window and screams, "Stop the truck!"

CHAPTER 13

"Libby!" Ryker shoves the apartment door with force, dislodging debris on the other side, but not enough to gain entrance to his sister's place. He hopes she's alright.

Ryker exited the grocery store when he heard the familiar sound of a missile cruising through the air. He thought maybe he was experiencing a flashback until he glanced in the direction the other patrons were pointing at. In the sky, she was arcing back to the earth, leaving a blazing trail behind her, not giving him much time. While everyone else gawked, Ryker transitioned into action mode. Seeing a mother nearby with a newborn strapped to her, he guided her back into the store and shielded them with his body behind what he hoped was a sturdy brick wall. The missile's shock wave ripped through the flimsy roof, sending parts of the heavy beam system crashing around them. With no wheels, he had to run to Libby's apartment, hoping he wouldn't find her crushed or seriously injured like so many people he passed along the way.

"Ryker!" Libby's hand grasps his through the opening.

Thank God. The tension between his shoulders relaxes a little. "Are you alright?" He lays eyes on his young, petite sister, her dark hair stuck up and disheveled.

"Yes. Are you?" Her tear-stained face betrays her confident answer, revealing all he needs to know.

"Stand back." He shoulders the door with more force, while Libby wrenches on the door from the inside. The door gives, and Libby falls back onto a pile of ceiling rubble in the tiny entryway. He pulls her up and examines her for broken bones.

"I'm fine. Just scared," she assures him.

He hugs her to his chest. "I'm here now." Guilt scores through him, knowing she endured that alone, but he moves past it and enters her apartment, finding it in shambles. The walls are partially intact, and the ceiling has held, but the cracks in the walls tell him it isn't safe here.

Ryker rubs his shoulder. "I'll go find my vest and suit up. You have hiking boots?" he asks, not waiting for the answer as he stalks further into her apartment.

Back at the store, he stuck around to make sure the woman and her child were safe and then wandered outside. The unmistakable mushroom cloud left little to ponder as the land belched smoke, but from his vantage point, he couldn't see from where. However, the trees on the boulevard were stripped of all their leaves and a few low-lying buildings looked intact. The sensation that he was back there, amid the ruins of a city in the sandbox, didn't sit well with him. People were limping or wandering around in shock and those mobile enough were walking the injured a safe distance away from the store. Then there were the bodies in random spots, sprawled out as if they'd dropped suddenly with whatever they were carrying. It became apparent that the severity of the situation dictated he grab those he cared about and hightail it out of the city, pronto. His sister was first.

"Where are we going?" Libby yells down the hallway behind him.

"I'll tell you when we're safe."

The diner is next.

***

Under the late afternoon sun, Libby squeezes Ryker's hand as he leads her through a neighborhood in Spokane Valley. She's petrified. The blood and carnage of the dead bodies they pass scare her. Unseen people moan and scream out in pain, exacerbating her terrified mind.

Her hiking boots pinch, but she doesn't complain because her psyche eggs her on to move faster. The streets look like a tornado has wreaked a path of violence on everything: homes leveled or barely there; trees uprooted; and abandoned vehicles, crushed or burning.

Ryker conceals his military vest and the weapons he carries beneath an oversized jacket. She wonders if his boots hurt, too. A woman with three children huddles outside their burning home. She releases the kids and stumbles toward them with a towel firmly held to her bloody head.

"That's far enough," Ryker says, placing himself in front of Libby.

The frightened woman stops, raising her hands in surrender. "Please, can you help us?"

"No, ma'am. Sorry." Ryker guides Libby along, circumnavigating the injured woman who stands dejected as they leave.

She doesn't understand her brother. *How can he be so unfeeling?*

"Please help my children," the woman calls out after them.

"Ryker, we need to help her." Libby twists to look back at the woman, but Ryker holds her hand firm and keeps walking.

"Libby, you can't help these people."

"Why not?"

He remains silent as they come to a park. Ryker steers them down another street, away from the grassy fields, but not before she spots the throng of people congregating around men and women with first aid kits and covered bodies. *Why are we not going to the park? We could wait for some kind of rescue. Isn't that what the army does? Set up tents and pop-up hospitals like they do in the movies?*

Crack! Pop! Ryker halts their momentum and tugs her to the ground with him. Panic sets in. Her heart thumps so fast in her chest, she must be having a heart attack. Her ears burn like her calf muscles. They've been walking for so long. She dreads moving forward while there's so much gunfire, but Ryker doesn't seem to be afraid as he draws her back to her feet and proceeds down the road in silence. *How is he so calm? We should go back to the park, where it was safer.*

Two men block their path on the street, causing her to gasp in fear. One is armed with a handgun, and the other, a baseball bat spiked with nails.

"Shit," Ryker says under his breath and steps in front of her again.

The man with the gun shakes his weapon at them. "Give us your backpacks!"

Ryker raises his hands. "Sure, man, anything, just don't hurt my girl. She's blind. I'll have to help her get it off."

Blind? What's he talking about?

Ryker turns, his eyes sliding downward, then back up. Libby's not sure what to do with that but nods. He stands behind her and unlatches the backpack from her shoulders, one strap at a time.

"Hurry up, then," the man with the baseball bat says, brandishing it like he can't wait to use it on them.

What's Ryker doing back there? Just get rid of the bag so they can leave us alone. The weight of the backpack lifts, amplifying a painful ache in her shoulders.

Ryker whispers, "When I throw it, close your eyes and hit the ground."

Wait, what?!

He stalks past her and approaches the men, holding the backpack aloft between them.

She spots the weapon in his hands. *Oh, shit!* Her heart jumps, and her breaths come in brief spurts, but she shoves the fear back down.

Ryker throws the backpack. The man with the baseball bat reacts too slowly.

Libby shuts her eyes and drops, and her hands smack on the rough ground. Four distinct shots rupture Libby's ears and dim the sound of her beating heart. As the seconds pass, her anxiety intensifies. *Could I squeeze my eyes any tighter?* The crunching of boots on the pavement causes her to tremble. Her fingers curl, forming fists.

"Libby? Open your eyes."

***

Smash! In the dwindling light, Ryker hurls a heavy rock through the front door, spraying glass into the diner. "It's Ryker. Anyone here?"

He leads Libby by the hand through the opening, with both their backpacks intact and his headlamp leading the way. Silence greets them. The subtle hints of food and leather linger. The reality outside doesn't quite mesh with the tranquility inside the diner they've stepped into. She spots the jukebox at the far end, dark and lifeless. Plates of food and mugs of coffee on the tables, untouched, waiting for someone to sit down and enjoy them. The absence of people heightens her apprehension. *Where did everyone go?*

As Ryker led her through the streets, he didn't even flinch when a weapon was fired, unlike Libby. She is still trying to come to terms with the death of those two men back there. Ryker embraced and soothed her with calming words. Thank God Ryker is with her. She isn't equipped to escape on her own or survive like him and is grateful he found her. She shivers, thinking about the dead bodies, again.

"Let's raid the fridge and take whatever we can carry," he says, seemingly undisturbed by their plight.

Ryker leads her into a dark kitchen, his headlamp trailing along the stove, to the prep counter and over the dishwashing station. The place looks like it was in the thick of a lunch rush. The grill is off, but food adorns the surface, ready to be flipped, and there are plates lined up in various stages of being dressed.

"Is this where your girl works?" she asks. When Ryker came home two nights ago, he wore a silly grin during dinner, and she knew it wasn't due to a new job. She'd like to think she grilled him like a sister should. Ryker certainly gave her enough ammunition to tease him with, and deep down, she thinks he enjoyed it.

He points his flashlight at the ceiling, leaves it on the counter, and takes her small hands in his. "Yes. Are you okay?"

"She's a lucky girl."

He laughs her comment away.

"No, I mean it. We've only known each other for, what, a couple of months? You've been like a rock to me. So caring. Attentive."

He listens but makes no move to reply.

"If you hadn't found me, I wouldn't know what it was like to have a big brother. Dad wasn't big on family stuff."

His guilt comes to the surface. "I'm sorry I left you and the others with him."

She was young when Ryker enlisted. He didn't visit the farm the whole time he served, but her father respected the military and praised Ryker, anyway. He never mentioned her other two half-siblings in the house, except as an insult. "We've gone over this, Ryker. You had to do you. You can't take care of others unless you can take care of yourself first. Stop feeling guilty. I'm fine. Or I was before this—" She waves her hand in the air. "—whatever this is."

He leaves her side, walks around the room, searches, and lifts objects. "I know a place where we can ride it out. Just have to get there."

"How far is it?" Her feet are hurting worse than before, so it'd better be close. She wonders what kind of woman caught her brother's eye. "Will she be there?"

Ryker stops and stares back at her. "I hope so."

"Then I can't wait to meet her."

He grins. Libby likes how it's only been a couple of months but she can already tell when he's anxious. *He's trying to shield me from something.* Perhaps he's worried about this woman he likes.

Drawers scrape open and close as he searches.

"What are you looking for?" she asks.

He pulls things out and bags them. "A can opener."

Libby gazes through the kitchen hatch, into the darkness of the diner. Black shapes walk past the windows. Fear creeps back in. Their precarious predicament washes over Libby as the last few hours catch up to her. "I'm scared."

He crosses the kitchen and encloses her in an embrace, his vest preventing her from getting too close. "Don't worry, I got ya. Let's go find the pantry and stock up."

Chapter 14

Carrie slaps Beth. Blinding light forces her to curl up as it consumes the blackness within the car. Glass sprays between her and her sister. A heavy force thrusts Beth in the opposite direction. Pain pierces her head.

Beth jolts, the back of her head slams into something hard, and she yelps in total darkness. *What the hell?* She listens but hears nothing except her own breathing. Her fingers trail along the smooth leather. *My couch.* She makes contact with something hard and unforgiving. *The roof?* She forces her hand through what little space there is and presses her throbbing forehead. *Sticky.*

Beth tries to remember what happened. *It's not a nightmare, is it?* She breathes in and coughs violently. *Earthquake?* They are on the Latah fault line, after all.

So, this is how it ends. A slow, agonizing death. It's for the best.

"Beth!" Colin's distressed voice cries, cutting through her morbid thoughts. Hope sparks, then resignation takes over. *Don't reply and you'll get what you want.* She pushes her optimism down. His feet shift on what sounds like sand. A light skims the edge of her tomb, and yet she stays silent. It sounds like rocks are tumbling forth. "Beth!" *If he doesn't find you, the nightmare will end.*

"Colin," Sean calls out, "check the back." *Sean, take them to safety. Leave me.*

"Is this happening?" Alejo asks. "I'm not leaving till we find our Beth, babe. Her phone's here. She wouldn't leave without it." *Damn Alejo.*

"We'll find her, A."

Why are they wasting time searching for her? Why isn't Sean preparing them? They need to find their gear and head out.

"She's not back here," Colin says, his voice fainter than before.

"What will we do if she's dead?!" Alejo's rapid breathing follows.

Feet shuffle as Sean says, "A, slow down, honey."

He's hyperventilating. Beth can't die knowing Alejo might be in trouble or, worse, die with her. "Alejo?" she calls out weakly.

"Oh my God, honey!" She senses his fear, sure he jumped at her words.

Someone lights up the couch, and with effort, they lift a piece of the roof. Dust scatters. Beth coughs again.

"Are you injured?" Colin pulls her into his protective arms, slides a gentle hand along her chin, tilts her head up, and gazes into her eyes. "Other than your head?"

I don't deserve those eyes.

Beth surveys her damaged apartment. Jagged cracks trail down her walls and disappear into the floor. The ceiling has collapsed and crumbled around her kitchen island, sprinkling the ground with an ashen powder. The apartment windows, meanwhile, are gaping holes, the curtains stripped off their rods. Under the living room window, the butterfly stuffy rests atop smashed picture frames and among shards of glass. The first stars twinkle through the wide-open hole in her roof. *What the hell happened?* She cuts back to Colin. The bridge of his nose is cut and bleeding. "No. You're injured, though."

"I'll survive." His hold tightens.

She breaks eye contact and looks at Alejo and Sean for answers. "Was it an earthquake?"

"It's like a horror movie out there! They attacked us!" Words tumble out of Alejo like verbal diarrhea, and he reaches out in need of comfort.

"What? Slow down." Beth escapes Colin's warm embrace to cuddle and soothe Alejo by stroking his back and shoulders. "What's he talking about, Sean?"

"A missile hit Fairchild."

The airbase? Crap!

"There was a flash," Colin says.

Beth exclaims, "Shit!"

Colin looks almost shocked. Beth supposes it's because she rarely swears out loud.

"Hold on, are you sure it was a missile?" she asks Sean. "It could have been a meteorite."

Sean shakes his head. "It arced across the sky, Beth."

Meteors don't arc. "Did you see where it impacted?"

"No, but the mushroom cloud was unmistakable."

Nuclear? If so, we need to stay indoors. "Any particles in the air?"

Alejo scratches his head. "Particles?"

Sean answers, "No."

"How do you know it hit the base?" Beth asks, afraid of what he's going to say.

"It's a calculated guess. The only structures west of us are the airbase and the airport, and who would care about our airport?" he says, confirming what she feared. Valid points.

"How is that possible? Who has the capability of hitting us this far inland without being detected?" Beth asks.

"Whatever hit us took out everything from Fairchild to Spokane. The blast upended the truck, so we walked here. What we've seen..." Sean touches her forearm. "Beth, what Parker prepared us for? It's happened."

What? No... Beth recalls a conversation she overheard. "If it wasn't a nuke, and there's no..." She peers out the shattered living room window at the rising twilight, and the word "Fallout" tumbles past her lips in a whisper. Outside, an eerie red glow impregnates the sky and highlights the billowing smoke as embers float by like fireflies. Fear blooms on her face, then she deflates as disappointment takes over.

Beth approaches the hole in the wall that was once her window. The surrounding two-story buildings are piles of rubble or standing half cocked, ready to topple over. Flames lick the sky here and there. People aren't loitering like she expected. She searches out the wall clock, its hands stuck at two thirty. The sun's down. *It's been what...six, seven hours? Too much time lost.*

A long sigh escapes. *Every time things get better... Why?* The second darkest day of her life floods her mind. Beth stares with steely resolve at a reflection of her teenage self in the bathroom mirror. She's emptied an entire bottle of pain meds into a glass full of water and is waiting for the tablets to dissolve.

Alejo's whiny voice hauls her back from the memory. "I don't want to go outside. We should stay."

She has to make them see. Civilization crumbles once the food stops moving. "No. We need to get away before it's too late."

"I second Alejo's suggestion. It's too dark out there." Colin shifts closer to her.

Her demeanor transforms from defeat to resignation. "Colin—"

"Beth is right," Sean says, crossing his arms. "We need to leave the city ASAP." She knew he'd be on her side.

Colin shakes his head. "We just have to stick it out. The government will restore some power in a few days."

"It won't be coming back on," Beth says in a prophetic tone. They need to leave before the looting and chaos begin. Those who have enough food and water to last a few days will hold on to the hope that the power will come back on, but if she's right, that missile had EMP capability, and those few days could stretch into months or years of no electricity. Beth raises her arm. The digital readout of her Apple watch, a gift from her uncle, is blank.

"Beth, you're in shock. You'll see. They'll bring out the National Guard and set up camps."

Beth rummages through the debris around the couch in search of her phone. When she sees it in Alejo's hand, she gestures for it. *The distribution of food will stop. If we're lucky, we have a few days before the looting, stealing, and killing will get really bad.* She swipes the screen. It's blank, too. "Definitely an EMP. You should all go." All eyes move to Beth with varying degrees of "hell, no."

"What?" Colin reaches for her, but she shrinks from him. "I'm not leaving without you."

Alejo crosses his arms and shoots an I-don't-think-so vibe her way.

Sean steps closer, looking pissed. "Beth, there's no way in hell we're going to leave you here alone!"

Her chest tightens at the thought of going outside. The idea of seeing car wrecks and death is already triggering her. She'd have no control. "I can't go out there. It's not safe for me."

Alejo wrestles her crossed arms apart and clasps her hands. His kind eyes seek hers out. "Can't we be your safe zones, baby?"

"It doesn't work like that, A." They don't understand. How can they? She's never lost it around them. Their general chatter distracts her when they walk with her or drive her places. But now, out there, there's too much for her to ignore.

Sean walks into her space and points a finger at her. "Parker would never forgive me, or you."

Beth turns away and gazes into her mangled kitchen. Thoughts have been invading her for days... *How can I survive without control?* "It's going to get bad, Sean."

Alejo looks from Sean to her. "Bad? Whoa, what do you mean by bad?"

I don't know if I can walk out of this apartment. She wrestles with the thought of Parker risking his life to rescue her and dying in the attempt. *Damn it, I can't let that happen.* If she sticks with her friends, she might make it. Right?

"Beth, we'll help you through this, but we need you to get us there," Sean says, sounding calmer now. "The guys taught you everything you need to know. I've never done the journey on foot."

She turns to the three men. They hold their breath in silence and wait. Beth advances to the fridge, fingers a photo of her family that, miraculously, has remained in place, under a butterfly magnet, and weighs her options. Sean's partially right. He knows how to use a map and compass but he doesn't know the lay of the land like she does. She can get them there faster.

If they stay, they'll die here. If they leave, they could die. Regardless, even Beth can see this place isn't a safe zone anymore.

She tilts her head in their direction. Alejo's heels aren't suitable. He is their weak link and will struggle to walk the distance. "We need to go south, head through the neighborhoods, and find a car, but we can't be choosy."

"Find?" Colin asks.

"We need to steal one that works and take the highway out of town."

Struggle fleets across his face, but he regains his composure. "I know how to hot-wire one."

"We'll head to Haven via Reed. Ten days on foot, if we're lucky. With a vehicle, we can cut that down."

Colin releases pent-up air in his lungs.

Sean's shoulders drop. "Doable."

Alejo raises an eyebrow. "Hon, these feet don't do mileage."

Beth's poise changes from expressing grimness to determination as she yanks the photo off the fridge, sending the butterfly magnet to the floor. She gazes at her friend. "They do now, A. Lose the shoes." She turns to Sean, ignoring Alejo's sharp gasp. It's a sure bet he doesn't own runners. "If we're doing this, we need to adapt and get through the city. Looting will be underway by now."

Colin stays her with his hand. "Hold on, what's Haven?"

Beth exchanges a look with Sean. Do they have time to explain this? It's so much more than a typical farm.

"The name of the farm. We'll explain when we get somewhere safe. Sound good?" Sean asks.

Colin frowns as he nods.

Sean animates and tugs Alejo along with him in double time. "We'll go dig our backpacks out of the rubble. Be back." They climb through the hole where her door used to be.

Beth yells after them, "Bring the crowbar!"

She senses Colin's stare, pulls a drawer open, and forages for anything sharp.

"Beth, if you want to stay, I'll stay, no question."

Beth wishes he was the one, but an image of Ryker fills her head. If she knew where Ryker's sister lived, she'd go get him and take him with them. But it wasn't possible, and her heart hurt from the loss of something that never was.

She forces herself to concentrate on the now. "Sean's right, Parker prepared me for this. We need to leave." She clears her throat and walks past Colin, not meeting his eyes, with her bounty, down what's left of the hallway to her bedroom. They'll need to take Colin to his apartment, if it hasn't collapsed, to pack necessary items and anything the rest of them miss.

Hurling objects onto the bed, she finds it odd when Colin follows on her heels. He's never been in her bedroom. She pushes this awkward realization aside and searches deep into her closet. She lifts her boots out.

"Prepared you for what?"

She doesn't have time to explain it to him. Beth hurls a rubber Faraday backpack, weighted down with essentials, into his arms and says, "Survival." She flings a heavy jacket onto the bed, drops to her knees, reaches under the bed, rips out boxes of ammo duct-taped together, and throws them onto the bed along with a black box. The lock clicks under her thumbs. She draws out a handgun, slides the magazine in, and checks the safety.

"Jesus, Beth! Why do you have a gun?" Colin throws the bag on her bed.

She ignores the question, grabs Ryker's velvet box off her dresser, and throws it into her bag. It's been a long time since she's felt so focused.

His arms envelop her, and she goes rigid. His whispered words cause her hair to stand on end. "You're scaring me. I want the Beth I know back."

This is the real me. She steps back and out of his arms. "I need to be strong or I won't be able to leave." She resumes packing. "Our priority is to survive and get our asses to Reed before the world turns upside down."

His eyebrows squish together in confusion. "I thought we were going to a...Haven? What's Reed?"

Chapter 15

Dressed in warm gear, the backpack weighs heavily on Beth's shoulders as she navigates far away from abandoned cars, not wanting to find more bodies. The sheer number of them is overwhelming. Amid the darkness, the flickering flames of houses and cars form an eerie path through the streets. They haven't seen a living soul since leaving her crumbling building complex, but moans and screams for help fill the air. The smashed windows and ransacked cars lead her to be cautious, and she scouts around each and every corner for any potential danger.

It all reminds her of that night. She was the only one left alive. *It's starting already.*

Beth tries to regain some control by taking deep breaths. Gunshots pierce through the wrecked city, and she freezes as fighting echoes off the surrounding buildings. She approaches the corner of a church building, snaps her head back, and steps backward into the shadows.

"What is it?" Sean asks from behind her. Alejo crawls up Sean's back in a panic, while Colin waits somewhere further back, shrouded in the darkness. They are dressed in warm coats and hiking boots for the trip. Spring is in full swing, but it gets cold at night, especially in the Idaho mountains.

"Desperation."

Her group isn't desperate yet, but out there, in the streets, those people are desperate. She glimpses a mother shielding her children while her husband tries to defend their belongings from a group of men; a few of the attackers are wearing policemen's uniforms. *It's every man for themselves now.* She signals the others to follow her in the opposite direction. "This is a no-go—"

Colin sprints around them and toward the fight with purpose.

"Colin!" Alejo screams, clawing at the air.

Sean yanks Alejo back into the shadows, his hand over Alejo's mouth.

Approaching the men, Colin says, "Hey, leave them alone!"

Beth's heart jumps into her throat, but she stands still, rooted to the spot. One uniform draws his weapon on her friend, and she panics.

Sean's backpack thuds on the ground behind her as he sheds his jacket, then he stomps out into the fray. "Don't shoot!" He pats Colin's shoulder. "Let's go."

The one with the gun says, "You're not going anywhere." He turns to Colin. "Give us your backpack!"

"No!" Colin says.

Never fight for possessions! Your life is worth more. Beth inhales sharply and holds her breath.

A moment of confusion lingers before Sean rips Colin's backpack off and dangles it in the air. "We'll give it to you if you let us go."

Beth motions for Alejo to grab Sean's bag and be ready to take flight.

"And the family, too," Colin says in defiance.

"Colin, shut up!"

"My gun says all of you drop your stuff and back off."

Sean backs up slowly and methodically, never taking his eyes off the group of men, and tugs on Colin to follow. The men advance. Sean throws the bag up in the air between the two groups. When the men rush to grab it, the family takes off, while Sean and Colin run in the opposite direction.

***

"Colin, what the fuck was that?" Beth says in a low, venomous voice. The words fuel her anger to explosive proportions as she paces, trying to catch her breath after running for what feels like forever, the burden of her backpack causing excruciating pain between her shoulders.

Sean and Alejo catch up and bend over, hands resting on knees, to gulp down vital air. Alejo's ashen complexion alludes to his fitness level: lousy. He stumbles into Sean's unprepared arms, unable to word his concerns, and rubs Sean, checking for injuries.

"We're okay, babe." Sean cups Alejo's face. "I'm here. I'm fine."

Love shines in Alejo's terrified expression for his partner. Beth looks away, willing herself to stay strong. *You aren't.* Her lips tremble and tears threaten. They need to find that vehicle fast or they'll spend another day in the city. Something they can't afford to do.

"We couldn't just let those men hurt that family," Colin says, arguing his point in a low voice.

That does the trick, lighting the powder keg of her frustration. She ceases pacing, rushes him, and while keeping her voice down, says, "We? Your need to be the hero almost got us killed!"

"Beth—"

Her hand comes out. "Don't." Her head's pounding, and her hands tremble as the rage scourges through her.

Colin backs down from the dressing down.

Beth shrugs but fails to find any relief for her shoulders; only irritation. She scans the surrounding area to make sure they are alone before she scolds him again. "You never go in guns blazing! I'm the only one with a firearm." And the know-how to use it; the irony being, she's too afraid to use it.

After a few deep breaths, she says, "Stealth is best. Appear invisible and get out. You follow that, and we might survive." She turns her back on Colin, paces forward a few steps, and rubs her temple scar, which settles her mind and helps her slow her breathing.

Sean says, "Beth, let Colin carry your bag."

"No." That's a hard pass. She doesn't want to lose the stuffy or the velvet box tucked in the folds of her gear.

Beth squints at the moon rising out of the southeast. Pros and cons. This year, the moon was full on her birthday and looked beautiful. Right now, though, that's a con as it's even more important they stick to the shadows.

Under the rising moonlight, a middle-class neighborhood reveals itself. *Time to rock 'n' roll.* Her uncle's motto doesn't relieve her anxiety as she signals them to cross the street, into the cover of the trees. The unlit street lights and the dark, shattered windows of the damaged houses they pass unsettle Beth. Gunfire has been the norm for some time, going off randomly like firecrackers on Halloween night, disturbing her, as does the noticeable lack of rescue vehicle sirens.

She systematically approaches one parked street car after another, pulling on the handles, sizing up what might work for their escape, but not finding anything suitable. Parker had once told her an older model diesel truck should work in the event of an EMP. The why was lost on her, and there were no guarantees. Even if they find one, they won't be out of danger. Driving will put a target on their backs, but then, so does walking with backpacks.

A vehicle door opens, but the absence of a faint interior light lessens their chances. Colin's stolen bag had the tools they needed for this plan.

"Side pocket of my bag," Beth says. "Screwdriver."

Colin pulls out the flathead and seats himself inside the car. Beth searches the nearby houses for movement while listening to the tool being jammed into the steering column.

Rowdy voices. Beth freezes. The surrounding trees light up in an orange glow. The hairs at the nape of her neck rise. *Hide.* A mass of people, torches held aloft, enter her view from a side street.

Beth's heart races. She tugs on Colin's jacket and hauls ass up a nearby lawn, praying her friends follow. Not finding cover in the darkness between the damaged homes, she frantically advances down the side of the house and into the yard behind a fence.

Colin, hot on her heels, races through the gate, followed by Sean. *Where's Alejo?* Panic sets in.

"Alejo," Sean says under his breath, racing back out the gate, but he slides into the ground as torchlight brightens up the darkness between the homes. Beth sees Alejo; he's pressing his body into the side of the parked car they were stealing as if trying to fuse with it, his face unreadable in the shadows. Colin scrambles out and drags an unwilling Sean back into the yard behind the fence. Alejo's shape dissolves into black as the mob draws closer to his position.

Sean sidles up next to Beth, his fingers clamped around her arm, watching it all unfold. She covers his hand and prays Alejo doesn't move or make a sound, as he's apt to do. Helpless, Beth holds the door ajar, not to mention her breath. *Please, don't let them find him.* Her heartbeat pulses in her ears. The others breathe just as heavily.

The side of the cars facing Beth lights up ahead of Alejo. *Shit!* Someone is walking along the sidewalk. Alejo's form solidifies. He's on all fours, like a dog, scaling the grass toward the trunk of the car.

Torchlight brightens up the spaces between the homes as the cocky mob passes on the road, not caring who hears them. A few of them drag luggage along, followed by rattling grocery carts laden with jostling monitors and TVs. The shotguns and rifles they carry scare Beth.

A few unsavory-looking men stop on the sidewalk by the front of the car. One lights a cigarette, while another cups his hands around the light, protecting it. Someone in the crowd calls out. The men skirt the front of the car and head into the throng of bodies. Alejo scrambles back around the car. Beth releases her breath.

Headlights from a vehicle flood the roadway, growing brighter and spreading wider, until gunshots go off. Glass smashes, the light wavers, and tires screech as the car veers away from Alejo's position to light up the house across the street.

It jumps the curb, charges up the lawn, slams into the house, and upon impact, the house explodes in a flash ball of flame.

Beth closes her eyes, trying to shield herself from one horror, only to face the memory of her parents burning alive. *Mom, Dad.* Screams and cheers cry out along the road. Beth doesn't need to see to know the occupants are dying in that vehicle. Her chest tightens with grief for those poor souls, as well as for her parents that night, long ago.

"No!" Sean says, forcing Beth's eyes to open.

Alejo leaps from his position, runs through the gate, and rushes into Sean's open arms, attracting light their way. She closes the gate, losing the warmth of the flames upon the click of the latch, and turns to run but hits Colin's solid chest.

"We need to hide," she says in a low whisper. Torchlight beams stretch up the sides of the houses as people from the mob investigate. Colin snakes his arms around her middle and hauls her away from the gate. Sean guides them to the back of the yard and behind a shed. There's barely enough space for all four of them, and Beth is all too aware of the shaking of the fence.

But with no other choice, Sean follows Alejo in. "Keep going, babe."

Colin wiggles in behind Beth, his familiar scent and arms surrounding her, and his face buried in her neck. She swallows, uncomfortable with his closeness. Long strands of her hair move under his heavy breathing. She leans her forehead against the rough wood frame of the shed, causing Colin's head to pull back from her neck. She takes no joy in pushing him away, but it has to be done.

"It was just an animal." The voice came from the other side of the shed, and Colin's arms tense up around her. "Let's go."

***

They are way off track according to the map Beth carries in her pocket, but she wants distance between them and the mob. The moon is higher, but it still hasn't reached its zenith yet. They're deep in a neighborhood with mature trees. She counts the city blocks to occupy her mind, but it's not working.

Not finding any trucks, Colin has resorted to hot-wiring several cars but without success. They've been walking for some time, dodging fewer and fewer people and finding fewer cars on the street. She's going to have to make the call to leave the city on foot soon. A whiff of fuel, smoke, and burning flesh assaults her nose, conjuring the horrifying sight of her incinerated parents, their bodies contorting in pain. Their piercing screams haunt her with each passing minute.

"Beth, look." Alejo points in a panic.

Beth glances up. Among downed trees, the fuselage of a large plane lies on its side, a jagged hole exposes the disarrayed seats and yellow ceiling masks inside. Moonlight illuminates a broken wing stretching high into the dark night sky. Bodies lie strewn around the crash site. In a stained yellow dress, Carrie stands before her, radiating hate. Beth shrinks at the sight.

Sean clamps down on Alejo's wrist and turns. "Beth!"

Carrie rushes her.

Trapped in the past, Beth retreats, trips, slams into her mother's burned body, and crawls to the back of a nearby vehicle before covering her head with her arms. "No!" The acrid smell of hot metal assails her. Arms curl around her body, yank her back, and rock her back and forth.

"I'm here, Beth." Sean's whisper registers, but Beth's torment tramples the present.

"Make it stop. Make it stop!"

"Alejo, find those drugs!"

A zipper zips, and plastic crinkles.

Carrie crouches, tormenting her. *You know what to do.*

Beth, trapped in her mind, stretches her hand out and says, "Forgive me, Carrie!"

Carrie swats her hand away in disgust. *You don't deserve it.* Beth leans her pounding head back, closing her eyes to it all. Her heart beats in her ears so loud. Focus…it's not real.

"Who is Carrie?" Colin asks.

"See if you can start this truck," Sean says. Beth realizes her back is against Sean's rising chest. His heart races like hers.

Glass smashes.

A hand forces her mouth open, pills pass her lips, and water trickles down her throat. Beth chokes, but swallows, then says, "More, I need more. Make her go away!"

The roar of an engine tears through her consciousness, waking her from the nightmare. Her eyes open to Alejo's sympathetic face above hers. His fingers caress her face. "You're safe, baby, sleep."

Chapter 16

With the drugs wearing off, Beth focuses on the roadside line in the side mirror of the borrowed Dodge Ram, her anxiety rising as she fears an accident. Next to her, Colin drives with one hand on the wheel as he uses the other to hold hers. The strength in his hand is comforting, but she hopes he won't read too much into it.

The truck swings wide, driving over the line, causing Beth to gaze upon the road ahead of them. They are dodging an overturned semi truck, its payload scattered across the road. Thoughts of them dying roll around her head. If an accident occurred, they'd have no help. She keeps repeating "We'll get through it" in her head, but it's not hitting the mark.

A deserted Greyhound bus in the ditch comes into view, the passengers long gone. *Sadie.* As they near, scattered bodies appear, triggering her once more. *Murderer.* She doesn't want to stop but she needs to know and squeezes Colin's hand. "Pull over."

He slams on the brakes. The truck skids past the bus.

Sean leans forward between the front seats. "Do you want to check the bus?"

Beth says, "If Sadie's hurt or needs rescuing, we need to know." *I need to know.*

"Sean and I'll go." Colin exits and bends to gaze in through the shattered window at Beth. He's not the one, but she admires how handsome he is in his beanie hat. "Take the wheel. Keep the engine running."

On edge, she slides across the bench seat, stares at the dashboard, and says, "Okay, but be quick." She's never driven before, but Colin doesn't know that.

How could he? He doesn't really know her. None of them do. As the two men advance toward the bus, she can't help but feel apprehensive. What if they find Sadie? How will she face Donovan? Liam?

They walk cautiously through the scattered debris, their headlamps leading them through a path of open luggage, garbage, and first aid remnants...and bodies. Beth shivers as sensations prickle her skin.

Colin climbs the bus frame, lowers his hand down to help Sean climb up, then buries his nose into his forearm as he steps across the frame precariously. *Death.* The memory of a crumpled yellow dress lying on the road. Beth scrunches her eyes as a moan escapes her lips.

Alejo, attuned to her in the silence, asks, "Beth?"

She's too wrapped up in the memory to reply. The scent of pine and wet earth. Beth shakes her head in quick movements and focuses on her hands clutching the wheel, her heart rate causing a rapid rise in her chest.

Alejo points past her. "Beth!"

She follows the trajectory of his finger out the front windshield and down the road. A ragtag group of angry people is approaching. *We've been spotted.* Beth searches for the boys. "We've got trouble!" she screams out the window.

Colin and Sean scramble off the bus.

Beth stares at the gearshift. "Which one is reverse?"

Alejo points. "The R, baby!"

She wrenches on the gear shift but can't get it in reverse.

Alejo yells, "Step on the brake!"

We're going to die.

"Which one is the brake?"

"The middle one!"

She presses on the pedal, tries the shifter, and it falls into gear. The Ram zips into reverse, running roughshod over bodies and debris. She stomps on the brake. The door swings open. Colin shoves her over before she can get it into drive. The truck lurches. He hops in, and Alejo pulls Sean into the backseat. Doors slam and belts click into place.

Beth says, "Whatever you do, don't stop, or we'll die."

The truck takes off.

Alejo clamps his hands over his ears. "Die? Whoa, I didn't sign up for this!"

They barrel down the highway. Beth's fight-or-flight mode kicks in. With adrenaline coursing through her veins, her heart pounds, and her mouth becomes desert-dry as she instinctively reaches for the handgun. With trembling fingers, she attempts to pull back the slide but fails to chamber a round. *Damn it, I can't shoot people! This is crazy...*

Alejo yells out to Colin, "Faster!"

"Foot's already on the floor!"

Something smashes into the windshield. Alejo shrieks. The truck goes through a wall of people as bodies strike the hood.

***

Warning lights from the truck's dashboard illuminate Sean's face. The engine knocks as they bump and shake. The Ram's single headlight cuts through the darkness, sputters out, and comes back strong, lighting up a crushed gravel road closed in by trees. They enter an empty parking lot. In the passenger seat, next to Sean, a tired Beth points into the dark. "Back into that spot near the trailhead. If we need to escape, we should face out." She feels light-headed, and it dawns on her that they haven't eaten all day. The adrenaline from earlier has drained her of her strength.

Colin's depressed voice says, "Don't think she'll restart, Beth. She took a lot of damage, and we have no way of repairing her."

As Sean backs up, Beth rummages in the glove box for the trail bars and hands them out. Foil crunching fills her ears as she savors the sweet, nutty flavor. Her thoughts wander to Sadie, her fellow musketeer. She's a rule breaker. Donovan always had a run for his money with her. Sadie's always known what she wants out of life, and Beth admires her for it. The only thing Sadie has ever faltered on is Liam. "Sadie wasn't there?" she asks. *Or her body.*

Sean reaches for Beth's hand. "No." Her shoulders slump. Sean's hand tightens over hers. "Hey, if she was on that bus, she escaped and started her trek. She'll be there waiting for us. Focus on that."

They each had their own escape plans. "You're right. I will."

After the highway incident, no one walking along the road bothered them. A few ran after them as they passed, hoping for a ride, but it had otherwise been quiet. No more dead bodies, which relieved her. *As long as my friends are with me, I have a chance. I can do this.* "We'll walk from here, then," she says, not convinced she sounds confident.

Sean cuts the engine. The fresh air wafts in with the night, mixed with the scent of decaying earth and pine. Despite their predicament, Beth smirks as she welcomes the more palatable memory of her BAMF dads during their camping days. Parker must be beside himself with worry right now. They all must be.

Sean's rich voice pierces the black. "We'll set up camp. You guys need help?"

Colin's deep, warm voice chimes in. "No. Beth and I'll be fine."

A few minutes later, with her headlamp on, Beth digs near a distinctive post in the trees. *Thud!* Beside her, Colin is helping when he hits something solid. "Bingo." He uncovers a long PVC pipe, swipes the dirt away, and drags it up.

Beth buried her cache of supplies for the trek with William and Hoss a long time ago. They each added a gift for her in the pipe and then watched her put it in the ground. No free rides. Everyone did their fair share in this group.

She pops off the cap. Various survival necessities slide out. Among them is William's gift of a tiny camp stove and lighter fuel. She smiles as she retrieves Hoss's gift, a wickedly curved Karambit knife with a large circle at one end so she can clip it to her belt.

"You know how to use that?" Colin asks.

Proficiently. "A little." The stress of the day wears on her as she flexes her sore shoulders.

Colin wraps his arms around her. She stills. "Who gave you the butterfly necklace?"

She doesn't dare look up. His question invokes the sensation of Ryker's fingers brushing her neck and the gentle touch of his thumb stroking her cheek. Goosebumps rise unbidden across her skin. "Customer at the diner." Beth didn't thank Ryker for stepping in with those men. She hopes he's alright. He can handle himself, but she can't stop thinking about him. Need to let it go. Focus on now.

"Beth, we'll get through this together. You and me."

She should have agreed to the date. Why didn't she say yes? *You know why.*

She mentally adjusts her mask when tears start to well. "Let's get back."

***

The sound of the crackling Dakota fire accompanies Colin's question, "So what's Haven?" As he stokes the flames, the smoky aroma intensifies. Beth licks her lips, tasting the last bite of her dinner. The military calls them MREs. They might not be the best meals, but after the day she's had, they taste like the finest food in all the land. Even Alejo, who is dabbing his chin with a paper napkin, didn't complain when Beth handed him one.

Sean's jacket rustles in the fluctuating firelight as Alejo leans into him. Sean answers Colin. "It's a bunker Parker buried in Idaho, protected under the shadow of a mountain."

Growing up, Beth knew about the farm but didn't understand her mother's word for Beth's uncle. She called him a prepper. At her young age, Beth thought he worked with pepper. Not until she came to live with Parker did she truly understand the term. By then, Parker had built the foundation and walls of Haven.

"And Reed?"

"A smaller one marked on your map. It's hidden beside Donnelly Falls, but we call it Reed to hide its identity. There's a code to get in. It's written in the top right corner of the map I gave you."

"I don't understand. Why build two bunkers?"

"Donovan always says you need a backup plan," Beth says, glancing Colin's way. "Parker built Haven for their retirement. Reed is Plan B."

Reed went up much faster with the help of her BAMF dads. The company they bought it from helped them construct and bury it, leaving the doorways visible to those who knew where to look.

"But why go to Reed when you have Haven?"

"Reed is closer to those of us coming from the south. They named it after Penny's late husband." Beth says into the fire. The thought of Penny makes Beth pine for her. She helped Parker when he took Beth in. Penny never wanted to replace Beth's mother, but Beth needed a woman around for intimate things Parker couldn't handle, and Penny has always been a natural mother figure. Recently widowed back then, Penny needed the distraction.

Alejo scrunches his shoulders together and says with delight, "Oh, I love Penny! I want this nightmare to end so I can have Penny hugs."

He's not the only one.

A burst of laughter echoes under the canopy of the trees, easing their tension, if only for a moment.

"Why didn't you tell me about this place?" Colin asks Beth.

The pained look he shoots her way forces her to look back into the small flames. It is a fair question. Why didn't she tell Colin? She told Ryker when they met. Colin is really asking why she doesn't trust him, but she does. That isn't the issue, or is it?

"Parker swore everyone to secrecy. It was on a need-to-know basis," Sean says.

"And I didn't need to know?" Colin asks with an accusatory stare at Sean.

"Look at it this way. If we'd told you what it was, we couldn't have enjoyed the look of shock on your face when we arrived." Sean glances back at Alejo.

Alejo pipes in. "That's blown now. I was looking forward to that."

"Beth, who is Carrie?"

Beth remains silent. She doesn't want to talk about her sister. She doesn't want to dredge up more memories and trigger that incessant voice. "Leave it, Colin."

"Beth's sister," Alejo confirms.

"Being outside too long is an issue for you, right? Was that what you meant by it would be bad for you out here?"

Beth sighs and dips her head. "Yes." For lack of a better answer, she hopes this satisfies him.

Alejo walks over and warms her hands with his as he sits between her and Sean. Alejo knows her story. Beth's not sure how much he's said to Sean, but instead of saying anything, Sean unzips his pocket, plucks out a folded map, and lays it out on a tiny, makeshift log table they set up next to the fire. "Let's go over the route just in case someone gets lost."

Beth's glad for the distraction.

"Oh my God, honey, don't say that!" Alejo says.

Sean rubs Alejo's leg. "A, baby, it's just a precaution in case we have to adapt. Don't worry."

Everyone gathers close. Alejo shines a light on the stark white topographic map of Idaho. His lips form a pout. "You said this trip would be fun. So far, I'm giving it a bad review."

"Alejo."

"Yes, dear."

"There are Marines at the end of this rainbow."

Worry creases Beth's brow. She reaches for the butterflies under the neckline of her shirt and wonders where Ryker is in all this chaos. *Is he okay? Alive?*

Alejo's expression dances from sadness to elated ecstasy. So easy to please. He sucks in an excited breath. "Thank God! I can't wait to see the end of this frickin' rainbow!"

Everyone laughs again, seemingly more relaxed already, except for Beth. Her eyes meet Colin's and she drops her hand from her neckline.

Chapter 17
May 23

At six foot two, Donovan Masters's leads the way, his helmet barely clearing the ceiling as he descends cement stairs in full tactical gear and fatigues. Looking much like the sergeant he used to be, stress weighs heavily on him as he turns to a doorway at the bottom. Thoughts of his daughters manifest in his mind. Gina has Bradley at least, but Sadie... He pushes the thought back, rubs the cold cement with affection, and flips a switch in the utility room. "Long time no see, girl. Wish it was routine."

Reed hums to life. Her lights illuminate William and the two others exiting the stairs in tactical gear behind him. Hoss's son, Liam, is a younger version of his father, but his good looks come from his mother. The other is Penny Reed, a short, blonde bombshell with warm, hazel eyes—John's widow. She's their rock when shit hits the fan. *Boy, has it ever.*

He cannot get the images out of his head. The destruction that flashed across the screen in Haven's security room was horrendous. Massive casualties, and cities wiped out. The world is FUBAR; f'd up beyond all repair alright. His two girls are in the thick of it, which doesn't sit well with him.

Donovan hands his helmet and rifle over to William, and Liam follows William into the main living area. Donovan rubs his smooth yet irritated face. This morning, he nicked himself while shaving; something he stopped doing since he arrived at Haven a week ago.

"I'll drop my stuff. Meet you in security?" Donovan gazes at Penny's solemn face.

"Yup." He follows her through a stocked, spacious walk-in pantry lined with shelving and freezers packed with food supplies. They exit out the other end and are met with the sight of gleaming, stainless-steel appliances in both fully equipped kitchens. Reed's nowhere near the square footage of Haven, which makes her more intimate and easier to secure. Donovan admits to himself that the place eases his stress. He breathes out as he skims the icy surface of the smooth island counter between the two kitchens with his fingers. His favorite activity: cooking. *Going to need it this time.*

Penny walks away from him, down a twenty-five-foot-wide main living corridor. Two communal tables stretch before him down that corridor, pointing to a big-screen TV on the opposite wall that is framed by two L-shaped leather couches. He remembers the frustration of assembling those tables and how his wife calmed him with soothing words.

A solitary door to security stands guard next to the TV, while four doors line the corridor on each side of the tables. The communal bathroom/laundry room sits nearest to him, on the left, with its washing machines and showers. They share every room except the two family suites at the end of the corridor. Penny enters the far left one.

William exits from the second door on the left. The workroom is a place for tools and locked weapons storage. "I'll go tell the boys to set up a perimeter." William heads to the security door at the end and disappears.

Donovan knows it's going to be a hard ride if the girls don't show soon. Patience, he's low on, but perseverance? Plenty.

He walks down the right side of the tables, past a gym and a women's bunk room, and enters the men's bunk room. Reed sleeps fifty-two people: twenty each in the bunk rooms, and six in each suite. He picks a bunk, leaves his backpack, and sheds his tac vest. Donovan leans on his forearms against the top bunk and reaches for the chain around his neck. *Give me strength.* Two simple gold wedding rings dangle, one thicker and one thinner. He'd search for the girls himself, but it would be futile; besides, he taught them well. They're Masters girls.

A memory of his wife breaches his defenses. Comfortable in their bed, his brave Tina is lying down, her head wrapped in a pink headscarf, her hand frail in his strong one. She barely gets the words out. "Save my ring for Sadie. One day..."

Donovan blinks rapidly, steps back, and runs a hand over his brown crew cut and down the back of his neck. *Stay on point, Masters.* He can't think about one day. He needs to be strong and keep the girls safe, along with anyone else who comes through those doors.

Donovan steps into the corridor and walks toward security. He glimpses Liam picking up a vial from the cabinet in medical, checking the label, replacing it, and repeating the action with the next one. He appears calm on the outside, but Donovan knows better. Liam's coiled up as tightly as the others, especially worried about Donovan's oldest daughter, Sadie.

"You worried about Jessie and Steven?" Donovan asks, mentioning Liam's brothers as a test.

"Yeah, half a planet away is too far."

Yup, Sadie alright. "They're with their unit. They'll find a way back to base."

Donovan withdraws and moves toward the end of the corridor. He spots Penny inside the doorway to her suite, gazing upon the wall, tac vest in hand. Pictures of everyone and their families in happier times adorn that wall. She caresses one of them. It's one of her and her late husband, his brother-in-arms, John Reed. *Gone too soon.*

Hearing him approach, she steps out to meet him with a sympathetic smile and, for a moment, they gaze upon each other.

***

William eyes the twins on a monitor. They're standing guard outside, dressed in their tactical gear. He keys the mic. "Security's up, boys." They both wave and take off like kids ready to hit the playground.

He leans back in the chair as thoughts of Beth creep in, causing him to stretch the tension out of his neck. He's the only one who understands her loss. Her trek will be an uphill battle. If she doesn't show, he'll convince the guys he's the one who should go find her. His hope is Jose has her with his family and they show up in the next week, safe and sound. They trained all the kids for this, but the reality of not knowing weighs on them. Something they didn't calculate when planning this place of refuge. Of course, no one thought they'd be using it for real; it was a pipe dream. When they grew fat and old, it was just supposed to be a place for them to retire.

They all wanted to rescue their families, but it was a futile mission, and they knew it. It took all his muscle to stop Parker from going rogue on them yesterday. The logging road was likely riddled with downed trees. Even if they could get out, it would have taken days to clear it. No, they had a plan in place so they wouldn't go off half cocked and be no use when their friends and family showed. They had to stick with the plan.

William leans forward on the desktop, clasping his hands against his lips. He finds it ironic that they were the ones who went off to war, leaving their families in fear they wouldn't make it home in one piece, and now, they're the ones left behind, wondering if their families will return to them.

Penny pops in and hands over her vest along with her weapon. Donovan strides in behind her and asks, "Hoss?"

"Doing rounds with the twins. Probably in his bunk by now, though. You need him?"

Donovan shakes his head and rubs his neck.

I wonder which of my brothers will crack next. Which one am I going to have to clamp down on after Parker?

William opens his mouth, but Penny steps up and reassures Donovan with a gentle squeeze. "The girls will make it, Don."

"I won't be right till they do."

"I'll make cookies."

Chapter 18

Mal stands guard by the trucks in the parking lot of a grocery store as gunshots go off around him. Sounds like trouble, but he stands his ground. Hunter leans against the Rite Aid, monitoring Mal and the others. Wendall's brother stayed back, opting to stay outside as the others entered the store. He wonders how Hunter got those nasty scars across his face, but more importantly, Mal isn't sure where Hunter's loyalty lies. Wendall and Gideon are his family, but Hunter acts morosely around them. Disenchanted. It could be because they've just lost their little brother, but Mal has a feeling there is more to it than that, and his gut is never wrong. Whichever way Hunter swings doesn't help Mal's plight, though. He's not sure he wants to stay with these people, but Wendall has made it clear anyone who tries to run will be shot. If the opportunity presents itself, Mal's out of there.

Gideon sits with their brother's body in the other truck. He's been quiet, keeping to himself since last night. They camped on a rural road outside the city. During the night, a few men took off, but their group is mostly intact from the day before. Gunfire kept Mal awake most of the night, and it was cold enough that they had to keep the fire going. It sure didn't feel like May.

He surveys what's left of the surrounding stores and spots the street sign. They are on Sprague Avenue in the middle of Spokane Valley. The chain stores are intact, but the mom-and-pop shops are leveled up and down the street. Except for one building. The metal frame of the awning is bent and hangs crookedly but, otherwise, it's not structurally damaged. He makes out the white lettering on the shredded vinyl fabric: *Parker's.* He finds it oddly satisfying that the building stood strong against the force that took the other buildings down.

"Look what I found!" Cain exits in new duds from the Rite Aid with bags of medical supplies and dragging behind him a scared young woman by the arm who is fighting him all the way.

"Let go of me! Help!" Her blue, terrified eyes dart between all the men in the parking lot, then she digs her heels in and yanks on Cain's iron-clad grip to free herself and flee.

Alarm bells go off in Mal's head as the wind shifts. *Shit.* This is not how he rolls. He scans the grocery store front for the rest of Wendall's group, but they're still in there. Upon closer observation, Mal discerns a strange pattern of blood spatter on the young woman's T-shirt. There is a void. It is a telling sign. Cain shot someone defending her, perhaps? She hits Cain with her free hand and kicks as he sidesteps and laughs at her. It is a futile attempt, though Mal can't fault her for it. He knows the orange jumpsuits don't scream exemplary citizens. She is bleeding from her mouth, and the burgeoning imprint of a hand gives her cheek an unnatural, pink glow.

"Shut it! There's more inside. I locked the women in the bathroom."

Jesus. Mal can't help closing his eyes for a moment. Cain didn't mention any men.

"Go get them. We'll take them with us," Wendall says, coming out of the grocery store. Trailing him, Sonny and the rest of the group haul out bags of food and stroll toward Mal with smiles a mile wide. They dump their loot on the tailgate of the truck and run toward the Rite Aid in high spirits, celebrating the windfall. Cain shoves the trembling woman into Mal's hands and takes off after them. *Me? Great...*

Mal can't chance her getting loose. He wouldn't put it past Wendall to shoot her in the back. Mal tightens his grip, makes a play, and backs her into the truck. Moving aside her long hair, he nuzzles her stiffening neck and says, "Don't struggle. I'm not like them."

She tenses but makes no move to flee. A whimper escapes, cutting out his heart, but he has to put on a show or he'll never be able to help her if he has the chance.

"Hey, no touching," Wendall says in an authoritative voice.

Mal stops and tilts his head but doesn't turn. "Why not?" He can't believe those words have come out of his mouth. The wind is tugging at Mal. Deep down, he's aware it won't end well for the women.

"Later." Wendall settles the question.

Mal backs off the frightened woman, hoping she's understood him, and mouths, *Stay close to me*. The fog of fear in her face seems to lessen.

Thank Christ!

Mal gazes up at the Rite Aid, expecting a group of women to emerge. Hunter isn't against the wall anymore.

Wendall calls out, walking through the parking lot. "Hunter?!"

Where did he go?

"Hunter!" Wendall yells again, ambling toward the storefront.

"Yeah." Hunter rounds the corner of the Rite Aid, zipping up his pants, and walks toward his brother as if nothing is amiss, halting his brother's advance.

Movement draws Mal's attention down the alleyway. Terrified women are jumping over a fence. Hunter stares directly at Mal, daring him to say something. Mal ducks his head and turns away with the woman still in his grasp. *Interesting.*

***

"Why can't we slow down?" Libby halts to inspect her shoe. "My feet hurt."

Ahead of his sister, Ryker continues through the trees, deep in thought, skirting an open farm field. After several tries, Ryker had found a vehicle he could jump-start, and they took off out of the city limits and drove till it ran out of gas, just west of Worley, Idaho. According to his map, the highway crosses the Python River through Swindon, so that's where they are heading.

Their water supply is dwindling. If he wants them to keep up this pace, they need to find a stream to replenish their stores. Their food is lacking more than it should be at this stage, too, and Ryker suspects his sister has eaten more than she needed. She doesn't understand the severity of their predicament yet. How could she? Libby is still a young adult, existing in a world that is no more. He knows better.

"Ryker!"

He squeezes his eyes shut. Might as well call out to every person within range to take what they have. Ryker twists and grabs her shoulders. "Libby," he says in a low whisper, "I told you to talk low. Stop yelling, please."

With a resigned sigh, Libby says, "This is too much. I can't keep up with you."

Ryker forgets she's not like him. He's used to mileage like this. "Sorry." He takes her by the hand, leads her to a clump of trees out of the sun, and unclips his dangling water bottle. "Here. Drink this."

Libby partakes of his offering and quenches her thirst. "Can't we stop and rest here for the night?" she asks with pleading eyes.

Ryker searches their surroundings. There's too much daylight left to do that. The longer they're exposed, the harder it will be to escape undetected. They can't slow down or they risk losing what advantage they have left. "We can't. We have to keep moving."

Ryker pulls out a map of Idaho he procured back in town, lays it out on the ground, and crouches to study it. Back in town, logic said they should travel south and not through Spokane Valley, into Coeur d'Alene. That way was too risky.

"How long?" Libby asks in a whiny tone.

"Till nightfall at least. We need to find a river to replenish the water we're consuming."

He estimates it could take a week or more before they reach this farm, if he finds it at all. His finger follows Highway 95, past Worley, toward the words *Lake Coeur d'Alene*. Beth said the farm was on the Canyon River, which feeds this lake on the other side.

"Can I have a chocolate bar, then?" She holds her palm out for the treat.

"We need to conserve our food," he says, occupied with reading the map. They'd cross through the city of Swindon. The bridge there spans the Python River. Highway 3 is on the other side and, hopefully, Beth. They'll have to be careful in Swindon and try to cross the bridge in the dark. The daunting task ahead is challenging, even for him, but he won't give up on finding this farm and providing safety for his sister. His finger follows the Canyon River, then backtracks. The words *Coil Trail* spring off the page. Voilà!

Libby's hand drops. "Can't we just steal more like we did this stuff?"

Ryker peers up at his sister. "There's no chance of that. It's too dangerous to approach a city unless we have to."

"It can't be that bad."

This is what he's been worrying about. Libby's underestimation is proof he needs to be more vigilant than usual around her. "Let's find the river and then we'll reassess whether we should stop. Sound like a plan?"

Libby turns her face to the fields, hiding her expression from him. "Okay."

***

Firelight dances off the faces of the hardened criminals gathered around the fire. They're glum over the loss of the women. Mal isn't. When the men came out of the Rite Aid empty-handed, Mal breathed a sigh of relief. He sits silently as the men discuss the women's escape. He has nothing to add. Incredibly, they can't figure out why the women would run from them. *Idiots.* Women are smart. That's one reason Mal gives them a wide berth.

He gazes at Hunter's quiet form in the glowing light as he stares at the flames. Mal sees Hunter in a different light now, but he is still a Greaves brother, and blood runs thicker than water.

As the day progressed, they acquired farming equipment, hit up a few hardware stores, and collected seeds for planting unchallenged. Mal figures they are going to farm, but where? He assumes it is on a need-to-know basis, and he doesn't need to know. Mal actively sought chances to escape with the captured woman, but Wendall tied her to the truck bed, forcing her to sit among the other men. He gave them strict instructions not to touch her or someone would lose a hand. It is something, but Mal knows Wendall's generosity won't last.

They are camping for the night by the side of the highway and made her cook and wash dishes. The men jeered at her, but Mal offered to help, which caught Wendall's eye. He threatened Mal with violence if he used the opportunity to get closer to her. Mal denied it, citing she couldn't do it all on her own. Hunter stepped in and offered to supervise Mal. That piqued Mal's curiosity, but he remained silent. Wendall relented and let them have free rein to clean up.

Cain asks, "What's the plan tomorrow?"

"We'll rob some more places along the way to the farm," Wendall says. "Our new home is in Idaho."

Suspicion confirmed.

"How long we going to be there, you think?"

"By the looks of things, could be awhile. The law won't be calling."

"We're farmers now?"

"Unless you want to starve like the people sticking it out in this town."

"Are there women in our future or are we all taking turns with her?" Dugal points at the scared woman tucked in behind Wendall, her hands bound by a rope that trails to the back of the truck. She shrinks in fear.

Wendall pulls hard on the rope, forcing her into the firelight, and scans the men around the fire. "She'll be up for grabs once we gather more women. Until then, she's off limits."

"Why do—?" Someone elbows a wiry fellow into silence. Wendall chooses not to acknowledge it and stares down at the woman tied up beside him. She shrinks away, pulling the rope taut between them. The last time she spoke, Wendall smacked her to the ground and kicked her. She lost her voice after that.

"Sonny, take her to the truck and tuck her in. She'll need her beauty sleep."

Chapter 19

A river snakes the edge of a field riddled with weeds. Idaho's picturesque mountains tower over a yellow farmhouse that's seen better days, and a blackened barn stands watch over the yard. Two dirty trucks jostle through the field, loaded with men, some still in orange jumpsuits, followed by a few SUVs and cars.

Gideon turns his back on the sheet covering Greg's lifeless body. Ever since losing him, Gideon hasn't spoken a word. Losing his little brother is like an open wound, festering in the cool May morning sunshine. The warmth of his heavy jacket can't thaw the coldness inside his dark heart.

The truck stops, then doors creak open and slam shut.

Wendall barks an order. "Hunter, dig a hole for Greg."

Hunter saunters to the tailgate, conveys a grim expression edged with sadness, and avoids eye contact. Men gather at the back of the truck alongside Hunter to collect Greg's tarp-wrapped body and carry him off. They follow Hunter with their burden. Gideon trusts his brother will bury Greg in the family cemetery at the back of the property with the rest of the Greaves. The place where they buried their grandparents. May they rot in hell.

Shorter than Hunter by a few inches, Wendall waits till Greg's body goes by before focusing his eagle eyes on the rest of the ragtag men they collected from the jail. His brother will rule with a firm hand. Wendall commands and does not bend to anyone. The men feel it even now because none of them meet his brother's gaze except one man.

"Mal, take the men to the barn," Wendall says. "You'll sleep there."

The man named Mal, in shades, bearded, his long dark brown hair tied back, stands up in the truck's bed and makes a noise that sounds like a hum to Gideon. It doesn't seem to faze his older brother. Mal's been too quiet for Gideon. The quiet ones think too much.

***

The stench of rotting wood and mold is overpowering as Gideon leans his chair against the wall, his boots resting on the edge of the worn, run-down dining table where his grandmother forced him to eat the slop she made. Notches line the table edge—ones he put there over two decades ago. He remembers well the beating he took from his grandmother for that while his grandfather sat to the side.

Wendall dangles his legs over the same table. "Send the boys out scouting for workers at nearby farms."

All his brothers witnessed his humiliation at the hands of his grandmother. His grandfather didn't even look up from his dinner. Perhaps it was out of respect, not bringing attention to it.

"How far should they go?" Hunter asks, staring out a fractured front window among threadbare furniture strewn around an open living-dining room. Curled wallpaper and skewed and faded pictures on the wall are the only reminders of the people who lived in this house long ago. All that's left are echoes, ugly memories of childhood, trapped in the rooms they grew up in.

Gideon gauges Hunter's mood as tepid, then glances sideways when Wendall says to Hunter, "Till they find one. Give more food to the ones that go south."

"What would they need food for?" Gideon asks. "It's an easy run." By vehicle, it couldn't be more than an hour on the logging road to the highway and then another forty-five minutes to the farming community of Swindon.

"I'll need the trucks. They can walk."

Where does his brother think he's going? The farm needs running, and the men need kicking to get the seed they stole into the ground.

"What if they have kids?" Hunter asks.

Of course he's more worried about kids than why Wendall wants the trucks. Hunter always had a soft spot for the little creatures.

"Use 'em as leverage. They'll catch on."

As expected, Hunter's expression sours with distaste.

"What about the women?" Gideon asks, pulling Wendall's eyes back to him. Losing the women back in town bummed Gideon. Even the one they'd managed to tie into the back of the truck had somehow escaped. Gideon needed a stress reliever, and women were his ticket to the promised land. He could have had a piece yesterday if it wasn't for his brother's controlling nature. Almost made him regret breaking Wendall out of prison.

"Keep the pretty ones for sure. We'll use the others for cooking and cleaning. Tell the boys no touching. I need workers who can function. Don't lose any men, either."

Gideon scuffs the floor with his boots in disappointment. Wendall gives him the eagle eye, forcing Gideon to lower his gaze. He's had his fair share of shit-kicking from Wendall. Boys will be boys, after all. The control bullshit, he can do without, though. Easier to bide his time and sidestep his older brother's rules by just agreeing for now, then doing things on the quiet when Wendall isn't looking.

Growing up, Gideon couldn't get enough pussy and screwed every girl willing to give it from dawn to dusk. Sometimes they weren't willing, but he'd smooth it over with his charm, and they'd beg for it in the end.

Wendall's cold eyes slide to Hunter. Gideon wonders how Hunter fared in jail. He certainly served long enough to suffer, but his face doesn't betray any feelings. Hunter's cold as ice. He learned that growing up here, like the rest of them.

"We'll divide the women here," Wendall says. "I want the crops in the ground before I leave."

Leave? Gideon's interest piques at this news, but Wendall doesn't elaborate further as he hops up, ending their conversation by walking through the kitchen and out the back door.

***

Through a scope, the sight line follows men walking between the barn and the farmhouse. Across the river, high in a tree, splayed out behind a sniper rifle on rough floorboards, Parker lifts his head and sighs. The abandoned farmhouse forms part of their property. Orange jumpsuits don't scream wholesome neighbors.

Parker's got a million things to do, but all he wants is to search for his niece and bring her home. It's too late for that, but it gnaws at him that she's not here. He envisions her injured, maimed, or worse, dead.

Chapter 20

As dusk approaches on their second day since the bombing, Colin lounges inside thick bushes along the side of a rural road. After leaving the truck behind and beginning the long trek toward Idaho, they stopped to rest. Even though he is tired, he wants the first watch—wants a chance to observe Beth fall asleep, to know she is safe.

It sounds to him like this Reed they are heading to is a safe place. Beth said Donovan would be there waiting for them and their task is to get there in one piece. He's taken it upon himself to add another task, however: to keep Beth safe.

Eyes closed, Sean says, "With no cell, I can't tell how many miles we did, but if my feet are any sign..."

In their winter jackets, under a mylar blanket, Alejo spoons Sean and pouts. "My feet hurt, too."

Dozing against the bush, Beth's head jerks up as she fights the sleep she so desperately needs. She pulls a can of food out of her backpack. Colin was happy she didn't reject him when she woke up in the car holding his hand. He needed her touch, needed her to be alright.

Escaping the city with her had been eye opening. Her knowledge of the streets and how to avoid people has revealed a side to her he's never seen. This is not the Beth he met in tango class.

She opens the can and polishes a spoon with her sleeve. "You'll get used to it, A. Gotta keep moving. Get as far from civilization as possible." She turns to

Colin and offers the can with the spoon. He takes the items with a note of gaiety. It proves she's thinking about him.

Alejo's lids grow heavy as sleep takes him.

"I'll take the first watch," she says, crossing her legs and wrapping herself in a mylar blanket.

Colin isn't having any of that nonsense. She took first watch the night before and didn't wake them till the pre-dawn hours. "No, I am tonight."

"You need your sleep."

"When was the last time you slept?" he asks, knowing the answer.

Her hesitation confirms it. She gazes at him. The wheels turn in her pretty little head, but she remains silent. She unzips her backpack and retrieves a worn-out butterfly stuffy. "I'll take the next watch. Wake me in three hours." Beth arranges her pack to sleep next to Alejo with the stuffy in her arms. He'd seen the stuffy in her apartment. She's never explained why she keeps such a filthy object, and it surprised him when she took it with her. *It's important somehow. Could it be her sister's?* She'd never mentioned a sister before. He remembers the picture with the two girls she had among the other picture frames. He'd assumed she was a best friend or cousin.

"Beth. Sleep here, beside me." Colin doesn't appreciate the doubt that crosses her face. "You won't be a third wheel with those two, and it'll be warmer."

He's not pleased when she hesitates, either, but she says, "Alright."

With the butterfly in tow, she nestles against him and draws her hood up, while he scoops out his first sweet taste of fruit salad. He savors the small gain with a satisfied smile and she shifts to get comfortable. She's had a few hard days, and the butterfly shows the level of her anxiety. He thinks the stuffy is ugly but wishes she'd clutch him as tightly. "Beth."

"Yeah?"

"Do you trust me?"

"Yes."

He's happier she didn't pause this time. "Put your arms around me. Let me give you a space you can trust enough to fall asleep in."

Under the fading light, she weighs his request, then leans into his open arms, laying her head on his chest. He relaxes. They haven't had a shower in days, but he recognizes the hint of raspberries lingering around her and enjoys her warmth in his arms. *Where she belongs...*

"Colin, thank you."

"Anything for you, sunshine."

Three hours later, Beth's head lies on her pack, curled up next to his leg, the stuffy forgotten. Colin places it in his lap. He wishes she'd let him in; give them a chance. The gift of being able to watch over her keeps him awake. In the darkness, he runs his fingers through her hair for a few precious moments and rubs the surface of the butterflies on the chain around her neck. Seems too intimate a gift.

He recalls the first day she walked into the studio. She wore a T-shirt with colorful butterflies, like her tattoo, jeans, and canvas sneakers. Next to a smartly dressed Alejo, she looked under-dressed, but to Colin, Beth was a breath of fresh air and came across as authentic. From across the room, he observed her bite her soft, pliable lips, not making eye contact with anyone. He hoped she wasn't dancing with Alejo. Luck was on his side. He couldn't hide the elation he felt when his teacher approached with Beth in tow.

It was electrifying when their hands connected. Up close, her freckles were cute and wholesome. When her green eyes dipped up shyly, it stirred him—made him pay attention in ways he'd locked away long ago. In that moment, he knew two things would happen. First, he'd have the perfect dance partner, and second, she would be more than just his dance partner.

Colin nudges Sean. "Your turn."

Sean sits up, stretches his arms, and yawns. "She's going to be pissed you didn't wake her."

"I know, but she needs sleep. She's no good to us if she passes out." Colin hands over his unfinished can of fruit salad to him.

"True. You did the right thing." Sean removes his beanie and accepts the can. "I'll get Alejo to do the next shift."

Colin slaps Sean's shoulder and passes the spoon. "Thanks. Lots of people walking on the road. Some toward the city, some not. We have neighbors in the bush to the left. Looked like a family with kids." Sean glances that way. Colin settles down for some shut-eye.

"See you on the other side." Colin places the stuffy in Beth's open backpack, zips it up, and settles down behind her, resting his hand on the center of her back. He takes comfort in what brief contact he has with her and the faint scent of raspberries as he fades off to sleep. He can't help grinning in the dark.

***

The next day, Beth glances bitterly at her companions as they walk in twos. Especially Colin. He didn't wake her for a shift. She twists, looks back, and sighs. They're being followed through a forest of tall standing trees by an unknown group.

"Beth, watch—" Colin says, grabbing her jacket, preventing her from colliding with a large oak tree. He looks behind her. "We should help them."

Beth ignores the statement, curbs the anger, and wrests her arm out of his gentle grip. She'd planned on waking everyone before dawn so they could put some distance between them and the growing number of people who chose the same spot to rest last night. Giving her more sleep might have cost them. Beth can't afford to have strangers following them to Reed. The fewer people who know about it, the safer they'll be.

She'd hoped entering the forest would deter this family, but they still trail behind them at a discreet distance. For how long? She wishes she could help, but her dads drilled into her not to trust anyone in this scenario. Beth needs to protect her people first, but how? She doesn't like the only answer that comes to mind.

"Ow, ow, ow! Hold up," Alejo flinches as he hops on one leg.

They stop. So do their stalkers. *Crap.*

Beth rummages through her first aid kit and motions for Alejo to hold his foot out. When he does, she takes his wool sock off, one eye still on their followers, finds his sore, and applies a callus bandage with fast efficiency.

"Thanks, honey."

Their eyes meet.

"No problem." She averts her gaze from the sympathy Beth finds there. *Am I that transparent?* Beth draws her weapon, turns the safety off, and says calmly, "Colin, stay with Alejo."

"Why?" he asks, standing straighter.

Sean eyes the stragglers. "What are you going to do?"

What I have to. "Sean, pull the rifle out."

Alejo picks up on that statement and shoots a wary look her way. "Why are we pulling those out?"

Colin asks, "Beth?"

Not meeting his gaze, she answers Alejo. "Don't like the people following us."

Sean squeezes support into her shoulder. *God, give me strength.* Beth acknowledges him, holds her head up, and walks with purpose toward the group. *Now or never.*

Colin lays a hand on her forearm, forestalling her advance. "Beth, they have kids."

She levels her eyes at him. "They do, so don't let it cloud your judgment." Even to her, that sounded cold. *This is not me.*

"They wouldn't—"

Beth rounds on him with a whisper. "Colin, you need to learn. Kids give them a reason to take what we have."

He's unhappy, but comes to terms with something and says to Sean, "Hand me the rifle."

That catches Beth off guard. Colin's not one to touch a weapon, but when faced with violence, everyone has a breaking point. He takes the gun with unskilled hands. *No way he can handle that thing properly. He didn't take the safety off.* "Give it back to Sean."

"No."

She's not willing to put up with his stubborn streak. "Colin, are you prepared to end a life?" His shocked look is all she needs. "Hand the rifle back."

He does as requested. "I'm coming with you."

Beth walks off, hearing the crushing of dead branches and leaves underfoot as Colin and Sean keep pace with her. The weapon is heavy in her hands, so, with her finger off the trigger, she stops between two sturdy trees. Her ears throb and her heart races in her chest. She swallows. *Keep it together.*

The group comes upon them, and it's clear none were expecting Beth. The women grab five orbiting children, signaling the men to regroup and block the group's more vulnerable members when they see the gun in Beth's hands. *Decent at least.* The men are in wildly different attire: one is in a suit, while the others are dressed for cooler weather, in hoodies and mountain jackets.

Sean draws up beside her, mimicking her stance, rifle pointed down. Colin steps in behind her. The moment of truth. *God, don't lose your nerve now.* "Stop following us. This is your only warning." Her words carry on the wind.

One man in a hoodie steps forward with a waxy smile. "Friends, have some compassion. We have kids." *The charmer.*

"I can see that. Changes nothing."

Greeting her with troubled looks, some of them are unsure how to play it. Beth prays they move on or she'll have to do something drastic. *Don't make me...*

The suit flashes a handgun and steps forward. "Sheer numbers. We could take what you have."

Sean raises the rifle slightly.

She knows an empty threat when she hears it. The children keep them honest; they would have acted already. Beth shifts her stance. "Don't force me to use this because I will not hesitate. You want the kids to see that? It'll be on you...friend." The last word drips with sarcasm. "You'll be the first to die."

Leaves rustle melodiously in the trees above them. Each group stares, unmoving, in silence as tension rises with each second. Beth's trigger finger slides down when the man moves a little. *Don't...*

A younger woman in a blue mountain jacket signals him with a wave of her hands. "Harold, think of the children. Let's go."

Another puts his hands up. "Put it away, Ron. Let's move on." The others turn with him and walk away. Ron walks a distance backward with a sharp eye on them before turning around to catch up with the group. Beth hopes they aren't lying about moving on but wouldn't bet her life on it. She doesn't move until they disappear from view. The breath she's holding in rushes out, and her chest heaves rapidly as she lowers the weapon.

Colin pulls her into his front as her legs shake so violently that she doesn't think she could walk away if she wanted to.

With warm breath, he whispers in her ear, "Lesson learned."

CHAPTER 21

Overseeing the men spreading seed, Cain emerges from the direction of the river. He breathes army even though the military was through with him long ago; dishonorably discharged like Hunter. For unknown reasons, Wendall saved this man back at the prison, but it's clear he's loyal. Gideon respects that.

"There's a fortress up near the mountain," Cain says, stopping a few feet shy of Gideon.

Gideon doesn't like that. You'd never know there is anyone over there, except for the few people working the land across the way. Used to be their grandfather's land till he sold it. Gideon didn't know to whom.

"Secure. High walls. Cameras," Cain continues. "Looks like they're planting the same as us."

"What are they growing?"

"Corn, looks like. Other kinds of crops, too? I don't know. They've an extensive vegetable garden behind a chain-link cage, and there are lots of blackberry bushes with sharp, hidden surprises." He wiggles his eyebrows. "And apple trees."

Cain strolls toward the house, probably to convey his intel to Wendall. Gideon scans the trees along the edge of the field, skirting the river between the two farms. His brother hasn't said when he's leaving, but Gideon hopes it's soon. Yesterday, Wendall sent out the teams of men to fetch workers, like he'd talked about doing. Some took off east, but Gideon doesn't hold up much hope. Not as many farms east; mostly cabins and people living off grid. More went south to fetch farmers on the outskirts of Swindon. Kaden was among that bunch. Cain still being here signaled to Gideon that Wendall didn't think he could handle the farm or the men alone.

Looks like there is more manpower closer than we thought. If Gideon plays his cards right, he could snatch some workers across the way and show his brother up. The vision of Wendall strutting in from his mysterious trek and his arrogant jaw dropping would please Gideon to no end. He'll have to concede that Gideon's not a fuckup in this family.

***

Beth stands guard while Sean and Colin dig up another cache behind her in the woods. On a nearby rock, Alejo gazes between Beth and the surrounding forest. "You think they're out there?" he asks in a panic.

As the wind blows, it hisses through the trees, creating a soothing rustling sound and a gentle touch caresses her cheeks. The sensation of being watched prickles her skin. Her senses are alive. They haven't shaken their stalkers. "A, don't ask questions you don't want the answer to."

Once they hit the trail, the hard work begins as the landscape transforms into mountains, fallen trees, and streams; hidden hazards waiting to be triggered. She will have to go over the way to navigate safely on the next leg with them. It'll take four or five more days to reach Reed, and the geography won't be the only obstacle they have to tackle.

Sean upends a PVC pipe, and the contents spill forth onto the ground. "You were right, Beth. More weapons and food."

"What's the bear spray for?" Alejo asks. "We're not going to—?" Movement. Her head tilts to the left. "Beth?"

"Time to move. Sean, leave the food on the rock over there." Beth says this without breaking her line of sight on the place where the shadow moved. They'll catch up soon, and she doesn't want to be within range of their weapons.

"Why?" Alejo jumps down and hikes over to her. "Is it them?" He steps to her backside, looks past Beth's shoulders, and uses her as a shield.

"Yes."

Sean and Colin lay out storage containers and bottles of water on the rock. Colin asks, "Won't they follow us if we give them food?"

She can't take them to Reed, but that doesn't mean she is totally cruel. The children must be starving by now. "They'll try, but there's a hidden shelter close by. We'll stay there till they move on, then we'll head north to the trail bridge."

"How do you know there's a shelter close by?"

Because I helped build it.

Her hesitation signals Sean to use this as a teaching moment. "All the shelters are on your map, marked with different colored Xs."

Each color represented the size of the shelter, ensuring they had room for their group. The larger ones for families included comfort items for the children.

Sean pulls out his compass. "Colin, let's get you familiar with the compass." Sean waves Alejo over. "You, too, honey."

"Do I have to?" Alejo whines.

Sean crosses his arms and waits. Alejo growls, rolls his eyes, and stomps forward.

***

In silence, Beth and Alejo trek ahead of the others. The trees are denser here, and she sways her head from side to side as she searches. It's been years since Beth's traveled to Haven. The landmarks have been obscured over time, but she's not concerned. Her dads travel around checking on the shelters regularly, so she's confident each one will be stocked. Still, she's worried those people might catch up to them before they can stow themselves away safely.

"What are you looking for?" Alejo asks.

Peace. The voices haven't returned for a couple of days, she realizes. She should be happy about that. *It never lasts.* "Looking for a particular landmark. It's a bent tree. Looks like a bench."

"How you doing, hon?"

"I'm fine."

"Sorry about the guy at the diner."

Ryker's never far from her thoughts. It's silly. She doesn't know him, yet she misses him. "Haven't thought about him," she lies.

Alejo comes at her with open arms, closing the distance. "Oh, hon—"

She holds her hands up, palms out. "Don't! I have to stay focused."

His arms drop, but his sympathetic eyes don't, and they resume their search in silence.

Soon, Beth stops...points.

Approaching the tree bench, Alejo rubs warmth into his arms, sits down, and pats the seat next to him in apology. She can't stay mad at him for long and lets him cuddle her while they wait for the boys to catch up. Beth's fingers seek the necklace in comfort as she constantly scans for threats.

"When I lost my focus, I left my Louboutins behind. No one's saying you need to lose your focus to miss someone."

Her heart cracks under a sad smile. "Can't miss someone you don't know."

"True, but you can mourn the chance you could have had together. It's okay to feel it."

Beth nestles her head into the curve of his neck. She blew it. She won't get that date or see Ryker again. "He was really hot, A."

Alejo's chest bounces. "My Louboutins were really hot, too, hon. It's a tragedy."

Chapter 22
May 26

At the top of a bluff, on their bellies, Colin studies the view as Beth gazes through binoculars. Last night, they slept in a shelter tucked into a cave high above the ground, accessible by a rope ladder they hoisted up after themselves.

"Damn it!" Beth hands them off to Sean.

Beth's language disturbs Colin. She's changed since the missile drop. Most of the day he's been silent.

"Could be a sniper." Sean passes the binoculars to Colin.

"No choice now but to go through Swindon," Beth says, sounding disappointed.

Swindon? Through the binoculars, Colin scans the calm lake spread out before them, pausing on the trail bridge they were supposed to cross. Beth said it's part of the Rattlesnake Trail that zigzags through the mountains of Idaho ahead of them. Colin spots a body on the bridge, lying down, unmoving. He recognizes the suit jacket fluttering in the wind. *No way...*

He searches further, finding no one else. The family had wandered by their hiding spot last night. They should have offered to take those people to Haven. They had children, for God's sake.

Beth hangs her head, frustrated, and says into the ground, "It's two...three full days away."

She means this Swindon town. He's learned cities are dangerous places to be right now. Colin drops the binoculars, feeling sick to his stomach, and gazes over at Beth. Why isn't she more upset about these people? She's changed somehow, and he's not sure how to bring her back.

Alejo takes the binoculars but speaks before having a peek. "It's only been...how many days since hell dropped on our heads? Can't be that bad."

Beth lifts her head. "It's been four days, A."

Sean confiscates the binoculars, preventing Alejo from using them. "Babe, four days without food... It's going to be bad down there." He tilts his head to Beth. "How do you want to proceed?"

She thumbs behind them, and they back up a distance, unfold the map, and smooth it out on the ground. Colin joins them. Beth searches out the butterfly necklace and strokes its colorful surface without thinking. Why is it so precious to her? Fatigue darkens Beth's eyes. As they progress further east, Colin worries about her more and more. She hasn't slept well since she was in his arms two nights ago, and he wishes she'd let him do it again. Beth's stronger than Colin thought and good at adapting to her environment, but the days weigh on her. Back at the apartment, she said it would be bad for her out here. That was an understatement after what he witnessed back in Spokane. It bothers him, this piece of herself she won't give up to him.

Sean drags his finger across the map's surface from the lake, down the long Python River, and into Swindon. "I've only driven to Haven from the north. There's only one bridge on the south side?"

She nods. "We have to get through Swindon first, then cross the bridge."

"Well, then, we have to hope we don't get noticed," Sean says.

***

Since the sun set hours ago, Ryker has marked the comings and goings on Python Bridge from a concealed position upriver. Without any light pollution, the darkness is all-consuming and earlier than he's used to. They skirted the

148

town, staying close to the railroad tracks and under the cover of trees, ending up where they were now.

A small band of armed men is detaining anyone who attempts to cross the bridge, escorting them out of Ryker's sight. There is another way upriver—a trail bridge that forms part of the Rattlesnake Trail system into Idaho—but he doesn't want to initiate Plan B unless it is necessary. The territory isn't familiar to him; only through the map he carries. The highway follows the Canyon River on the other side, but he's aiming for the Coil Trail, so he wants to stick with the current plan.

He glances down at Libby dozing in his lap, her breathing soft and steady, and enjoys the moment, despite still being furious with her. Ryker's first mistake was trusting her with the food and, two nights ago, during her watch, he expected she'd stay close as he slept. She didn't.

He smooths her hair and caresses her cheek. During the night, Ryker awoke alone; Libby was nowhere to be seen. Adrenaline shot through his body like the spike of an energy drink. He had a sudden sensation of dread and launched from his sleeping position in search of her, repeating to himself that everything would be fine. He couldn't call out to her without alerting anyone to their presence, so, in the dark, he whispered her name as he scoured the area surrounding their camp. Ryker found her, cold and shivering, and crushed her body against his own before promptly scolding her for leaving him without warning. When Ryker calmed down, she told him she walked off in search of a place to empty her bladder and didn't want to wake him.

Even now, he can't believe she did that. Ryker's job is to keep her safe. With his trust in her shattered, he hasn't slept for the past two nights.

Two men stand guard on the south end, closest to Ryker, well armed. Two more join them, and the group confers for a few minutes. It's too dark to make out what they look like. *A shift change?* The town must be under some sort of rule; it's only been four days. They are letting people in, but Ryker's seen no one leave.

Regardless, they need to get a move on. He's afraid of what will happen if they can't cross the bridge. They're running out of food, and the cornfields across the river give him hope. A few dozen ears stuffed in their backpacks would sustain them for days until he could find this farm Beth talked about.

Movement on the bridge snatches Ryker's attention. *Bang!* The white flash of a muzzle blast lights up a man escaping across the bridge. The piercing cry on the night air startles Libby, but Ryker remains still as she shoots up and says, "What—?"

Ryker clamps her mouth shut. "Shh."

Loud voices carry down to them. "Did you get him?"

"He yelped, didn't he?"

"Find the flashlight."

They didn't know for sure if they'd tagged the fleeing man. This information was useful to Ryker.

***

Under the beam of his headlamp, Ryker finds the service door under the bridge locked tight. He swears under his breath, switches the light off, and waits until his eyes adjust. For once, he'd like a break. With no way to open it, he makes a change of plan and pulls Libby in for a hug to cut the sound of his voice to those above. "We have to cross the bridge in the open. Not one word when we go topside. When I signal, walk silently, and whatever happens, don't run."

"I'm scared."

He squeezes courage through his arms. "I'll be right behind you."

"What if something happens to you?"

He pulls back, cups her jaw with both hands, and leans his forehead against hers. "Libby, nothing will happen to me. I promise."

"Okay." She doesn't sound sure, but they have no choice but to cross.

On all fours, they crawl up the hill to the bridge deck and behind a concrete barrier, Ryker draws Libby close to his side. The red glow of a cigarette swings up through the air as a man takes a drag. It brightens, then dulls. The glow flicks in the dark and drops still in the man's grasp, next to what Ryker assumes is his thigh. He gauges the man to be shorter than his counterpart. The darkness obscures any more detail, but Ryker's been in these situations before. All he needs to know is where to strike if things go sideways.

"I have to take a leak," a man in the darkness says.

Their chances have just improved. Ryker yanks on Libby's jacket and signals for her to move before putting a finger to his lips. She nods and goes to leave, but the flash of a light crosses their position. *Christ!* Ryker wrenches her back and ducks as his heart does a double flip.

"Jesus, Rick. You just went."

Rick illuminates under the soft light and dances from foot to foot. "I know, Ned. I'll be quick." Rick hands his cigarette to Ned and runs off to the side opposite Ryker's position. The other man hefts more bulk than Rick, but a knife in the hands of an expert doesn't care.

Ryker gives Libby a gentle shove, then advances toward Ned, the cold metal in his hands warming beneath his touch. This is familiar ground for Ryker, like riding a bike. He's done it so many times. Other than the two men in town, he's never taken the life of an American civilian like this. His morals fight him with every step, not wanting to do the man harm, but does he have a choice?

Ryker chances a glance north, down the bridge. The moderate light helps him see the bobbing of his sister's backpack as she walks steadily to the halfway point. The body of the man is off to her right. His sister and the dead man remind Ryker why he has to do this.

Her retreat extinguishes with Ned's light, and the darkness hides everyone from view. Ryker's eyes adjust. He refocuses on the man standing before him. The enemy has changed. Unknown to Ned, death is three feet from him if he so much as turns around.

"You done yet?" Ned says. The light from the cigarette slides up to his mouth and brightens as he takes a long drag.

"Yeah, where the fuck are you?"

Ned doesn't reply, and steps away from Ryker, leaving the flashlight off. Ryker's guard goes up, as does his heightened sense of hearing. A slight breeze tingles his neck, bringing with it the fresh scent of earth and pine. In the distance, the faint glow of firelight lights up a building in town. The spring melt has turned a lazy river into a churning mess under the bridge as the pressure of so much water jams between the bridge legs. Ned snickers.

"Ned? You better not be scaring me again." Rick says, ahead and to the left of Ryker's position.

Leaving them to their game of hide and seek, Ryker retreats, steering clear of the dead man on the bridge as he follows in his sister's footsteps. It's pretty clear to him now that the rules of engagement have changed and it's every man for themselves.

***

May 27

Beth stands in a field of wheat, waiting for him, her long brown hair floating on the wind, swirling around her face. The smile he enjoyed back at the diner graces her freckled face and stunning, overjoyed green eyes greet him. His head jerks up, and he blinks rapidly, unable to process where he is. It takes a moment for him to realize he'd fallen asleep.

The vision he conjured dissipates as the flames of the small fire he built in a deep pit materialize before his eyes. Libby stands over him, wrapped in an emergency blanket. The forest and their escape from Spokane... Swindon sharpens in his muddled mind. "Libby, don't get too close. You'll catch fire."

Libby tilts her head. "I won't burst into flames, brother."

Ryker's too tired to take the bait. He dozed off, but he needs to stay awake. After crossing the bridge, Libby thought they were out of danger in the trees. Ryker shut her down when she tried to talk to him, and she's been miffed ever since. They made it to the highway without further hindrances and stuck to the road for some time before entering the woods for protection. They passed several farms, the windows dark, but collected the corn they needed to sustain themselves without interference.

He can't go on this way, but a little further north, then he'll rest tomorrow.

"Ryker, you need to sleep," she says, taking a seat across from him, in a knitted hat and puffy winter jacket, her face illuminated by the flickering flames.

"I'm fine," he assures her. In the crisp night air, the smell of pine lingers. The nights are chilly, but the days are gradually getting warmer as June approaches.

"You're not fine. I'm taking the next shift," she says, rubbing her hands over the fire pit.

"No. Get some sleep."

She relaxes her hands in her lap. "How can you function without sleep?"

"Did it all the time. You get used to it." He lies. It was a bitch to keep his eyes open, but the threat of someone killing his fellow Marines was a great incentive to stay awake during watch. They had tricks to help with that, anyway. Caffeine, he was low on, and he didn't have any nicotine, but he could run through push-ups and squats to keep the blood flowing. Looks like he'll be exercising tonight. He can't let his guard down.

"I'm sorry I worried you." Her apology is sincere. She comes at him with an emergency blanket and wraps his shoulders with it. Ryker tries to push her away, but his reflexes aren't as sharp. Libby wins this round. He accepts her help and cinches the blanket between dirty fingers.

"Danger is present. Need to keep you safe." Ryker's eyes droop with heavy sleep.

"Sleep. I'll keep you safe, brother," her melodic voice floats around him.

His mind fights, but his eyes war with him. Perhaps just a little nap will help and then he'll get them through another day. He gives in. "Okay, don't leave. Just give me fifteen."

Chapter 23

Sean trails Beth up the slope to the road leading to Python Bridge. He gazes north of their position as they slouch behind the concrete barrier. Alarm bells go off in his head. No one is guarding the bridge. It is empty.

They tried the service door under the bridge moments ago, finding it locked. Beth shook the door handle, then stood for a moment, gripping the bronze knob tight. Sean knew what she was thinking but kept silent. The pry bar was in Colin's lost backpack, but there was no use crying over spilled milk.

On their way into town, tractors and armed men blocked the road. Alejo tumbled backward into a ravine. Sean's heart seized. They combed the underbrush until Alejo was located, and Beth administered first aid from her pack for the scrapes and bruises, while Sean clutched his love.

He glances down the hill at Alejo, who hugs himself with worry next to a vigilant Colin. Sean waves them up and shakes off his apprehension from the thought of losing Alejo. "Why isn't the bridge guarded?"

Beth dips her head. Sean waits her out. She's slept poorly the last couple of days, so he treads lightly, knowing she's doing the best she can. "I don't like it. We should wait till dark to cross."

"Hey!"

Their heads turn in unison to the unfamiliar voice at the south end of the street into town. A whistle blows. Fear grips him, sending waves of adrenaline through his body.

"Shit! Time to go!" Beth jumps over the concrete barrier and hightails it north, across the bridge deck. Swift and athletic, Colin clears the barrier with ease. Alejo lags, his expression one of fright, but he and Sean hit the bridge deck and run together. More men come at them from the north side of the bridge, tightening a noose none of them saw coming. *We're doomed!*

Beth and Colin halt midway across the span. As Sean reaches them, Beth eyes the water, then scales the railing. *Really?! Is this our only option?!*

Metal rings as bullets make contact with the bridge railing. Colin howls and stumbles.

"Colin!" Beth's shrill voice cries out.

Shit! I got you, buddy! Sean yanks Colin up and partially drags him until his legs return.

Alejo catches up, out of breath. His face is dark red, and his purple-tipped hair is in a messy bun. "Are you insane? We'll die!" he says to Beth but clambers over the railing, anyway.

"We'll die if we don't. Jump!"

Colin reaches for Beth's hand. "Beth, wait!" Their fingertips brush.

Sean tracks her fall straight into the turbulent river below. He twists his head as the sting of a bullet caresses his cheek. *That was close!* Sean scrambles over the railing and gazes back as the mob hits the bridge deck on both sides. *Fuck, we're doing this!*

"We're jumping, grab Colin!" Unceremoniously, Sean hauls Colin over the railing before Alejo can object, but his boyfriend surprises him and helps carry the load. They leap.

Alejo screeches till the cold water swallows them.

***

Beth loses sight of the bridge, engulfed in the flow of a raging river sweeping her around a bend. Her backpack pulls her under, impeding her ability to swim.

Lose the bag. Panic sets in as she struggles to keep her head above the frigid water and fight the current to get to the river's edge. *No, I can't!*

Sucked beneath the choppy surface, all sound cuts off, replaced by churning bubbles. Beth's body twists, over and over, confusing her which way is up. Sunlight fades as the river claims her, dragging her down.

A memory she doesn't want to remember comes up: the anguish of loss overtaking her mind, breaking her as she weeps and screams in the backseat. Her arms tighten around a soft, furry object as fire rages unhindered in the car across from her. The high-pitched screams of her parents died long ago, replaced with crackling metal, acrid smoke, and a sweet, putrid taste. Misty rain cascades under the streetlights, but not enough to douse the flames. *I was alone.*

Beth's lungs protest, but her mind commands action, and her limbs reply as she claws her way up from the river's murky depths. Light charges at Beth, and the river spits her out. She gasps and chokes, still caught firm in the river's grip as white noise assaults her.

Sirens rang in her ears that night, aggressive and invasive, as pain tore through her broken and battered teenage body. Swaddled under blankets, her arms were bound to a stretcher.

Desperate to grab onto something, Beth's arms flail, and her hands reach out, but she's moving too fast in the flow. Not finished, the current rakes her body over jagged rocks, tosses her around, pulls her under, casts her out, and sweeps her over rapids without compassion. Pain registers, it's everywhere; she can't pinpoint any place she isn't hurting. *Why fight it?*

"Whole family was wiped out, man. One survived," said someone, pushing body bags into the hospital elevator from the hallway. One of those should have been for her. This punishment, brutal and just, is appropriate for her crime. Beth gives in and lets go. *This is what I deserve...*

Chapter 24

A dense forest frames angry rain clouds in the dark sky. The wind carries crisp mountain air over a river swollen with a fast-flowing spring runoff, causing turbulence along its center. Colin wakes disoriented to white noise coming from the water. He peels himself off the ground and onto his elbows. Warm air escapes his trembling lips as he eyes the river through the soaked strands of his blond hair. *I fell into the river.*

His brain's half-firing, piecing those last memories together. *Beth fell first.* Burning pain draws his eyes down. Colin twists his leg for a better look, prods his dark pants, and discovers two wet holes. His fingers come up bloody. He stumbled on the bridge, and the guys helped him over the railing. *They must have shot me.*

Wide awake now, he scans the river's edge from left to right. *Where is she?* He spots a body downriver, face down. Colin's stomach drops as his mind reels. *Oh, God, no!* "Beth!"

Colin scrambles up through the searing pain, but the fear of losing Beth overrides it. *Please don't let it be her.* He hops toward the body, lands, and turns it over. He falls backward as his hand shoots to his mouth. The stench! *Poor bastard.* Without the dress shoes, Colin wouldn't have known the swollen body was a male.

He rises, favoring his wounded leg, scans the river again, and concludes he's alone. That needs to change. Colin hobbles downriver, determined to find his friends and Beth. If he made it out of the river, surely they did, too.

A short time later, under heavy rainfall, Colin climbs out of the wet foliage of the riverbank and onto blacktop, using a large branch as a crutch, and sighs. From the protection of a hood, he observes that no one is on the road. In the distance, atop the hill, he spots a farmhouse. Across the slope, hayfields stretch between them. "Too open," he says under his breath.

Back at the river, Colin found a few corpses here and there, but not his friends. Seeing dead bodies no longer affects him, and this realization disturbs him. Less than a week ago, he was celebrating Beth's birthday and looking forward to their next tango dance class together. Now, he'll be glad if he never sees a dead body again...or a raging river.

Beth... His chest tightens at the thought of not finding her. Colin struggled in the river's grip to reach the edge. He's never choked on so much water or had so much anxiety over possibly drowning before. He sailed past Sean, clinging to a downed tree over the river and, by then, he'd lost sight of Alejo.

Colin squares his shoulders, glad his heavy coat gave him some protection from the elements, but he'll have to dry out all his clothes for them to be effective. *You'll find her.* He has to. Sean taught Colin how to get to Reed and that's where Beth will be, so he'll follow and, hopefully, find her safe and sound. He just needs to familiarize himself with the compass and the map in his pocket. Colin's thanking his lucky stars they insisted he learn while they were together. Perhaps he'll find them down the highway and won't need the compass. In his precarious position, this wish is the lifeline he clings to. Colin didn't learn in case he got lost; he did it to impress Beth.

***

Longing for this nightmare to be over, Colin stops and holds the map up against the wet bark of a tree. The rain has tapered off, but the air is chilly. He can barely feel the map in his icy hands. Earlier, he filled his water containers to the brim, but he needs food if he's going to get to this Reed place. Colin looks left, down the slope, and glimpses the highway below. Choosing to follow the road for hours has kept him going in a northerly direction, but there are no Xs near the road on the map. His friends aren't following this path either, or he'd have found them by now. Colin has considered the possibility that following the road isn't a good idea, but he's unsure about using the compass. Beth will be at one of those Xs on his map, and his hunger pains are telling him to find a shelter. He needs to start a fire when he finds one.

Movement on the road catches his eye. Bedraggled and looking exhausted, a wet Alejo trudges on, dragging his feet along the pavement. Joy slams into Colin at the sight. "Alejo!" He waves his arms, elated to have found one friend, raising hope that they'll find the others.

Alejo glances up and, with a big grin, welcomes Colin with a frantic wave, like he's greeting Colin coming off a plane at the airport. As Colin waves him up with a smile, Alejo shakes his head and waves him down with a serious expression. Colin sighs. He's going to have to be firm with him. There's no way around it.

Colin's grimy finger slides across the map and locates the closest shelter, but it's far. He takes out the compass and glances up the slope. With no choice but to use it, Colin starts up the waterlogged slope, believing Alejo will follow if he's as hungry as Colin is.

***

Beth's pink cheek, dappled with freckles, lies on the sand, her wet hair plastered to her forehead, encircling a dark temple scar. Raindrops spatter sand into her face, rousing her. Panic floods her thoughts, then twists into disappointment. *I'm alive.*

She picks at her wet clothes as she rises, unsteady at first. Anxious eyes search up and down the river, then across to the opposite shore. No one. Fear wells to the surface. *Everyone leaves me.* She blows warm steam into her cold, shaky hands. Beth needs to find a shelter and she won't reach one till nightfall. *I can't do this alone.*

She unzips her pocket, partially pulls out a compass, flashlight, and waterproof map to make sure they're there, and shoves them back in. Something on the ground attracts her attention. *Damn it!* She bends down to retrieve it. A rush of water gushes over her head.

She swings her waterlogged backpack around and spots the rip. *No!* She reaches into it in a rush and finds the interior of the bag empty. Carrie's stuffy is gone. Beth strikes the sand with the bag and cries out in frustration. It was the one thing she had left. The thought of never holding it again crushes her. For good measure, she kicks the bag. A metal sound clinks underfoot.

She picks up the bag, checks the side pockets, and sucks in a dramatic sigh. Great, all the homemade weapons she took from the apartment are still there, like she'll ever need those. *Oh, no!* She seizes her holster. Empty. *Damn it!* With a heavy sigh, her head dips and shoulders slump as her new reality sets in.

Beth brushes water off the photo of her parents hugging her and Carrie, places it back in her pocket to protect it from further damage, and zips it up. "Ow!" She hisses, drops the bag, snatches her caught finger back, gazes at it, and rubs the pain out. She hoists the ruined backpack upon her shoulders, scans the forest, pulls her hood over her head, and wipes her drenched face. Rain pours steadily as she sprints into the trees.

Not far in, pressure causes her to stumble forward. Her cheek plummets into earth. The weight of someone on top of her forces the air from her lungs. She reels, confused, as raindrops clog her vision. A crazed man has jumped on her, the sting of steel sharp against her throat forces a strangled cry out of her. She rakes her hand through the ground, desperately searching for something, anything, as his wild face nears. Her fingers curl around soil. She hurls it. He shies up, unbalanced.

Beth bolts into the forest. The man's heavy breathing grows louder. He latches onto her, tackling her to the ground. She clambers to rise but is pushed forward. The rough bark of a tree scrapes her cheek as her shoulder slams into the trunk, and she goes down. Hands yank on her jean pockets. She twists and kicks with everything she has, connecting with the man's chest. He topples backward but stays upright.

The roar of an enraged animal echoes. *Bear!*

Terror pauses her movement. Her voice cuts through the silence, sharp and shrill, and says, "Oh, fuck!"

On instinct, her body restarts and scrambles backward like a crab until she smacks into a tree. The bear charges them and clamps his wide mouth down on the man's shoulder. The man's howls pierce her ears as he attempts to fight the bear. Blood sprays. Her horrified eyes pinch closed and she waits—

Nothing happens.

Her body trembles violently as she peels her eyes open to a vision that defies belief. Opening its powerful jaws, stained with blood, the bear drops the body onto the forest floor. In a display of power and triumph, he lifts himself onto his hind legs and lets out a thunderous roar, declaring his victory over her attacker.

This is it. Drenched and shivering, she can't tell if it's from the cold or from fear. Beth forces herself to stand on her wobbly legs and surrender. *Give me release.*

The bear's eyes lock onto Beth, recognizing her as a threat, and it lets out a fierce, bone-chilling bellow before charging toward her. The ground shakes. She hears her own heartbeat in her ears. Terror spurs her legs to move. No time. She braces. A huge paw flies at her, causing stars to burst across her vision. Her head strikes the tree, rendering her senseless. She tumbles downward, pain courses through her head, then nothing.

***

Beth is trapped in her parent's car, her arms tight around a furry object. Misty rain drifts through the harsh lamplight. Pain scores through her ribs and legs, but she can't lift her throbbing head to see. Water drops pelt her face, so she closes her eyes. There's no noise. No one disturbs the silence.

Dead air hangs as moist precipitation, and the scent of trees overpowers her senses. Her eyes open. Tears trickle down her cheeks. Warm air escapes her lips under the streetlight, creating puffs of white smoke at steady intervals. Cold seeps into her limbs. Why can't she move?

Beth jerks awake, shivering, and finds herself on the forest floor, wet, exposed to the elements in pitch-black darkness. It was a dream. She moans her disappointment aloud. *I don't deserve this life! Why can't you just let me die?*

There was a bear. Beth remembers bracing, the ground shaking...then her memory runs a blank. She's not sure how long she's been down and investigates the pain in her jaw with quivering fingers, senses wetness there. *Blood, maybe.* The wild animal used her as a punching bag and must have batted her around with those huge paws.

She reaches her cold hands into her pocket for her flashlight, draws it out, thumbs the soft, ribbed button at the top, and toggles it on. Beth's heart jumps out of her chest, along with a scream. Her attacker's contorted face stares back, covered in blood. She scrambles backward and catapults off the ground, only to fall back to the earth, her head pounding and her limbs cold and stiff. *Have to find shelter...and relief.*

CHAPTER 25

Ryker stares into space, ignoring the bubbling melody of the water. He found Libby by the stream, her body against a tree as if she had fallen asleep peacefully to the soothing sounds. But she hadn't. Her end had been nothing but peaceful.

He awoke at dawn to find her missing. He hoped he'd find her like the last time, cold and lost. When that didn't materialize, he retraced his steps and used the one thing he knew would lead him to her. Tracking is a skill Ryker's father taught him before he died, which was honed further by Elias and his older brother.

Her tracks indicated she'd gotten lost and attempted to backtrack but ended up moving further away from their camp. Libby had wandered far and alone, until she wasn't.

Sharp sunlight slices through the trees, highlighting natural perfection. Libby's beauty was flawless; her smile, infectious. Her innocence... Libby's light is no more. She'll never grace him with it again. *My fault.*

The other tracks tell him more than he'd like. There were four of them. Two wore heavy-tread boots, and the others wore the same patterned shoes with a flat sole.

Birdsong echoes every once in a while as the animals communicate with each other through the trees. A vision of Libby standing at the kitchen sink comes unbidden. His sad smile bursts through. Ryker walked in on her shaking her hips to music, singing and orchestrating with yellow gloves, a scrub brush in one hand and a cup in the other. God, how he wishes he could go back to that day. To reverse this dark path he now has to blaze.

His lips tremble. Hot tears score down his cheeks, only to be captured by the recent growth of his beard. He gazes down, picks up a rock, and lays it with a clunk on top of other rocks. Numb, he picks up another rock and repeats the unnatural sound on autopilot.

One man was taller than the rest. Ryker's jaw tightens. All the footprints lead to her body. Two deep holes are entrenched in the mud where their knees were. He holds back tears and swallows back the knowledge of what he's gathered from those tracks and blocks out the unnatural way he found her. It torments him mercilessly. *My fault.*

He straightens on his knees and flexes his shoulders back; the effort forces a tired groan from his parched lips. *Forgive me.*

Before him lies a solitary pile of rocks in human shape. The stabbing in Ryker's eyes continues after he closes them. He mourns the loss and wishes he was in someone else's nightmare; longs to wake up and find her sleeping beside him. The emotion will pass. Ryker welcomes it, knowing with every fiber of his being that the next emotion will be rage. He needs to unleash vengeance and wipe the slate clean. Nothing else matters anymore. Only his need to avenge her.

He reaches out with a soiled hand, and his dirty fingers cover a smooth rock that reads *Libby* in black Sharpie. He made a promise by this stream, and he plans on keeping it.

***

Beth stares at the roof of straight branches held together with rope, moss, and leaves. Her memory of locating the shelter is fuzzy; she can only recall that the journey was cold and wet. Her flashlight helped, though it wouldn't surprise her if she'd found it without it. They camped at night sometimes, and her BAMF dads would send the kids off to find the shelter in the dark. Beth rubs her elbow, sensitive to the residual pain of a fall she took one year. Traipsing in the dark wasn't without its pitfalls. This particular shelter had been made for two people, or three if you were okay with being cozy. She and Parker were to use the ones marked on her map, in red. It pains her she'll never see him again.

Hunger disrupts Beth's bleak thoughts. *I don't need to eat.* Pulling herself up, she shivers as the chilly morning air seeps through her damp clothes, and cautiously, she looks around. The forest around her comes alive. The voices of the birds filter in, and streams of rising sunlight splinter through the branches, burning off the morning dew in wisps of steam. She's glad her nightmare didn't come back. Her sister's lost stuffy was a blow among the horrors of the day before. One more reason to stop this farce of a life. One she shouldn't be living. She's no use to her friends now. They'll be better off without her, anyway.

Beth brushes away debris and eyes a flat basalt rock lying on the earthen floor. Knowing what she'll find underneath, her shaky hands lift it, revealing a hole lined with more rocks and a camping cooler nestled there. Removing the lid, she grabs a first aid kit, unzips it so it flays open, and stares at a white bottle of pain meds. *My family would be alive if it wasn't for me.* Beth fingers a leather-bound journal, picks it up, and flips the pages till she finds the last entry. All the shelters have one, to see who's been there, and to give encouragement. Two fresh entries glare back at her. The first is from her uncle, Henry Livingston: *I see we're the first here. It's good I'm ahead of you. Don't worry about injuries and such. We'll be ready for you. Stay safe and dry.*

He is one of her mother's older brothers. Growing up, Beth wasn't close to them. Uncle Henry and Uncle James lived far away with their families at Camp Pendleton. Parker had lived there, too, once, but with no children, he moved back to his hometown of Spokane when he retired. Never one to let the grass grow, he opened the diner and began building Haven, the place they called the farm. Beth's not sure how he could afford to build it. Those were things they didn't talk about after he took her in.

Beth reads the second entry by Hoss's son, John Henry: *You've done this trek many times. What's one more?* She grins despite her mood, relieved he and Rita made it with Steven's wife, Lisa. After that, the page is blank. Gina and Brad haven't visited this shelter yet. That bothers her.

Beth closes the journal and plucks out the bottle of pills, but it doesn't feel right. A heavy sigh escapes her lips, and her shoulders slump. She flicks the lid off with her thumb and upends the bottle. A few pills tumble into her hand. *Crap, not enough.*

Beth stares down into the hole at the ready-made meals and fights the urge to eat. She could just lie down and die, but how long will that take? Less painful with a bottle, which is why Beth chose that method as a teenager. With a heavy heart, she drags out the map and locates the next red X. She'll have to start a fire and dry her clothes to make it to the next shelter. *What's one more day?*

***

Beth walks among giant trees and mossy roots, taking in the surrounding forest. *I knew it would get worse.* She fought for years to vanquish her destructive thoughts. Tried to conquer them through control of her environment; by creating safe zones. Sometimes, the voices crept up on her, but she had a therapist and friends. Here, out in the open, she has too much time to think. That's why she avoided Haven, as well as it being the burial place of her failure. Beth trips, catching herself, going down on a knee. *Crap!*

A densely wooded forest contains many treacherous traps. One minute, you're progressing well, and the next, you've twisted your ankle with no way of getting help. The words "slow and steady" echo in her mind. It was Hoss's mantra as they trudged through the trees. One year, he'd given them a challenge in which he'd pretended to be injured, so they—still just teenagers—had to carry him out with no help from the other adults. You don't know what you're made of until you're in those situations. *I was strong back then...*

Twigs snap... Her head perks up, and hope fills her. The boys? Several snapping sounds echo, leading her to believe that more than one person is approaching. A whiny child's voice calls out. "I'm tired."

Her hope dwindles. With a sense of urgency, Beth scours her surroundings for a hiding spot, eventually finding solace under a fallen tree, and hastily gathers debris to conceal herself. She may want to end it, but not by someone else's hand. She holds her breath as a blond man with a backpack walks by with a little boy, who is carrying a child's backpack. The man seems too focused on his son to notice her lying there, terrified.

"I know, son. We'll be safe at the cabin in a few more days."

The boy jumps up, all smiles, and yanks on his father's jacket. "Will Gramps and Nana be there?"

A tickling sensation crawls across her neck. This is the worst time for a creepy crawly bug to use her as a highway. She doesn't dare move, but the urge to flick it away grows stronger with each passing second.

With a long, sad sigh, his father says, "I'm not sure, son."

The boy stops abruptly. "Can I have my surprise now?"

The bug crawls further behind her ear, causing mayhem. Her fingers itch to move, but she can't.

"When we camp, you'll get it. Now stop talking, son."

Yes, please stop and keep walking. Her last thread of sanity frays as the bug tickles her inner ear. Her fingers ascend up her body in a painful, slow journey to be rid of her tickle monster.

They walk out of her field of view. She swipes at her ear and shivers. The forest sounds don't return as they should. Beth's intuition tells her not to move, so she retreats further under the tree, gathers more forest debris around her, and buries herself until she can't see anymore. With her ears alert, footsteps approach as the ground shakes. She doesn't dare move, doesn't dare breathe. Something or someone is out there. Animals aren't the only threat she faces.

CHAPTER 26

Approaching the tree line under the afternoon sun, white noise fills Beth's ears as she shades her eyes and scans a flat, open expanse of rocks. Even with the spring runoff, the river seems tame. Uprooted trees and a few truck-sized boulders litter the edges of the riverbed. Beth shivers at the thought of meeting whoever or whatever walked past her back there. She hopes her friends are okay and prays they make it to Reed.

Beth risks exposure and walks out of cover to spot the way across upriver. She doesn't need the compass to know where she is; Parker taught her how to identify the shapes of the trees back when she was a carefree teenager. They're still recognizable. Beth recalls the last time she was here.

"Girls! Watch your step." Five sets of eyes cast glances at Hoss, relaxed at the far edge, waiting for them to cross like he had all the time in the world. The musketeers—Gina, Carrie, Sadie, Sonia, and herself were crossing the stream. He waved his hand sharply to their right as if he could sweep them over in that direction. Hoss's four handsome sons were watching, too.

Beth had a crush on Hoss's second son, Jessie, and him watching them bolstered her confidence. It also raised her heart rate. She didn't think it was that treacherous. *What a weirdo I was!*

Sonia was ahead of them, hopping from rock to rock with ease. Gina was more interested in bugs than boys and was holding Carrie's hand, leading her across, one rock at a time. Slow and steady. Gina took this advice and changed their direction to the right. Beth was upset that day because Carrie had played damsel in distress earlier with Jessie, knowing it would infuriate Beth. She was behind her sister, holding onto Sadie's hand.

Sadie made her first mistake and lost her footing, grabbing onto an unsuspecting Beth, who lost her balance and fell backward. They would have plummeted into the water, but Donovan hauled them up from behind, shouting over the sound of rushing water, "Keep your eyes on the rocks, girls!" Donovan always knew what they were thinking, and in Sadie's case, it was probably Liam. Donovan wasn't as fun as Hoss.

The little boy from earlier dashes out from behind a boulder in the riverbed.

Crap! Beth crouches down, unsure whether he spotted her. Where's his father? Cut off from her crossing, she scans downriver for another way but sees the next set of rapids. Human sounds amid the river static draw her attention back to the boy's position.

Shit! Beth crawls back into the tree line, finds comfort in the shade, and stretches her neck for a better view.

A man with tattooed arms catches the child by the collar and drags him to the rock. A terrified voice carries on the wind, but she can't make out the words. Another man with long, scraggly dark hair rips the backpack from the boy's shoulders, rousing her anger. *He's just a child.*

He dumps the contents onto the rocks and pilfers through the items, tossing the boys' trinkets and toys in favor of the water and food. The tattooed man shoves the boy to the ground and walks out of sight behind the boulder. The boy cries out in terror, infuriating her further when his tiny hand reaches into the air toward the rock. She guesses by his reaction that something unpleasant has happened.

The same man reappears, brandishing a blade, followed by two equally intimidating men. Her breath hitches as her mind recoils in fear. *God, no, don't!*

They accost the boy and push him over before they take off across the river, whooping loudly with their newfound loot. The air she's been holding in suspense rushes out of her lungs. *Assholes...*

Not wasting time, the boy scrambles behind the rock on his hands and knees.

Beth wants to know what happened, but interacting with unknown people goes against her training.

"When faced with the prospect of strangers, don't approach them," Donovan said on that same camping trip. "It's too dangerous to trust anyone on the way to Reed. You're not safe in the forest. There are animals out here and they aren't friendly," he said as he paced in front of the children lounging around the fire pit they'd set up for the night.

Stretched out with them, Hoss whispered in Beth's ear, "People neither. Remember that, my little musketeer."

They were kids back then. She's not a kid now. They taught her to listen to her gut, and it was telling her this was the right thing to do. Faced with the prospect of going against Hoss's warning, she bolsters her nerve, takes a deep breath, walks out from the tree line, and down the slope.

Rounding the boulder, a hand on her concealed knife, she spots the father lying against the rock, severely wounded, clutching his bloody abdomen. The vision of Carrie's broken body leaps out of her memory. She forces the image down. The sight of the boy clinging to his father and wailing brings her own cries for help into sharp focus on that lonely stretch of road nine years ago. No one answered.

Beth's heart tightens. Tears escape, but she wipes them away. She's certain the father's wounds are a death sentence. He shoves his son behind him, cries out in pain, and pays the price for that. *Protective till the end.*

"We have nothing," he says, spitting his words out with effort.

"I want nothing. Can I help you?" Beth approaches, guarded. She scans her surroundings for those men or any other threat.

Any misgivings he was having vanish and he shoves his protesting son toward her with hope in his desperate eyes. "My boy! Please take my boy."

Take him? Beth's mind reels at the prospect.

The boy objects. "No, Daddy!"

He transports Beth back to that night, and she reaches for the scar at her temple. She awoke in the sheared-off back half of the car, open to the elements under the ghostly light of a street lamp. The sight before her crushed her. It took one second to know she was truly alone. It was futile, but she called out for her parents, anyway. Beth scrunches her eyes, trying to block out the next image she wants to bury. *Need to end this.*

"Son. Shh...you need to be brave."

Beth takes in his words and refocuses, opening her eyes to the man stroking his son's cheek. *Be brave.* With an eye on the tree line, she crouches ten feet from them and wars with herself. Can she take care of someone who reminds her of her loss? She can't take care of herself, much less a boy.

In a weakened state, the father waves her over. "I can't help him now. Please don't let my son..."

The word he leaves out hits her in the gut. He's right. The boy would perish out here. Beth can't help but gaze at the child. The boy's head shakes, his dirty cheeks stained by tears, as he denies his father's words. *Crap!* Her heart breaks, like it did years ago on a wet road in Spokane. Beth kneels beside the man. She couldn't live with herself, knowing she had the means to save the boy and didn't. *I can do this, I have to.*

"He needs a home," he says.

So did I. The memory of Parker standing beside her hospital bed rushes in. Sadness and grief etched across his features when he said, "When they release you, I'm taking you home with me."

Upon her reluctant nod, the injured man grabs his son by the shoulders and commands him in an authoritative tone. "Neil, son, focus. You need to go with..." The man looks at her for confirmation.

"Beth."

He looks back at his son. "You need to go with Beth."

The man coughs up blood, which incites the boy. "I don't want to leave you, Daddy!"

Beth continues to be vigilant as the drama plays out. "We have to go, Neil," she says, praying those men don't hear them and backtrack.

He caresses his son's chin. "Son... Shh... No more talking. I won't make it. You need to live... Keep..." He licks blood from his lips and swallows. "I have something." With shaky hands, he pries Neil's palm open and places a beautiful, shiny, black Hematite stone there. "Was going to give...later... You've been good. Keep it safe." His eyelids grow heavy. "Stay alive... Promise."

Neil looks between his dad and Beth, clutching the rock tightly in his tiny hand. "I promise."

Beth's heart shatters completely. The pain is too much for her to handle. *I never said goodbye.*

"Love you...little monster." He yanks his son to his chest as tears tunnel down his ashen face. Neil's declaration of love gets lost in translation against his father's chest. The man spits up more blood, and his lips peel back in pain. He looks at Beth. "Bag." He points at his upturned backpack on the rock bed. "Didn't take everything. Promise me... Take care... Love him."

"Neil will be safe with me. I promise," she says, and gathers his meager possessions back into the bag, happy for the distraction.

"Go! Treat her... Obey Beth."

Neil doesn't move but looks at her with doubt in his vulnerable blue eyes. His world just imploded. Like hers did. The same hell she went through nine years ago is reflecting in his expression. Beth opens her arms, hoping he'll come to her of his own free will. "Neil, I won't harm you. Trust me to get you somewhere safe."

Hesitation, doubt, and fear ripples through his tear-stained face.

"Please," she pleads.

Relief washes over her when he sprints into her welcoming arms, encircling her like a lifeline. Stroking his hair for a moment, she gives Neil time to process what is happening. His father's face softens. She extends her hand to touch the man's shoulder; a gesture he accepts with an understanding smile.

"Go get your bag, Neil."

Once he's out of earshot, she turns to the man, and, overcome with emotion, says, "Don't worry. He'll be safe at the place I'm going to."

"Where?"

"To my family in the mountains."

"We...cabin. Take him one..." He coughs up blood, not able to finish that short sentence.

She's sure they won't be looking for this cabin, but she placates him. "We will when it's safe."

He lets out a sigh of relief, which troubles her, but Neil's arrival, with his little backpack strapped to his back, chases her questions away.

Beth leaves them, gazes across the river, and spots their exit to give Neil time to say goodbye. She tears up knowing what's happening behind her, but she can't look and finds it hard to breathe. Her head tilts as a cold, tiny hand slides into hers. Neil's trembling betrays his outward demeanor as she leads him away from the only person left in this world he knows. Rubbing the stone every few feet, Neil turns sideways to look back. His father reassures him with a smile or a weak wave. *At least he got the chance to say goodbye.* Beth wonders if he understands that's the last time he'll see his father. She didn't. They navigate across the river one rock at a time.

Neil stumbles. Beth rights him and asks, "You good?"

He nods through a veil of sadness.

On the opposite side of the river, Beth scans the tree line before them and finds what she's looking for. "Take my hand and don't let go."

The two of them crouch to hide inside a bush while she surveys the opposite edge. Against the boulder, Neil's father sits, slumped sideways, his head touches the ground. It's done. *May you find peace.* Beth doesn't know if Neil should see his dad this way, but she needs him to know he didn't suffer long. She swipes newly formed tears away. He's not her dad, but it feels cathartic to cry for him, anyway. *This is hell.*

"What are you looking for?" he asks, rising to get a better look.

She draws him back down, not looking him in the eye. "Neil, can you do something for me?"

"Uh-huh."

"There are very dangerous men out here." Beth offers a reassuring hug, and with her chin on top of his tiny head, says, "We're going to play a silent game. I'll teach you a special sign language, and we'll practice, okay?"

This piques his interest. "Special?"

"My uncle taught it to me when I was young. He's a Marine."

"A real Marine!"

Her heart jumps in her chest as she covers his mouth. "If you're silent all day, I'll have a prize for you tonight to eat. Deal?"

He nods with gusto. That was easy. "Good. Let's go. We have little daylight left." *And hopefully, we won't stumble upon those men.*

CHAPTER 27

Near a concealed lookout hole, Beth leans against a wall, surrounded by the scent of cedar, and watches Neil devour his reward—a chocolate bar—and rub his stone. The shelter's leather-bound book sits open in her lap. She finds it arresting that he's rubbing his stone and she, her necklace. They found the shelter as dusk settled. This one is a well-built tree house, hidden under camouflage. She opened the first aid kit when they arrived for a Band-Aid and saw the pill bottle, feeling the need to take it.

Jose's son had made an entry in the journal, which gave her hope.

Neil glances over at her. "I'm scared."

Beth can't blame him. She lays the journal aside. The day was grievously tragic. They won't be safe until they get to Reed, but she keeps that to herself. "Come here. I'll keep you warm."

He drags his backpack over the floorboards and makes himself comfortable in her lap. She goes with it, tucking a mylar blanket around him, though he has other ideas and reaches over the mylar, retrieves his dad's backpack, and pulls out a scrapbook. She'd planned to go through the bag and transfer her stuff over but didn't have the heart to do it on the eve of his father's death.

Beth recalls the day Parker took her back to her parents' house. It was something she wasn't ready for, but she couldn't tell her uncle that. Parker walked into the house, keys in hand, and said, "Let's start packing your room while we wait for the guys." He hadn't understood the turmoil swirling in her teenage mind and had walked further into the house none the wiser, out of sight, in search of her room. Beth had stood outside, grounded to the spot, terrified to enter. She'd have to pass her sister's room. The voice tortured Beth from within as guilt ripped through her. She deserved every moment of that torment.

A heavy object lands in Neil's lap, snatching her out of the past. "What's this?" she asks, gazing at a handmade cover decorated with sports stickers and happy rainbows.

"My family. Wanna see?" His enthusiasm tugs at her emotions. *We've both lost our families.*

"How old are you, Neil?"

"Ten."

Younger than I was. God, it's not fair.

He opens the book and points at a picture similar to the one tucked safely in her pocket. Neil's parents are standing on a boulder with clasped hands, surrounded by orange fall leaves and with some arranged in a pile in front of them as two kids prepare to jump into its depths. The other child is smaller. A sister... *No.* She closes her eyes. "What a lovely family."

"I miss them."

Tears well, and she wills them to go away. "I miss mine, too." She unzips her coat pocket and pulls out the worn and cracked picture. Her sister was younger, but they could have passed as twins; their coloring and features were similar. She kept this photo because, out of all the others, she found it in one of her father's old wallets; where it once was close to his heart.

Neil plucks the picture out of her hands for a closer look and asks, with a hint of innocence, "Where are they?"

Beth's eyes slide to the pill bottle that calls to her from the first aid kit. "Gone, like yours."

"To heaven?"

For lack of a better answer, she says, "Yes."

His sympathetic gaze crushes her as he passes the tiny picture back. Then his eyes dip. "Your necklace is pretty."

Observant. Ryker's smile fills her mind and regret follows. "Thanks. You can show me more tomorrow. Let's get some shut-eye, okay?"

He pushes the book back into his father's bag and snuggles into her without another thought. So trusting, children are.

***

Dragging a mylar blanket, Colin crawls into an A-frame shelter made from branches. Its rustic appearance blends seamlessly into the surrounding wilderness. *Finally.* He collapses, out of breath. It took him the better part of the day yesterday to figure out how to stop getting lost. Sean taught him "red in the shed," lining up the red needle and aligning it with the orienting arrow, but he forgot about the magnetic declination—the angle between magnetic north and true north. He wishes he had Sean's experience at trekking through the forest. He hopes for Alejo's sake that his friend isn't injured or worse.

After locating their shelter last night, they wasted no time in starting a fire to combat the bone-chilling cold, their frozen fingers fumbling to hang their damp clothes. They shivered as they reached for the survival blankets in their tiny refuge, but the warm flames from the fire soon thawed them the rest of the way.

Today, they made headway as Colin lined them up for this dwelling. The color coding for the shelters meant something on the map. Blue was for singles, red was for two and the purple Xs were for families. This was a red X.

"I'm not sleeping in there," Alejo says.

Already lying on the shelter's hard, unforgiving floor, Colin lifts his head and focuses on the outline of Alejo's legs standing at the entrance. It's near dusk, but Colin's so exhausted that he cannot possibly rise again. Hunger is the only thing forcing him to move, otherwise he would have said to hell with it and let sleep take over. "You can sleep with the night creatures out there, then."

Alejo crouches down and, cautiously, crawls on light limbs like he's in fear of catching something from the ground. Colin smirks at his friend. *Didn't take long.* Alejo shrinks in fear of a leaf grazing his forehead but gets past that intrusion and clings to Colin for warmth.

He says to Alejo, "See, cozy."

His friend shoots a sneer his way, and Colin figures Alejo has never been one for roughing it like his partner. Colin wouldn't mind if there wasn't a subtle sense of peril in the air.

Colin moves to his side, slides his fingers over a rough stone, and prays it's the one he's looking for. Lifting the stone, his fingers touch a cooler entrenched in the hole. A silent prayer passes his lips. He reaches with trembling hands for the flashlight in his pocket, clicks it on, and digs. Alejo leans on him during this task, so Colin hands him a bottle of water and a snack. He's never experienced so much joy from hearing the crinkling of a wrapper before and lies down to devour his own energy bar.

"What happened to Carrie?" Colin asks, hoping Alejo will spill the piece of the puzzle that's been dogging Colin since Beth uttered that name.

"Her sister died a long time ago... Car accident," Alejo says in between chewing.

"Why does Beth want forgiveness?"

Silence. Colin's grateful he got that much out of Alejo, but the unanswered question remains. Forgiveness for what? Did they have an unresolved quarrel?

Every muscle in Colin's body aches, but his jaw hurts the most. He chews with the last bit of energy he has, savoring the sweet taste of raisins and choco-late. The crinkling noises cease beside him, and Alejo breaks out into his familiar vibration of soft snoring. Colin doesn't mind the intrusion tonight and closes his eyes. Denying him sleep, his brain fires up as he lies there. Beth materializes as she was before he kissed her on their date. He circled his arm around her small waist and drew her softness into him. Colin can almost smell the raspberry scent she wore, which somehow warms him in this damp environment. He's held her close before, but dancing isn't like a first kiss.

Beth bit her lip nervously. He braced himself for rejection, but she closed her eyes and leaned in, her touch gentle and reassuring. Her lips tasted like cocoa from the chocolate cake she'd eaten earlier that night. He'd sought entrance between those sweet untouched lips and, for a few moments, she granted his wish. Their tongues mingled: his, urgent and needy; hers, submissive and eager. He wants that moment again.

Affected by the memory, Colin shifts uncomfortably and unzips his pants, allowing for some room. He wants her so badly that just the thought of her arouses him. He hopes she's safe, for the thought of living without her is unbearable.

CHAPTER 28

Beth drops Neil's dad's backpack near a stream, draws in a deep breath of fresh crisp morning air, studies the trees, and listens to the gurgling water. She thought Neil would be more of a problem, but he's proven to be a fast learner, and above all, the offer of a prize keeps him silent.

She crouches by the stream, places her filtered bottle in, and traps the cold water. Kneeling next to her, Neil does the same with his children's bottle while gliding his tiny hand in the flow. She follows his example and glides her fingers across the fresh water in wonder, almost forgetting the reason they are here. Beth takes a moment to ponder what it would be like to be a mother.

At Steven's wedding, she'd dreamed of being in love with someone but she'd never thought past that romanticized idea. If they made it to Haven, there would be no one to marry or have children with.

She notes the quiet of their surroundings, with no birdsong or rustling leaves to break the tranquility, only the soothing sound of the stream. Her eyes comb through the scenery until they settle on a motionless, unkempt man on the other side.

Crap! Flight or flight kicks into high gear, leaving her breathless and on edge. With fear coursing through her, she shoots up in alarm.

"Hey, pretty girl." He holds his hands up in surrender like he's corralling a filly in a stable, not wanting to scare her off.

That was the wrong thing to say. Expecting the others to jump out, she searches in a frantic state for more threats. She won't be able to fight all of them...or fight at all. Neil steps defiantly in front of her and yells, "Leave—"

No yelling! Quick to cover his mouth, she commands her heart to calm down, and says quietly, "Remember our game. Get behind me."

Neil does as she asks, but along the way, he grabs her forearm. Beth appreciates that he's protective, but she transfers his hand to her belt loop, slides her thumb into the circle of her blade, and waits, hoping she doesn't need to pull it. Her eyes slide to the backpacks. She hooks a finger into the loops and drags them as she and Neil back up.

The man advances. "No need to leave, pretty girl."

You can take him.

I can't.

"Neil, is there anyone behind us? Check." She's hoping that's what he's doing, not wanting to take her eyes off this man.

You have no choice.

"No," he says.

"Take our stuff and wait by the trees."

Stop being a coward.

"But—"

"Neil, do as I say!" She forces the words through gritted teeth, irritated by the alienating voice. *No time for drama, Little Man.*

The backpack drags over her feet. He's strong for a small guy. She senses Neil reach the trees when the man transfers his predatory eyes solely on her. "You can't outrun me, so you should just give up."

She juts her chin out. "I'm not running. You're going to leave."

His evil grin deflates her bravado. "You know I can't do that." He circles right, trying to cut her off from Neil.

Oh, God! This isn't happening. But while her mind is terrified, her body has a different agenda; her thumb tightens on the ring, and her trembling hand yanks the curved blade out as a challenge.

The man's no fool and loses the grin in favor of a malicious smile, knowing he has the upper hand.

Damn him. She circles right to defend Neil and their stuff, bringing the man closer to her position. Worry consumes her as she scans around him, expecting company. *Why hasn't he alerted the others? He wants me first.* The unwelcome thought makes her skin crawl and courage crack.

You're weak.

Not now, damn it!

Movement catches her eye in the trees behind the man. The others...

The man advances.

Sharp and unexpected, a dirty hand forces the man's forehead back, exposing his neck. The flash of a blade slashes the throat in a singular motion. A mixture of terror and shock fills her as blood rains down on the riverbed.

She breaks for Neil. Beth's heart races as she picks up the man's desperate gurgles and the sounds of his body thrashing in the stream. She rushes toward a scared little boy, his eyes wide with fear, as if they might burst out of his skull. *Fuck!*

She snatches him into her embrace and twists, knife out to meet this new threat. A man she doesn't recognize. Dirty, dressed in fatigues and a tactical vest, toting a backpack, and armed with a bloodstained combat knife, Beth's new threat scans the forest. He looks worried, like her, but steps over the dead man like he doesn't exist. "Are you okay?" he asks.

Did she hear him right? Something about him is familiar, but she keeps the blade poised between them.

"Beth?" His eyes widen. Delight spreads across his face, causing his cheeks to lift. "Beth, it's me."

The man before her has a full beard, but the voice... *Oh my God! It can't be.*

"Ryker?" She drops her hand as the sudden relief causes her body to shake. How did he find her?

"Stay back!" Neil steps in front of her, his fists up, ready to duke it out. She stifles his mouth but is amused by his response and makes no effort to move him.

Ryker's gaze settles on Beth. The air between them charges. His gaze craves her, igniting a strong desire in Beth; a need she was missing. Desperate to melt into him, she wants to close the distance between them.

Blood rushes into Beth's limbs, the urge to pounce being the only way to describe what her body wants to do, but Ryker signals to stop, alerting her to danger. *How did he know?* She yields, wrenches Neil's body to hers, holds her breath, and grips the blade with nervous anticipation. As she listens to the bubbling stream and stirring leaves, her own heartbeat pounds loudly in her ears.

Ryker migrates toward them in quick steps. Beth's inner heat intensifies. He stops short. Disappointment surges through her. Ryker's intense eyes travel up her body, causing parts of her to dance once more. He points behind her and says, "Walk straight that way, and I'll catch up."

"Where are you going?"

"Hiding the evidence."

Her eyes drift to the body lying face down in the stream like a rag doll. A vivid image of her sister's contorted body lying face down on the pavement crashes into her mind.

Neil tugs on her forearm, chasing the illusion away. "Let's go."

With Ryker's instruction clear, she pockets the knife, hoists her backpack up, and lets Neil lead her away from the one person she wants most.

***

Beth's head is swimming. *Is he really here? How did Ryker find me?* After all this time, her visceral reaction to him shocks her. *What does it mean?*

Neil's tiny hand tugs rhythmically on her belt loop as they trudge through the underbrush. He's been quiet; too quiet. She stops and crouches down. "Neil, you're very good at this quiet game, but I need to ask you something, okay?"

He appears reluctant to speak but nods. The boy loves his surprises.

"Did you see Ryker kill that man?"

He nods, not meeting her eyes. *Crap.*

"Do you understand he did that to protect us?"

He shrugs his tiny shoulders.

"Tell me what you're thinking." She rubs the back of his hand, hoping this coaxes him out of his shell. "Are you afraid to tell me?"

His head bobs up and down while he scuffs the bottom of his shoe on the ground.

"Did you tell your mom everything?"

He confirms with a curt head bob, then raises his head, looking fearful and unsure. "You're not going to leave me, are you?"

Beth envelops him in her arms, in part so he can't see how that's affected her. After she moved in, she asked Parker the same question. Beth hadn't trusted Parker to stick around if he found out what she'd done and distanced herself from him and the others. She can't let Neil do that and gives him the same answer Parker gave her. "No way in hell am I ever going to leave you."

Neil hugs Beth, warming her from the inside. She skims the surrounding trees and hopes Ryker isn't having any problems. They've walked for some time in the same direction with no sign of him. Maybe she conjured him up.

"Beth."

She twists, separating herself from Neil. Her heart thumps loudly. The world disappears. Ryker navigates the forest toward them, brandishing that big wide grin she likes. Beth throws all decorum out the window and runs.

Ryker opens his arms, and her heart soars when they connect. He stumbles backward, but recovers, and buries his face into her neck. Everything about this feels right. She soaks up his strength and loves the way he holds her against his body. The vest is a hindrance, but he doesn't let go, like he needs a minute just to be with her. Beth takes in his earthy scent mixed with sweat and can't believe he's here in the flesh. It's euphoric. His warm breath tickles her throat, and his lips brush her neck, sending shivers up her spine.

"Hey," he whispers.

"Hey," she whispers back and laughs at the familiar greeting. She's never loved one word so much.

Chapter 29

It's too late in the day for the sun to warm their hiding spot at the base of a western white pine tree, camouflaged by thick, low-lying branches. Wrapped in blankets, Beth and Neil relax on boughs cut from nearby tree branches for padding. He glances her way. Hunger escapes her. She offers her half-empty MRE of hot macaroni and cheese, but Neil declines it, favoring the trail bar in his small hands instead.

Once Ryker set up their shelter, he told her he'd be back late. Her anxiety hit the roof, and she needed answers. Ryker calmed her with his touch and promises of later, so she's been listening for him ever since, like a schoolgirl waiting to see her boyfriend in the hall. He's been gone too long. Happy with his reward, Neil munches away on the trail bar; he hasn't said a word since Ryker led them to the shelter. She digs a little. "Today was rough. How are you?" The level of violence Neil has witnessed must weigh on his young shoulders.

He hands her the empty foil wrapper, reaches into his backpack to retrieve the scrapbook, and conveys what he wants with hope in his eyes. He hasn't forgotten her promise.

"Sure." Anything to get him talking and take her mind off Ryker.

Neil hugs the book to his chest like it's precious, crawls over, and makes himself comfortable in her lap again. She peers over his shoulder as he turns the pages and points out various people.

"This is my mom." The picture labeled *Samantha Stuart* is of a pretty, petite woman cradling a swaddled newborn.

"Is that you?"

"Yeah. Dad said I was tiny." He sounds worried about this.

She grins at the back of his head. The scrapbook is handmade, by his mother, she assumes.

"This is my dad." He points at a picture of the man she met, which says *Garrett Stuart*. He looks nerdy in glasses but still handsome. She listens as Neil talks her through the various photos of camping trips, car trips to famous places, Disneyland, and holidays in Hawaii. There's a sadness in his voice that she wishes she could heal. Beth remembers some of these adventures with her own family. It's a painful road, but she lets him talk and reminisce, giving Neil the space to savor his memories. He flips a page, and a group shot in front of a cabin catches her eye. "Is this the cabin you were going to?"

"That's Grandpa and Nana's house."

Beth remembers his dad saying they weren't there, but the question remains, why was Garrett relieved when she said they'd go there? One picture of a little girl in a pink dress catches her eye. "Is this your sister?"

Someone approaches. Beth signs stop. Neil obeys. He's learned the few military hand signals she's shown him quickly. Beth lets out a breath as Ryker crawls in on hands and knees; the space is large enough for three adults to sleep. Their eyes meet. Sudden heat washes over her face under Ryker's admiring gaze. Neil closes his book with a thud, dragging her eyes away. He places it back in his bag without a word but doesn't give up her lap.

Ryker relaxes against the tree trunk and points at Neil. "You've got quite a protector there."

She fusses with Neil's hair. "Neil, this is my friend Ryker."

Ryker extends his hand. "Nice to meet you."

Neil crosses his arms.

"Neil, that's not nice."

He glances up at her, pouting, not ready to play nice.

"It's okay, he'll say hi when he's ready," Ryker says, defusing the situation. Remembering the meal she made, she offers Ryker what's left.

He takes the pouch. "Hmm, left the military to get away from those." He rips it open and digs in, not taking his voracious eyes off her.

Beth blushes. If Colin looked at her this way, she'd say it was a predatory gaze. But with Ryker, it looks like he's starved of her. Somehow, this makes Beth's heart expand with joy. *You have no right.*

Ryker pops hard-shelled candies into his mouth, one at a time. Beth finds it difficult to concentrate as she fixates on the crunching and sucking sounds he makes, then switches her thinking to questions. "Where did you come from? How is this possible?"

Ryker tears another pouch and takes a bite of a cracker. His eyes travel to Neil, then back up to her.

"Neil, I need to talk to Ryker. Lie down and rest, okay?"

After the activity of the day, Neil doesn't protest. He twists and wraps his arms around her in a warm, inviting hug, which she reciprocates, then he crawls out of her lap and lies down.

Beth turns her full attention back to Ryker, yearning to connect with him, but she doesn't seek his hand like she wants to. She craves the longing look he gave her back at the diner. Thinking of the diner, she grins. "You owe me a secret."

He smirks. "I do, don't I? I have a question for you."

"Question?"

"You ready to go on a date with me?"

She stifles a rush of laughter.

Ryker sighs. "I've missed that."

She wasn't expecting that, either, but his words warm her heart. In the brief time she's known him, Beth has missed him, and she's not sure why. She's only met Ryker twice, but she wants to know more about him, to touch him and smell him. That last one makes her feel weird, like it's somehow wrong to miss that about him. *You don't deserve him.* "I'm not ready yet."

He gazes down with a smile and lets out a deep breath. "Geesh, for a second there, I thought you were going to say yes." He pops another cracker past those kissable lips and crumbs tumble down his shirt.

She chuckles. "Do you have a secret for me?"

His chewing slows, and his pleased expression falls, replaced with sadness. Beth braces for something bad when he reaches out, holds her hand, and rubs her palm with his thumb. "I'll wait."

"Why?"

"Because I need you to get some rest and take the next shift while I'm gone."

"Gone? Now? Where?" she asks, not liking this turn of events.

"We'll talk when I get back."

"I thought you were back."

He reaches out and caresses the curve of her jaw, moving down to her chin. "I confess, I couldn't wait till later to see you, so I took a break."

The light touch of his fingers tingles her skin, stirring a desire she's never experienced. In a husky voice, she says, "A break from what?"

Ryker pauses. His eyes brand her; the yearning is unmistakable. Then he severs the contact. "Rest now, talk later."

***

It's almost dark as Ryker sits at the entrance of their shelter. He can't believe he's found her. Of all the scenarios he's dreamed up in the past few weeks, none of them came close to this one. Best case: he'd find her at the farm once he located the right one. Worst case: he'd never find the farm. Nightmares of that scenario had depleted Ryker's optimism every night since the missile dropped. He never thought for a second he'd find her out here.

When Beth ran to him, all he could think was she'd be in his arms and, once she was there, he didn't want her to leave...ever. She fit into him perfectly. Ryker had to rein in a powerful need to kiss her and settled for her quick pulse thumping under the surface of his lips. He was conscious of the fact he was dirty, but it wasn't enough to stop him. All that mattered was Beth was there, in front of him, safe and sound.

Ryker turns to look at the boy nestled in her arms. Jealousy wriggles to the surface; Ryker wishes he could be in Neil's place right now. He would have pegged her too young to have a child Neil's age. What was he, eight? He's not sure what age Beth is, but he has to guess she's in her midtwenties, which tells him she was young when she had Neil. Back at the diner, she didn't have a wedding ring on. Did some asshole get her pregnant and leave? Is that why Beth was shy at the diner? Then it hits him. Neil is the reason she doesn't date. But why would Beth's friends push her into dating? Neil puts a wrench in Ryker's current plans. Makes his mission difficult but not impossible.

Beth's soft moans pull his focus away from Neil and back to her. They aren't nightmarish moans; they arouse him and inspire ideas. He wants to hear those soft sounds for sure in the future. He scoots over, lies next to her, leans on his elbow, and looks down, admiring her pretty freckles. Despite his reluctance to bring this moment to an end, he says, "Beth."

Through the haze of her dreams, she whispers, "Ryker." He greets her with a grin when her drowsy eyes land on him. *Fuck, that is hot.* Desire lingers in her eyes, which he senses all the way to his groin, and he swallows. She's killing him, but he's a glutton for punishment. *Ride it out, Kensington.*

"You're intoxicating, you know that?" Under his heated gaze, her cheeks redden. "Especially when you blush. Time to get up."

Neil shifts in her arms, giving Ryker the opportunity to detach the boy from her. They crawl to the entrance, out of earshot. The night air is chilly. He reaches into his backpack and pulls out his oversized brown jacket and shoves his arms into it. "Keep watch. When I get back, I'll take the next shift."

Beth halts his movement to leave with a gentle touch on his forearm. "You need to sleep."

Ryker loves the softness of her hand. Her words echo the sentiment expressed by his sister. She'd be alive if he'd listened. "I'll catnap when I get back if that makes you feel better."

"It doesn't." Beth rubs the sleep out of her eyes. "Are you going to tell me where you're going?"

When he doesn't reply, Beth tugs out her necklace and rubs it. The gesture warms him. Ryker's not sure he can, but he needs to explain. "After the missile dropped, we went to the diner first. No one was there. We took as much food as we could and came looking for you."

Her empathetic, olive-green eyes lock onto him. She gets it. He fights to keep his emotions locked in; perceives her fear as she scours the confines of their shelter out of instinct. "We? Where's your sister?"

The memory of how he found his sister lying broken against the tree forces its way through. *Libby... God, give me strength.* Shame makes him avert his eyes. "I buried her," he says, and reins in the tightrope of emotions.

"Oh my God! You shouldn't have come looking for me."

Shit! I didn't mean... Using those quick reflexes, he cups her chin with a gentle touch and locks eyes with hers. "Don't go there. It's not your fault. It's mine."

Beth bleeds shame and recrimination as if she killed Libby herself. He identifies himself in those tortured depths. He hadn't expected that.

She changes the subject and asks, "What did you do with that man?"

He drops his hand, breaking their connection. Beth shouldn't care about that piece of shit, but he's glad she gave him that distraction. Ryker wants it, needs it, to fuel his anger. "Don't worry about him. He got what he deserved." Ryker had lied about hiding the body to protect the boy. The question lingers in her eyes, and like he's privy to her thoughts, he gives her the answer. "He hurt my sister. One of them, anyway."

She pales in fear. "One of?"

"Four men. Now there's three." He doesn't like the anxiety in those beautiful eyes and vows he'll remove that feeling from Beth's life. "I've been tracking them. I caught up with them today. Don't want to think about what might have happened if I hadn't."

"Oh, Ryker."

He loves it when Beth's warm fingers curl around his hand. In return, Ryker turns her palm up and strokes his thumb over the quick pulse in her wrist.

"Killing them won't bring her back."

"No, but justice is what she deserves, and I'm going to serve it to every one of them," he says with conviction.

A fleeting moment of guilt passes across her face as her eyes lower. Beth has nothing to feel guilty about. It's all on him.

CHAPTER 30

June 1

Fighting off a brutal headache, Kaden leans against a tree and taps a branch on his thigh while Jace looks on from beside him, spooked by the scene they've stumbled upon. Dugal scowls from his crouched position by the base of a tree in the morning light.

Drag marks lead to Jax against a tree, his neck slashed. Among blood trails, written in Sharpie, his chest reads, *I've done unspeakable things for my country. Imagine what I'll do for the one you took from me.*

Kaden's not happy losing a man like this. Gideon won't be pleased. Jax didn't deserve this. They have an angry man hunting them and now he understands why. He's not worried, though. No man will ever best him.

Jace, younger than the rest, his beard coming in patchy, speaks up first. "It's that girl, isn't it? You just had to mess with her, didn't you, Dugal?"

Kaden is tiring of Jace's cocky attitude of late and, by the way Dugal rises, he's not the only one. *Time to rein this guy in.* "Jace, let's go."

"You're just going to leave him here?" Not an excellent reader of people, Jace doesn't realize his mistake.

Dugal swings into Jace's space and jabs a gun under his chin. "You want to join him?"

Christ! "Dugal," Kaden warns. Jace catches on quickly and shakes his head repeatedly.

"Shut your mouth, and we'll get along fine." Dugal lowers his weapon and trudges off back to camp.

"Let's get a move on." Kaden's agitated. They won't be back at the farm for a few more days, so he needs to keep those two apart till then, and he'll need to keep this asshole from picking them off.

***

Beth covers her ears, but there's no sound. Fire trucks approach her position, followed by an ambulance and police vehicles. Carrie stands in the street, her yellow dress torn and bloody, flashing blue and red. Her sister's hateful eyes bore into Beth as she screams, "You're a monster!"

Beth cries out in distress, fighting to escape, but she's enclosed in warmth, her arms trapped. A male voice cuts through the horror. "It's a nightmare, Beth. You're safe... Breathe." Not daring to open her eyes, she inhales the smell of wet rain and fresh air...and the faint scent of spice. *Ryker.*

Strong arms encompass and hold Beth close. She calms. Her hands snake around his biceps, needing an anchor to this world. She opens her eyes to the head of a reaper tattoo on his forearm, a knife between the reaper's teeth. *Hmm...* After a moment, Ryker pulls back, tilting his head to look into her eyes. "You with us? You okay?"

Beth attempts to disengage, but Ryker won't let her, and instead, searches her eyes. He frowns, then settles with her against the tree, secures her in his lap with protective arms, and makes eye contact again. She could get lost in those eyes. Ryker's five o'clock shadow at the diner has grown into a dark, unkempt beard, but it suits him. Her eyes trail down a neck scar she hadn't noticed before now, which disappears into his shirt, then back up to his bloodshot brown eyes. He's burning the candle at both ends.

"You're freaking your son out."

Her son? *Crap!* Beth links eyes with Neil's. He burrows his head into her chest, wrapping his tiny arms tight around her as she soothes him. "I'm okay. It was just a... I'm okay now." She dares to dream that they're a family, the three of them huddled together; a moment where Ryker gazes at Beth like he's her man, comforting their son together. If it were only real. *But it can't be...*

Neil's head pops up. "I'm hungry."

The tension lifts for a moment, amid tired smiles.

"We have to leave," Ryker says.

"Pleeeeaasee."

Ryker sighs and gives in. "It's not food, but check your backpack."

Intrigued, Neil crawls on all fours to his backpack and searches inside his bag by touch.

Ryker murmurs, "You want to talk about it while he's distracted?"

Neil runs excited fingers over the smooth surface of a stone the size of his hand. Another auspicious moment. Beth loves that he did that for Neil. She swivels her head back to Ryker and she's rewarded with one of those grins she loves so much. Ryker seems like he's waiting. *Did I miss something?* When Beth says nothing, he asks, "You want to talk about your dream?"

Her eyes dip, and Beth shakes her head. *You'll see who I really am.* "I need to clear something up."

"What?"

"Neil's not my son."

Confusion reigns for a second, then Ryker's concern greets her. "Who is he then?"

Should she tell him? Beth's not sure it would help.

"What's wrong?"

For someone she barely knows, Ryker sure picks up on her moods fast. "Those men killed Neil's father a few days ago."

Before her, Ryker's face hardens, the pain visibly sharp, and his head twists away from her. Hatred pours out of his soul, then sadness when he looks over at Neil. Ryker has no words. Her heart aches for him in that moment; she senses Ryker's a good man with a tremendous amount of stress on his shoulders. She caresses his beard, and her touch causes his eyes to slide back to her. "Neil's lost. He needs support to control the chaos inside him." *I called someone Dad once.*

"For a couple of days, you sound like you know him well."

I do.

His brown eyes narrow. "Why are you out here alone?"

She evades his stare. Envisions Alejo dragging himself out of the river. *God, please don't let him die.* "I wasn't. My friends and I got separated after we jumped into the river."

"Jumped into a river? That was risky."

Her insides melt at Ryker's concern for her. "Yeah, well, when you have no choice... Being shot at helped." Beth remembers the last time she saw Colin. They shot him. She let go of the bridge railing and cascaded backward. Colin reached out... He grew smaller and smaller, till the cold water sucked her in.

"Why aren't you following the river to the farm, then?"

She snaps out of the replay, sits up, and soon regrets moving away from Ryker's warmth. "Here we go again with the questions."

A slow smile plays across his face. "Only way to learn what I'm up against."

"And how you're going to get around it?"

His smile broadens. "Now you're getting the hang of it."

Beth likes his eyes on her. Her body itches to scoot back into his arms. Even shaggy and dirty, he looks damn hot. She sighs. "The highway follows the river. Roads are dangerous. The plan is to rendezvous at Reed. It's closer."

He tilts his head, intrigued. "What's Reed?"

Right, he doesn't know. She'll have to fill him in if he's coming with her. The realization that Beth won't be alone up at Haven hits her. Her body hums a merry tune. "It's an underground shelter we buried near the falls. Should reach it in two or three days," she says, "I have a map in my backpack."

Ryker stills. "A survival bunker? Show me." He bends across Beth and gathers the map from her bag. Her eyes follow a chain with dog tags and a ring dangling from Ryker's neck. She wonders who the ring belongs to. Looks handmade, some kind of metal.

"My BAMFs...my uncles, are there waiting for me."

Ryker places the map in front of her and leans in close as Beth points to a *Reed Falls* written there. His finger glides over the paper from Reed to their position. Beth gazes up as he calculates in his head. "Everyone has a similar map and this—" She points to a number at the top of the map. "—is my code to get in."

After some silent moments of thought, he folds the map and announces. "You're coming with me."

"With you? No, we're going to Reed."

"I don't want them to get away."

Get away? She can't risk Neil's safety. Beth's priority is to get them somewhere safe, not hunting these men. Her thoughts stray to Donovan and Hoss. They'll be at Reed, waiting for their kids. "We can get more help at Reed."

"This is my fight, not theirs."

If Ryker's bent on doing this, she can't stop him, but Beth can't risk Neil getting hurt or, worse, seeing the men who traumatized him and killed his father. "I can find my way. I don't need you to take us."

Ryker smiles at no one, sighs, then tenderly grips the back of her neck, forcing Beth to stare into his arresting eyes. His thumb skims gently across her skin and over the chain around Beth's neck, causing delicious mayhem in her. "Probably, but I've found you and I'm not letting you out of my sight. No man worth his salt would allow his woman to be out here alone. When they veer away from Reed, I'll take you there first, then finish my mission."

Did he just say his woman?

Chapter 31

Cross-legged, Beth eats from an MRE with Neil smack dab in the middle of her lap, needing her like a security blanket. They made camp in the shelter she located for them; an upgrade from the last one, with rough floorboards and more legroom. It could accommodate four grown adults if they lay side by side, with room for their packs to stay dry in the back. A fallen tree created a roof between two rock walls, where a natural dip in the earth gave them enough room to sit, but not stand.

With his legs outstretched, ankles crossed, Ryker openly admires her from across the shelter.

True to his word, Ryker didn't leave her side all day. The way he tracked these men fascinated her. Ryker knows their names, their habits... It's mind-boggling how much information he has garnered from the few footprints he found at their last campsite.

Ryker taught Neil along the way; said he had potential. If Neil had questions, he didn't voice them, staying true to their silent game for a prize.

They kept a slow, steady pace until midday, when they caught up with Ryker's targets. She didn't want Neil to see them, so she kept him back while Ryker slid forward and observed the men setting up their camp from a distance.

In the shelter, several opened meal packages lie between them. Ryker drops his finished meal into a bag. "Shelter's handy. Parker's a hunter?"

Beth noticed the change in Ryker as he observed the men today; focused, fearless, and filled with purpose. Beth hasn't known him long, but she knows military training when she sees it. One thing is obvious: each of those men in that camp will pay for their crime.

"No, a prepper. I helped build this one when I was twelve." Beth says this like it's completely normal for a child to build shelters in the forest. For her cousins, it was; it is how they grew up, molded to be ready for when the world fell apart. She was late to the party, but she soon caught up.

Ryker jerks his head back in surprise. "Really?"

The thought that he's impressed with that causes Beth to hold her head high. "Donovan and Hoss took their kids to Haven on foot a lot. I was...included."

Ryker raises a brow. "This is quite a trek for kids. Haven's the farm you mentioned at the diner?"

Beth nods with pride. "They prepared us for this situation. Did it in a way that was enjoyable. We all chipped in and did the work. Built lots of shelters out here."

"All stocked like this one?"

She remembers the load they all carried becoming lighter as they stocked various shelters along the way. This one is larger than most, so they stocked it for the families. "More or less." She throws her garbage in the bag.

"Is your family up there?"

Beth stares down at her palms. *Yes.*

Beth recalls the last day she was at Haven. She didn't attend the funeral, but Parker wanted her to see where her family was buried before they left for the city. Numb, she stood apart from Parker in a small white-fenced graveyard surrounded by trees, near an old stone church. They stood over the three fresh graves of her family in silence, her eyes dry and lifeless. She didn't want to look up out of fear. If she did, he'd know. Somehow, Parker would see her sin.

She shakes the image out and points at the ring around Ryker's neck. "Whose ring?"

His hand stretches to touch it. "My sister's. I made it for her in shop class out of a coin."

Insert foot in mouth. Beth tries to lighten the mood. "Aren't you handy?"

His eyes betray a hint of sadness as a faint smile forms on his face, but her joke falls somewhat flat. "I told her I met a beautiful dishwasher." He glances across the shelter. "She wanted to meet you."

Guilt shreds her again. "I'm not beautiful."

"I beg to differ."

"You have a sister?" Neil asks.

Forgetting they had a listener, she smiles at the back of Neil's head in her lap. It's funny how you think children aren't listening, but in reality, they hear more than you think.

"I have three," Ryker says in reply.

He didn't say had. He is shielding Neil. Beth applauds Ryker for that.

Neil asks, "Did they make you mad?"

Beth thinks this is a strange question but stays silent. She hopes Ryker will gain common ground with Neil if they talk more.

Ryker crosses his arms. "All the time. Drove me nuts, especially the older one."

Neil plays with the stone his father gave him and doesn't look up. "I was mad."

Beth exchanges a worried look with Ryker. He asks, "At your sister?"

Neil's little frame trembles as he nods. "I killed her," he whispers.

The familiar phrase coming from Neil's lips throws Beth for a curve. She strokes his head. "I'm sorry you feel that way, Neil."

Ryker interjects, wearing a serious face. "Why do you think you killed her?"

Neil's breath hitches. "I pushed her, then Daddy yelled."

"Did she get up after you pushed her?"

The tiny shake of his head threatens to take Beth's walls down, but she holds fast to the belief that it isn't true that this little boy could have done this intentionally.

Neil glances up at Beth, looking distressed and tearful. "I'm going to hell."

Beth embraces him, touching her lips to his crown. "Neil, don't say that."

He leans back and cranes his neck up to her. "Nana says when you do bad things—" He catches his breath. "—you go there."

Time to get this situation under control. "You're not going there." She wipes his tear-stained face and tries her best to reassure him.

"Are you sure?"

Tears well, but she blinks back her emotions. "I'm sure. You know what else I'm sure about?"

"What?"

Beth hopes this does the trick. She needs to steer him to a happy place after that revelation. "That we're going to see a waterfall."

He straightens and twists around to stare at her with saucer-sized eyes. "A waterfall?"

"Yes, a waterfall. And guess what? We're going to sleep under it."

This news pushes Neil into an excited posture. "Really?" Beth signs for him to calm down with her hands, and Neil complies.

"Okay, I know you're excited, but it's time to sleep."

"Ahh…"

"The sooner you sleep—" She points at him. "—the sooner we see the waterfall."

Neil, happily distracted, accepts her reasoning. "Alright." He surprises her, cups her face with his little hands, and kisses her cheek, melting her heart.

Relishing his display of affection, she says, "Say good night to Ryker."

Neil makes do with a reluctant wave, shuffles over the floorboards, and climbs under the mylar blanket they'd set up in the corner of their space.

Beth glances at Ryker, and the tenderness in his features warms her. It's a look she's not worthy of. He tilts his head to the entrance, and she follows him.

"Nice save," he says out of Neil's earshot.

"Why did you come looking for me?" Beth asks.

Ryker hesitates for a moment. "I wanted another chance to ask you out."

She blinks in surprise. "Idaho's a big place."

He grins. "You told me where it was at the diner. I would have found you eventually."

"You don't give up, do you?"

On impulse, Ryker kisses her forehead. "Nope. I'm a Marine. I'll be back. Don't leave the shelter."

The darkness outside swallows him up. Her half smile drops. Libby would be alive if he hadn't come searching for her. She says into the evening air, "I wasn't worth looking for."

***

The dwindling sunlight will make it harder to see inside soon. Beth and Neil sleep beside him. Beth has a candle and a single match ready to use once the darkness takes over. This shelter, smaller than the last one, provides just enough space for them to lie side by side. Made of rough-hewn boards and covered with moss and leaves, it's built into the hillside, hidden from anyone who passes it.

Neil ate in silence earlier and passed out. The day's mileage is taxing on all of them, but Ryker needs to keep up pace with his targets. Last night, he didn't get a chance to take one of the bastards out. They were sticking close to camp.

The boy's tiny hand dangles, his arm resting across Beth's waist. Sleep eluding him, Ryker lies next to them. He enjoys the sound of their slow, steady breathing. He's been watching them for a while. Can someone fall in love this fast? He has nothing to compare it to. No one to talk with.

This brings up thoughts of his sister. At first, Libby was hesitant with him when he reconnected with her. He left when she was eight, so it made sense. She slowly warmed up to him in the end. He didn't have enough time with her. His mood darkens, so he refocuses on Beth.

Maybe Beth needs to get used to him. Neil definitely does, but that's understandable. Ryker knows what it's like when your foundation collapses underneath you. The world dims. You hold on to whatever connections you have left; in Ryker's case, Elias and his five other siblings, three of whom were too young to understand their own situation. Trust in others diminished fast for him, and eventually, there was only one person he could trust: himself. It's good Neil has Beth.

Beth stirs. Their eyes connect. She blushes on cue; peaceful to shy in two seconds flat. Ryker finds this super cute. "Hey." Ryker lifts his head and leans on his arm to gaze down upon her.

"Hey," Beth replies in a husky whisper which arouses him.

He squeezes his thigh to prevent himself from touching her. Too soon. "Am I worthy of a date now?"

An I-don't-think-so grin spreads across her face. "Worthy, but no."

It was worth a try. She'll say yes one day. Until then, he'll keep asking. "Your beauty is truly captivating."

Beth hesitates, then a slow smile spreads. He hit the right button.

Ryker's tempted to reach out. He needs a distraction and asks, "Who did you escape with again?"

Worry shrouds Beth's face as she looks left. "I hope they made it. Sean and Alejo are a couple that lived in my building."

Her eyes light up at the mention of their names. "I miss Alejo. He's so much fun to be with. He can be childish at times, but that's what I like about him. Alejo owns a hair salon."

Ryker remains silent.

Beth continues, "The coffee you drank at the diner is Alejo's. He has a side business, selling his secret beans as he calls them."

"That was good coffee. Alejo sounds like a card."

"He'd call you hunky."

Ryker's hands flourish down his chest like Vanna White showing off a new car. "Yeah, I mean, what's not to like about this bod, eh?"

He chuckles when she rolls her eyes, but a red tinge appears on her cheeks. He finds it adorable. She tells him a little about the men in her life whom she calls her BAMF dads. They all seemed to be honorable and protective of her, as they should. Ryker would have thought less of them if they weren't.

He remembers a question he wanted to ask. "I've got to ask, what's with the pencils in your backpack?"

She feigns anger and gives him a gentle slap. "You looked in my bag?"

He shrugs. "Of course. The sight stumped me." The pencils aren't the only sharp pointed objects in the bag.

She dampens her smile. "Hoss says you never know when you might need a good...writing instrument."

"I'm liking this guy more and more. So you lost Alejo and Sean at the river?"

She hesitates.

"And Colin..."

Ryker's learned that when Beth hesitates, it's not good. Colin sounds like someone he needs to worry about. "Who's Colin?"

She hesitates again.

Okay.

"Alejo signed me up for tango lessons to meet guys. Colin's my dance partner," she says with a sadness Ryker can't quite pin down, but the news makes him burn with jealousy.

Ryker's hand tightens into a fist. He tries to keep his face neutral as he asks, "Is Colin your boyfriend?"

Beth pauses before saying, "He wants to be."

"Has he asked you out?"

"He did."

He recalls Sophia's words: "Holds things close to the vest." *No shit! Gonna make me work for it.* "Did you go out with him?"

"Why do you want to know?"

Stubborn. "It's always good to know your competition."

Beth rolls her eyes. "He's not."

"You didn't answer my question."

"Maybe I don't want to." Beth challenges him with a stare.

The hair at the nape of Ryker's neck rises. He unclenches his fist and aches to touch her. *I fucking love saucy.* Ryker swallows as warmth travels to places that have been cold for far too long.

Beth draws inward, hugging herself. *Damn it, too far.*

"My friends pressured me. I told you, I don't like being pushed."

"Sorry. You don't have to ans—"

"I wasn't ready. After the date, I told him we'd only be friends."

"That must have hurt." Is it okay that he's glad about that? *Hell, yeah. I feel possessive as fuck.* So much so that Ryker's blown away by his own feelings. This is all new. He needs to calm down and focus on her.

"Ryker, we're going off course. We need to take Neil to Reed."

"What? No, I don't do half-assed jobs. I need to finish what I started."

"I'll take Neil myself then."

"I don't want you out there alone." *I need to protect you.*

"I told you, I can get there without you."

"No Beth, it's too dangerous." *I don't want to lose you, too.*

She turns the tables on him. "Did you always want to be a Marine?"

He sees the ruse of her change in subject and sighs. "No, but my circumstances changed, and I signed up the first chance I got."

"Seventeen?" she asks, her eyes going wide.

He nods in silence.

"Wow. That's young."

"Military was good for me. Gave me what I didn't get at home. A better family."

"Do you miss it?"

He doesn't look her in the eye when he speaks. "I miss the family part. I won't see those guys again. Makes me sad."

She rises to mirror his stance, head held in the palm of her hand, which catches him off guard. "I shouldn't have asked. Sorry."

It's getting hot in here. They stare for a beat and soak each other up. His heart races with excitement. The yearning on her face is apparent, and he's not hiding what he desperately wants.

His eyes dip to her lips. "I'm fascinated by the color of your gorgeous eyes."

His words force her eyes downward.

"I have this incredible urge to kiss you right now."

She blinks. "You have to wait till the date's over to get a kiss, and I haven't said yes yet."

It was a good attempt to deflect, but Ryker has a comeback. "Isn't dating a time when you get to know someone?"

"Yeah..."

"Then we've been dating the last two days, beautiful."

He has her when she bites her lower lip nervously. *Now or never, Kensington.* He leans in.

"That's not dating and stop saying I'm beautiful," she spits out.

The conflict in her is palpable, but he's started his advance toward those desirable lips and aims to claim them. "I figured a way around it."

Before she can react, he cups the back of her neck and draws her in. His soft lips brush against eager ones, then he nibbles and tastes them. *Delicious.* Beth shifts closer. He sucks on her bottom lip, then bites. Hunger awakens and rushes through his body like a drug. *Feels spectacular.*

Ryker pulls her back with him. Not wanting to lose the connection, her hands coil around his neck. Every part of him tingles. He yearns to venture deeper, eager to satiate a thirst he's missed. Then he remembers–

Ryker's lips disengage. He regrets losing her warmth, but they have to stop. Her mouth continues to seek his out.

Ryker holds her back.

Beth dips her chin and tries to retreat.

Embarrassed? She has no reason to be. He cups her face with his hands, and his eyes probe hers. "Hey, don't misinterpret my intentions. There's nothing more I want to do right now than to lose myself in you." He brushes trembling lips against hers. She moans; tingling sensations return. "But Neil's right behind you," he whispers and caresses her nose with his, dropping tender kisses on her.

He releases her with a sensual, dark-toned promise. "I'll never stop telling you how beautiful you are. To me, you were worth looking for. If I didn't have to leave, I'd show you how much. And if we were safe, you wouldn't be."

She opens her mouth to say something.

Bang!

Their heads jerk toward the sound. "Stay here!" Ryker sprints from the shelter.

Chapter 32

Kaden, Dugal, and Jace aim their weapons into the trees. Mal trudges into their camp, under Kaden's guarded gaze, with two men in tow and no captives.

"What the hell, man?" Mal asks, enraged, lowering his hands.

Kaden relaxes his shoulders. "I didn't know it was you!"

"Jittery much?" Mal says, using the comeback to hide how royally ticked he is.

"No luck?" Kaden fires back, hiding his mistake under arrogance.

When they'd told him to kidnap farmers, Mal hadn't been down with that plan. Not his thing, but he needs to eat, too. So far, they've found no one. Luck? Definitely. "No farms this way." Mal looks around, equally audacious. "Looks like you have the same luck."

Kaden appears to back down, switching to a serious expression. "Walk with me."

Doesn't sound good. Mal scans the faces of Jace and Dugal, finds no sign of trouble, and follows Kaden away from the warmth of their fire. He doesn't trust anybody but himself.

"You good at tracking?"

Good? Mal learned from the best; his father. He gives Kaden a side glance. "Yeah, why?"

"We have a stalker."

Mal stops to face him. "What?"

"We found Jax dead two days ago."

What the hell? Hope is disappearing fast with this group.

"Went to do his business. Didn't return."

And just like that, the opportunity isn't knocking anymore. "Why's he stalking you?" Mal scans the forest ahead as they walk again.

"Dugal killed a woman."

Mal halts. His head snaps back to Kaden, and he grinds his teeth.

Kaden ignores Mal's stare. "We took turns with her." He licks his lips and grins, relishing the memory. "A fighter, that one." Kaden drops the smile and peers back at the men. "Dugal wanted to be last, so we left him with her."

Fucking unbelievable! Mal does his damnedest to keep from losing his shit. "Wendall said no touching."

Kaden faces Mal's stony expression, puffs up, then walks back to the fire. "Just find the fucker, Mal!"

The hair on the back of his neck stands up, and somehow, he knows he's being watched. *Fucking hell!* He wrestles with his emotions. He can't even imagine what happened to that woman, but damn it, the fear and pain they caused. Mal's lip curls up in disgust, and his nostrils flare in anger as he strokes a pink fuzzy rabbit's foot key chain hanging off his belt loop. Time to jump ship. The only question is when.

***

Mal stands and stretches his legs before the fire. Wind fans the embers, casting a red light upon the men snoring around him. In prison, he never really slept. During the day, he was always on guard, waiting for the next threat. He was surviving in prison. But out here is no different. A stalker is a threat, so Mal volunteered for the first watch after the sun went down. He relies on no one but himself.

Mal listens to the forest. The buzzing and chirps of the various night crawlers have stopped. *He's out there.* Mal's hair stands up at the nape of his neck. Their stalker is waiting for his opportunity. Mal's waiting for his.

"You got some of that jerky left?" Jace asks, absorbing heat from the fire against a log, with his palms out.

Mal's only reply is to say, "Back in a minute." He steps without a sound as the darkness swallows him and gives his eyes time to adjust before he goes further. Back at the farm, when they were young, Elias furthered their father's teachings and taught the boys to track animals for hunting; a skill he and Ryker perfected on their own when they were old enough. They'd make a game out of it by tracking each other. Mal won most of the time. He hasn't seen Ry since he enlisted and wonders where his brother is in all this crap. Mal stops, tilts his head, and listens to the right. Eerie silence greets him.

The knuckles of a solid fist make contact with Mal's jaw, causing sharp pain before he loses consciousness.

***

Just beyond the reach of the fire, shielded by the darkness of the trees, Ryker waits for his moment, one knee to the ground. His thumb brushes over the reaper tattoo on his forearm while he tightens his grip around a cold steel blade. There's always an opening, but one has to be patient. The one called Kaden awakens too soon and tosses around on the ground, trying to fall back to sleep. Ryker could kill all three men while they sleep, but they don't deserve clean deaths. What they have a right to is a painful and torturous one, like the one they dealt his sister. He isn't one who typically enjoys tormenting people, but in this case, he is all in.

Ryker grappled with uncertainty regarding his brother. His surprise at seeing Mal acquainted with these men wasn't a pleasant one. Too many years separate them for him to trust Mal just yet. He knows Mal wasn't part of this group's transgression, but his association with these men has raised doubts in Ryker. Still, Mal taking the first watch is fortunate as it grants Ryker the time he needs.

Jace yawns and surveys the camp under the firelight. This one mentioned crude details of what he did to Libby and laughed about it to the others. He wasn't gentle.

Ryker's jaw hurts, his eyes burn, and he's been nursing a headache all day. He catnapped a few days ago and managed a few hours last night, but losing sleep is catching up to him. Ryker knows better, but the fear of Beth ending up like Libby haunts him, so he denies himself sleep to keep Beth safe.

Kaden's soft snoring carries on the wind. After punching Mal, Ryker listens for any movement from his brother's body, hears nothing but soft breathing, and prepares. His moment has arrived and he won't be gentle. The darkness expels Ryker, like the reaper he is, knife in hand. Jace recoils and opens his mouth to yell but isn't fast enough.

Chapter 33

P-taff... P-taff...

Rubbing the back of his head, Mal wakes with a groan on the forest floor as the scent of damp earth and moss wafts through the morning air. *Solid hit. The next one's mine.*

He sits up, scours his surroundings, and turns his head toward the gunfire. Moments later, Dugal, gun in hand, rushes by, disturbing the ground, not noticing Mal in the underbrush. *What the hell?* Dugal traipses into their camp, and bends over, with hands on his knees, to catch his breath.

Mal closes his eyes momentarily as he stands. The pain in his head throbs.

"Did you get him?" Kaden's distant voice asks.

Mal follows Dugal into camp, massaging his sore head.

Dugal spills words out between breaths without looking up. "Asshole's...bleeding... Couldn't find him."

From a crouching position, Kaden twists toward Mal. "What happened to you?"

Kaden's next to Jace's lifeless body. Someone inflicted a savage slash to Jace's throat, leaving his hand stiff in a middle-finger salute.

Jesus. "Found our frenemy on my rounds last night."

Kaden's hand points to the body. "There's a message on him."

Mal steps closer and reads the black words penned on Jace's chest: *Come find me. Ry.*

Son of a bitch! Well, that answers that question. Mal gazes back the way he came from, hiding his expression. *Why is Ry killing them? Hell, who was the woman?*

Dugal rises to his full height and scans the message. "What the fuck does that mean?"

Kaden slides his hand over his head in frustration. "He's taunting us. Can't be far. He's bleeding." He stares plainly at Mal. "I want this guy dead."

He's hurt? Shit! Opportunity is knocking, and Mal is happy to answer. "I'll take care of it."

***

Hugging his body protectively, Ryker forces a smile and rushes toward Beth. She rises with her hands clasped from the entrance of the shelter. Neil peeks out from behind her, his angelic face ashen, afraid to come out. No time to waste. He'd like nothing more than to sit and rest, but his brother will track him. A fire has been lit, and Ryker needs to stay ahead of the flames. He reads Beth's concern for him.

"Were those gunshots?" The fear in her voice is unmistakable as she reaches out to him.

He kneels, bringing her down with him, and flinches, out of breath. "First aid?"

She scrambles past a frozen Neil staring at him. Ryker pulls the quick release on his vest and drops it next to him.

He needs support. "Neil, gather our stuff and be ready to leave."

Ryker breaks out in a sweat. The wound torments him, but he keeps it together and focuses on the boy instead of his rapid heartbeats.

Neil's eyes question Ryker. "Are you going to die?"

The little guy doesn't mince words. He can handle me being direct. "No."

Neil doesn't move. Understanding Neil's need to be reassured, Ryker cups his tiny chin and says gently, "I need you to be brave for Beth, alright? Promise me."

Beth jostles Neil on her way out, not seeing their silent exchange, and unzips the first aid kit. "What happened?"

Ryker doesn't answer Beth as he keeps his eyes fixed on Neil, waiting. The boy nods, then vanishes inside.

There's no way to sugarcoat it. With some effort, he yanks his bloodstained shirt over and off, exposing a pectoral tattoo of a Marine eagle, globe, and anchor symbol, which Marines call an EGA...and his bloody wound.

"Oh my God!"

Yup, she's never seen one. "I'll patch it up. We need to run." Ryker probes his front, above his right hip bone, for an exit wound. His body jerks, and he shuts his eyes tightly and clenches his jaw. His vest stopped one from making contact, at least. It was a clean shot and hurt like hell. He'll need the adrenaline to keep going. Ryker digs into the kit and pulls out Quikclot gauze.

"Patch it up? They shot you!"

Thank God for military guys. Civilian kits don't always have these kinds of items. He isn't kidding about running and regrets he has no time to comfort her. "We'll head to the next shelter. I'll keep us safe."

"Safe? No! We're going to Reed."

He can't have this argument now. "Beth, we've talked about this and—"

"No, you've talked about it! I grew up with BAMF Marines, and they're at Reed!" She bends close and stabs his chest over the EGA. "You're my priority now, and I say we're fucking going to Reed!"

Wow! Does she know how gorgeous she is when she's mad? "I don't know whether to be angry or turned on."

She pulls back in confusion.

Behind them, Neil's scared voice asks, "What's at Reed?"

Even angry, she looks cute as hell when she doesn't miss a beat and says, "Penny's chocolate chip cookies, I hope."

Sophia said Beth loved cookies; helped with her stress somehow.

"I vote for cookies," Neil says in a shy whisper.

She crosses her arms and tilts her head like they voted. *Delightful.*

Ryker senses he's lost an unseen battle. She's right. His wound needs medical attention. Reed will have meds, antibiotics, and when Mal tracks him there, backup. He decides he's not angry, closes the gap, and pulls her in for a hungry kiss, then releases her in a flustered state. "I think I've found your hidden superpower. You win." Ryker welcomes the distraction and asks, "How many Marines will be there?"

Anxious, she looks him up and down. "I'm not sure, but it'll probably be three or four."

Ryker brushes his sleeve across his sweaty forehead, acknowledging symptoms of shock creeping up on him. He licks his lips. *Getting shot fucking sucks, big fucking—*

She grabs his arm. "You okay? You're scaring me."

They need to concentrate on getting to Reed sooner rather than later. He calculates they could arrive before nightfall if he pushes them. She won't like it, but it's too risky to spend another night out here with Mal in pursuit.

She rubs her necklace, which gives him a warm feeling.

"I've been wounded before," he says, his voice filled with a hint of pain. "It hurts like hell every time." He sucks in air to clear his nose, but the tension in his body remains. Ryker reads her fear, walks his fingers over her shoulder, and coaxes her to his good side. He kisses the top of her head, enjoying the feel of her being there. "I'll be fine."

"Everybody leaves me," Beth says.

He speculates she's talking about her friends, but he doesn't like her saying things like that. He lifts her chin. "I'm not going anywhere. You hear me?" He looks at Neil. "Both of you."

She nods, not looking convinced, but he'll have to take it for now. He captures her lips, to which she responds with equal enthusiasm.

"Your charms are wearing me down."

Amused, her laughter vibrates against his lips.

"What I wouldn't give for five minutes, safe with you and those lips."

"Ew," Neil says, scrunching his nose. They laugh. Ryker grimaces as pain threatens to take over.

He admires her for a moment, wanting to bottle her laughter. *Three or four Marines, huh? Possibly this Colin guy, too.* "Can you wear the clean shirt in my bag when we get to Reed?"

"Why?"

He thinks it's cute that she puzzles over his request. "That shirt's ruined." She gazes down at the bloodstains on her top, then shrugs like it's not important. "Indulge me. Hmm? Let's get going."

She supports him as they rise together. He drapes his good arm over her, and they walk forward.

Neil begins another barrage of questions. "What's a BAMF?"

CHAPTER 34

Outstretched on a couch, a paperback in hand, Liam's foot moves to the music they uploaded to the sound system. He lays the book on his chest and stares at the ceiling of the bunker. Donovan's been observing his best friend's son for a while now while drying dishes with a dishtowel. He's trying to keep busy, not allowing himself to wonder why his girls haven't arrived yet.

Didn't take long before other people started showing, though. Parker's brother Henry and his family arrived first, so Liam's mainly been spending his time treating broken bones and superficial wounds. As a military combat medic, Donovan's sure Liam's seen some pretty gruesome and dire situations, but he always persevered through them because people depended on him to do his job. Liam's good at what he does, but Henry is their resident doctor, and losing him would have been devastating.

Hoss's youngest son, John Henry, showed up with his and Steven's wives. They told of some harrowing events they escaped from which only riled the men up. They kept those stories from Parker. He didn't need more to worry about on top of everything else he was dealing with up at Haven. It weighs on Donovan, but he can take it. He works well under pressure. Parker is trying to get the farm up and running, and that is more important than anything to their survival.

Penny walks down the corridor and heads into her suite. She is a lot like Donovan in some ways. If she had enlisted, she'd be a force to reckon with. Penny takes the stress of the world on her shoulders and carries it for everyone else when their spouses and children are in trouble. Despite all the losses she's experienced, she still puts everything aside and offers help wherever it is required. Penny is Donovan's hero, and there's nothing he wouldn't do for her.

Liam's military brothers, the twins, Alex and Miles, saunter out of the bathroom, freshly cleaned, towels draped over their shoulders. They salute Donovan as they cross the corridor and enter the men's bunk room for the night. They don't need to salute him, but he doesn't discourage the practice. Donovan earned his stripes and takes it as a sign of respect. They arrived back today after delivering the first group safely to Haven three days ago. Every time a new group arrives, their job is to get them to Haven in one piece, and they've been executing it well.

Liam's sigh carries down the corridor. The boy suffers like him over Sadie not being there yet, but he can't do anything for him. They all live in their own private hells.

Jose was a different story. Donovan is still processing—

An alarm blares throughout the compound, and Donovan's hope flares. *Please be them.*

Penny reemerges, looking focused. "Show time," she says as she walks into the security room. Liam throws the book aside, vaults off the couch, and follows her with Donovan on his heels.

***

The large metal door echoes closed. Drenched from the falls and bathed in red light, Ryker rests against Beth in a very sterile four-by-eight hallway made of cinder blocks. Neil's soaking body trembles.

Ryker snakes his arm around Neil's neck and reassures him with a chest rub. "It's okay. We're safe now."

The red lights become an intense white one, forcing them to huddle close and shield their eyes.

"Beth! You alright?" A woman's tense voice sounds hollow over the loud-speaker.

"Penny, is Liam or Henry here? Ryker's wounded."

The confidence in Beth's tone is positive, and Ryker enjoys hearing it. *She's with her people now.*

"Liam's here. You need help, or can Ryker walk?"

Like hell I need help. He's not showing weakness now. Ryker cranes his head up and talks to the speaker. "I'm good. She's overreacting."

"Okay, you know the drill, Beth. Ryker showers first."

Fuck, an actual shower! He pumps his fist. His wound stabs him, and he slows, but he deals and says, "Yes!"

Beth becomes still in front of him. He curls his fingers around her neck and squeezes. "We made it. I'll be fine."

Taking in his words, Beth narrows her eyes at him. "Don't take all the water."

He flirts as he caresses her face. "We could conserve. I'll scratch yours..."

Beth blushes and turns to Neil. "While we wait, let's find some clothes for you to wear."

"Clothes?" Neil asks.

"Yeah, we have bins of clothes here."

***

The shower warmed Ryker's cool skin, but he protected his wound from the cascading water, cleaning only what was required. With a clean shirt draped over his shoulder, Ryker strolls in gingerly, trying to manage his pain. He spots the radio equipment and computer monitors on the wraparound desk displaying a wide scope of things happening outside. He was expecting a cold, damp, dark dungeon when she said bunker, not this bright, sophisticated setup. These guys don't mess around.

Standing in front of the desk, a bearded man of Ryker's height appears stoic, his hands clasped in front of him. Ryker turns to the only woman in the room he assumes is Penny, who strikes him as friendlier. Her white-blonde hair, untouched by gray, gives him the impression she's young, but the wisdom in her hazel eyes tells a different story. Her slender frame stresses her curves in all the right places. "You must be the cookie queen I've heard about. Ryker." He thrusts his hand forward.

She clasps his offer with a firm grip. "Penny. Got a fresh batch. I'll save you some."

"Thanks." Ryker sizes up the jarhead haircut on the bearded man. He rarely meets anyone taller than himself, so he's curious to know which Marine this one is. *Intimidating enough to be a sergeant.* He guesses it's Donovan.

The man tilts his head at the shorter, muscular blond man off to the side and, without taking his eyes off Ryker, says, "This is our medic, Liam."

With a warm smile, Liam steps forward and peels back Ryker's dressing. "Found some love out there, I see."

The EGA hasn't gone unnoticed, so Ryker postures, stares straight at the bearded man, and says, "Nothing I can't handle."

Yup, a sergeant alright. Intense and non-blinking. Ryker attempts to keep his composure as Liam prods. He endures the prick of a needle and prays the drugs kick in soon.

Past this man, the radio comes to life. "Scout to Reed. Is the package secure?" Ryker's sure that is code for the three of them. From the use of the call sign, he's not surprised these men have a lookout. Someone to cover their backs as they take the last few steps before disappearing into the falls, in case they are followed by unfriendlies. It's comforting to Ryker; a feeling he's missed and welcomes again, like a familiar blanket.

Donovan clicks the mic and says, "The package is secure."

"Donovan!" Beth's cheery voice floats through the pain and attracts Ryker's focus.

Hmm, BAMF Dad Number Two. Beth runs into Donovan's arms. Donovan's eyebrows rise at the sight of her wearing Ryker's oversized Superman T-shirt. *Nothing gets past this guy.* Ryker stifles a smug grin at Donovan's disapproving look.

"Glad to see you're safe, Chickie."

He blinked. The man is human. Ryker finds Beth's nickname endearing.

Penny opens her arms. "So glad you're safe."

Beth launches herself into Penny's gentle arms. Ryker's heart tightens, affected by the scene in front of him. She soothes Beth with a back rub and inaudible words, for only her to hear. *Motherly, like Sophia.*

Snippets of memory lay into Ryker. His mother's caress to his cheek, smoothing his unruly hair before letting him run into his father's arms on base. Snuggling on the bed and listening to her read his favorite book. Opening his lunch kit at school to find a chocolate chip cookie with a note littered with hearts and the words *Love Mom.*

"Cookies?" Beth asks like a little girl and wipes away her tears.

Ryker swallows his memories. Donovan stretches his neck uncomfortably.

"Waiting for my girl to show." Penny squeezes her with affection. "Where's the boy?"

Ryker, like everyone else, turns back to the shower room.

Neil ogles them from the doorway. His small hand rests on the frame. Once the attention drifts his way, Neil takes cover from their stares.

"Neil, it's okay. These are my friends." Beth calls out.

He stays hidden.

Ryker halts Liam's ministrations with an upheld hand and treads over to fetch Neil. He can't kneel like he wants, so he lowers his shirt over his wound and ambles in. "I don't know them, either, but they have cookies."

Still unsure and unmoving, Neil asks, "What kind?"

Ryker glances at Penny through the doorway. Her dimples show as her lips curve up. "Hmm, not sure which ones you'll like. I have different kinds. Why don't you come out, and we can find some?"

Neil's distrust wavers like a teeter-totter. The road Neil's on will be tough, but with a little love and more room to trust, he might be okay.

"You know," Ryker says, "if you give them a chance, they might surprise you." Ryker walks back in, leaving the choice up to Neil, and a tiny hand slides into his. He smiles at the victory. Neil glances around and eyes Donovan with open apprehension. *I feel you.*

Penny steps forward and takes a knee so her eyes are level with Neil's. "Hi, I'm Penny. What's your name?"

He backs up warily into Ryker. "Neil."

She stands, hand extended out, and waits. "Let's go find some cookies."

With fear in those wary eyes, Neil asks Ryker, "You aren't going to leave me, are you?"

Ryker shakes his head with what he hopes is a reassuring smile. "No, we're right behind you. Save me some cookies." He gets Neil's toothy grin.

Once Neil disappears with Penny and the door clicks, Donovan asks Beth, "Who's the boy?"

Ryker returns to Liam under Donovan's watchful eye. Beth didn't mention Liam, so Ryker's not sure what to make of the blond man, but he has steady hands. Ryker can tell Liam's not had much sleep though by the dark circles under his eyes. *Guess there are still people missing.*

"He watched his family die, one by one. I promised his father I'd take care of him."

Silent understanding dawns in Donovan's eyes, and he squeezes her shoulder as if communicating some unspoken language between each other. *Fatherly.*

"Tell me Alejo, Sean, and Colin made it."

The moment of truth.

"Two arrived yesterday. Alejo's here." His eyes slide over to Ryker. "And lover boy's been itching for you."

Ryker's nose flares. *Nice shot...* Donovan smirks at Ryker's discomfort. He approves of Colin, then. *Not going to happen.*

Her intake of breath is audible. "Sean?"

"No sign."

Beth deflates. "Sorry, this is Ryker. He's—"

Donovan holds up his hands. "We'll take care of Ryker." He points to the door and says, "You go in, settle Colin down."

She turns to Ryker, offers her hand, and smiles. He likes this one because it's only for him.

"Liam, is Ryker going to be okay?" she asks, her eyes never wavering from his. The worry in her voice disturbs him. If it's in his power, he'll erase that emotion soon.

"He'll live, don't worry," Liam says, not glancing up.

"I'm right behind you." Ryker pours optimism into his words as he squeezes her hand. She hesitates, nods, and turns to leave. The door clicks behind her.

Donovan refocuses. "How's our boy here?"

Ryker narrows his eyes. *Boy?*

"Through and through. No visible infection, yet." Liam finishes his handiwork and peers up. "Gave you the good stuff so you can rest easy."

"Thanks."

Donovan shifts. "Probably best that Superman slows down."

That brings Ryker's eyes back to Donovan. *Someone's a little threatened.* They glare at each other.

Chapter 35

Colin paces down the corridor, parallel to the tables. The minute the alarm bellowed, he prayed to God it was Beth. Penny came out with a nervous child, which punctured his optimism, but not Liam, so someone was still in there. The waiting gnaws at his nerves; her absence tortures him. He's not looking forward to another sleepless night.

Alejo waits with Colin in quiet excitement, wearing a pink onesie and sitting on the edge of a chair with his hands between his knees. Colin is happy he found Alejo, even if he has no sense of direction and certainly doesn't understand the compass. Sean's still missing, and Alejo is suffering. *How can a forester get lost?* Colin rubs Alejo's shoulder and says, "Won't be long."

The security door opens. Alejo jumps up as someone ambles in. "Beth!"

Her expression says it all: I missed you. She opens her arms as Colin sucks in a sorely needed breath and seizes her with both arms. He swings her around, needing her touch, and breathes in strawberries. *I missed you so fucking much.* Beth clutches him tightly, sending a thrill up his spine. *She misses me, too.*

Alejo asks in desperation, "Is Sean with you?"

Colin bends down for a kiss, but she squirms out of his arms and pulls a distraught Alejo in. He washes down the slight because it's Alejo. Her sadness is unmistakable, and he can guess the answer before it passes her lips.

"He's not, A."

Alejo's joy diminishes and he soothes himself, running his hands through her hair.

"I'm so happy you both made it." Beth points at Colin's leg. "Are you okay? You took a bullet on the bridge."

Her concern warms him. He needs the contact, so Colin hugs her with Alejo. It's the best he can do until he gets her alone. "Grazed my leg. Liam gave me antibiotics for it yesterday."

"Not finding my baby has been awful, hon. I was so scared out there." Alejo's expression bleeds with sadness. Still, he's improved in the last day. His rainbow of Marines has distracted him, and Colin's sure Beth will raise Alejo's spirit because she's certainly raised his.

Beth leans her forehead against Alejo's. "He's an experienced woodsman, A. He'll find his way."

Enjoying the moment, Colin gazes down at the S on her shirt. "What're you wearing?"

***

"Your shirt on Beth?" Donovan asks point blank.

"You know it."

Pleased at Ryker's confidence, Donovan rests against the desk. "Smart move. Don't think Colin'll miss that. How'd you know he was here?"

A bold smile spreads across Ryker's face. "I didn't. Just don't want any question of who she belongs to."

So he knows about Colin. Donovan stays silent on the subject.

The corner of Liam's lip quirks up as he surveys his handiwork. "You're done. See you in the morning, gentlemen."

"Thanks for the patch job," Ryker says.

Donovan's focus shifts to Liam. Once Sadie shows, he's going to have to pay close attention to him. They think he doesn't notice their mutual interest but they've been sniffing each other since she turned eighteen. *Nothing gets past me.*

"Night," Donovan says, the word hanging in the air as the door shuts with a resounding click. He'd like to interrogate Ryker further, but Donovan's tired. He sighs and checks his watch. Time to sleep, but he won't. Donovan hasn't slept right since the missiles dropped. He'd rather forgo the nightmares his overburdened mind conjures up.

"What's on your mind?" Ryker asks, his poise challenging Donovan.

Here we go. Donovan pushes off the desk. "Marine, huh?"

"The EGA says I am."

Cocky... They'll need every able-bodied man; especially if he's a Marine. "Still active?"

"Nope."

Does he have the mettle to stand up to me? Donovan tests that theory by stepping into Ryker's space, eye to eye. "Only going to say this once, Bethany's special to us. You mess with her, you answer to all of us. Am I clear?"

Ryker doesn't flinch. "I had sisters, so I know where you're coming from. Crystal."

Quick wit. Donovan's eyes narrow. He likes Colin, but this guy seems like a better fit. Not that he's going to give him a hall pass or anything. If they make it through the gauntlet, they're worthy of dating Beth. That thought brings up Brad and his daughter, but he wills that thought away. Not knowing has been plaguing him for weeks now. Just like the alarm has. Every time the damn thing goes off, his heart rate ramps up along with his blood pressure.

Donovan stands back and extends his hand. "Welcome to Reed, Superman."

***

Backed by Donovan, Ryker steps with confidence into the main corridor of Reed. The aroma of a home-cooked meal lingers in the air. Penny sits at a long rough wooden table, watching over Neil, who is savoring chocolate chip cookies, his hand clutching a glass of milk. He follows Neil's vigilant eyes toward three people hugging each other, and the rest of the room ceases to exist. The caveman reaction he experiences seeing Beth between two men comes as a surprise. A tall man with blond-tipped hair, and a shorter man exuding the same greedy vibes. *Not yours, mine.*

He quells this line of thinking but finds it interesting that he jumped to a male's basic instinct of possessiveness. He doesn't like the nervousness that radiates from her, so he doesn't quite relax just yet. They're safe, but it doesn't feel like it.

"Wow, hunk-o!" The tall one in pink fans himself.

Alejo. She was right about the hunky remark. He looks like the energizer bunny minus the oversized head. He finds Alejo's jet-black hair dipped in blond striking and flashes a smile his way. "You must be Alejo."

Alejo clutches his face in delight. "Holy shit, that voice, those tats, my dreams. Tell me you swing my way, and I'll freakin' die!"

Ryker chuckles, then hisses, forgetting his injury. "Sorry, Alejo, your dreams are just that, dreams."

Alejo's lips form a pout, which Ryker finds endearing. Without warning, Alejo's expression changes from pouty to concerned. "Are you hurt, honey? You should sit down." He slides a chair out at the end of the table.

"I'm okay," Ryker assures him and scans the main area they're standing in. The place impressed him more and more by the minute. Two L-shaped leather couches stretch out to his left, pointing toward two long wooden tables with seating for a large crowd. At the end of the rectangular space, two kitchens mirror each other, a door and a lengthy island snug between them, with top-of-the-line appliances. Yes, this is quite the setup indeed.

Beth asks, "Is the suite empty? It's been a long day."

There are suites? The place went up another notch in Ryker's eyes.

"Yeah, you want it, it's yours," Penny says, rising and wrapping her arms around Beth. "You must be exhausted. We'll catch up tomorrow." Beth answers with a tight squeeze. Penny kisses Beth's cheek and strolls toward Ryker. "Night everyone. Ryker, the bathroom is three doors up. Towels are in there. Light's always on." She places her hand on his forearm, squeezes, and says, "Thank you for bringing her back to us." She exits through the door to Ryker's right.

If he was firing all cylinders, he'd be more curious about what's behind the doors on both sides at regular intervals down the corridor, but he was growing weary.

"Ryker, this is Colin," Beth says, her eyes low as she rubs the necklace with fidgeting fingers. He doesn't enjoy hearing the distress in her voice.

He catches the sting of jealousy in Colin's demeanor but remains neutral and waves with two fingers. The air in the room grows tense, and the blond California surfer straightens, but his arm remains around Beth's waist. It's a challenge. Neither man says a word. Ryker wouldn't be friendly, either, if he saw a threat to his woman, but he waits to see what she does. Ball's in her court.

Neil must be feeling the tension in the room because he squeezes in between Beth and Colin, disengaging Colin's grip. Ryker takes pleasure in the way Colin frowns at Neil. *Good boy.*

Beth goes down on a knee. "What's up, my brave bodyguard?"

"Can I sleep with you?"

You and me both. They've been sleeping together, so it stands to reason the boy doesn't want to be alone with strangers. Beth's eyes seek out Ryker for confirmation. His heart rejoices. *Fucking absolutely, he's sleeping with us.* He dips his chin, yes.

Donovan takes this as his cue to approach and kneels at the boy's feet. Neil steps back into Beth and coils his arms around her neck. Ryker smiles at the intimacy.

"Name's Donovan. Do you know how to cook?"

"No."

"Hmm... Everyone pitches in around here, and I have an opening for a cook. Why don't you come out early tomorrow, and I'll show you how to make breakfast for everyone?"

Sergeant has a soft spot for children.

Neil's head turns to Beth, the hope in his eyes unequivocal as he asks, "Can I?"

She squeezes his little body. "You sure can."

Neil runs to Ryker for a gentle hug and stares up, unable to contain his excitement. "I'm going to cook!"

Ryker's pain subsides as the meds kick in. "I hear that, Little Man, but first let's get you to bed, okay?"

Everyone's watching this play out in happy silence. *Except Colin, I suppose.* Kids can do that. Calm you in high-stress situations. Seeing the tenderness in Beth's face as she rubs the necklace makes his heart swell. She's never looked so beautiful as she does now, her eyes only for him.

"I'm tired, A," Beth says. "I'll fill you in later?"

Alejo hugs her. "You'd better." He blows kisses to Ryker, says, "Night hunky," and enters a darkened room across the way. *One more ally.*

"Ryker, follow me." Donovan's deep voice yanks Ryker's attention away from Beth. Ryker doesn't budge.

"No, he's with me in the suite," she says, pointing at the second door on Ryker's right.

Colin's head cuts to Beth. Ryker suppresses a victory smile and dips his head. *Ooh, that hurt.*

Donovan steps to the opposite side of the room and says, "Okay, you three hit the sack. I'm turning in. Colin?" He's trying to defuse a confrontation. *Hmm...*

Beth walks toward Ryker, then turns midway down the corridor to Colin and says, "Night." *Not even a goodnight hug.*

With every step Beth takes toward Ryker, Colin looks a little more crushed. She guides Neil into the suite as Colin catches Ryker's eye. He nods at Colin before following Beth in. *She's mine, so hands off.*

Chapter 36

The last time Beth had visited Reed was during their camping adventures growing up, back when the place didn't have furniture. So tonight, Beth is eager to discover what lies behind the suite door. She finds a comfortable living area painted in warm blue, a couch, and bunk bed, and through another door, a bedroom. It appears homey—sparse, but functional for its intended purpose: to calm families who've been through hell to get here.

Neil climbs the ladder to the top bunk with his scrapbook and a confiscated teddy bear from the lower bunk. There, another teddy bear sits among various children's books that are splayed out. Losing her sister's stuffy cut Beth's heart; the sting of regret is sharp. On her sister's tenth birthday, the family took a day trip to the Woodland Zoo in Seattle. They had many exhibits, but Molbak's Butterfly Garden was the reason they visited, and upon their arrival, her sister insisted they go there first. For Beth, it is a memory she will always cherish. It was one of the few times she didn't fight with her sister, and the day her father took a beautiful shot of them holding a butterfly in their hands.

The suite door clicks, collapsing the adored memory, unsettling her. Beth's been in survival mode for weeks, so it comes as no surprise that she's tired and highly strung all at once. It dawns on her that Neil's fully clothed, but Beth doesn't want to risk running into Colin, so abandons the thought of searching for nightwear for him. "We'll get you some pajamas tomorrow, Neil. Take your clothes off and slip into bed."

Neil cocks an eyebrow her way like she said something crazy.

"It's okay, Neil." Ryker startles her. "You're safe. No one's going to hurt you here." He was closer than she'd thought.

"That man was big," Neil says, meaning Donovan.

Laying her hand on the bed frame, Beth cranes her neck to Neil. "I trust Donovan with my life. You never have to fear anyone who's here."

He contemplates this, the wheels constantly turning in his cute little head. "I don't like the blond man."

Beth sighs. "Donovan's an early riser, so go out when you wake up. He'll be waiting for you."

Neil strips down to his new underwear and slips under the covers uninhibited. The way his eyelids droop, it won't be long before he crashes. It amazes Beth how fast she's become attuned to Neil's habits.

Ryker clears the items off the lower bunk. The thought of sleeping alone in that bedroom intimidates her. If she offered, would he sleep with her? Beth puts her hand on his shoulder and shakes her head. He straightens and says, "I didn't want to... Are you sure?"

She's not but she doesn't like the alternative. Not knowing what to say, she nods.

Ryker pats Neil's hand. "We'll be right through that door if you need us." But Neil is past hearing.

They walk into the bedroom. The queen bed occupies the center, flanked by nightstands and functional lamps. There are two tall dressers on either side of the room. In theory, no one should ever be here long enough to need them, but they're there to keep up the illusion of home. Once again, the door clicks behind them, but this time, she senses Ryker's eyes on her.

"Was this for Colin's benefit or mine?" he asks.

The air between them charges and warmth rises in Beth's cheeks. It's the first time they've been truly alone. "Mine," she says, tired of being scared out there...and in here.

"He's got it bad for you."

"I know."

"He's not the only one."

Their eyes connect. Beth longs to believe in the want reflected there. *Why do I have to fight my feelings all the time?* She longs to touch him, but the voice of doubt seeps in. *You have no right to feel.*

Ryker moves toward her.

Not ready, she blurts out, "I've never been with a man. I mean, I don't know what to—" She turns, mortification flushing through her. *Now I want to die.*

Ryker's hands slide around her waist as he whispers in her ear, "No pressure. You want to wait, we wait. I'm happy to be with you, whether it's just for your company or those bewitching lips."

His words induce tingles, drawing a smile. The scent of his freshly showered body envelops her. How does he calm her anxiety and, in the same breath, make her feel cherished, safe?

Ryker leads her to the bed. They lie down on top of soft sheets and face each other, his fingers entwined with hers. Thoughts and feelings swirl in Beth's mind. What is this spell he has on her? She wants to experience those lips again. His touch isn't enough. She wants more.

"What happened to you nine years ago?" he asks, running a thumb over her skin.

Beth gazes up, feeling exposed. "How did you—?"

"Jose hinted at it."

What did Jose tell him? The pit of her stomach grows cold. *If he knew, he'd leave me.* She tries to withdraw her hand, but his clamps down, halting her retreat.

"None of us are perfect. I want all of you. Beautiful and ugly." His unwavering stare and patience give her space.

What can she tell him? Her friends know some of it, but no one knows everything. Not even her therapist. *Maybe it is time I own up to my mistake and face the consequences.* She is tired of carrying the burden. She retrieves the photo of her family out of her back pocket, caresses the weathered surface, and wishes she could hug them one more time.

He scoots up to the headboard, hauls her with him, and leans against the pillows.

Offering the photo, she says, "This was my family."

"What happened to them?"

Her anxiety compounds. Beth's not sure she can speak her true feelings out loud yet. But he deserves to know she isn't a good person, doesn't he? Beth fidgets with her index finger and continues. "I was in a car accident on my fifteenth birthday. My family died around me," she whispers. It isn't the whole truth, just the truth she can swallow. She glances up.

Under a soft gaze, he says, "I'm so sorry. That's why you don't celebrate it?"

"They crowd me on my birthday. They're afraid I'll slip again."

"Slip? How?"

Beth clams up, not sure if she should explain further. *Shouldn't have said anything.*

His hand quells her fidgeting fingers and asks, "Can you trust me?"

Can I? He's not glaring at her like a freak. With a heavy sigh, she says, "On my sixteenth birthday, I was...not in a good frame of mind. I OD'd on pain meds." There. Beth's second worst shame is out there between them. To her surprise, Ryker encourages her to go on with a squeeze of his hand. *How does he know I'm holding back?* "My therapist... She helped me create, um, safe zones... My apartment, the diner. Places I feel secure in."

"PTSD?"

Beth nods. "I have issues traveling between them. Everyone pitched in; drove or walked with me. I was never alone outside those zones."

"Coming here was a challenge, then?"

She's impressed he came to that conclusion so fast. It gives her courage. "When I'm not in my safe zones, I, um, slip." Beth glances down and resumes fidgeting. "I took a bottle of pain meds from the first shelter, but there wasn't enough to do the job. So, I headed to the next shelter, hoping there would be more."

His deep voice asks, "Did you find more?"

"Didn't have a chance. I picked up Neil before I could get there. Then you happened." Beth wants to look up but feels too embarrassed.

"Are Reed and Haven safe zones?"

She shakes her head. "Not like the ones in town. I haven't been here since... The voice is stronger when I'm alone."

"What does this voice tell you to do?"

She doesn't know how to answer that. *He won't understand.* "I made a huge mistake. Stopped going to my therapist." She glances up. Ryker raises an eyebrow at her but stays silent, giving her room to talk. "I thought... It seemed like I was better. The voices were under control. I moved out, found friends. But then my birthday...it's a trigger."

"Why do you want to die?"

She bites her lips, not wanting to say it out loud, and reaches for the necklace. The moment engraved in Beth's memory appears clearly in her mind's eye, like it has so many times before. Beth wakes up disoriented in the back of the car, surrounded by screams and the acrid smell of smoke. The sheared-off other half held her parents captive. Smoke drifts up from the engine as flames lick the hood, snaking toward them.

Beth attempts to move but cries out as intense pain courses through her ribs. Then, heartbreaking disappointment consumes her. She can't save them. Her head swivels to the empty seat beside her, and Beth screams out her frustration as remorse and shame twist around her like a noose.

"There's that one second...when everything stops... It took one second to know I was alone and that the car accident was my fault." Her goosebumps spread over what feels like the full surface of her skin.

"That's a lot to put on yourself. It wasn't your fault."

When she closes her eyes, Carrie reaches out to strike her. Beth shakes her head as war rages within her. "That's what everyone says, but they don't know."

"Don't know what?"

The images speed rewind in her head to before the accident. Beth retaliates and unhooks Carrie's seatbelt. Her sister lunges. Beth's eyelids bear the weight of tears as she pushes the next words out in a whisper. "I distracted my father, and I...undid my sister's seatbelt."

Ryker slides down and wraps his arms around her in a tender hold. "You didn't know the accident was going to happen."

His words release the tension she's been holding in. "I couldn't save her... I...I murdered her. Them." The floodgates of emotion burst open. Tears spill, and thoughts swirl into a cyclone of shame and regret, spurring the voice on. *It was all on you.*

"Hey." He searches her eyes out, willing her with his own to listen. "You didn't murder anyone, beautiful. You made a mistake that cost you."

"I don't deserve to live."

He crushes her against him. "God, Beth, don't say that." He pulls back. "I can't lose someone I care about again. Please don't do that to me. If you die, I'll be alone."

Alone? Why would he want anything to do with her after that confession? She wiggles out of his hold. "I'm sorry. I shouldn't have said that. You lost your sister—"

"Don't apologize."

"I have to. If you hadn't come looking for me—"

"Don't. It wasn't your—"

"Yes, it was! I'll understand if you want nothing to do with me. I'm a monster."

"Beth!" Ryker cups her face. "Stop listening to the voice and listen to me. You didn't murder your sister. It was an accident. Those men out there—" He points away from them. "—it's their fault. They took my sister from me, not you!"

How can he dismiss Beth's part in their sisters' deaths so easily? She'll never get forgiveness or closure from either of them.

Ryker strokes her cheek with the most loving eyes she's ever seen. "Beth, I don't think I could breathe without you."

Holy crap! Her heart jumps into her throat.

"I want you to talk to me. I need to know what's in your head."

Beth pulls her emotions back and attempts to lighten the mood. "So you can find a way around it."

Ryker smiles before dropping it again. "Promise me you won't leave me."

First Neil, and now Ryker. Despite her confession, he's asking her to stay? Beth realizes her answer is fundamental to Ryker's sanity, but she can't promise him that. Agony, mixed with longing, hovers in his eyes, so she whispers, "You make me feel safe."

He grins with open desire. "I want to make you feel more than that."

Beth savors those words, longing to taste his lips again. Her breath quickens, and she swallows. *Every time things get better...* Tired of the voice, she trails her fingers through Ryker's soft beard and says, "I want what you promised me."

Her words bring warmth to those brown eyes, and Beth wants more. Her lips explore his, tentatively at first, then brashly. Feverish excitement mixed with anticipation electrifies her further when his arms surround her. *Is it supposed to feel this amazing?*

Ryker pulls her under him, still on his side, not breaking their connection. His hand trails around her waist and squeezes her ass, then slides further down her thigh to bring her leg alongside his. His lips flinch.

Shit, he's hurt! Beth pulls back, lowering her leg, and swipes the back of her hand against her swollen lips. *He's going to think I'm scared, like Colin did.* The fear that Ryker's eyes will reflect the same displeasure stops her from looking up.

"Too fast? We can stop."

Beth dares to gaze up, but there's no disappointment in his face, only concern. *For me?* "You're hurt... I don't want to hurt you," she says.

The grin she adores radiates from Ryker, yet his eyes remain laced with hunger. "I'll figure a way around it." He rises and sits on the edge of the bed. This change of position piques her curiosity. He pats his thighs. Beth's not sure this is a good idea.

"Trust me." He welcomes her with open arms.

Beth straddles his lap, and for a moment, their eyes connect; a moment that bonds them, strips them bare, and increases a mutual need to cement their union. Ryker slides a hand up her back, into her neck, and with a gentle push forward, claims her lips greedily. Her body electrifies as his tongue skims her lips, seeking permission to enter. She grants it, and her desire skyrockets. Beth pushes out every thought, focusing instead on his body hardening, molding to hers, and the delicious sound of Ryker's groans. She tugs at his shirt. Wants more, needs more.

He releases her lips and changes course. Ryker's whisper tickles her ear as he asks, "Beth, are you sure? We can stop, take it slow."

Beth loves that he's concerned for her but she knows what she wants, and there's nothing in this world that will stop her from attaining it. Need propels her to help him remove his top. "I want more. I want you. This." Her lips trail down his neck scar as her fingers glide over Ryker's chest tattoo and explore further down, skimming over his toned abs. *He feels so good.*

Not wasting a moment, Ryker's hands move under the Superman shirt, graze over the curves of her breasts, and tease her erect nipples, firing every one of her nerve endings. Beth moans under her breath, yearning for him to explore further.

He pulls back, their eyes connect, and he whispers, "Right now, all I want—" He tears the shirt over her head, baring her breasts and vulnerability to his eager eyes. "—is you under me...safe." Feasting on her nakedness, Ryker's rough fingers glide over the necklace, then halt under her collarbone.

My tattoos. Beth's arms shoot up as she attempts to cover them.

He cups her face. "Why do you hide from me? You're stunning."

"No one's seen my tattoos."

Ryker pushes aside her crossed arms so he can have a better look. His warm fingers glide over the fallen angel under her left collarbone. "What does this mean to you?"

She relaxes, but not completely, as heat rushes through her cheeks. "She's been through rough times but isn't jaded by life yet."

"I think I know you finally, and then you surprise me." Ryker's finger scorches as it traces the tattoo of Carrie's name over her heart. "Your sister's name?"

She nods shyly. His calloused fingers continue to burn a trail between her breasts, causing her body to hum with desire. Beth yearns for more. She gets her wish when his hands backtrack up, across the angel, and over her shoulders. Lust swirls in the depths of his eyes: pure unadulterated carnal desire. *For me?* It excites her, causing her body to dance internally.

Ryker fists her hair, draws her head back, and bares Beth's neck to his tortuous, slow, hungry kisses. He trails his wet tongue over the butterfly necklace, down her collarbone, and over her tattoos. Her skin ignites as Ryker teases her nipples with his sensuous mouth and devilish tongue, one at a time, in slow, agonizing circles. Passion courses through her, forcing her to shiver. She's going to black out from his attention. *Fuck.*

He wraps both arms around her, lays her down, pushes her body into the mattress, and lavishes urgent kisses on her. "Beth."

Hearing her name on his lips causes mayhem, urging her hips to lift and move rhythmically against him. His need for her is unmistakable. She reaches out, desperate to touch him, but he denies her and restricts her arms. She strains against her bonds, captures his eyes, and asks, "Ryker. Am I safe?"

A mischievous smile plays across Ryker's lips as his head dips down and he begins a slow, torturous descent, eventually releasing her arms. Every kiss, and the trail of his lips over the curve of her breasts, sets her on fire. His tongue scorches a path, further and further, until his answer drifts over her lower belly, eliciting her intake of breath. "No."

***

Half lidded and numb to any pain, Ryker's chest rises and contracts as he lies on his side. He basks in the afterglow and caresses a satiated Beth, her eyes closed, facing him. *God, she turns me on.* The only sound: their heavy breathing. *So intoxicating.* He doesn't want to stop touching her.

Ryker didn't want her first time to be awkward; he wanted to cherish her and make it the most amazing experience. Her spasms and moans forced him to lose control eventually, however, catapulting him into the heavens. *It was so fucking hot watching her peak.* He hopes she did. Beth's quiet. She sounded happy when she crested the first time.

Caught in the sheets, she turns onto her back, faces the ceiling, and breaks out into a wide smile. "That was fucking amazing! I never knew it could be so...wow!"

Ruptured laughter escapes his lips before Ryker clutches his side and rides the discomfort. He'll endure it. "Shit, Beth, that's just what a man wants to hear!"

Chapter 37

In the wee hours of the morning, Beth emerges from the communal bathroom, showered and feeling relaxed. Soft lighting guides her way back to the bedroom, reminding her of the light strips on a plane. She hasn't felt this energized since before the accident. *Too good to be true.* Before the thought finishes, she's already chasing it out of her head. *Don't ruin it.*

"Still have those nightmares?"

Beth startles and grabs a table chair to steady her nerves. "Geesh, William. You scared me."

"Sorry, honey," William's soothing voice says from the shadows of the living room.

After expelling the air from her frightened lungs, Beth asks, "Do they ever go away?"

Hefting his heavy frame off the couch, William beckons her forward with a one-sided grin under the soft glow of the floor lighting. Beth cocoons herself into his welcoming arms, leans her ear to his chest, and relishes the fresh scent of the forest. His slow and steady heartbeat calms her down.

"No, but they lessen as life moves on. I'm glad you're safe." He combs his fingers through her hair, sending shivers up her spine. Beth hasn't seen William since he moved up to Haven with Pauline a year ago. He married the year Beth lost her family. She misses his strength and tenderness. The last month must weigh on William after his loss, but he appears well. His grip loosens, and he tenderly brushes a stray hair over Beth's ear, evoking another round of shivers. "Parker's been worried. Heard you took a river detour."

The awful memory of choking on water comes to the surface. "It was horrible."

"Heard you got a man, too," he says with disapproval in his words.

Her BAMF dads didn't vet Ryker first, but she's hoping Donovan's endorsement will be enough for them to forgive Ryker. "He's a Marine."

"Hmm," he says as he steers her to the couch. "Sit, Chickie." Is this a chance to catch up or a lecture? The others are still asleep. She sits. William seeks the couch across from her. "How long have you known this guy?"

"Two weeks," Beth lies. She's only seen Ryker for seven of those days.

"What do you know about him?"

Interrogation? Okay. "Ryker's a second gen Marine. He's intelligent, has quick reflexes, came to my defense at the diner, and he's saved my life."

William soaks that info up, not alluding to approval or not. "What do you like about him?"

"He has a good moral compass and cares about family. He's protective but, also, respectful."

William smirks. "When he kisses you, how does he make you feel?"

She drops her gaze to the floor and says, "I don't know."

"Yes, you do. Don't be coy. Tell me."

The memory of Ryker's tongue searing her skin comes to the forefront. "Like I'm on fire." Her lips twist as her eyes raise to glimpse a contemplative William.

His eyebrow lifts. "Fire, huh?"

She fidgets under his studious gaze, wanting to be anywhere else but on the couch.

"Donovan filled me in, but I'll reserve judgment till I meet him. Not that you need my approval."

No, but she wants it. Of all her BAMF dads, he's the only one that understands her. Donovan and Jose are controllers, while William and Hoss are the opposite: laid back and calm.

"The most important question is, does he make you happy?"

Ryker's smile comes to mind...and his tongue. The things he did to her last night. "Yes."

"I'm glad. You deserve happy, sweetness."

"Did you watch us come in?" Beth didn't tell Ryker or Neil but she knew they were being watched as they rounded the plunge pool and headed toward the wall of water that hides Reed's front door.

"Yup. Hoss, too, I expect."

"In his usual spot?" Beth asks.

"Yup. We're on shifts till we account for everyone with kids." That's always been the plan in this scenario: collect and transport the most vulnerable first. "Where did the boy come from?"

The memory of the man smiling through his pain filters in. "They were heading to their cabin when they were attacked. The attackers gravely injured his father."

"You up to taking the boy on?"

The last few days with Neil bring a smile to her lips. "I am. When his father suggested I take him, I was concerned at first, but it was the right thing to do."

"He's younger than you were," William says, referring to Beth's loss at fifteen.

"Yes. I know where he's at and where he's headed."

William raises his head. "No question about that."

"Why are you sleeping out here?" she asks.

He lies back and closes his eyes. "You better get back to bed. Your beau's worried."

William must have got the short stick on this one. *They don't trust Ryker.* It irks her, but she accepts it as a protective measure. A silent test Ryker has to pass in order to gain their trust.

"Ryker's asleep."

"He's not."

"How do you—?"

"He came out, gained a feel for the place, loitered outside the bathroom for a spell, and then went back into the suite."

The men may be overprotective, but Beth loves each of them in her own way. She rises, bends over, and kisses his forehead. "Sweet dreams, Dad." Her endearment earns her a grin and fills her with joy. She's a poor substitute. He deserves his children back, but that will never be.

"Sweet dreams, my Chickie."

She walks to the suite and an image of Parker gently brushing her hair in her hospital room comes to mind. He greeted her with a smile as she awoke the morning after the car accident. Donovan would have relayed to Haven that she was safe, but perhaps... Beth's hand hesitates on the door handle, and she twists her head to the open security door.

"William, can you show me how to use the radio?"

***

In the chair next to her, William flips switches and hands her the mic. "Press the side button on the mic but don't hold it too close to your mouth when you speak."

She raises the heavy mic, presses the button, and exhales. "Reed to Haven."

Silence follows.

"Parker's probably sleeping in the bunk across the way." William reasons. "Give him a minute."

She gazes at him. "Why would he be sleeping there?"

"He has slept nowhere else since we got here," he says, his meaning clear. Parker is worried about her; something she's never seen. Parker has only ever shown her a relaxed attitude, even when she knew he was under extreme stress—some of which she'd subjected him to over the years.

"If we hadn't intervened, he'd have gone looking for you."

"Haven here. Is that my Little Chickie?" Parker asks, full of exuberance.

"Uncle!" she says, and not able to contain her enthusiasm, she squeezes William's forearm.

"You had me worried. You okay? How was the trip?"

William places his hand over hers, leans in, and says, "I'll leave you two alone." He kisses her forehead before exiting into the main area of Reed.

She clicks the mic, wishing he was here with her. "I'll be okay when I can hug you again."

"Same here, girl."

"We met with hostiles yesterday. Need a couple of days to heal before making the trek up there."

"Who's we? S with you? I know A and C are there."

They never use names on the comms, Hoss's name being the only exception, which has always confounded Beth. Her friends don't have call signs, so her BAMFs have clearly opted for using their initials. "No, S is MIA at the moment."

"Not good. Hope that gets resolved soon."

Donovan didn't tell Parker about Ryker and Neil. She loves Donovan a little more for that.

Beth leans forward and speaks into the mic. "Uncle?" She doesn't know how he's going to take her news. The whole time she lived with Parker, she never brought a boy around. Her complicated life left little room for anything so normal.

"Now I'm worried. What?"

With a clenched jaw, she expects his reaction with dread. "I met someone. He's here with me."

"*With you*, with you?!"

Oh, boy... This is unfamiliar territory for both of them. "Yes, *with me*, with me."

"He'd better be Osmond approved," Parker says, using Donovan's familiar call sign.

Beth rolls her eyes but dangles a carrot. "He's a Marine." She sits in silence for a beat, biting the inside of her cheeks in apprehension.

"I see." He sounds cautious. Possibly still undecided about someone he's never met.

She strengthens her case. "He's defended me and saved me."

Silence. Is she losing ground? "You don't need saving, do you?" he asks.

"Chili and Sophia both liked him and offered to give him a job." Chili was Jose's call sign. That alone should give Ryker a seal of approval.

"No names on the comms," he reprimands, but it gets him talking. "Sounds like he might be good enough for my Little Chickie." Emphasis on the might.

"I've adopted a little boy, too."

"Come again?"

***

Laid out on her front, palms cupping her chin, Beth studies Ryker on the bed. She's never had a boyfriend before, but she likes the way he makes her feel: beautiful, appreciated, and safe.

Sleeping peacefully face down, Ryker's arms are out at ninety-degree angles, bent at the elbow, his dark hair disheveled. She marvels at how long his dark lashes are. A tattoo on his right shoulder blade reading *1/6 Hard* stares back at her, as do various scars. He surprises her, too, it seems, and she wonders if it refers to Ryker's unit. Beth's eyes wander from his shoulder, down his nicely curved bicep, and along the tattoo she didn't notice last night. Finally, she can feast her eyes on all that is Ryker. Beth rises on her hands, cranes her neck, and spots the reaper tattoo she saw before on his inner arm. *Fascinating.* Another tattoo, a dagger coiled by a snake, reveals itself to her wandering eyes on his other forearm. *I wonder what they mean to him.*

Ryker catches her scrutinizing him and, in a gruff voice, says, "Hey."

The clear hunger in Ryker's look makes Beth all too aware that she's wearing nothing under his Superman shirt. A thrill zings through her body. "Hey."

His hair a mess, Ryker rises like a scruffy cat, yanks Beth down with him, and winces. Ryker nuzzles her neck and breathes her in as his hand trails down and spreads over her curvy bottom, sending her senses into overdrive. Beth loves his fascination with her body a smidgen too much, as well as the way her frame molds to his without question. *It's getting warm in here.*

With an audible sigh, he mumbles into her neck, "Is Donovan family?"

That question throws her. "He served with my uncle. Why?" When Beth saw Donovan's appearance yesterday, she knew Sadie and Gina hadn't arrived yet. He's never had a five o'clock shadow before, much less a beard. Donovan would never let himself go like that unless something was wrong.

"He challenged me."

Beth erupts into laughter. She tries to suppress it but fails.

Ryker lifts his head back, gazes at her, and feigns offense. "He was mean to me."

Her mouth opens, and her eyes widen. "He was not."

Ryker laughs, hisses, then clutches his ribs.

Beth drops the smile. "Ryker?"

He squeezes her ass and slides his arm out from under her. "I'm okay. Just need to keep the pain at bay." Ryker groans as he turns to sit up.

Beth shakes a leg and arranges the pillows behind him.

He tilts his head. "What're you doing?"

"I'm helping you get comfortable."

Desire drips from eyes that seek hers out. "That better be because we're going to have some mind-blowing sex again."

Beth raises an eyebrow, displaying a flirtatious smile. "Was that what that was?"

Not rusty on the reflexes, she shrieks happily when Ryker strong-arms her back into the mattress. He takes her lips hostage in a long carnal kiss, pulls her leg up to tease her with his need, and breaks contact. "Remember now, brat?"

Infused with desire, she teases back. "Hmm, I'm new to this. Perhaps you should refresh my memory."

CHAPTER 38

Beth exits the suite, her hand in Ryker's, and walks the familiar corridor. Memories of her time at Reed linger. The only furniture out here back then was sleeping rolls. She wishes she could go back. Good times...before they weren't.

One of the two tables is buzzing with morning activity. His nose in a book, Liam passes meds across the table as Beth settles in beside Ryker. She notes the dark circles under Liam's eyes and the deep wrinkles of frustration in his forehead. The unkempt beard's new, as well.

Ryker slides his arm across the back of her chair and accepts the bottle of pills with a nod of thanks. The heat from his hand covers hers once more on the smooth tabletop.

Alex and Miles are concentrating on a game of chess. They both look up; Alex winks, while Miles smiles. This is the first time she's laid eyes on the twins. She understands they own an apartment up at Haven. Up close, they appear the same in every way, but she identifies Alex by the scar Liam talked about, slicing through his left eyebrow. A story she's not privy to.

As Miles decides his next move, Alex eyes his brother's plate. Miles pushes it forward, seemingly thinking nothing of it. Alex snatches a piece of bacon with a satisfied grin. New faces... There's bound to be more.

Thinking of fresh faces, she looks at Ryker. Beth directs her attention back to the people in the room. "Do you know what happened out there?"

Liam lays his book aside. "From the SAT feed, it looks like the world bombed itself. No rhyme or reason. Nobody's claimed credit for it, either."

That's disheartening.

Miles moves a piece on the board. "There was a delay between targets. The US was first, then the rest of the world a day later. Bases and major cities suffered heavy hits. Got graphic. We cut the feed to the apartments up at Haven."

"The feed's gone dark, too, now." Alex gazes up at Ryker. "Colin said a missile hit the base?"

"Saw it myself, an Auntie. A shock wave took out the valley. Not much standing after that. So I'm guessing some of our military's FUBAR."

Beth can't believe that was just a couple of weeks ago. If the boys hadn't forced her out, she'd still be there. She turns to look at Ryker. They were fortunate to find each other. The aroma of bacon compels her to lick her lips.

Liam drums his fingers on the tabletop as he frowns. "No reports of nukes used, either."

Miles leans back to wait for his brother to make his move. "Good thing they used the antimatter weapons, or we'd be looking at a different world out there."

He's got that right. But why not nukes? Aunties annihilate matter but without destroying the planet. For some fanatical group to do this but not claim they took out the world... It doesn't sit right with Beth.

Alex looks up from the chessboard. "Makes no sense."

"Yeah, we'd never bomb ourselves," Miles says, gazing down at the board, biting his inner lip. Unease fills the air as the men shift awkwardly.

Worry weighing on her, Beth glances into the kitchen. "Donovan, who's still out there?"

Under the soft sound of sizzling food, Donovan slaves away over the stove top, a tea towel draped over one shoulder and a spatula firmly in his grasp. From a three-step ladder nearby, Neil pays close attention. *Neil would have died if I hadn't been there.*

Donovan speaks over his shoulder. "We're waiting for Sadie, Gina, and your uncle James's family, and then we'll pack up. Head to Haven."

Beth's eyes keenly observe Liam's reaction when Sadie's name comes up. A wave of tension passes through him causing his eyebrows to furrow. Without missing a beat, Alex squeezes Liam's shoulder. Beth hopes, for Liam's sake, Sadie shows soon, or he'll go AWOL. And she prays her uncle's family will be alright as she glances at Neil. Her uncle's youngest child is Neil's age.

Ryker squeezes her hand, drawing her eyes back to his handsome face. He gives Beth a soft smile.

She returns the sentiment and glances back at the kitchen. "Gina can't be far behind me. She was waiting for Sadie." Beth turns back to Liam. "How about your family, Liam?"

"Jessie and Steven called Dad from Spain before everything went down." He toys with the book in front of him. "Don't expect to see them again."

She hopes that's not true. *They must find a way home.* The prospect of Hoss losing another child weighs on her. Liam's mention of Steven brings John Henry to mind. "I saw the entry from John Henry. Did he make it with Rita and Lisa?"

"Yeah."

So many people to worry about. Beth's grateful her uncle created this place for them. Without Parker, they wouldn't be here. They survived the trek, but what about their future? How are they going to keep afloat? "What about Jose and Sophia? Saw the family's entry."

The sound of Donovan scraping the pan with the spatula comes to an abrupt stop. He transfers hash browns to a plate, hands it to Neil, and squirts a small mound of ketchup on it. "That's all there is to it, Little Man. Head to the table with that."

She smiles at the new nickname they have for Neil. He appears to be less scared of the men today as he settles next to her at the table with his breakfast. She brushes his hair aside, needing the connection, as he digs in.

"Beth, come into the pantry." Donovan turns the stove off and disappears through the door between the kitchens.

That didn't sound good. The men around the table avoid her questioning eyes. On instinct, she reaches for the smooth surface of the cold metal necklace under her fingers. With a concerned expression, Ryker extends his hand, and she accepts his offering. Beth's anxiety builds with each step closer to the pantry. Sophia and Jose would have been at the diner when it happened. Everyone had their own escape plans. Theirs would have been gathering the four kids and making the trek to Reed. She doesn't want to hear what she thinks Donovan's going to say. They've got to be alright. She saw their entry, didn't she?

Hands in his pockets, Donovan's fascination with the pantry floor scares her. He's never like this. When his eyes slide up, she knows she has to prepare herself. Her chest tightens, pulse quickens. Ryker envelopes his arms around her, bracing her. *Please, God, no...*

"Jose was in terrible shape when he showed." He shifts his gaze to Ryker. "Sophia didn't make it."

Beth covers her escaping gasp and crumples in Ryker's arms, clutching his shirt. Memories flood her mind as she weeps: Sophia laughing at the diner with customers, and barbecues in Donovan's backyard. Her smile, the way she called everyone hon. Jose and her fooling around in the kitchen like sex-crazed teenagers. *Apple pie.*

***

Ryker places a gentle kiss on the inside of Beth's palm as he leads her down the corridor, giving her time to compose herself. He's so gentle with her, and the passion between them is undeniable. Does she love Ryker?

He pulls out the chair next to Neil for her. Sympathy radiates from the guys around the table, and Beth realizes they've already had time to grieve for Sophia in their own way. Her thoughts steer toward Jose. *This will have crushed him.* She wonders how their children are faring.

Neil must be feeling the mood swing because he runs over to hug her. "It'll be okay," he says. *Sweet and sensitive.*

The boy takes her hand and leads her to the chair, then seats himself, picks up a handmade paper airplane, and swings it around. Everyone returns to their devices, and the mood shifts back to normal.

"En passant." The twins' chess game attracts her away from her mournful thoughts. Alex reaches across to take Miles's rook and conjures a satisfied smile on his face.

"This is quite a setup," Ryker says with a flourish of his hand.

Liam smirks. "If you think this is impressive, wait till you see Haven."

Haven. Beth wipes her nose on her sleeve. Their new home now. She mourns the loss of her old life. The apartment, the diner, and the people she has lost. Sophia was like a mother to her in a lot of ways. She was sweet to Beth, but she pushed, too. Sophia urged her to stand up for herself and take life by the horns. Something Beth struggles with. She truly appreciated working alongside Sophia. Tears threaten to spring forth, but she breathes in and squeezes her nose, containing her emotion for a little longer.

Miles moves another piece on the board. "Farming's going to be a bitch to secure."

Farming. *How are we going to learn what to do without starving first?* They have an extensive stockpile of food, but it won't last forever. The whole reason they were reuniting up at Haven that weekend before the missiles was to help Parker and the guys with planting the seed. The year before, the crops had failed, and it didn't surprise anyone; none of them knew how to farm. Hoss had responded by saying, "That's what that YouTube thing is for."

Adapt, improvise, and overcome. This is the way they come at any problem, and Beth loves them for it.

"Why?" Ryker asks.

"It's a lot of acreage to oversee. We aren't the only people heading into the wilds to escape the cities. And we have more than most. You'll see."

Penny comes out of her apartment, peruses the food on the table, beholds Beth, then looks at Ryker. "Don told you?"

An audible intake of air leads Beth back down the road to tears, and Penny hugs her. She is a nurturer, unlike Sophia. Penny grieved the loss of her husband around the same time Beth's life changed. After Beth tried to take her life a year later, Penny recognized their shared predicaments and came out from under her veil of mourning. Through their shared, unhealable wounds, they supported each other, emerging even closer. At the time, Beth didn't see it, but Parker and Penny filled the void her parents left behind.

Penny smooths Beth's hair. "I'm sorry, Beth. We'll all miss her." She takes the empty seat on the other side of Ryker. "Alejo's up late. I could use a boost."

Alejo's coffee. This perks Beth up. But she's not surprised he's still in bed; she's never seen Alejo up early. He argues he gets up early but it takes a long time to look that hot. The thought puts a tiny smile on her face.

Donovan transfers hash browns to a plate. "What can I make you, Pen? Powdered eggs? Bacon and hash browns?"

"Bacon and hash will do," Penny replies.

"And Ryker, what do you want?"

"The same for me," he says and rubs Beth's hand. The intense hunger in his eyes evokes the vivid memory of their passionate encounter that morning, igniting a fiery desire within her. *Getting hot again.* Heat flares in his brown depths. *God, can he read my mind?*

Swallowing, she focuses back on the chess game. Alex makes a move and gazes up at his brother with a see-how-you-get-out-of-this look. Beth grins despite the sadness swirling inside her. Focusing on them helps. Miles cautiously rubs his chin. Beth glances at the board. *Take the queen.*

The aroma of oranges drags her out of Ryker's arms, and she glances down at a plastic glass of orange juice. Beth follows the hand that brought it and gazes up at Colin's handsome face.

"From Donovan," he says, through the tail end of disappointment, before a wide grin graces his square jaw.

Beth returns the sentiment.

A longing gaze betrays his outward appearance before he breaks eye contact and kisses the top of her head. "Morning, sunshine." She lets him caress her cheek and trail gentle fingers down to cup her chin. "Sorry about Sophia." His eyes come up to Ryker in challenge before he walks away.

Colin! Not able to do anything about his feelings, she refocuses on the chess game. Miles takes Alex's queen. *Touché.* Alex's expression falls.

Beth catches Ryker narrowing his eyes as Colin moves away. She doesn't know how to deal with jealousy. It's an emotion she used to have with her sister, but they were children. These are two grown men. She gazes down at the juice and sighs. Beth would like to think Donovan views her as one of his daughters. He's a hard-ass sometimes but then he does something sweet like this, warming her from the inside. "Thanks, Donovan."

"Anything to make my Chickie happy." His words invoke the feeling of a blanket being wrapped around her with love.

Neil is busy folding paper beside her. He's hers now, no matter the way he fell into her world. Sometimes, she wonders if things happen for a reason. Was this the answer to her cry for death?

He peers up at her and smiles, then returns to his paper airplanes, which now litter the table. She's happy there is something for him to play with and takes the juice in hand. "I love orange juice," she says to him. "So...much!" They have other substitutes, but it won't be long before they run out of the fresh stuff.

Liam peeks over his book. "Freakishly so."

Beth sticks her tongue out at him.

The oldest of her "cousins," she met Liam when he was seventeen. She likes his powerful sense of justice and compassion for others. At Donovan's various barbecues, Liam didn't tease her like his three younger brothers did. Instead, they talked. He had a way of bringing her out of her shyness. He enlisted the year she lost her family.

Liam laughs her off, then returns to his book. Beth teases him by raising the glass to her lips and moaning with pleasure. Ryker enjoys the show, while Liam rolls his eyes and grumbles.

Under an enormous sigh of defeat, Alex says, "*Scheisse*. Mate in four moves."

There is a smile plastered on Miles's face. "Actually, in three."

"What? How?" Alex studies the board, twisting his lips in concentration.

Everyone makes Beth feel more at home, and she upends the glass.

The light goes on in Alex's head. "Well, I'll be—"

Colin slams a cereal box down on the table.

Beth jumps, and juice dots her shirt. *What the hell, Colin?*

Ryker shifts and points his accusing eyes toward Colin. Liam and the twins sit forward, alert, and brace for a fight. Neil sidles up to Beth and squirms his way under her arm. Ryker loses Beth's hand as she smooths away Neil's fears by stroking his head.

All eyes turn to Colin.

CHAPTER 39

Colin drags a chair out from under the table, causing a sharp, grating sound to pierce the air. Once seated, he pours a generous amount of cereal into a bowl. "Beth's never mentioned you." He scoops a spoonful into his mouth while directing a resentful gaze at his rival.

What is wrong with you? Beth opens her mouth to give him a piece of her—

"No? Hmm." Ryker turns to Beth, then glances at Neil under a veil of calmness. "Beth and I met two weeks ago at the diner." He slides calm eyes to Colin. "I've heard you're good...friends."

Okay, everyone, calm down.

Colin's lips purse flat, creating a thin line of tension on his face. She feels the weight of his accusing gaze as his eyes slide over to her.

What was that for?

"Cool it!" Donovan slaps a plate of food in front of Ryker, startling Beth. He drops plates for Beth and Penny, as well, on the way to his seat at the end of the table. He swings a leg over the chair next to Penny, plops down with a fork poised over his plate, and eyeballs Colin and Ryker, daring them to disobey that order before taking a stab.

Beth encourages Neil to continue with the plane making. The twins arrange the chessboard pieces and start another game. Liam lifts his book, and everyone else digs into their food in silence.

Donovan. Always the voice of reason. He commands the room when he enters. Everyone toes the line, and no one ever challenges him. As a teenager, he intimidated Beth until she found his soft spot. His girls.

A metal door clicks closed, echoing slightly, and is followed by the rhythmic sound of boots slapping stairs as two distinct voices grow louder. Beth stares down the corridor along with the others.

Hoss and William, dressed in tactical gear, saunter into the kitchen with an air of confidence. Hoss is carrying a sniper rifle across his strong shoulders and follows William into the weapons room to unload, calling out without a glance, "Oorah!"

The guys and Ryker respond in kind. Colin marks Ryker's reply with scorn.

The year after her world crashed, Hoss and William influenced her more than the rest of her dads. Amid the tension between Ryker and Colin, she fights the sudden urge to run and bury herself in their safe arms.

The two men swagger back out lighter.

Hoss halts and sniffs the air, wearing a T-shirt that reads, *Hold on... Let me overthink this shit*, and says, "God, I miss recon! What the hell do I smell, Osmond?"

Unable to sit any longer, Beth wipes her face and springs up from the chair. Even though she talked to William last night, his eyes light up, and an enormous smile appears. "Hey, look what the cat dragged in!"

"Holy shit, if it isn't my Little Chickie! Come in for a squeeze, baby girl!" Hoss gestures for her, acting like he didn't know she was here.

She runs. William tosses her around first, then his concern shows. He brings her in close. "Donovan told you?" Beth confirms with a sad nod. "It's a blow we all feel." He gets in another bear hug before he hands her over like she weighs nothing.

Hoss squeezes her and says, "A sight for sore eyes! I was thinkin' of sendin' out a search party. Can't marry you off if I can't find ya." His eyes pass over Ryker. "Who's the guy?"

Always direct and unapologetic. And yet, Beth loves him because he doesn't push her but gives her space and guidance when she asks for it. Above all, Hoss makes her laugh. She glances down. *Love the shirt.*

Catching her gaze, he smirks.

When her dads interrogated Colin at the dance studio, Hoss took her aside and asked if she wanted to learn some defensive moves. She was a Tae Kwon Do student before the accident, so she said yes. It's been very interesting and entertaining.

Spotting something beyond her, Hoss's eyes light up. *Neil.* He points an accusing finger Neil's way. "Whoa, who are you?" He has the same soft spot as Donovan.

Neil crawls on hands and knees and takes shelter in Ryker's lap, looking terrified, while everyone around the table stifles grins at his expense.

Not fazed by Neil's apprehension, Hoss plops down with Beth securely in his lap at the end of the table. "Let me guess. George Washington?" With a serious expression, Neil shakes his head. "George Clooney?"

This gets a reaction and a childish giggle. "No, my name is Neil."

Hoss narrows his eyes in contemplation. "Hmm." He eyes the paper airplanes on the table. "You building airplanes?" This gets him a nod, but Neil stays put. "Watch this." Hoss picks up one of the finished planes, not taking his eyes off Neil as he bends some angles. With each fold, Neil's eyes widen at the miraculous transformation until he crawls back to his seat under Hoss's slow smirk. Hoss tosses a fighter jet Neil's way.

Internally, Beth laughs; a spectator who appreciates Hoss's way of making friends with children.

"You make more of these, and I'll show you how to turn 'em into all sorts of things. I'm gifted that way." He reaches across Beth's lap and tousles Neil's hair.

William approaches Ryker and asks, "What year were you born?"

This is William throwing Ryker off, but she's impressed when Ryker answers without missing a beat. "Nineteen ninety-eight."

"Hmm, did you know the Yankees won that year?"

"Defeated San Diego, right?"

William lends his hand to shake Ryker's before walking around the table, keeping one eye on Hoss. William raises an eyebrow. Hoss waves him off. These men are different in their ways of accepting people. She guesses it was a thumbs-up.

Alex offers William his seat. "Duty calls."

Hoss holds up a hand in midair. The twins slap him on the way past as he says, "It's been quiet the last two days, but keep vigilant." Not missing a beat, Hoss directs a question to Ryker. "How you figure in with Beth?"

Donovan answers quickly, "Ryker's Beth's boyfriend. Neil's hers, too."

Keeping his eyes on Ryker, Hoss leans into Beth and whispers with a grin, "Glad to hear you're gettin' laid."

Her hands leap to her face. "Oh my God, Hoss!" She glances at Neil, hoping he doesn't understand the phrase, but he's busy unfolding the plane Hoss made for him. She relaxes.

Ryker busts a gut laughing, then quickly flinches and clenches his jaw.

In equal measure, bitterness darkens Colin's face.

"And he's a Marine, too. I could cry." Hoss puffs up with pride.

Of course he would. According to Hoss, there are three kinds of men: Marines, the other branches, and everyone else. She knew he'd be okay with Ryker from the start.

Beth takes a seat between Neil and Ryker, leans into him, and whispers, "How'd you know the answer?"

Her ear tickles under Ryker's whispered response. "My dad was a big Yankees fan."

"On your birthday, you didn't mention a boyfriend on the phone, Chickie," Hoss says, his way of giving her a hard time. He winks down the length of the table. Beth follows his gaze to a blushing Penny. *Who said old dogs couldn't learn new tricks?* She wonders if that meant Penny said yes.

Beth avoids looking in Colin's direction. She doesn't want to answer but she has no other choice. "I didn't know Ryker, then." Technically, she didn't when they called.

"How'd you find him? Can't be too many of our kind wanderin' around in the forest."

"She picked a fight with the trash I was—" Ryker's eyes slide to Neil. "—tracking."

Donovan narrows his gaze, the mood at the table shifts, and silence saturates the room.

Having finished her breakfast, Penny lays the utensils on her plate and gets up. "Neil, I have a few games in my room. Let's go find something to play."

Neil refers to Beth for permission, and she grants it with a smile. He swipes his arms across the table, collects his planes, and jumps up with an armload.

Donovan thanks Penny with a squeeze of her hand before she leaves the table. She graces him with a tender smile, takes Neil by the hand, and enters her suite. When the door closes, Donovan focuses back on Ryker. "Tracking?"

"More like depriving them of their existence," Ryker says with a hint of disgust.

Hoss leans forward, all business, and asks, "How many?"

"There were four."

With wide eyes, Hoss asks, "Only four? Are you sure you're a Marine?"

"I was taking my time with them on purpose."

Colin's face turns white, and his eyes dart to Beth. She understands what Ryker did. His sister deserves justice. *So does Carrie.*

Donovan slides his plate forward and clasps his hands, fingers laced, on the table as he asks, "Why?"

"It's amazing the pain you can inflict on someone when you're defending your sister's honor."

"Respect, brother," Hoss pipes in. "That's how you got the injury?" Hoss exchanges a troubled look with Donovan.

"Yes, but I'll deal. I'm not done. Two left. I'm here to charge up before finishing the mission."

She doesn't want him to leave, but this is something he needs to do. What those men did deserves punishment. If they were in the normal world, the law would take care of them, but in this new world, there is no law. Deep down, she's scared. What if he gets wounded again? Who will look out for him out there? He won't ask for help. Perhaps she should approach Donovan later.

Catching Colin's acute focus on Beth, Hoss says, "Hey, Twinkle-Toes! Looks like Beth's in expert hands."

Colin's chair scrapes the floor. Bristling with bitterness, he leaves the table without a word and stomps off toward the gym.

Damn it, Hoss. She doesn't believe in kicking someone when they're down.

Hoss smiles back at her. "Now that *mia famiglia* knows I'm here, I'm gonna rack out!" He gets up and points at Donovan across the table. "Osmond, you gonna make mac for lunch?"

Donovan waves his hand in a ya-ya response.

Hoss fist pumps his approval, swaggers to the men's dorm, stops, turns, and points at Ryker. "By the way, good one scorin' Beth. But, brother—"

"I already gave him the speech!" Donovan says.

Hoss moves his finger back to Donovan. "You the man!" Then he swaggers into the men's dorm.

Half awake, Alejo stumbles out of the girl's dorm in a pink bathrobe. "Who keeps shouting?"

The thought of her future coffee perks Beth up, causing her to smile in anticipation just as Hoss sticks his head out again.

Alejo shrieks as his hands fly to his face. "Holy crap, honey, you need a trim on that hunk-o beard, but otherwise, you're doing it for me in a bear kinda way."

Hoss leans on the door frame, thumbs in his belt loops, with a cocky grin. "Well, you make me that Foxtrot coffee, A, and I'll let you trim me shirtless."

Alejo's expression turns serious. "Fuck, honey, I'll be ready in ten!"

Everyone laughs as Hoss flees with uncanny quickness, and Alejo jumps to the kitchen with gusto.

The alarm blares. Ryker stiffens next to her. Donovan and Liam burst into action, heading toward the security room.

"Going to see what's up." Ryker kisses Beth and follows.

She turns her attention to the gym.

***

Gideon wipes his brow and enjoys the warmth of sunlight on his skin. He'd forgotten how much farming takes out of a man. They need more workers. With his hoe supporting him, he gazes at his blisters and winces as he flexes his hand. If his grandfather could see them, he'd say Gideon is becoming soft. *Dick.*

"Gideon," Wendall's voice echoes across the field. Gideon turns. Wendall stands in the area between the house and the barn.

Gideon lets the hoe fall to the ground and casually walks up to his brother. "Yeah, what?"

"You hold the fort down till Hunter and I get back."

Confusion overshadows Gideon's excitement. "From where?"

"Hutchison Farm."

That farm girl from way back? His brother can't be that stupid, can he? It's been over ten years since Wendall laid eyes on her. Gideon would never voice it out loud, but she's likely married and popped out a dozen kids by now. Certainly not worth going after. Instead, Gideon asks, "For Kessie? Why?"

Wendall stares down his challenge. "I'm bringing back her relatives and hired hands to work the farm."

Gideon lowers his eyes. *Fucking hell.* "They'll sabotage us at every turn."

"Can't sabotage what you need to survive." He has a point, but still...

"Why you bringing Hunter?"

Hunter ran away as a teenager. Wendall searched high and low for him but came up short. Gideon never understood Wendall's need to find Hunter. If he didn't want to be a part of this family, then good riddance. It would be just one fewer brother Gideon had to compete with. But Wendall is tenacious, and one day, he returned to the farm accompanied by a gloomy-looking Hunter. When Gideon inquired about the matter, Wendall remained tight-lipped, and that had marked the end of the conversation. Gideon, not one to shy away from uncovering the truth, confronted Hunter. All he gleaned was that something had transpired between Wendall and Kessie's father. The mystery of Hunter's involvement intrigued Gideon, but he never unraveled it.

"Leverage, Gideon, leverage."

The desire to ask why burns within him, but Wendall's violent tendencies make Gideon think twice about provoking him.

"Try not to mess things up while we're gone," Wendall says before walking away.

Chapter 40

Liam perches on a chair, his finger resting on the talk button of the mic. Behind him, Donovan stands, gazing down his nose at the security monitor display in front of them. Ryker leans in for a closer look. Feeling a little shocked, but pleased, he sees a confident Mal staring back at him through the security camera above the entrance. If he didn't know any better, he'd say his brother looks like he's just hopped off a motorcycle with what he's wearing. *Looks like Mal's attitude hasn't changed after all this time.* His brother always appears undaunted by what life throws at him. Ryker's never been able to get through Mal's exterior but he's sure that what's underneath is anything but confident.

Over the radio, one twin says, in a hollow voice, "He's armed but approached with confidence, like he knows where he's going. Does he have a code?"

Liam speaks into the mic. "No."

Ryker says, "He won't. Mal's my older brother."

Donovan faces Ryker, crossing his arms in scary sergeant fashion. "How'd he find us?"

Ryker reins in his need to flinch as he straightens and meets Donovan's gaze. "Mal rendezvoused with the men I was tracking. He was on the wrong team, so I gave him an out and let him follow me here."

"Let him?" Donovan holds out an open palm. "Hold on, I have people to protect here. You trust him?" He points at the monitor.

I used to. "In this matter, yeah."

Liam swivels in the chair. "How can you be sure? He could still be in their camp."

I'm not. "Because I have the advantage."

Ryker watches Donovan weigh up his options. Trust is everything to men like Donovan, and Ryker can tell he doesn't give it easily. Now, the question is, does he trust Ryker? *Maybe he shouldn't.* His brothers in his unit did and look where that got them?

"The first sign of trouble and he's out." Donovan pushes a button, and the buzzer sounds.

Ryker breathes out the tension he's been holding in, grateful for Donovan's answer. He's relieved and humbled by the trust being shown. "Understood."

Ryker turns to the monitor. Mal steps inside cautiously, not letting the door close behind him just yet.

Liam gestures for Ryker to take the mic. He hasn't spoken with his brother in twelve years and, as his finger hovers over the talk button, he's at a loss for what to say. This is the one person who protected him growing up, the one who stood strong when their lives fell apart, the one Ryker looked up to.

He shakes his head and says to Liam, "You give him the speech."

***

Mal yanks the laundered Henley over his head and tunnels his arms down the soft sleeves. He runs his hands down the wood-finished cabinet, which offers various sizes of clothing. Mal's curious to know what this place is for. There was no sign that this bunker existed on the outside. When the tracks led him under the waterfall, Mal wasn't sure if it was a dead end or a trap. It took a moment for him to have the guts to walk through the steady flow of water; whoever thought of hiding this place underneath it was a genius. One thing's for sure: Ry's tracking skills have improved since their childhood. It wasn't easy, but Mal concluded his brother had wanted him to follow while trying to slow him down; didn't want him catching up too quickly. But why?

Carrying his unloaded weapon in a bag, Mal dumps his stolen biker clothes into the basket and strolls into what looks like a security room.

Ryker grabs Mal's attention immediately by stepping forward and saying, "Give the bag to Donovan."

When this request had come from the disembodied voice at the front door, it hadn't been to Mal's liking. He'd kept the metal shiv he'd acquired back at the prison in his boot, not wanting to be exposed while greeting whoever was on the other side. Prison taught him paranoia well. Always expect the worst in people and you're never disappointed when it happens.

He assesses the room and the two men in it. The unfriendly man next to Ryker screams military and stands like his father used to, hands clasped out front. His likeness to Mal's namesake elbows him into nervous territory. All of a sudden, this is a place Mal doesn't want to be; it's exposing painful feelings of loss over his old man.

Mal sighs and drops the bag on the desk. He's never enjoyed being told what to do, and it's stranger still that the order is coming from his little brother. He remembers a different Ryker growing up. He was seventeen and shorter when they parted, but he's sprouted since then; high in stature and able-bodied. *It's been too long, brother.*

Ryker brings him in for a hug. Mal softens, pulls back, looks Ryker up and down, and gives his jaw a shake. "Good hit, Ry. You've improved. It shocked me to see the message."

"Likewise, to see you with those animals."

Mal breaks their contact to gaze upon all that is Donovan and says, "Had no choice. It was go with them or die in jail."

Donovan crosses his arms and frowns. The crew cut gives away his obvious occupation, and the cold-shoulder rubs Mal the wrong way. *This one's right-*

eous. Mal's stepfather looked at him like this after Mal caught Elias hurting his mother.

"In jail? What for?" Ryker asks point blank.

Mal wanders the perimeter of the room. The dark screens behind the old man say they don't trust him with their security yet. He wouldn't either, but then, Mal knows who he is. So does Ryker.

"They thought I was guilty of stealing something," he lies. A little one. He stole something, but it wasn't an object. It was a life.

Ryker crosses his arms. "Care to elaborate?"

Disapproval is something Mal understands and knows well enough to ignore. He leans on the desk across from them. "Nope. Nice security."

Ryker's eyes dip down as he asks, "And did you steal something?"

If Ry wants to play Twenty Questions like his asshole stepfather, Mal will fire back short, vague answers. "They thought so."

"Where were you when the missile dropped?"

The question invokes the claustrophobic feeling of the cell he was stuck in, the smell of gunpowder, and the ultimatum Wendall gave him. The uncomfortable memory causes Mal to shift as he says, "Trapped in a jail cell."

"Which prison?"

Mal hesitates to answer, then decides he has nothing to be ashamed about. "Doleridge."

Ryker's eyes widen. "A maximum security prison?"

Tell me something I don't know.

"How'd you get out?"

Mal appreciates the concern that crosses his brother's face, but not wanting to expand further, Mal perches on the desk and reclines backward on his hands to stare directly at Ryker. "Rescued by other prisoners. They were free, and I wasn't."

His brother pauses, tilting his head. "How'd you shake those men?"

Switching tactics? At last. "Didn't have to. They wanted me to track you. I did. Look, who's the dead girl to you?"

The ever-silent Donovan seizes the opportunity to speak. "I'll give you the room."

Were we boring you with our banter, old man?

Ryker nods, and Mal relaxes as the grumpy old man exits. He detests authority figures; they remind him of Elias. He says, "Heard you have an injury."

Mal's surprised when Ryker says, "It hurts like hell."

His concern comes to the forefront as he eyes his younger brother up and down. *Seems to be alright.* Ryker lifts his shirt and exposes his bandage.

Shit. "It looks like hell. You going to be okay?" Mal asks out of concern.

"People have shot at me before."

It isn't right that his brother says it's normal to be wounded. When Mal's twin, Krystal, said she was running away, he told her she wasn't going without him, but they couldn't leave Ryker with Elias. They waited until he was old enough to enlist, then they all ran. "Didn't hear from you. Thought you were dead. You still serving?"

"Got out a couple of months ago."

Mal leans forward, placing forearms on his thighs. "Message was cryptic. You didn't need to knock me out."

"I needed to know where your loyalty was."

A wide smile graces Mal's face. "Well, you know me. In the wind."

Ryker gives Mal a once-over. "I do. Where's Krystal?"

Mal covers his hand in shame. Guess now's as good as any other time to unload his failure. His twin. The one person he should have protected. *I fucked it up.* Mal glances around, anywhere but at Ryker, when he says, "While I was on the inside, her boyfriend got her hooked on heroin. Sis OD'd back in 2019."

After the lamentable pause Mal expected, Ryker says, "They say twins feel things."

A pain I can never heal. "They're right, I felt it." Mal lowers his gaze, disgraced. "And when I got out, I made her shit-bag boyfriend feel it, too." He mumbles under his breath, "It was worth doing time for that."

"You won't like what I have to say."

Mal becomes suspicious and straightens up. *What could be worse than not being able to save your sister?*

"Those animals killed Libby."

Mal slumps, head bowed in disbelief. The blow strikes him with the force of a freight train. *What the fuck!* He recalls Kaden's words, "We all took our turns," and exhales. Mal fluctuates from anger to sadness. *She was only, what, twenty?* He clenches his fists, and his nostrils flare. *Innocent.* His dark eyes come up to Ryker's. "She was with you?"

"Yeah. After I got out, I moved in with her. We escaped the city together."

Mal discerns Ryker's haunted stare. *Like looking in a fucking mirror.* "If she was with you, how did they get to her?"

Ryker averts his eyes. "It was my fault. She didn't understand the danger. Walked away while I slept."

He understands Ryker's burden all too well, but he's lived with his guilt longer.

"I should have…" Ryker's tortured gaze lifts to Mal. For a beat, their eyes connect with grief.

"I know where they're going. When do you want to head out?"

"Tomorrow. I have to leave Beth here."

Mal sits back. *Beth?* He sniffs trouble where women are concerned, sensing manipulation when they get all touchy-feely. Like a noose. "Who are these people?"

"Beth's family and friends. I vouched for you, so don't fuck it up for me."

He recognizes the anxiousness in his brother's eyes and smiles. "For you? Ry's got a girl. Go figure." *Sucker.* Mal never thought he'd see the day his gangly, pimple-faced brother would have a girl, much less a woman. He can't wait to meet the one Ryker's taken with.

"Wait till you find yours, then you'll be in trouble."

"Fuck that! I don't want to be trapped." *I won't hand my heart to a woman again.*

***

Alejo holds a mirror aloft as Donovan comes back into the corridor. Bare-chested, sitting in a chair, Hoss inhales the steam coming off his mug of coffee. He checks his neatly trimmed beard in that same mirror and says, "Outstanding, A."

A front view of Hoss's chest reveals a mass of tattoos Donovan's familiar with. The outline of a great white shark circles his right chest, and a panther circles the names of ten children over his left chest. Hoss believed in meanings so the tattoos weren't random. A skull and crossbones adorned the middle of his abs in black outline. He only had one that was in color.

Donovan reclines against the counter with his arms crossed. Ever since Hoss first tasted Alejo's coffee, he's been saying it's ruined any other coffee for him. Donovan admits Alejo's coffee is to die for but he doesn't enjoy catering to Alejo's ego too much. He thinks Hoss has a secret crush on Alejo, but he hasn't been able to nail that down yet. Wouldn't surprise him, though. Hoss likes everyone. Except Colin, which Donovan aims to change. *Two birds with one stone.*

Alejo turns the mirror and flatters himself in its depths. "I am." Looking pleased with himself, Alejo rounds up his salon stuff and kisses Hoss's cheek. "Enjoy, hon." He skips to the women's dorm.

Hoss eyes Donovan up and down. They've known each other long enough; shared difficulties in life as friends first, then as brothers-in-arms. Hoss can always tell when something's up.

Donovan doesn't waffle. "I need you to take Colin under your wing."

"I'm…" Hoss cups his ear. "Sorry, I thought I heard somethin' funny come outta your mouth."

Donovan knows why Hoss doesn't like Colin, which is why he's perfect. He just has to convince Hoss he's right for the job. "When we get to Haven, we're going to need more security."

"Why do we, sorry, I need to give him direction?" he counters.

Despite Colin's love for Beth, Donovan thinks he's a good guy. Now that Ryker's in the picture, Colin will need a distraction. The last thing Donovan needs is another problem on his hands; he's got enough to deal with. The image of his two girls skipping toward him—one is dirty blonde, and the other, auburn colored—comes to the forefront. He tucks that vision aside for safekeeping. "You're the only one who can relate to him."

"Relate to a yoga-dancer? What the hell you talkin' about?" he sputters.

Guess I'm going there. "Two words: your ex."

Hoss raises his hands in protest. "Really? You're going there?"

Hoss's ex did a number on him, which he hasn't forgiven her for. Donovan smirks. *He's going to resist now.*

"You know I don't like him." Hoss paces in front of the chair he was sitting in moments before.

"You don't like him 'cause he's got the hots for Beth, yet you're okay with Ryker?"

Hoss stops and holds his hands out, palms up. "He's a fucking Marine!"

"We can mold Colin into one, too."

Hoss juts his chin out. "Maybe he don't wanna be one."

"Only one way to find out." *Wait him out, Masters.*

Donovan can see Hoss wrestling with that thought. It bounces around his friend's head as he weighs the pros and cons, but in the end, Donovan knows he's right. Colin's no slouch. He's fit, young, and works with his hands.

Resigned to his fate, Hoss rolls his eyes as a big sigh escapes. "God damn, you're an asshole, you know that?"

Donovan shoots a rare, endearing smile Hoss's way. "I know, but I'm your asshole."

"Fuck, man, that sounds so wrong." He's annoyed, but Hoss laughs anyway.

Chapter 41

"You're going to need a thick skin around Hoss." Beth's voice echoes in the gym space.

Eyes closed, Colin meditates on a gym mat and doesn't respond. He used to be happy when he heard her voice, but now he wants her to leave.

He visualizes her the day they went on their first date. Beth was a vision in a blue dress and dainty flats. Her lengthy brown hair, clipped high, cascaded in wavy locks around her shoulders, framing that beautiful smile for him. He'd hoped they would be a couple. Then Beth shows up with this Marine guy, whom she barely knows. *Taking what's mine.*

He opens his lovesick eyes only to regret it. Beth leans against the rail on the mirrored wall across from him. Her beauty and sensuality strike him a devastating blow, reminding him he's not the one she moans for. She did when he kissed her that night. The thought of it still stirs him; being her first, it's like a drug. His eyes caress her hourglass curves, landing on those sensual green eyes he loves so much. He recognizes the sympathy in them; it pierces his heart. Anger comes to the surface as he asks, "What's he got that I don't?" Rejection hurts. *How did I end up here again?*

"Don't be like that."

"What's wrong with me, Beth?" *Wasn't good enough for Amy, either.*

"There's nothing wrong with you."

He gazes away. "I hoped with a little time, you'd change your mind." Amy refused his proposal after two years of living together; she wasn't ready to settle down, she'd said. It crushed him; took him a year to move on. Cut him so deep that he ended up leaving Portland to try to escape the memories.

"It wasn't in the cards for us," she says.

Since their first date, she's fought against the idea of them being a couple. He's been too blind to realize it, desperate as he was to have someone in his life. Someone who truly loves and wants him. *She's trying not to hurt me, but it does.*

Spokane was supposed to be a fresh start, but he rushed things with Beth. Seems he isn't ready, either, but he can't just turn his feelings off. Living in close quarters with her at Haven might kill him. *How can I go forward?* He doesn't like the situation but he's not ready to accept it or Ryker, either. "If he hurts you—"

Hoss strides into the gym with purpose and a scowl of disapproval. "Beth, can you give us a minute? I need to talk to Colin."

Great, just what I need right now.

Astonishment crosses Beth's face as much as it crosses Colin's, but she hugs the bastard and says, "I'll leave you to it, then." In the same breath, she points a finger in his face. "Be nice." She may not be Colin's girlfriend but she is still in his corner. It comes as no consolation to him.

Hoss follows her as she walks away with his eyes. *What could he possibly want to talk about?* Sitting cross-legged, Colin glares up at Hoss and waits. The constipated look Hoss directs back at Colin doesn't ease his resentment for the man.

But then, there's a shift. Hoss takes an audible breath and concentrates on the floor. Hands in his pockets, apparently reluctant to speak but resigned, Hoss forges ahead in a flat monotone voice, like he's reading off a cue card. "We're gonna need more security. You interested? I've got the skills and I know there's a brain in there somewhere."

Colin stares deadpan at Hoss. Of all the things to say, he didn't expect that! "Wow, your skill at winning me over is incredible." His eyes narrow. "Did you lose a bet?" *Could be a trap.*

Hoss raises an eyebrow. "What?"

"You never talk to me. You must have lost a bet." There's no way Hoss would volunteer out of the goodness of his heart to do anything for Colin.

Hoss's lips twist and he sighs. "Cut the shit, boy. You in or not?"

Colin laughs. "You really lost a bet, didn't you? Donovan?" He's curious to know how Donovan strong-armed Hoss into it. Must have been a doozy.

Hoss glares back at Colin.

He is right, of course. They'll need security up there. On one hand, Colin's competitive side wants to show up Ryker, but in the end, he needs the distraction. Security would get him outside and away from her. His skills as a mechanic will keep him busy, but not all the time. "You've aroused my curiosity, so sure, I'm in."

Hoss's eyebrows rise, satisfying Colin. He enjoys catching the prick off guard.

Hoss throws a knife and says, "Alright, let's see what you can do with that. No time to waste."

Colin catches it easily, disappointed he won't be learning handguns first.

***

Mal follows Ryker out of security and into a long corridor filled with furniture. Nothing special, but the doors interest him. Perhaps when everyone's asleep, he'll cruise the place. The door at the end, past the island kitchen, draws him like a moth to the flame. Reading the word *Pantry* summons up thoughts of food, tantalizing his taste buds and forcing him to swallow. There are certain foods he hasn't tasted in quite a while. Mal wonders if they have ice cream...chocolate.

A pretty woman comes out of one of those rooms and into the corridor, halts, and scrutinizes them. Ryker's demeanor changes in her presence. He closes the distance between them with a slow smile that builds, reaches out to her, and says, "Beth, come meet my big brother, Mal."

Ryker's proud of her and wants to show her off. *So, this is the one.*

Mal's eyes roam over feminine curves that stir his senses as she saunters into Ryker's arms. *Hello.* If there are more women like her here, he'll like this place a hell of a lot more. She looks at him distrustfully, uncertain of what to make of Mal. He wonders what Ryker has told her about his big brother, if anything at all.

Ryker hugs her close, strokes her arm, and whispers in her ear, "I'll catch you up later."

Not much.

Mal's never seen his brother so devoted before. She looks good on him. *Sexy eyes.* Mal goes for his low, husky voice, laying on the charm, not taking his eyes off her as he says, "Wow, a knockout, Ry. I see the appeal."

Beth blushes. *Cute.* Mal doesn't like the virginal types. He fancies women who have a mind of their own with a dash of sass mixed in.

"Don't be fooled by his charms," Ryker says with a twinge of jealousy. *Ripe for the picking.*

Beth's eyes travel up Mal's body. *Of course, she likes what she sees.* He took care of himself, both inside and out of prison, and he took pleasure in flaunting it. *Time for a little teasing.* "I don't know, Ry. Looks like she might prefer me over you."

Ryker glances at her. Her cheeks burn red as she casts her eyes to the floor. Ryker gazes back at him and says, "In your dreams, brother."

Mal laughs as the unfamiliar smile stretches his cheeks. *Oh yeah, this is gonna be fun.*

Chapter 42

Gideon holds court, one arm draped over the back of a dining chair, the other rests on the table, his index finger taps the table top rhythmically. Appearing unfazed, bored almost, Dugal casually leans back in a chair under the lamplight in the dining room. Meanwhile, Kaden stands, eyes downcast like a berated child, opposite an angry Gideon at the head of the dining table. *At least he knows his place.*

So far, Gideon's kept his replies short. He hates losing control. Kaden has recounted his disastrous trip, and Gideon's deciding whether he should kill Dugal or not, but he can't afford to lose the manpower. *Fuck!* He senses a headache coming on. When Wendall finds out, Dugal won't be the only one to suffer his wrath.

His brother took off in the early morning with the vehicles, Hunter, and a few men. The rest of them have finished planting in one pasture and are preparing to break ground on the next one. Wendall sent Cain and a few others out to hunt for more workers, much to Gideon's relief, because he needs time to erase what these idiots did.

Kaden fucked up, but they've been together long enough for Gideon to know where he's at emotionally. Dugal is new. The thought of Wendall's anger mixed with Dugal's attitude pisses Gideon off.

He rakes Kaden over the coals. "First, I told you, no touching. Second, you lost three fucking men I needed! And you?!" He points accusingly at Dugal.

"What the fuck? I need workers, or we don't fucking eat. Pussy was in the cards, but not for you to kill!"

It is pointless to destroy something valuable, and women are a commodity he doesn't have and sorely needs. He wanted to kill whoever let the kidnapped woman escape back in town.

"I got carried away. Happens." Dugal throws out the word like it's no big deal.

Gideon jumps up, crosses the divide, and forces Dugal back. The chair smacks the wall along with Dugal's head. "Shit, doesn't 'happen' to me! You fuck up again and I'll kill you myself. We fucking clear?!"

Dugal, cradling his head, his jaw tight, stares for a beat. "Clear."

Gideon draws up, unclenches his fists, yanks his shirt down, and seizes control over himself. He turns his attention back to a subdued Kaden, his face obscured in shadow. "You brought this lunatic to our door, you idiot!"

"No, Mal's taking care of it."

"Mal?" Another of the men his brother rescued. Mal is too self-confident for Gideon. He's never liked the quiet types.

"He's tracking the problem."

"Alone?" Gideon doesn't like the idea. He doesn't know Mal; can't trust he'll take care of it. If he doesn't return, it'll be another man down. Gideon has no choice but to beef up security with what men he has left, which will further delay the tilling they need to do.

"Yeah, said he'd handle it."

As much as he can't stand Cain, Gideon wishes he was back already; he could use the ex-military guy's expertise right about now. Gideon's not sure Mal has the skills to cope with this stalker, but Cain could erase the problem with efficiency. He's seen it firsthand.

Gideon points an accusing finger at Dugal. "If we get any more women, you're cut off till I say so. Tell me you fucking heard me."

With some hesitancy, Dugal nods.

"Get out!"

***

Beth yawns on the couch, her legs outstretched across Ryker's lap as he strokes lazy circles over her sensitive skin. Gazing between Ryker and Mal, she notes their features are similar. Ryker's hair is lighter and shorter, while Mal, who is taller, carries more muscle and keeps his long, dark hair tied back. He certainly has charm in spades, but she can tell it's a cover. He's guarded in a way Beth has not encountered before.

Alejo preens himself in a pink housecoat next to an unimpressed Mal and runs his fingers through the new man's hair. "This animal has to be tamed, Mallory. Let me do it for you."

Mal swats Alejo's hands away like he would an annoying fly. "Stop touching me. I like it just the way it is. And stop calling me that."

Mal's somewhat sexy voice drew Alejo out of the women's dorm earlier like a magnet.

Alejo looks at her and says, "Someone's a little cranky. Nothing will deter me. Tell him, Beth."

Once he'd closed his gaping jaw, Alejo introduced himself, offered Mal coffee, and gushed over him. But hunky or not, she knows Alejo's distracting himself from the fearful thought that Sean isn't coming back to him.

Beth smirks at Mal's expense. "He'll hound you until you let him."

Mal turns on the charm. "If you hounded me, I'd let you do anything to me."

Ryker pipes in. "Hey, go find your own girl."

Mal's throaty laugh echoes around the corridor.

She glances at Ryker. *Possessive. First Colin, now Mal.* Mal's hot, like a bad-boy hot with his dark looks, but her eyes are only for Ryker. *Can't he see that?*

Mal smirks. "He's just testy 'cause I stole Barbra Stilton away from him in high school."

"You did not!" Ryker says, a tad quickly.

Ah, the piece that completes this puzzle. Makes sense now.

"See...testy," Mal says, but his laughter fades a bit. *Ryker wasn't the only one hurt by Miss Stilton.*

"Who's Barbra Stilton?" Beth asks, not able to resist the tease.

"Ryker, Mal." Donovan pops his head out from security and gestures for them to come in.

"Saved by the old man, Ry?"

Ryker punches Mal's shoulder as they stand up.

"Hey, don't ruin the merchandise. Beth might need me later."

Ryker takes a swing again on their way to security, but Mal sidesteps, and Ryker misses. Mal goads him on with a laugh and a pointed finger in jest.

It all seems so petty now, the fighting. She'd give anything to see her sister again. *Your life?* the voice says. Her smile dies.

Ryker jogs back to Beth, bends, touches his lips to hers, brushes over them, and leaves her breathless. *God, I could get used to this.*

The minute the door clicks closed, Alejo shoots over to Beth in a pink blur and shifts the couch. His head swivels, checking for eavesdroppers, then he whispers, "Okay, start talking."

"Talking? About what?"

"Where in God's name did you find that amazing creature?" He points at the security room.

"You mean Ryker or Mal?"

"Ryker."

How to begin? "Remember the guy at the diner?"

His hands fly to his face. "You're freaking kidding me! How in the world...?"

"I told him at the diner where the farm was. He used the info and escaped the city with his sister to find me."

Alejo leans forward with sad eyes. "Oh, I heard about his sister. I cornered him in the bathroom. Poor thing."

She envisions Alejo doing literally that and stifles a chuckle. She'd missed his levity while trekking through the wilderness.

"What is it with you and Marines, Beth? They're everywhere." He rubs his head on her shoulder and snuggles into her side.

"How you holding up?" she asks.

He fidgets, scraping at the chipped nail polish on his fingernails. "I feel bad."

"Why?"

He rises, looks her straight in the eye, and says, "Sean proposed."

A shot of happy grips Beth as she seeks his hand for support. "When? What did you say?"

Alejo's sad face and droopy mouth give her the answer. Beth's happiness disintegrates. "Oh, A."

"I wasn't sure. I didn't want to get hurt."

Alejo's father left him and his mother when he was twelve, and it left its mark. He's always waiting for the other shoe to drop, afraid Sean will leave him. She thinks this might be the longest relationship Alejo has ever had.

"Sean adores you. He told me it was like the Fourth of July fireworks when he met you two years ago."

"I know."

Beth mulls over something encouraging to say, then remembers Alejo's pep talk in his kitchen, which seems so long ago now. "This is salvageable. When Sean shows, you're going to say yes."

Alejo sends her a tender smile. "You think he'll show?"

"Of course he will," she says, trying to sound hopeful. Inside, she's not.

Her encouragement spurs Alejo on to say, with some sadness, "He won't ask me again."

"No, you're going to ask him."

Alejo shakes his head repeatedly, waving a hand, warding away that image. "No, I can't do that."

Beth holds him to the spot. "A, do you love him?"

Pink spreads through Alejo's cheeks as he stifles a satisfied smile. "Yes. But—"

"There are no buts. A comfort zone is a beautiful place but nothing ever grows there."

Confusion pinches his face. "Where'd you hear that?"

"Next step in therapy: getting out of my zones."

"Getting out, honey?" Alejo waves his hands around. "I think you are the only one benefiting from this scary apocalypse thing. You burst out of that zone with hunky for sure."

***

William and Hoss lounge in chairs in front of the monitors as Donovan takes the empty seat next to them. Ryker rests on the desk, while Mal stands back from the group, preferring to keep his back against the wall. He's never been keen on others being in charge. The only person he trusts is himself. Everyone else has their own agenda, and it never coincides with his.

Alarm bells go off in Mal's head when Donovan faces him with questioning eyes. "These guys you were with. What's their aim?"

Once Mal and the other convicts were on the road to the farm, they robbed places and stole what they needed. Mal was down with that, but when they started kidnapping... That was a line he didn't cross. Ever. "Captives for farming...mostly."

Wendall had had his eye on Mal. He would have run, but Mal's intuition told him to stay. Mal had wanted to help the woman but didn't want to eat a bullet doing it. Things took an interesting turn when Hunter intervened, though.

"Where are they taking them?"

"Wendall and his brothers grew up on a farm. Heard them say they used to hide there when the law was after them. Why?"

"What's the farm look like?"

The old man's questions dredge up a past Mal would like to forget. He hates being grilled, finds it tedious, and it rubs him the wrong way. He glances at Ryker and receives encouragement to answer. "Faded yellow farmhouse. Front porch. Barn."

His minimal answers don't seem to bother the old man. "Is it near a river?"

Mal pushes himself away from the wall with surprise. "Yeah, why?"

Donovan's head drops. "I know where they are." He turns to Hoss. "Parker spotted men in prison orange at the farm the day after we made the trek here. He's been monitoring them for weeks now."

"Thought you buried Haven," Ryker says. "There's a farmhouse?"

Buried? That intrigues Mal.

"Across the river. It's yellow." Donovan says.

Haven. The other bunker they told him about. Another place like this one with more inventory interests him. Could be opportunities there, but he won't get too excited just yet. Mal wants to wait and see where the wind takes him. Hasn't failed him yet.

The alarm blares. His brother flinches, then recovers a second later. *Jumpy?*

Every eye scans the monitors, and Mal follows their lead. A bright white light illuminates two scared children on the security screen. An unwanted memory of Ryker and Krystal jumping up from their seats in the hospital waiting room eats at Mal. Their terrified eyes still haunt him.

Blood drains from Donovan's face. "Fuck! It's—"

"James's kids. Shit!" Hoss slams a wall lock and runs into the shower room.

On the screen, the kids cry out and run into Hoss's welcoming arms. The scene brings back the memory of Mal walking out of his mother's hospital room in a shocked haze, not able to process her dying words yet. His teenage heart hardened in that waiting room, knowing his stepfather hadn't bothered to show and witnessing the torment rip through his siblings as they charged him. He was their lifeline back then; a safe harbor.

Mal slants his head Ry's way. Memories reflect in Ry's eyes, or so Mal would like to think, raising the hair on the back of Mal's neck. He wishes he could forget her words and the promise she made him swear. He doesn't like to admit it, but on that fateful day, his siblings were his lifeline, too.

Chapter 43

With Donovan by his side, Hoss watches Penny tuck James's kids into one bunk bed with tender hands. Understandably, the kids are reluctant to separate from each other, still shaken. "Good thing James taught his kids how to find Reed," he says to Donovan. "There was some kind of distraction. Told them to run here."

"Means they passed us," Donovan says, resting on the opposite side of the doorframe.

Hoss chatted with James's girl, Lily, earlier, while Penny was tending to the boy's cuts. Her message passes through his mind and dredges up dread. Hoss isn't sure how his best friend is going to react, but he has to come clean.

Lily asks a question, and Penny ponders the answer with a finger to her lips. Hoss cherishes those lips.

"Lily said scary men came and took them. James told her they were going to work on a farm."

"Same one?" his friend asks. There are other farms and communities out there on the Idaho landscape. They'll need to catch up to them fast if it's not the one across from Haven. Ryker said he and Mal could track these people, so Hoss's itching to get on that.

Hoss reaches out to brace Donovan for the news. "She mentioned Gina's with them."

Donovan takes the punch to the stomach but only shows it as tiny, almost imperceptible ripples cross his face. Hoss gives his friend credit. He didn't showcase the same control when they found his daughter amid the ashes of her apartment.

"No mention of Brad or Sadie?" Donovan asks.

Hoss shakes his head. "He wants us to hurry 'cause Lani has an infection."

James's meaning spreads between them.

"Let's keep that to ourselves for now," Donovan says. "Sophia's death is still fresh. Beth doesn't need to know her aunt is in danger, too."

Penny shows empty hands to the kids. The boy yanks a book from its hiding spot amid giggles as Penny exclaims surprise and raises her arms in the air. Hoss has kept their relationship on the lowdown for a couple of weeks now.

"Penny's good for you," Donovan says, unearthing his intel. Hoss turns away and scrapes the door frame with his finger. "You don't need to hide it from us."

Hoss shrugs. "Just didn't want you thinkin' badly of me."

Donovan grips Hoss by the shoulder, forcing his friend to glance up. "Hey, Kathryn and John have been gone a long time. Nothing wrong with wanting happiness again. What do your kids think?"

"They figured it out faster than I did." He scratches his neck, then directs Donovan with a palm up and out toward Penny. "What's not to like?"

They both listen as Penny breathes life into the story, and her charges, transfixed, hang on her every word with wonder in their eyes. Penny isn't a Marine, but she knows how to take care of herself. After all, she is the widow of Hoss's former sniper partner.

"Sucks, she never had kids of her own," Hoss says. She and John tried for years, until one day, they stopped hoping. Hoss remembers the beers he and John had over the sad news. Didn't stop them from loving on each other, though. He's glad she made John happy.

The life of a Marine's wife can be lonely, but Penny made the best of it. She offered help on the base wherever it was needed, connected with the other wives, and always took part in various committees or social events. Losing Kathryn and then Tina was hard for her too.

Donovan says, "My kids were lucky to have her. She was my rock after Tina died."

Was she ever?! Cancer took Donovan's wife two years ago. Penny took up the slack 'cause Donovan's two youngest were still in high school. She gives so much and expects nothing in return but hugs and kisses. Her other side, though, is far from sweet. It's a side she rarely shows, but the men know better.

Hoss grins proudly. *She's mine now.* "My kid-lets think she's the bomb," he says with a twinkle in his eye.

"With your record, I'm surprised you lasted this long, horn dog."

The last five years since Kathryn's death are the longest Hoss's ever been without a woman. Dry spell's over, and he doesn't want to be without a woman ever again. They're so damn soft and smell so good. Even he can't believe he waited this long.

Beth comes up behind them with Neil. The men part to let her pass.

"Gather the men," Donovan says. "We need to plan a rescue."

Hoss backs off. "On it."

***

On his elbow, Ryker overlooks a map of the area that has been laid out across a sturdy, boardroom table that spans the width of the multi-purpose room. He is surrounded by six Marines, active and former, his brother, and Colin. Nothing adorns the walls except the flags of the USA and the Marine Corps. The first half of the room is reserved for medical.

Donovan slides a pointer across the surface of the map. "William, Alex, Miles, and Pen will escort the vulnerable to Haven. Colin, you're going with them. The rest of us will track—"

"Why can't I come with you?" Colin asks, then glances over at Ryker.

Donovan's eyes come up.

Ryker gives Colin credit for being eager, but if he knew what was likely to be involved in their planned extraction, Ryker doubted he'd ask that question.

Donovan dismisses him. "You'll be better off with the others."

"What's the point of training me, then?" Colin asks.

Hoss shuts Colin down. "You aren't ready."

Hoss's answer is in line with Ryker's thoughts. Colin is still in the dark about his training and what it will lead to. He's as green as they all were at one time.

"We're training you to help with security up at Haven, not fighting in CQC," William says.

Colin's confused by the reference, but not wanting to appear weak, he doesn't ask the question so blatantly apparent on his face. Close-quarters combat is something Ryker did a lot during his time as a Marine. *Has it really only been two months since I left?*

Ryker's not sure why Colin wants to help with security all of a sudden, but Colin has guts. That's clear...and useful.

Ever the closer of an argument, Donovan lays out his gospel on the subject. "Colin, you're here because this is something you need to learn. Over time, if you get through all that Hoss throws at you first, then you'll be ready for missions like this one."

Beside Ryker, Mal slides his arms off the table. An undercurrent of restlessness rolls off him. Mal wanted to head out yesterday. Ryker used Beth as an excuse, but his injury was the real reason he held them back. But now, with the children showing up, everyone has realized their enemy might be a common one and that they need to act. He'll cope with the pain if it means pursuing these dangerous men.

He glances around the table. The older generation of Marines stand relaxed, if you can call it that. They've been out of the service for some time but they've kept their skills sharp. The newer Marines in the room appear tense but focused. Ryker senses their edginess, not unlike his own; eager to get the job done. The meeting feels right, and Ryker can't help but be surprised at how happy he is.

There was no question it was time he retired from the service, but he'd felt lost afterward, like he had no purpose. But these men have accepted him, and he is grateful for it.

"Parker said the men are farming across the way," Donovan says. "A large group took off in their vehicles, leaving a skeleton crew behind. We suspect they will take the people we've been waiting for to the same location, but we'll see where their tracks lead us. We'll head out at first light."

Ryker studies Donovan, whose expression is tight and controlled. Beth mentioned she hopes Sadie, Donovan's oldest daughter, is with them. Never having had children, Ryker can only surmise this whole situation weighs heavily on Donovan. Neil pops into Ryker's thoughts. The boy hugged him longer than usual before bed tonight.

CHAPTER 44

"So, nothing's changed. He's still an asshole?" Mal asks.

"Farm over family," Ryker says with disdain over his shoulder as they exit the bathroom, Liam trailing behind.

His brother has said little since the meeting. So far, they've only touched on one subject pertaining to the past: Ryker's visit back home with their stepfather. When he brings up Krystal, the last twelve years, or practically anything else from their upbringing, Mal shuts down. Perhaps it's because they have too many ears, but Ryker doubts it.

"Okay, again." Hoss's voice echoes down the corridor.

The three of them stop short and gaze up.

Looking relaxed, with one arm resting on the table, Hoss oversees Colin practicing knife maneuvers. Colin's shoulders slump as he sighs. Ryker almost feels sorry for him. They've been avoiding each other as best they can in such a small bunker, which suits him just fine. They're both in their corners. The only difference is that Beth's in his.

"We Jenkins do nothing over family. Touchy-feely bunch," Liam says, adding his wisdom to Ryker and Mal's conversation as he crosses the corridor between the tables. He pats his father's shoulder along the way. "Night, Dad."

Hoss tips his chin at his son. "Goodnight, son."

Mal asks, "Family first kinda stuff?"

Liam twists his head back. "Yup." He disappears into the men's dorm.

It was like that under their dad's watch, but it died with him. Their stepfather influenced them in the other direction. Ryker hopes Mal will thrive up at Haven and not resume his nomadic ways. He's the only family Ryker has left.

With their two-day trip to Haven on the horizon, most of the compound has already called it a night. Ryker's not sure how long they'll be out tracking Wendall's men or where they'll end up, but he's glad Beth will be safe with her family and friends. Once they find Donovan's daughter and James's family, he'll concentrate on his original task with Mal and hunt down the two remaining men on his list.

Beth waltzes out of Penny's suite, searches, and lays those beautiful green eyes on him. Ryker's heart beats faster when she casts that flirtatious smile his way, capturing him, hook, line, and sinker.

"Neil down?" Ryker's glad Neil has other kids his age to play with now. It's another positive in his trauma recovery.

"He's excited about the sleepover, but he's fine, so Penny kicked me out. I hope the rest of them are okay."

Beth wears her concern for her young cousin, Elena, and best friend, Gina, on her face still. Ryker remembers the shy, young girl at the diner, so full of youthful enthusiasm. Her abduction feeds his anger. Ryker reaches out, pulls Beth gently into his arms, and plants a kiss on her; something she reciprocates quickly. This is a hunger he enjoys savoring.

Hoss says, "Colin, focus. Again."

Colin yells out in frustration, "Damn it, Hoss, I've been practicing."

"Not enough," Hoss says with a calm that Ryker respects. "You're slow as molasses, but you'll get better."

"When can we move on to real weapons? I'm ready."

Hoss's eyebrows arch upward in disbelief. "Real weapons?" Without missing a beat, he calls out, "Beth."

"Yeah?" Beth answers with trepidation.

"Come, show Colin why he's not ready."

Ominous. Her hesitation piques Ryker's interest.

Radiating nervous vibes, she approaches Hoss in slow steps.

Why is she cautious? Ryker picks up Colin's confused look, exchanges a quizzical look with Mal, then turns back as Hoss hands her a practice Karambit blade. He remembers how she'd had a real one in her hands during the altercation with that piece of shit by the stream.

In an authoritative voice, Hoss says, "Cut and disable, Chickie."

No way. His lips part.

Colin eyes her with a sidelong glance, his eyebrows furrowed with suspicion.

She says, "Hoss, I can't do—"

"Stop, you know you can."

Why is she so reluctant? Beth squares her shoulders and stills before them. Her head lifts, determination solidifies on her face, and in quick succession, she swings the blade through a series of moves. His jaw drops the same instant his body stirs. *Holy shit! My woman is a badass.*

She uses Colin's shock against him, disables him, and drives him to the floor with little effort, then steps back, blade poised to strike, and awaits further instructions. Hoss taps her out, and Beth relaxes. *A well-oiled machine.*

Mal adjusts his stance. "Man, I think I'm in love."

Ryker's chest fills with pride. *I know I'm in love.*

Beth helps Colin up in shy silence and keeps her eyes averted.

"Beth? How? That was..." Ryker's still processing what he's witnessed. She turns away, so he turns to Hoss. "How long have you been teaching her?"

"Ever since she moved out. Beth was a junior black belt growin' up." Hoss turns in her direction and says, as though reprimanding her, "But she holds back."

Beth hangs her head in response, the badass attitude disappears, and her bashful eyes glance Ryker's way.

Ryker and Colin both voice the same sentiment. "A black belt?"

Hmm, Colin didn't know, either. That makes Ryker feel better somehow.

"That was holding back?" Mal asks, looking astonished.

Beth dismisses their comments with a shrug, not meeting their eyes. Her body language reminds Ryker of how she looked when he intervened with those idiots back at the diner. She could have defended herself back then, but she didn't. Why is she embarrassed about defending herself?

Erotic images of play fighting skip through his head, forcing him to adjust himself. *Christ, that was arousing.*

Hoss says to Colin, "I'm hittin' the hay. So should you. O six hundred comes fast."

Sounds like a good idea. Ryker's surprised when Hoss enters Penny's suite. *Good for him.* With naughty thoughts flooding his own mind, Ryker says "Tomorrow" to Mal, slinks over, and grabs Beth. She shrieks. Her hands dash to her mouth, embarrassed by the noise she's just made. *Time to hit something, but it ain't going to be hay.*

Beth lets him drag her to the suite. Along the way, Ryker calls out to Mal in jest, "If you hear screaming, don't bother coming in, I got it!"

Mal emits a throaty laugh. "Don't worry, Beth, when he doesn't satisfy you, come see me."

Fat chance, brother. After the door closes, Ryker pushes her against it with a playful glint in his eyes. "That was hot as fuck, my badass girl."

"I'm not a badass."

Ryker holds back his retort and runs his fingers through her hair, taking a moment before saying, "Well, my not-so-bad-ass girl, you sure know how to keep things interesting."

Beth throws her head back, and Ryker enjoys the amusement in her full-bodied laugh.

***

Mal hears Beth's laughter faintly from his side of the door and turns his attention to Colin, who appears sad, with downcast eyes. "You should let her go."

Colin glares back.

"Just saying how I see it. She doesn't reciprocate the love you feel. It's an illusion."

"Speaking from experience?"

He doesn't take the bait. Mal's seen jealousy on many men, but not himself. Never going to let a woman get that deep. Love is the illusion Mal's managed to avoid so far, and he means to keep it that way.

To keep Colin from trying to goad him further, he changes the subject. "What'd you do before?"

"Heavy vehicle mechanic. You?"

"Farmer, mechanic, among other pursuits."

"Valuable skills now."

Mal flourishes his hands up and down in Colin's direction. "You doing all this to impress her?"

"I was till she just kicked my ass."

Mal stifles his smile. *This guy has it bad.* Normally, he wouldn't get between two men vying for the same woman, but this is his brother. "For what it's worth, there's other fish in the ocean."

"Well, this ocean has dried up. There won't be any women up at Haven for you or me."

Colin might be speaking the truth, but Mal's not looking for a relationship. An unemotional single woman with needs would be perfect, though.

Chapter 45

There's a flurry of activity as the first group prepares to leave. True to his nature, Mal doesn't think of himself as a part of the crew, only an observer. He's felt this way ever since high school. What he saw of it, anyway. His stepfather yanked him and his sister out early; needed a farm worker and a babysitter, instead.

Alex adjusts Alejo's tactical vest and slaps his back gently, while Hoss fine-tunes Penny's vest as she holsters a weapon in the strap on her side. *Beth isn't the only tough woman in these parts.* William and Donovan take in the sights from the sidelines, next to the three kids with backpacks on. It's like everyone's getting ready for school.

Mal's had little interaction with William. All he's managed to garner is that he's a workaholic and doesn't show signs of slowing down. He sleeps, monitors the screens in security, or goes out patrolling with Hoss. *To each their own, I guess.* It's not like Mal's the friendly type, either.

Donovan stands out more than the rest. He reminds Mal of his old man: regimented and principled. What he remembers, anyway. The image of his distraught mother standing in the front yard as they jumped off the school bus with a Marine sergeant and chaplain standing stock still behind her interrupts his train of thought. He was seven when he had to grow up and lost the only man he ever looked up to. He glances over at Donovan again. Mal respects the big undertaking these men have taken upon themselves. *Family first.* Wishes he was like them. Never will be.

Beth captures his attention as she exits the suite with her vest on. Mal's body tingles as an image of her walking down the aisle slinks into his consciousness. She'd be his sister-in-law, and he'd welcome it. He catches Ry's look of desire.

Alejo prances around Beth in a circle, wearing the vest and dressed in black clothes. "I don't know if this is me. What do you think?"

"You look totally dangerous, A."

Does the man need more encouragement?

Alejo jumps, all giddy. "I feel dangerous."

Mal's on the fence about Alejo. He doesn't enjoy being pawed but understands Alejo's sadness about his partner. The one they call Sean. This conjures up a vision of his sister. His partner. His failure.

Ryker steps into Beth's space, fusing their bodies. He squeezes her ass, brushes his lips over hers, and whispers, "Should have worn that earlier. You look hot."

Colin averts pained eyes.

She melts under his brother's words. "You're incorrigible," she says, somehow managing to look bashful even after last night's tour de force. Mal's never met a woman who possessed that kind of power, yet held it back. He likes it when they own it and wonders why Beth doesn't.

Ryker's lips brush her ear. "That's why you like me. That and my smokin' hot bod."

There's a phrase Mal hasn't heard since high school. Ry hasn't changed. Inside, he's still the teenager Mal remembers.

"Be careful with my smokin' hot bod."

Mal steps forward, sporting a wide grin. "Don't worry, I'll protect your toy."

Ryker shoves Mal playfully. He's missed moments like this with his brother, and Mal's grateful they're tracking together, just like old times, even if the reason they must do so is not palatable.

The weight and feel of his harnessed rifle is unfamiliar; heavy and cold in equal measure. He prefers handguns. They're easier to conceal. Still, Mal admires the hardware these guys have handed out for the mission. *These could be valuable back in town.*

Hoss slaps William's arm. "The FNG doesn't know much, so go easy on him."

Should I be taking notes? Mal leans in, elbows Ryker, and in a low voice, asks, "What's FNG mean?"

Ryker bends to Mal's ear and says, out of Colin's earshot, "Fucking new guy."

"Ah," he says, finding it difficult to keep up with their secret club language.

Hoss eyes Penny and encircles her slim waist with one arm. Mal pegs her as being in her fifties based on her demeanor, but she doesn't look a day over forty. He doesn't like blondes much but he'd find it hard to say no to her. Besides, her cookies alone would lure him in.

She responds with a gentle hand on Hoss's chest and a warm grin. In a quiet tone, Hoss asks, "Move your stuff in, okay? Leave the heavy stuff for the boys." He gives her ass a gentle squeeze and takes her lips like a boss.

Beth blushes in Ryker's arms, Liam beams proudly, and Donovan approves with a nod. By their reactions, Mal figures this is the first time these lovebirds have shown affection so openly. The only one not showing any interest in Hoss and Penny is Colin. The craving in his eyes longs for Beth. It's like watching a train wreck. *Love is for losers.*

Once Hoss comes up for air, Alejo pecks Penny's cheek and hands Hoss a thermos. "Made Foxtrot coffee just for you, hon."

Mal learned that Foxtrot means fuck in military speech. Logically, it's their way of swearing in front of the kids, but he's not sure why they would call it fucking coffee.

Hoss winks. Unlike Donovan, he is charismatic and empathetic. On the surface, anyway. Under his swagger and weird shirts, Mal has realized that Hoss is cunning.

Alejo grips Mal's arm and leans against his shoulder, much to Mal's chagrin. But he has to give it to Alejo, the man doesn't give up when he wants something. If he toned down the pawing, Mal might let him cut his hair. *Might.*

***

In the darkness, sleep escapes Mal as he lies next to the other men in his uncomfortable tactical vest. Ryker shifts beside him. Mal can't block out the day's turn of events. Tracking is a skill he honed long ago, so while it took a while to locate the patterns the children left, the trail eventually revealed itself. Ryker and he had split up at one point, and they thought they'd lost the path, but Mal found it again. They soon made headway, and for the better part of the day, the signs Mal traced led them east of Reed, not north toward the farm.

He removes his hand from atop his helmet to seek the warmth inside his blanket. It took time to get used to hearing their voices through his headset, and the weight of the vest isn't particularly pleasant, but on the flip side, he has everything available to him in the various pouches. He's not sure how his back will be in the morning after sleeping in all this gear. Donovan told him this is the way they sleep out here, so Mal has realized he wouldn't have been any good in the military if he'd had to sleep with all this stuff on every night.

Liam's face materializes above the faint glow of their small fire as he shoves his hands forward for warmth over the flames. They didn't ask Mal to take a turn on watch. Trust: he hasn't earned it yet. On some level, this bothers Mal, but it shouldn't. He doesn't need their trust. Or does he?

After following the tracks for a few more miles, they came across the place the children had run from. Mal was the first on the scene. The sight of the bodies caused him to pause; he felt disturbed and sad for the poor souls. Mal made quick work of figuring out the scene before the others arrived. Once they did, he'd be hard pressed to hold them back. When the rest of the men did show, there was a moment of collective heartbreak, confirming to Mal that these were, indeed, some of the family they had been waiting for back at Reed.

Mal helped entomb the bodies in rock graves with crude crosses laid over them. Pressed for time, it was the best they could do. They'd come back and bury them properly later. Mal had observed the group around each grave with interest. He doesn't know these men well enough to read their emotions accurately, but he understands mourning.

Donovan crouched over what Mal learned was his son-in-law's grave. Whoever this Brad was, it confirmed that his wife, Donovan's daughter, is with this gang. The image of what they had done to the man sticks in Mal's head. They executed him on his knees. *Brutal.* Mal wouldn't wish that on anyone.

Ryker had stood over another grave with the rest of the men. This was Beth's aunt, he was told. By the looks of her body, before they'd buried her, she died of multiple injuries; not from the journey, but from before.

Before they had left to make camp, Donovan radioed the other group, though he kept their intel to a minimum. Guess he wants to avoid upsetting anyone until everyone is safe.

There's been a lot of sadness today. Mal raises the blanket a little higher, up to his chin. *I wonder if anyone will shed tears over my grave.*

***

William lounges next to Beth, a rifle on his lap, his back against a tree. Alejo's snoring is soothing but not enough to lull her to sleep. The light from their buried fire pit dwindles, and the aroma of burning pine lingers in the air. An owl hoots to her left, and a creature laps at the water across the tiny lake they're camped by for the night. William reaches out, and Alejo's rhythmic sound dims for a spell, then resumes, softer than before.

It all brings back cherished memories of their camping trips, although Beth hasn't missed the feel of the hard earth. William's warm, weathered hand curls around her head, and he caresses her cheek. Once they set up camp, William radioed Donovan to say they were safe. Donovan relayed the same in return and cut contact. It was an unsecured channel, so chit-chat was short and sweet. He didn't say if they'd found Gina or not.

This is one reason she is still awake, but her friend is with Brad, so Beth takes some solace in that. The other reason is her fear of being attacked like her uncle James was. Penny says the kids told her Elena escaped with her siblings but exposed herself to give them time to escape. Brave. *Unlike me.*

Despite being young, the kids kept up with the adults and were the first to get everyone going again after resting for too long. The men obliged their request, finally calling it a night near a lake just as they made it past the midpoint of the journey from Reed to Haven. As the men set up camp, the boys cultivated an interest in the rocks they found near the water's edge. During the trek, Neil had taught his new friends the silent game, so Beth rewarded them after the nighttime meal for a job well done. They voiced no complaints when bedtime was called.

She assumes Ryker is alright and that his wound isn't giving him trouble but she can't help but worry about him. When he finds those men, she has no illusions of what will befall them. All she can hope for is that Ryker won't get further injured during the confrontation. And that her family will be okay.

"Sleep, my Chickie, sleep," William serenades. The darkness hides the smile that spreads across her face. She's grateful he's with her.

They'll arrive at Haven tomorrow. Her smile withers. They will have to pass the church: the place they buried her family. It's a moment she's dreaded for years. Will she have the courage to face her fear? Does she really have a choice?

CHAPTER 46
June 7

R yker feels like shit. He didn't have the slightest bit of good sleep last night, and the few dreams he had were nightmarish.

They resumed their expedition early after a hurried meal, seeking to catch up with their quarry. Donovan's daughter is with those bastards. Ryker remembers Gina only vaguely from their brief encounter in the diner, realizing it's because he only had eyes for Beth that night. The sight of her husband in that condition resurrected the haunting memory of how he found his sister.

He gazes at his brother's back at the front of the line. Mal's head sweeps back and forth as he extracts answers from the tracks left behind. His brother hasn't spoken a word since their gruesome find yesterday. Witnessing dead bodies is not something you got used to, and it's sure to be yet another memory that will keep Ryker up at night.

He scans the forest and inhales the fresh mountain air, alert to any danger that might be present. Afternoon sunlight pierces through the heavy rain clouds, yet no drops fall. The others trudge along ahead of him, their weapons ready as they move through the dense forest. To his left, Hoss ambles along with a sniper rifle strapped to his back in a drag bag. They haven't encountered hostiles, but Ryker expects they will soon enough. They have the advantage of speed; the kidnappers aren't as agile, bogged down as they are with captives. Plus, they're not expecting company.

An unfamiliar voice in Ryker's headset says, "Pinkie to Osmond, over."

Donovan signals for everyone to halt. "Osmond, go." Everyone obeys the command, taking a knee on cue, except Mal, who continues to scan the ground.

"The friendlies you seek are at the pool."

Mal pauses and jerks his head toward the group. The pool is their codename for the farmhouse. No need to track now the situation is clear. Time to regroup and come up with a new plan.

The voice says, "They're in the bar." *Codename for the barn.* "What's your position?"

Donovan checks his watch, gazes at the trees around him, mulls things over, then says, "We'll line up for the bar and grab and go before the sun sets."

"We'll be ready for you."

Ryker's not sure what that means, but neither is he not privy to what awaits them at Haven. It's a piece of the puzzle he's missing.

Donovan adds, "I'll relay intel when the time comes."

Mal moves toward them. As the only one without a military background, Ryker can see his brother has questions.

"Roger that, out," the voice says, ending communications.

Donovan signals everyone in and says, "Liam, keep watch. Let's hash this out."

Mal approaches with a puzzled expression on his face. "Who's Pinkie?"

Hoss unfolds a map as the rest gather around.

"Parker. He runs Haven." Donovan makes a point of glancing at Ryker. "And Beth's uncle."

Ryker catches the meaning in Donovan's words and hopes he lives up to Parker's expectations. Parker is BAMF dad number one, and Beth is everything to this man. Ryker needs to make a good impression.

"We'll approach the house from the south." Donovan points at a hand-drawn map of the farmhouse and barn. "Hoss'll scout ahead of us on the north side of the farmhouse to give us a body count. You heard Parker. They're keeping the captives in the barn."

"Don't you have men up at Haven who can strike from there?" Mal asks.

Donovan shifts, not used to being grilled. "Mal—"

"Son," Hoss interrupts, "you're looking at them."

Mal's jaw tightens, but he doesn't move.

"We know why you want to hoof it in double time," Hoss says, looking between Ryker and Mal, "but this isn't about revenge. Our top priority on this mission is getting our family back in one piece."

Donovan refers to the map. "Now, we'll focus our energies on the barn and extract the captives. Just knives for now. This is a silent grab and go operation and I don't want a showdown at the ok corral."

Mal frowns. "What about Gideon and his men? Aren't we taking them out?"

Ryker reads Donovan's face. He has a reason to kill, too, but these men don't kill for the sake of killing. Getting his daughter home safe is Donovan's priority. They will stick to the plan and not much else unless fired upon. Civilization may have become unhinged, but it doesn't mean they will resort to that level of crazy.

He meets Donovan's eye.

"We'll leave a boat for you," Donovan says. "Cross the river when you're done."

***

Miles and the kids are quietly making their way through the tall grass ahead of Beth, in a small open area with no trees. Penny follows behind him. They are within a few miles of Haven now, and the closer they get, the more intense Beth's anxiety is becoming. She searches the surrounding forest, missing the relaxed atmosphere of Reed...and Ryker. Her feelings have deepened, and it's like she's lost her security blanket. *He's under my skin.*

Behind her, William and Colin take up the rear. Beth locks eyes with Colin. He flashes a smile laced with worry, seemingly picking up her mood. She lights up a grin, hoping it will bring a sense of calm.

"Do you think Sean's okay?" Alejo asks, snaking an arm around hers, luring her away from Colin's gaze.

Penny twists toward them with a finger to her lips. Under normal circumstances, Beth would love to chat with Alejo; he keeps her out of her head. But out here, they need to be quiet. Beth pats his hand, and Alejo mouths *Sorry*. Parker relayed earlier that Sean was at the farmhouse, which caused a ripple of hope through her friend.

Parker also made it known that Gina is there, as well. Beth prays her friends are okay. This is not how she'd envisioned the world turning upside down. The plan they'd trained for and the reality they were experiencing were vastly different, and Beth's anxiety has risen. She squeezes Alejo's arm.

The forest sounds still. Miles raises a fist in the tall grass, signaling the group to freeze. Beth turns her head to look at William, who is scanning the forest for the threat, his weapon ready.

In an act of self-preservation, Alejo takes cover behind her, while Penny comes to stand beside them, brandishing her firearm. Beth's adrenaline kicks in. Craning her neck, she searches ahead for the children, but they're hidden from view, further ahead than she'd like. *This isn't good.*

The area is depressed enough for Beth to see Alex coming out of the forest ahead of them on higher ground. He is taking point today and scouting out the path before them. All the adults, except Colin, have made this journey so many times, she's sure they could do the trip backward in their sleep.

Penny motions with her hand to follow her toward Miles and the children. They slink forward.

Gunfire erupts from their left flank, cleaving the group in two. Alejo collapses, disturbing the ground, and leaves Beth exposed. She freezes. Keeping her weapon close, Penny rushes toward Miles and the children, parting the tall grass.

Beth glimpses Miles yanking the children back in retreat. Bullets make contact with his vest. His body jerks backward. They topple over and disappear. *Neil!*

Fear explodes in Beth, but before she can take one step, William pulls her out of harm's way. He faces the threat and fires his weapon, ejecting shell casings in rapid succession.

Colin shields Beth with his body, showing no regard for his own safety. William takes a hit in the thigh and falls sideways. Terror grips her. With strength she never knew she had, she pushes Colin aside and scrambles forward. "William!" Using her weight, she leans on his thigh. Blood gushes through her fingers. *Can't stop it! Fuck!*

William pushes her out of the way, his blood spurting from his wounds, and yells, "Get back!"

He's trying to protect me, like Neil's father. "I'm not leaving you!" She strains to get to his wound, but his grip is solid.

"You can't help me. Do as I say! Colin, take her to the trees!"

"No! I need to put pressure—" Colin drags her away, but unbalanced, she falls backward on her ass. William's body propels backward as he takes another hit. *This isn't fucking happening!*

William's weapon goes silent. He doesn't rise. Beth attempts to crawl back to him. Disheveled men stride out of the foliage from different directions. *Outnumbered.* Blood sprays as one of them drops dead.

Someone's firing from the front of the line. *Alex? Miles?* She can't see them.

One man walks through the chaos of bullets whizzing by and zeros in on her. Afraid of him, her body goes rigid.

Penny screams. Beth turns toward the sound. *No!*

William's secondary. Beth scrambles to reach the handgun at William's lower back.

Rough hands yank her backward, dragging her away. Colin lunges for her. His eyes widen.

Bang! Colin flies backward, disappearing into the tall grass.

"No!" Her rage bubbles to the surface. A dirty hand muffles her screams, and the world goes black.

***

Excruciating pain slams into Penny's head as she plummets to the ground. Stars cloud her eyesight. Bullets crackle, and before she can figure out what's happening to her, someone grabs her ankles. She's without her weapon, and the ground is moving beneath her. The tall foliage of the fields disappears, and a canopy of trees appears above her. The gunshots lessen.

With effort, Penny lifts her head to see a dingy man above her, grunting. Dry leaves crunch under his feet. He won't drag her for long; she refuses to let them capture her. His cold eyes meet hers. *Showtime.*

Taking hold of his shirt sleeves at the wrists, she brings her legs close to her chest. He stumbles forward, clearly not expecting her strength. A pistol tucked into his pants captures her attention, and she lunges for the weapon. He grabs her arm, but not before she detects the roughness of the grip in her slim hand. He yanks. In one swift motion, she pulls the trigger, and the echo of the gunshot resonates in her ears.

He moves back a few paces, his face twisted in pain as he clutches his groin. She takes aim from the ground and squeezes the trigger once more, sensing the recoil in her palm. His body swings backward and hits the ground with a vibrating thud. She crawls away, her senses sharp as she vigilantly scans the environment, looking for signs of danger. Not seeing any, she launches up and makes her way back.

From the edge of the trees, Penny scans the field, the weight of the handgun providing a sense of protection. Silence engulfs her as she moves forward with caution, mindful of not startling her companions or alerting any potential threats.

"Cookie," Alex calls out, hidden in the tall grass.

She responds to her unfamiliar nickname, her voice filled with confidence. "Pretty Boy? We clear?"

"Yes, but not safe." Alex materializes unharmed near where William and Colin were when everything went down.

Relief floods her at the sight of him, but she doesn't want to acknowledge the sadness on his face. "The kids?"

On her right, Miles's voice breaks through the silence, filled with strain. "They're with me." Her head turns. Miles's legs protrude from behind a tree, unmoving. She hastens over to his position, following the bloody drag marks, dreading what she'll find. *He's been hit.* As Miles comes into view, her heart races. Somehow, he'd propped himself against the tree as he guarded the children, his grip firm on the rifle despite his obvious pain. The kids cuddle up to Miles, scared out of their wits. A noticeable dark stain on his lower leg confirms one contact, demanding attention. The kids look ready to bolt, but she stays them with a hand, and they relax back into Miles. He'll need warmth when the shock kicks in, so without knowing it, the kids are helping.

Penny hears Alex approaching but turns to confirm it's him anyway, clutching the weapon close to her chest. With a bloody lip, he kneels beside his brother. The distinct sound of Alex tearing his medic kit from his back fills the air.

"How many?" she asks Miles, not wanting to alarm the children.

"One," he says through gritted teeth. "Foxtrot burns."

The absence of William and Colin fills her with dread, and Alex's sad expression implies there is more to be said.

Preparing herself for his disclosure, she says, "Give me the lowdown, Alex."

As he works on Miles, he takes a breath. "Alejo fainted. I got three hits, two made contact."

That's too many down for Penny's taste. "And the bad news?" Her words hang in the air like a dark cloud.

***

Alex tastes blood, along with his failure. This is a call Alex doesn't want to make but he has no choice. When Penny asked for the bad news, he thought that would be the hardest intel he'd ever have to relay…until this call.

You never know who has their ears to the ground, and he doesn't want to communicate the message more than once, so he asks Parker to switch to the other team's channel. "Pretty Boy to Osmond."

He glances at Miles, cradling his rifle, leaning against a tree with a bandaged leg, and scanning the forest for any threats. Penny zips up Alex's first aid pouch. For a split second, the visual of Miles's plate armor taking one of those vibe checks, as Marines call bullet contacts, causes Alex physical pain. He thought he'd lost his brother when he disappeared under the heavy foliage, and Alex's heart stuttered when the children took a nosedive after him. He's glad they weren't hurt. Having the higher ground afforded Alex the advantage of hitting targets as those bastards approached his friends until he had to take cover from the gunfire himself.

Penny blocks the children's view as Colin drags a body out of the underbrush, severing Alex's painful memory. Alex directs him to move it further so the children don't see it.

"Osmond here. What's your status?" Donovan asks.

"Pinkie has ears on this channel." Alex shuts his eyes as he takes a deep breath. This won't be easy. "We were ambushed."

He and Miles have been in CQC plenty, and he can deal with that. But this, this was something else. They crossed the line, engaging with women and children present. Penny whispers soothing words to the three distraught kids beside Miles. Alejo sits nearby, his head wrapped in a bandage, a physical manifestation of his descent to the earth.

"The girls, kids?!" Hoss sounds distressed.

Penny locks eyes with Alex.

"The littles are safe here with Cookie. Chickie was taken. Tell Superman I'm sorry. Twinkle tried to protect her but ended up catching a round."

Colin's lips curl back in pain as he straightens and rubs his chest under the vest with red-stained hands. The blood isn't his. Alex tries to rub away the phantom pain in his own chest.

Donovan's commanding voice says, "We're on our way."

Penny contradicts him. "No, stay on course. Pretty Boy and I have it under control."

Parker says, "You need rescuing."

"No, Pinkie," Penny says in Alex's ear, "we don't. We'll get ourselves home."

Uncertain of their ability to reach Haven without succumbing to more issues, Penny's unwavering determination provides Alex with a flicker of confidence. When he saw the women being taken earlier, his breath had caught in his throat. He's never felt so helpless. Then, out of nowhere, this unassuming, gentle woman surprised him when she twisted herself free, a weapon held firmly in her grip.

Hoss says, "Cookie—"

With a commanding tone, Penny says, "I got this. Chickie needs you."

"Are you sure?" Parker asks, his voice filled with emotion.

Under a grim expression, Alex walks to a tree and takes a knee. He can't believe he's going to say this. Miles distracted Alex, and it cost him. *He failed.* He releases a heavy sigh. "Osmond, Scout didn't make it."

He lays a hand on William's shoulder. Slumped against a tree, he sits in a relaxed position. *Brother.* Alex supported the man till his last breath, when he added William to a list of good men he'll never forget. He also gave William his word: Alex would end the bastard that took Chickie.

***

Ryker's world shifts... "Chickie was taken." *My Chickie.* His heart quickens, and Ryker struggles to breathe. His mind betrays him, hurling the memory of Libby at him, her body naked and beaten. Except it is not Libby, but Beth in her place. He can't go through that again.

Donovan turns from them, slumps, and stumbles to a nearby tree for support. Hoss reels back in shock and grabs Liam for support.

Ryker's mind pumps out another memory of him mourning over two bodies in the morgue, covered in American flags. *Elvis. K-Man. And now William. He was a good man.*

Ryker can't process what else is going on around him as he uses what brain power he has left to focus on functioning. It's a losing battle, because he can't keep it together, and fights the crushing feeling that he's failed yet another person he loves. *Can't lose her. Not on my watch.*

Silent, like the grave, each man stands locked to the forest floor, dwelling in their own private hell.

Mal's voice forces its way through. "Ry?" Mal shakes him. "Ry, look at me."

Not knowing why, Ryker obeys the command and turns to Mal. His brother's determined, icy stare pulls him into the here and now. "Focus on the mission. We'll find her."

Mission... Libby... Beth...

Donovan straightens and says in a gruff voice, "Cookie, the minute you hit home, we get a call. Copy?"

"Copy. Out."

Donovan turns damp eyes to Ryker and says with scary conviction, "We're pushing through to catch up to these fuckers."

Chapter 47

Out of the trees and into an open field, Beth stumbles along, tied to a rope, with two more captives in their twenties: an African American man, and a redheaded woman. The shock having worn off, Beth fights the voices again, and a massive headache. She's worried about William and Colin. Deep down in her gut, she believes they are dead. *Nothing lasts.*

Ahead of them, the man the others call Cain saunters along, in full control of their rope. Beth deduces their captor is a military man by the way he carries himself. Not the good kind, either. She can still taste the blood on her lips. The result of her testing the boundaries with him.

Two men splash through the stream behind Beth. She was afraid the men would attack her once she came to, based on the redheaded woman's terrified demeanor, but it didn't happen. They ogled her as they trudged through the forest, though, proving she wasn't misreading her predicament. Beth reaches up, stretches the rope, unable to reach her throat, and mourns the loss of her necklace. It was likely torn from her neck during her scuffle with Cain.

The farmhouse looms ahead of them. The last time Beth glimpsed it from across the river, it seemed tired. Now, the dilapidated building is almost pleading to be whole and loved again. She notes the wooden walls of the barn, standing strong though they've darkened with age. Escorted between the house and the barn, she spots a man sawing wood near a fence and another repairing a tractor. Beth squints against the sun and spots men working the field in the distance. She stops, rooted to the spot.

A barrel-chested man gazes at them. *Uncle James!* He slaps a thinner man on the back, who straightens and glances over. *Sean!* A weight Beth didn't know she was carrying lifts, and she sucks in a hint of hope. Her arms propel forward without her, and her body crashes to the ground.

A man reeking of sweat appears overhead and helps her up. "This one looks promising." He's wearing a Black Sabbath shirt. A carpenter's pencil protrudes from behind his ear.

Beth gasps, enraged, and shrinks from the man's grasp. *He groped me.*

"Too bad Gideon cut you off, eh, Billy?" Cain says as he reels her in by the rope and out of Billy's grasp.

"He may have cut me off but he didn't say I couldn't watch Chase here fuck 'em," Billy says while looking at a tall, muscular, tattooed man who is licking his lips and humping the air. Beth's stomach lurches.

Under a sheepish smile, Billy strolls back to the fence, where the other man laughs at her expense, picks a long-handled screwdriver off a table of tools, and dives back into the engine.

Cain ties the end of the rope to the tractor, unties the male captive off the line, and drags him into the barn, leaving Beth and the woman behind. Separating the women isn't a good sign, but now she knows the men are in the barn. The more information, the better when planning an escape. *I'm capable of getting myself out of here, but how far will I get?*

With Cain gone, and opportunity knocking, the two men by the tractor approach, crowd the girls, and rub up against them. The redhead panics, her body clenching as she sobs, when Sabbath Shirt kisses her neck roughly.

Beth's heart races with anticipation as the pencil from behind his ear drops.

The tattooed man pushes a fearful, trembling Beth against the tractor. His hands invade her body, squeezing and probing. She closes her eyes at the sight of his rotten teeth and the sour smell of his breath. The people in the field protest on deaf ears. Beth endures it. She has to.

"Back off!" Cain exits the barn and eyes the men with suspicion. They yield, taking the pressure off. Tools catapult skywards as Beth upends the table and tumbles to the ground.

Cain slaps the men on the way past, under protests of "Hey!"

Unfazed by their whining, Cain yanks Beth up. "You're a clumsy one, aren't you?"

***

Cain leads Beth and the redhead up a neglected set of stairs, down a dingy hallway, and past a room with a four-poster bed, the lumpy mattress stripped of sheets and bare. Beth tries not to imagine what happens in that place as she's drawn into the room across the hall. Angst hangs in the air as Beth enters a bedroom on the shady side of the house. The room smells of sweat mixed with a damp earthiness. Mold? Beth tumbles forward, shoved from behind.

"Tie them up like the rest," Cain says, handing her off to their guard. Just like the other men, he oozes stale body odor and breath that could kill.

Three disheveled women rise from the floor, each tied to a post of the four-poster bed, which has been stripped down to its metal frame. She senses the women before her would bolt if they had the chance. There's still fight in them. Her teenage cousin, Elena, rises last, her fear unmistakable. A short-lived relief washes over Beth.

"Hands!" Beth jumps before raising her arms slightly, wrists facing each other, praying he doesn't tie it too tightly and works fast. The less time she's around his stench, the better. The itchiness of the rope mixed with the need to vomit irritates her. She's tied to a post shared by an older woman with long, brown, wavy hair; fear mixed with exhaustion radiates off her. On the guard's way out, he teases each woman, Beth included, with stray touches, like he's petting dogs in a kennel.

314

As the door clicks shut, Beth recognizes Gina by the damaged window. "Gina!" Beth's heart fills with joy, but her hope crumbles when her friend doesn't acknowledge her. *Something's wrong.*

"Beth, I'm scared," Elena says, tearing Beth's eyes away from her fellow musketeer. On one hand, Beth's glad Elena's safe. On the other, it confirms the urgency that Beth needs to figure a way out. "I was at Reed when your sister and brother showed. We'll get through this." *I hope so, anyway.*

Her words draw out a sigh of relief, and Elena bows her head, and her shoulders go slack. *She's too young for this kind of strain.*

The floorboards squeak and groan. Gina startles Beth with a quiet hug. Tied, she can't reciprocate, so Beth squeezes with her neck and picks up the fresh scent of lavender soap. *She's clean.* Beth views the others; they're dirty like her. "Why aren't you tied up?" Up close, Beth can see there's a fresh bruise on Gina's cheek and eye. "What happened to you?"

Gina averts her eyes and strolls back to the window as if she didn't hear the questions. *What's wrong with her?* Brad wasn't with the men. Is he injured, perhaps in the barn? "Gina, where's Brad?"

The older woman nudges Beth. "Name's Melanie. Who's Gina to you?"

"Best friend."

Melanie nods at the woman closest to Elena. An understanding crosses the divide of the bare metal frame, and the woman distracts Elena with some questions. Melanie checks on Gina, then says under her breath, "They killed Brad in front of us."

Beth inhales sharply as a rush of air leaves her lungs, and her head whips around in surprise. *Oh my God!* "Gina." *What a blow.*

Her attention comes back to Elena. *God, she witnessed that?* Beth reaches. The rope tightens around her wrists. The loss wounds Beth as she longs to give both of them comfort. Gina's distance makes sense now. She's grieving and numb. Beth can't fathom how her friend is functioning at all. The thought of losing

Ryker that way causes her to cast the thought aside in favor of scanning the room for escape options.

Aside from the bed frame, no furniture adorns the room. From her vantage point, it looks like they've nailed the window shut. *Smart.* The worn wallpaper, marked with water stains, appears cracked, and remnants of ceiling paint are strewn across the exposed floorboards beneath her feet. Beth takes comfort in the weight of the weapons up her sleeves: the warmth of the pencil and coolness of the screwdriver she pilfered. *But do I have the courage to use them?*

The woman nearest to Elena says, "It's okay, honey. Your dad's outside. Take comfort in that."

Beth sure was happy to see her uncle James and Sean, but the woman's words uncover a painful realization. "Where's Aunt Lani?"

Overcome with grief, Elena wails, collapsing in a heap on the dirty floor. The women are quick to shush her, their fearful eyes darting to the closed bedroom door.

Beth scrunches her face in frustration as despair closes in. So much death, so much pain. Sophia, Brad, and now Lani. "I'm sorry, Elena."

Beth tracks back to Gina at the window and marvels as a tiny sliver of sunlight stretches to reach this side of the house, cascading over her friend's honey-colored hair. A memory of Gina standing in her wedding dress springs forth, the sunlight glinting off the pearls laced into her golden hair that day, only a year ago. Brad was so good for her; a match made in heaven, they said. *Not enough time.* Beth swipes away her tears as best as she can.

Scrutinizing the derelict window behind Gina, Beth figures if she can get the ropes off, an escape could be possible. But can she do it undetected? When Gina crossed the room, the floorboards creaked. Beth stares at the floor, tests the theory, and shifts her weight back and forth. The boards groan loudly. This might be harder than she thought. Beth gazes at Gina's back. *We need to keep our heads.* "They're coming to get us, Gina. We need to hold on." *God, please hurry.*

Gina turns to Beth, a glint of hope sparkling in her otherwise dead eyes.

"Gina, I—"

The creak of the door elicits fearful moans from the women. Their guard steps in and calls Gina with a wave of his hand from the partially open door. "You're requested downstairs. Get."

Frightened into action, Gina brushes past Beth. *Why does she leave willingly?*

After the door slams shut, an atmosphere of despair floats over the women, leaving only a dreadful silence. Beth scans Melanie's facial bruises and asks, "Where's Gina going?"

The other woman converses with Elena once more, distracting her as Melanie whispers, "To Gideon."

"Who's he?"

"As far as I can tell, he's the leader."

Beth's afraid to ask. "Why did he summon her?"

Melanie checks Elena before she confides, "She's his."

The horrible implication of that statement dawns on Beth as she stares at the closed door her friend has just slipped through. The bruises. *God, no! Why doesn't Gina escape?* Haven's across the way. The meek person who hugged her was not her friend. *What has he done to her?*

"We arrived this morning. Today has been...hard."

Hard? The redhead's knees weaken. She crumples to the floor in a state of panic and buries her head in her arms, tied to the bedpost above her head. The other women implore her to quieten down.

"They took Gina away first." Melanie lowers her haunted eyes. "When she reappeared, she was...changed." She doesn't elaborate further, but the implication is clear.

Despite their shattered nerves, the women still try to entertain and distract Elena. They can't undo the physical and emotional trauma they've suffered, but for Elena's sake, they are doing what they can to put up a good front.

Beth whispers to Melanie to protect Elena's ears. "They haven't touched—"

"No! But prepare yourself and pray you don't get Dugal. He's the sick one."

The name sounds familiar. "Sick?"

"The men brag about a girl he kidnapped and did things to...while she died."

Ryker's sister.

Beth's fellow captive says, "No, no, no!"

The vision of Ryker's sister's last moments horrifies Beth. She tastes bile. Swallows. Ryker said he wanted Dugal to suffer the most and was saving him for last. Knowing he's here ramps her anxiety into high gear. Beth prays she never has to meet this animal face to face, but fears it might be inescapable.

Chapter 48

Parker stands in the late afternoon light, outside the compound wall next to his straight-laced brother, Dr. Henry Livingston. Under his black-rimmed glasses is an accomplished Marine. The only part of him that's part rebel is his non-regulation mustache, which Henry enjoyed flaunting after he served. Parker's proud of his little brother and glad he and his wife made it with their children unscathed. Henry's skills as a surgeon are invaluable, irreplaceable, and a major key to any hope of them living here in Haven successfully.

Under the soft sound of goat bells, Alex and Alejo appear through the trees supporting a hobbling Miles, his arms curled around their necks. His bandage is tinged with a blotchy red patch. John Henry and three younger men follow. They had met the group on the other side of the river with the zodiac inflatable boats. As they near, Parker witnesses the sweat on Miles's brow. It was an arduous journey, but they've made it. Not having time for pleasantries, Henry moves forward, relieves Alex and, with Alejo, conveys Miles toward the single steel door in the wall.

Brandishing William's rifle, Penny leads three shaken, tired children up the path toward Parker. The kids' dark moods turn to smiles when their eyes settle on the large compound wall. Seeing Haven for the first time usually elicits a mixture of wonder and shock. *No one's ever prepared for what's beyond the wall.*

Parker tugs Penny in for a brief hug and a kiss on the forehead, noting the dark circles under her eyes. "Go in, settle the kids. I'll catch up with you." Silently, she squeezes his arm, then escorts the children into the compound yard. The trip has taken a toll on her.

Over the radio, Alex conveyed that with the loss of their numbers and most of their group injured, it wasn't possible to carry William's body with them. He lies under a temporary pile of rocks, like the others, for a future extraction. Losing a brother always unsettles those who remain. It will be bittersweet when they finally bring him home to rest in the cemetery, up at the church, next to his recently deceased wife.

But there is no time to mourn the loss of his friend. Parker and the guys will grieve when the mission is complete. The family they have left is their priority. William loved Beth like a daughter and would have understood.

Sadness hangs on the faces of the last two men to approach. Parker assumes the blond man with Alex is Colin. Alex explained on the comms he and Colin were meeting up with the others across the river. He wants retribution. They all do.

Parker hands over weapons and extra mags to Alex.

"Thanks," Alex says as he straps on the extra gear, and frees his hands for the soft cloth of food and bottled water Parker passes over.

Parker turns to Colin. "We haven't met. Parker." He stretches out his hand and presents another soft cloth and water to him.

Colin stands taller upon this admission, takes the offering, and shakes Parker's hand. "I'm Colin. Beth's...dance partner."

Good grip. Colin's confidence pleases Parker. "Ah, yes, I've heard good things about you. Glad you made it." Donovan's suggestion to train Colin was sensible. He is green, but they'll soon see how well he does under pressure.

Parker man-hugs Alex. "Bring our family home, Pretty Boy."

Parker came close to going rogue after discovering that someone had taken his Beth. Like Alex, he was itching to pick up a rifle and retrieve her. Parker hasn't cried since the day Beth choked those pills down. Guilt ate at him, then, not because she'd wanted to die, but because he had failed her. Beth was his by blood and that meant more to Parker than anything in this world and he vowed on that painful day he would not fail her again. But he isn't that young kid with an "invincible" complex anymore, either, and Parker rubs his slight paunch with a four-fingered hand.

"Will do, Pinkie," Alex says in kind, before leading Colin away.

Henry's footsteps sound as he steps up beside Parker.

Parker had responsibilities now, and badass brothers on a mission. Men invested in the same goals and who love Beth as much as he does. *All for one, one for all kinda shit.*

The men disappear through the trees.

"I wish I could go with them."

Henry grips Parker's shoulders. "I know, brother, but Beth can't lose you, too." He's referring to Parker's heart condition, the reason he had to leave the service long ago. "She may have Ryker now, but she'll still need you when she comes home. All that matters is our family comes back to us, brother. We'll rally, like we always do."

***

Long shadows stretch across the field to the yellow farmhouse, and light seeps out of the barn, darkening the outer boards and bringing Ryker's view into sharper focus. The scent of freshly tilled soil fills his nostrils as he focuses on the farmhouse. Its cracked second-floor windows appear vacant. *Hold on Beth, I'm coming.* He wants to rescue Beth himself, but Donovan has other plans for Ryker and Colin, so he's reluctantly placing his trust in the sergeant, hoping it is the right choice. In theory, he understands the reasoning, but every minute he's not with her is painful and he'd like that to stop.

Colin and Alex joined up with them. Alex avoided any eye contact with Ryker when they arrived. He doesn't blame Alex. There's nothing he could have done except what Alex did: protect what he could. Ryker's been in Alex's shoes.

Left with his thoughts between Reed and their rendezvous with Alex at the farm, Ryker's emotionally shredded. He replays happy memories over and over in his head: the first time Ryker heard her laugh back at the diner was music to his ears; Beth's tongue licking her lips in concentration was a sight to behold; the one he repeats most often is Beth's cute freckles, enticing green eyes widening, her breath hitching before the orgasm shook her. He refuses to think of anything but happy moments because, if he doesn't, he might just lose his shit and go mad, which won't help Beth or him. The urge to leave these men is strong, but he's aware they fight together, not alone. Beth matters a fuck of a lot. It kills Ryker that he didn't tell her his true feelings.

Donovan wasn't happy Colin was there, but he insisted. Ryker finds it harder to look at Colin. They took Beth on his watch, and Ryker finds it hard to swallow. But they say Colin took a bullet for her, and Ryker respects this selfless act. He's done it and seen it countless times during his military career, but it doesn't always end well for everyone. Finally, Ryker chances a look at his rival. *No, I should have escorted her myself, and it's a mistake that could cost me everything.*

"Hoss, peepers on?" Donovan asks through the mic. Hoss is out there, watching and waiting. He'd gone ahead and scoped out what they were walking into.

"Eyes on you. Candy and I are snug as bugs. Three captives in the bar. No packages sighted." Their nickname for the women. The absence of them concerns Ryker. The captives are the men.

Mal asks beside him, "Candy?"

Ryker pats his rifle in response, not wanting to miss the conversation between Donovan and Hoss. Some men name their guns, unlike Ryker. Mal shakes his head under an audible sigh. Mal was always the one in the corner, quietly absorbing the energy of the room without engaging. His brother's participation, even to be critical, is a positive sign.

"Two hostiles in the bar," Hoss says. "One hostile front of the pool. No eyes inside."

"Packages must be in the pool," Donovan says in the comms.

"My guess, too."

Ryker feels his chest constrict when he thinks about the last time he saw Libby, then he shoves the thought aside. The tension in him is so tangible that he desperately seeks a way to ease it. Despite his dislike for everything right now, he understands that this is the new reality they must face. With no order comes violence. Ryker's trying not to dwell on the prospect of what they'll do to Beth, only what he's going to do to them.

He's not subtle with his jaw clenching and knuckle cracking, either, so Ryker supposes the surrounding men understand what he's thinking. In this new world, they might even take part, but there's no doubt as to the level of violence he's willing to go to for Beth. One hair messed on her head, and he won't be accountable for going berserk on those dead men walking.

"So not a grab and go, then?" Donovan asks of no one in particular. No one volunteers to answer him. Instead, they remain in position, awaiting further instructions. Not as simple as they thought, but adapting is what they do best. This is fine with Ryker, who's ready to rain fire now.

Donovan blows out air and turns to Alex. "Pretty boy, you and Rask are with me in the pool. Check your weapons. Knives won't be as useful now."

Mal's jaw tightens at the use of his new nickname: Rask for rascal. He doesn't like it, but no one ever has a choice.

Donovan turns to Ryker and says, "You and Golden—" He's referring to Liam. "—extract the captives, like we planned. Use the silencer."

"You'll need help," Ryker says. "I'll take Rask's place and come with you."

"No. Rask has seen the layout of the house, and I need someone with CQC experience in the bar."

During a mission, you keep your emotions at arm's length for good reason. Emotions get you killed. Ryker swallows the lump in his throat, not liking the situation, but Donovan speaks with logic. Liam is a medic, trained to do what he does best: keeping men like Ryker alive during combat. Ryker has to do his part.

"Once you've reached the river, we'll sweep the house clean and secure the packages."

A twinge of jealousy sears through Ryker as he bumps into his brother's shoulder.

Mal bumps him back. "Don't worry, I'll get her out."

To shed the jealousy, Ryker instructs Colin. "Twinkle, stay behind me. Once bodies start dropping, search 'em for guns and ammo."

Colin scowls at him or the nickname, he's not sure which. Ryker volunteered to take him under his wing for this mission since Hoss was busy. Keep your friends close but your enemies closer. Simple to see Colin as the enemy, but the new norm forces them to live in close quarters. All about tactics. Ryker needs to be the better man because Beth's happiness is his priority. "Check the safety, secure 'em like Hoss taught you."

Plus, Donovan's plan to make Colin one of them is solid. Their situation demands every non-disabled man to defend and be able to fight if it comes to it. He's too green to be of much use right now, but Colin will learn. "Don't get in my way unless you want to catch a round, copy?"

"Since you took my weapon, that shouldn't be hard to follow."

Of course he did. Why Hoss gave him a handgun without proper training is beyond Ryker. *Christ, just what I need, an untrained civilian with a loaded weapon. Especially on my six.*

Donovan looks sideways at Colin. "Superman's your superior on this mission. Do we have a problem?"

Ryker takes pleasure in Colin's discomfort. Normally, Ryker wouldn't think Superman was a great nickname. His last one—Slash—was more appropriate, but worse. *Perhaps this one will do, then.* Besides, it reminds him of Beth in his shirt and nothing else, so he'll take it, but he doesn't have to let them know that.

"No," Colin says with a sour look.

"Good. Let's roll." Donovan jumps up, and the others follow him along the tree line into the approaching sunset. "Hoss, try to miss us this time," he says in parting.

Ryker raises a disturbed eyebrow as he jogs in time with the others. "This time?"

In a serious tone, Hoss explains, "It's tradition, Superman. He always opens with that line on a mission."

***

Gunfire kills the sounds of the forest. Trees splinter around Beth as unseen bullets pass through the air. William fires off rounds. Beth covers her ears. Sounds warp but continue as William stumbles in slow motion like someone has pulled the rug out from under him.

"William!" Beth compels her limbs to spring toward him. She needs to save him.

The warped sound stops.

Steel arms enclose around her. She gazes into Colin's scared eyes and her anger flares. "Colin, move!"

Applying pressure on a man's wounded leg, blood gushes through her fingers. It keeps coming. *So much blood.*

She glances up, expecting to see William lying there, but Colin's unseeing eyes stare back at her. She propels backward in fear. *Not Colin! Where's William?*

Beth rises, scans the trees. She's alone.

Beth's pulled away. Foliage encloses around her, blinds her, and covers her. "No!"

A hand covers her mouth.

Beth wakes to Melanie's hand tight over her mouth. She says in the softest whisper, "They just took the woman you came in with."

Chapter 49

In the shadows, Alex and Donovan slit the throats of two armed men at the back door of the farmhouse with cold accuracy and deposit their bodies in a nearby bush. *Damn, these guys are scary focused.* Mal's glad he switched sides. After seeing the efficiency with which they dispatched those two, he feels a little more confident this will play out in their favor.

Donovan sidles up to the kitchen window, glances inside, and says, "Standing by, Superman."

"Copy," Ryker answers through the headpiece.

After what seems like forever, Liam says into the comms, "Entering the bar." Mal bleeds out the tension by dropping his shoulders. Another minute stretches into the next, and then Liam relays intel: "Os, no packages, three captives. Two targets, one armed."

Mal might not know their secret language but he understands that statement: the women are upstairs.

Alongside Donovan, Mal peeks through the window and is afforded a clear view of the dining and living room, lit by lanterns, beyond the dark kitchen. Cal and Joe are standing guard further back—always together, just like they were in prison—while Gideon is sitting at the head of the dining room table. To his left, a woman sits at the table with him.

At the sound of muffled screams filtering down from above, Mal's body tenses up again.

"Eyes on three targets, two armed, and Musketeer G," Donovan confirms, letting out a breath.

Mal focuses on Musketeer G, Donovan's daughter, Gina.

Gideon talks, his left hand disappearing into Gina's lap, and Mal fills with outrage. Under the lamplight, as Gideon dangles meat off his bent fork under her nose, Gina fixes her eyes straight ahead at the kitchen wall. She remains unmoving, like he didn't even speak. He plops the fork into his mouth and continues to talk while he chews. She appears to be fine, but appearances can be deceiving. There's no food in front of her. Gideon's head turns to Cal and Joe and then he leans in to Gina and says something. She flinches, and Gideon smiles. *Asshole's torturing her.*

Hoss's voice rings in his headset. "One incomin', front door!"

***

The bedroom door swivels and creaks on its hinges until the doorknob smacks the wall. Beth twists her head. A short, confident man walks in and begins inspecting them, a coffee mug in his grasp. The air is thick with fear on a whole new level, and Beth's gaze travels over the women. They cower to appear smaller, especially Elena, who is squeezing her eyes shut. *Dugal.*

Beth tries to quell her own fear as Dugal struts to the window, gazes out, and brings the mug to his lips. Beyond him, the setting sun paints vibrant colors on the trees and mountains. If she were at the window, she might see the fields across the river. *Haven.* So close, yet so far. Ryker will track them here, but will he make it in time to save them?

"Thought you lost your privileges?" Cain saunters in with a satisfied grin, dragging the disheveled-looking and emotionally shattered redhead into the room. He unceremoniously ties her to the bedpost, where she balls herself up on the floor. *Bastard.* The other women cower, avoiding his eyes.

Dugal continues to gaze out the window. "Reinstated."

This satisfies Cain. Beth stares him down until he disappears from the room. She wants to comfort the redhead but can't reach her.

What's she going to do if they pick her? She closes her eyes to the insanity of it all. *They should be here by now. Where are they?*

"Hell of a day." The women cringe at his voice. "Man works all day to put food on the table and expects a good fuck. Heard there was fresh blood in today." Dugal raises his mug, and his Adam's apple bobs with every swallow.

Sinister eyes turn to Beth, devouring and assessing her. She recalls the same asshole smacking Neil around the day she found him. Beth's skin crawls under the unwanted scrutiny of his malevolent gaze, but she challenges him with a bold stare. Hoss's voice speaks to her: "Never show weakness to an opponent, even when you're quaking in your boots, missy."

Dugal's greedy eyes slide away from her. Beth's heart races, anger flares, her eyelids widen. *Don't you dare.* Her head swivels toward Elena's pleading, wide-eyed expression.

Beth's memory flashes to the moment the car spun out of control. Her sister's terrified face. "Beth, help me!" Carrie cries out before the gravitational force sucks her out of the car.

Beth reaches out, but the sharp pain reminds her of the rope and where she is. Her heart collapses, painfully aware she can't help Elena. *Even if you were free, you'd be powerless to help her. You're weak.*

Dugal abandons the mug on the windowsill and advances.

Beth grips the bedpost. The rope bites. Her voice is loud. "Take me!"

He cackles like her request is ridiculous. The women closest to Elena scatter, forcing their bonds to tighten and causing painful cries to escape their lips. With ease, he overpowers a frightened Elena and unties her rope.

No, no, no! "Let her go!" Beth spits.

Dugal drags a distraught Elena by her hair around the bed and shoves his black-hearted face into Beth's. "I'm going to enjoy this one, and then you're next, my little spitfire."

Beth uses the only thing she has and kicks, but he sidesteps out of her reach. His brow creases with intense anger, and he points at her. "You little bitch! She'll suffer because of you."

Elena's wails chill Beth to the bone. He slaps Elena hard across the mouth, silencing her, before hauling her over his shoulder. The bedroom door shakes the walls as it slams closed, cutting her off from her cousin. An uncontrollable rage pours into Beth, forcing her to howl at the ceiling.

***

An outraged scream floats down from above, drawing Mal's eyes up. *Beth? Fuck, time for action!*

Next to him, Donovan's clenching his jaw. Urgency compels him to ask in the comms, "Ready? Now or never."

Mal eyes a wiry man as he hefts a lantern down the hallway and shuts the door to a bathroom under the stairs. *Walter.* No love lost there. *Four...*

"Hoss, is the porch empty?" Mal asks.

"Negative, different guard just came out."

Five... Whoever came out, came from upstairs. *Possibly six...*

"Ready?" Hoss says through the comms.

"Engaging," Liam relays.

Mal moves to the back door. Donovan's arm strikes Mal's chest, freezing him in place.

***

Elena's cries... Beth can't let her suffer but she can't fight them all, either. She doesn't deserve to suffer. *I do. Why didn't he just pick me?*

Melanie shakes her head. "Bastard. I hoped she'd be spared."

329

Her choice of words sucks Beth back into that hospital room. From a relaxed position, William regards fifteen-year-old Beth picking at her food and asks, "Did it ever occur to you that you were spared?"

Beth gives him a look as if he has lost his mind. "I wasn't spared. They left me."

"They didn't choose to leave you."

No, I did that for them.

William leans forward and says, his voice barely above a whisper, "You were spared for something greater."

She turns away from him.

"I've been in that dark hole, Beth. I understand your struggle."

"You don't know."

William's gentle hand slides under hers and squeezes. "Keisa was nagging me one night. We ended up arguing. She said I was lazy." He is talking about his first wife. "I was so mad. Had to leave or I'd regret saying more than I already had."

Her eyes make their way back to William's bowed head as he strokes Beth's fingers. "I was drunk at the bar down the street when the fire engine drove by." His eyes lift to meet Beth's. "My lazy ass hadn't replaced the smoke detectors. Jordan was six; Janet, four. I killed my family, Beth." He enunciates his next words: "I...know...your struggle."

Beth's teenage heart fills with love for the man, for his loss, his courage to come back. Can she do the same? "How did you get out of the hole?"

"It wasn't easy." His head dips back down as he sighs. "Took years to get my head out of a bottle...and my ass." He leans back in the chair. "But I started climbing. You will, too."

Beth blinks herself back into the present and scans the women staring back at her from around the metal bed frame, each one holding their breath in terror.

Hoss's gruff voice says in her head, *First thing you have to do is shed the fear. When you fear, you give them the power.*

You aren't strong enough.

No! Beth ignores the horrible voice.

The rope itches. She tests the strength of it. Used to being saved and protected by others, a new thought materializes. *I don't need to be saved.* William had the courage to face a bullet for her, and so will she. For Elena. *I am strong enough.*

"It's time to climb," Beth says to no one in particular. Fueling her anger, she battles against the searing pain, forcefully tugging and yanking her restraints until she loosens the rope enough to squeeze her hands out and finally breaks free. She thanks Hoss for making her go through these exercises. He taught her well. *I have to do this.*

Melanie gawks in shock as the rope falls to the ground. "Climb?"

Beth endures the burning agony in her wrists as she starts on Melanie's rope. "We're going to get ourselves out of this hole."

***

Intense and driven, Beth wrenches the bedroom door open. The women spill out into the hall, and with brute force, rush their unsuspecting sentry. Melanie smashes Dugal's heavy mug over the back of the guard's head, knocking him senseless, and they drag him into the bedroom. From the door frame, Beth monitors the stairs, praying no one comes up. She can't afford an altercation that takes her away from her objective. The aroma of food drifts through the air. Saliva floods her dry mouth, causing her to swallow as thoughts of hunger overpower her mind. Floorboards moan and groan under many feet behind her. She gazes back and takes in the moment as Melanie and the redhead drop their guard to the floor, then one straddles his face while the other sits on his chest, robbing him of oxygen. The last two women jump on him and restrict his movements so as not to raise the alarm as he thrashes.

Beth turns back to the hallway and focuses on the room she passed earlier. Peeled paint shavings rest at the base of the closed door, blocking Beth from seeing what's happening behind its cracked panels. Familiar hesitation bubbles up, but she fights herself for control. *You can fucking do this!* With adrenaline pumping and her mind on one purpose, Beth coerces the pencil to slither down her arm. *I hope this works.* Hoss made her practice enough on ballistic gelatin.

Melanie scoots up behind Beth. "What's the plan?"

"I'll free Elena. Come across, force a window open, and get the girls onto the roof. I'll distract them while you escape down a tree." Beth points west. "Head that way, cross the creek, then head north to the river. Walk west, and when you see the rapids, cross there."

"What about you?"

What she's about to do is bold and stupid, but at least Beth will give them time to escape. "I'll be fine. There's a bunker across the fields on the other side. Walk north until you find the wall."

Melanie hesitates. "Wall?"

"Yeah, you'll know it when you see it. They'll see you coming anyway."

Melanie goads her on with a wave of her hand. "Okay. Go save her. We're right behind you."

Beth's not sure why their movement hasn't raised the alarm but she has no time to worry about it. She pulls Melanie close. "Whatever you do, do it quietly and keep watch on the stairs for anyone."

"Good luck."

No luck needed. Beth prepares herself.

"No!" Elena cries from the other side of the run-down door.

"Sit still, bitch!"

Beth turns to the door to see her sister waiting, silent as the grave. Beth's bravado falters, but she doesn't push the panic button. Beth faces Carrie, daring her to get in her way.

***

Through the slats of the barn, the last of the sun streaks across bales as Ryker takes cover. The god-awful stench of rotting hay assaults his nose, but he swallows the bile threatening to come up to take a quick gander so he can assess his next move. Three men are huddled together, awake in a stall at the far end of the barn, their arms tied with rope. He deduces the barrel-chested one is Beth's uncle from the diner. He's not sure which of the other two is Sean.

James sits on his haunches like a caged animal, intense and ready to make a move, as the man in the Black Sabbath shirt converses with a tall, tattooed man by the barn door. The tall one strikes a match and lights an oil lamp. Sabbath Shirt says, "It ain't fair. It was just a joke." *He's armed.*

"Don't matter now," the tall one says, placing the lamp on a wall nail. "We need to keep our heads low. We'll get our chance with the women another time." He walks out of Ryker's line of sight. *Not armed.*

Using the shadows, Ryker stalks without sound along the hay bale wall, fixating on Sabbath Shirt. Hugging his weapon close, Ryker's perception of his surroundings heightens: with the suppressor, his weapon's center of gravity and weight have changed; Liam at his back comforts him, while Colin's loud footsteps threaten to reveal their position as he lags behind, ready to collect any dropped weapons. Their light dissipates, replaced by the glow of the lamp. The musty smell of disintegrating cedar mixes with the stench of decaying hay. The ground underneath him is uneven, but soft in areas and littered with rotten wooden boards. *Tread lightly.*

Ryker catches James's eye as he slinks forward, and James shimmies out of his bonds as the others cower. The bulky man snatches a bundle of rope off the wall with intent. *Once a Marine, always a Marine.*

Sabbath Shirt yawns.

Ryker slows...aims...

James's movement distracts Sabbath Shirt. *Winner, winner, chicken dinner.*

Ryker fires.

There's a spray of red mist where Sabbath Shirt's head used to be, and his body crumples. The silencer did its job, but it wasn't totally quiet in this space. Ryker prepares as he comes up to the corner. Although the other man wasn't armed, it doesn't mean he isn't armed now. *Never assume.*

"Watch out!" James yells.

The swing of a metal hook threatens to take off Ryker's head. Losing his grip on his weapon, he tumbles backward to the earth after clearing the arcing weapon. Ryker grits his teeth as the jarring pain from his newest injury intensifies but he pushes through and quickly finds the gun again. As James comes closer, swinging the uncoiled rope, Ryker scrambles away.

The tall man raises the hook to strike. James's rope flies. Ryker draws a fist full of earth and raises his weapon.

Chapter 50

B *ang!*

Beth's hand pauses on the tarnished metal door knob. Hoss's words trickle in: *Always be at least one step ahead of your opponent.* She clenches painted wood in her left hand, the straight edge under her thumb.

She has one job. Her brain registers the sharp crack of a weapon firing, but she discards it, twists the handle, and shoves the door into the room. Floral wallpaper is peeling off the walls, stained with the shadows of missing picture frames. She notes that the window to the right is unhindered by nails. The springs of the bed groan as Dugal launches himself off Elena, who has one arm tied to the metal frame. *I'm not too late.*

Beth raises the carpenter pencil skywards, sharp end out and enters. Dugal's surprise lasts but a second before he rushes her in a murderous rage.

They collide. Dugal seizes Beth's wrist, yanks her to his body, and twists her hand. The pencil clatters to the floor. His smile cries victory over her. She revolts against his foul body odor and yellow teeth, taking a precious second to comb the bed. Elena is struggling to untie herself.

Dugal clamps Beth's arm behind her back. *One step ahead.* She tightens her fingers around a plastic handle and says, "Go to hell!" Beth drives the screwdriver into his body with her free hand, surprised at how easily it penetrates him as liquid coats her fingers.

Pain slants Dugal's offensive smile. He didn't see it coming. *Neither did Ryker's sister.* "Bastard!" Anger fuels her as she tears out the rusty screwdriver with cruel intent and thrusts it back in again. Dugal stumbles backward, clutching his side. She didn't come up with a plan beyond injuring him and hopes she hit something vital. There's so much blood, but is it enough to kill him?

Elena scrambles off the bed. Their eyes meet. "Window," Beth whispers with urgency.

Elena bolts. Dugal extends his hand, but the injury has weakened him. Beth snatches her cousin and pushes her toward the window. "Window!" *Where's Melanie?* Beth's urgency to flee undetected grows stronger every second. Should she be concerned that he might raise the alarm?

Dugal's eyes darken, rage builds, and then he coils. The last of Beth's confidence fizzles out, and she backs up into the door frame. She needs to protect Elena. *This is it.* Dugal pounces. His feverish hands fuse around Beth's throat, impeding her ability to breathe.

Beth's brain jars as Dugal slams her head into the wall. Pain pierces her skull. His hands squeeze. No air escapes her lips. Her fingers go numb. The screwdriver strikes the floor, sending a tremor up the wall. Beth's body slides up, and her feet leave the ground, but her legs still fight as her boots slam into the wall. Beth's vision blurs.

This is the reason she's here, why she didn't die before. Beth needed to save Elena.

But it's done now. She's ready to die.

Light-headed, her consciousness wavers and eyelids flutter. The pain dulls. As she fades, Ryker's words fill her head: *Beth, if you die, I'll be alone.*

I had no choice, Ryker. Forgive me.

***

Hearing the gunshot, Mal has a fleeting moment of worry for his brother, but Gideon shifts Mal's focus when he yanks Gina up from the table kicking and screaming. He drags her into the living room, throws her into an armchair, and with his boot, shoves the chair into the wall. She recoils under his accusing finger. Through the cracked window, Gideon's angry words rend the air: "Stay the fuck there!"

Cal and Joe, guns in hand, gawk by the fractured front window. Gideon barks orders. "What the fuck? Go to the barn! Find out what the fuck's going on!"

***

The metal hook whacks Ryker's leg as the man plummets, brandishing a new hole in his forehead. "Son of a bitch!" Ryker grabs his thigh, thankful it landed with the sharp end up. *That's going to hurt.* He searches for the shooter and finds Colin looking like he wants to throw up, a 9MM pistol in his shaky hands. So much for the element of surprise.

"Hmm, maybe there's promise for you, after all," Ryker says through gritted teeth.

Hoss's urgent voice comes over the comms. "Two armed guests arrivin' in five seconds, Superman! Can't take the shot."

Ryker makes a call and jumps up. The pain in his leg threatens to cripple him, along with the searing pain of his healing injury. *Adrenaline, don't fail me now.* "Everyone, back through the hole! Hoss, try to miss us in three!"

James grabs Sean and the other captive by their collars, and they run like hell. Ryker lags a second behind them, happy he'll soon be rid of the revolting stench of this place, and pushes Colin forward.

***

"Time to close the pool," Donovan commands. "Alex, take the one in the bathroom. Mal, guard the back door."

Mal's fine with that. No sense getting involved when you have trained killers who can do the work for you.

"Fire in the hole, boys." Hoss calls through the comms. A powerful gunshot thunders...twice.

Four...

Donovan uses the distraction, taps Alex and Mal's shoulders, and leads them in. "Entering the pool."

"Yard's clear," Hoss says. "One lying low on the porch. Repositioning."

They enter a tiny kitchen with tile floors, sticking to the dark recesses. The two men split: Alex takes the hall, and Donovan, the dining room.

The bathroom door swings open. Alex crowds Walter back inside. Light dances with the shadows across the tiled floor as Mal holds his breath by the back door. The light goes out. Alex exits, securing a blade. Mal exhales with relief.

Three...

Mal's senses magnify: Gideon's whispered words to Gina sound muffled; the aroma of food alerts his stomach to the fact he has eaten little in the last twenty-four hours; the floor creaks above, signaling the movement of other potential threats. From the shadowed corner of the kitchen, Mal watches Alex, his steps inaudible, move down the hallway and toward the front door. *Handy skill.*

"In position," Alex says.

"Copy," Donovan confirms.

Mal witnesses the moment Gideon spots Donovan stalking in, weapon raised and radiating a different level of hate. Gideon hauls Gina up as a shield and points a gun to her temple. *You fucked with the wrong man, Gideon.*

Mal beholds a chain reaction in slow motion like he's never experienced before. Alex distracts Gideon, aiming at him from the hallway. Gideon faces both threats with Gina out front. And then the mission takes a different turn. Blood sprays across Mal's field of vision.

Four... Fuck, he miscalculated! From the dark shadows of the kitchen, Mal whispers in the comms, "Old man's down." His mind reels as he tries to make sense of what he's witnessed. Someone else is in the dining room. "Need backup now, Ry."

Gina's like a wildcat in Gideon's arms, screaming for her father. Donovan's down for the count, possibly dead. *I have to do something.*

Hoss's urgent voice comes through. "Incoming, front door!"

Shit! Mal sweeps the hall for Alex. Like a spectator, Mal watches Cain, armed and brazen, throw the front door wide and barrel forward. Alex fires, and Cain propels out the way he came in.

Three...

Before Mal can swallow that scene, a round of bullets slams through the dining room wall with Alex's name on them. *Who's the unknown man?*

Alex sprints up the stairs, whispering into his comms, which project into Mal's ears: "Fucker tagged me."

I'm the only one left. With no time to think, Mal shoves his weapon into the back of his jeans. *Better to go in looking unarmed.*

His brother's calm voice comes through on the comms: "Rask, we're on our way."

Mal rips his vest off and says into the comms, "I'll get you the time, Ry." Mal sheds the helmet, exposing himself, and enters the dining room. "Gideon! It's Mal, don't shoot!"

***

Melanie rushes into the bedroom and comes to an abrupt stop as the other women scurry past her. Beth's mind yells *Stop, save yourself* as Melanie jumps onto Dugal's back and bites his ear. He stumbles backward as her weight unbalances him.

Beth's body collides with the floor, and her coughs echo throughout the barren room. Under several grunts, the other women jimmy open the window, and cool mountain night air wafts in. The aroma of freshly turned earth awakens Beth to what's happening around her.

Dugal claws at Melanie's head, determined to rid himself of her, but Elena enters the fray and kicks him in the groin. Blood drops sprinkle on the floor. With a cry of pain, Dugal yanks his ear out of Melanie's mouth and bends over in agony. Melanie slams into the bloodstained floor, which loosens her hold on him.

Clutching his groin with one hand, Dugal seizes Elena's throat with the other.

Elena! Dazed and angry, Beth snatches up the bloody screwdriver.

Chapter 51

Kaden points his weapon at Mal from the corner of the dining room. *Doesn't know if he can trust me. Makes sense.* If he knew Libby was Mal's sister, Kaden would have killed him on the spot. His sister didn't deserve to die that way, and Mal fights the urge to rush Kaden. The inability to take his revenge burns, but Libby is gone and Gina needs him. She's his priority right now. *I've got her, old man.*

Glancing down, Mal looks at Donovan on the floor at his feet, blood pooling from wounds he can't see. "Jesus, Kaden! Who's this?" He steps over Donovan's still body, trying to appear as uncaring as possible.

"Don't know. Was that you shooting outside?" Kaden asks, relaxing his gun hand.

When Mal's gaze connects with Gina's frightened eyes up close, a long dead craving hits him like a Mack truck. Donovan's wife must have been a knockout because, even disheveled and bruised, Gina's gorgeous. He's not sure if it's her vulnerability that hits him in the chest or her beauty, but whatever it is, it unbalances him. Heat rises in places he prefers it not to. Gina's bleeding lip and bruised eye incites a rage in him so powerful, he veers toward the hallway opening, curbing the desire to punch Gideon.

"Where'd you get the clothes?" Gideon asks.

Shit. Mal thinks fast. "A trapper cabin I stumbled upon." Mal spies Cain's body on the porch and searches up the stairs for Alex. Sweating and holding his own in silence, Alex nods when their eyes meet. He notes the dark red stain carving a path down Alex's leg. *Time to finish this.* He wonders where Dugal is, the bastard. He's the one Mal wants to kill the most. Slowly and fucking painfully.

If Mal has a chance, he'll take out Kaden. Just looking at him sets Mal off. "One down in the hall. I got two, but I think there's another one out there."

Gideon shoves Gina into a surprised Mal's arms. "Take her and guard the door."

That was damn easy. With Gina in his grasp, he can't take out Kaden, but her soft skin under his hands and the hint of lavender are a fair trade-off. Something inside him softens.

Gideon turns to Kaden. "Pull this guy over, see if we can get some answers out of him." Kaden bends down to move Donovan.

Ryker stalks in from the darkness of the kitchen, followed by Liam. Gideon raises his weapon. Mal launches into action, pushing Gina into the furthest wall and shielding her with his body. Four gunshots go off in the room. *Goddamn, that was loud!*

Ryker says, "Ground floor clear!"

Alex's strained voice cries down the stairs: "Guys, upstairs now!"

Possibly one left.

Ryker, Colin, and an unknown, barrel-chested man charge up the stairs. Liam bends down beside Donovan. A shy, young African American man clutches the door frame to the kitchen behind him as a Hispanic man in a dirty plaid shirt lays his hand on the young man's shoulder. *Must be Alejo's partner.* Mal tries to shield Gina from seeing Gideon and Kaden's bodies.

"Let me go!" Gina fights Mal like a wild animal but isn't able to break through his firm grip. He can't let her get in Liam's way. Not wanting to hurt her, he corrals her just enough for his message to get through. "Gina, stop! Let Liam work on him."

Breathing hard, she ceases to fight.

There is blood sprayed across the wall, and Mal remembers Donovan hitting his head on his way down to the floor. He hopes for Gina's sake that the old man is okay, otherwise he'll have to grip her harder when she cracks. It's something he's not sure he can handle witnessing again.

Liam's experienced hands tear up green packages, exposing gauze, which he presses on Donovan's wound. He places his fingers on Donovan's neck, looking for a pulse, and leans down to listen for his patient's breathing. He adds more gauze, continues to apply pressure, and then slaps Donovan's face a few times. "Donovan? You here? Donovan?"

***

Ryker takes the stairs two at a time, feeling vulnerable. He pushes against the vision of Beth looking broken and battered, lying against the walls in a pool of blood. He tosses the fear aside completely when he spots Alex, dragging his injured leg, in obvious agony.

"End of the hall, left." Alex points at a doorway.

Ryker rushes past with James and Colin shadowing him and slides into the doorframe, rifle raised, ready to do battle. He takes in the room and the carnage.

Bleeding from her head and out of breath, a woman lies against the bedroom wall, while more terrified women stare in from an open window to the porch roof. He follows a trail of blood across the room to a man covered in red, his jugular pumping out blood in regular spurts.

"Dad!" Elena screams, reaching out.

James runs to the window.

"Beth!" Colin moves.

Ryker yanks on Colin's vest, preventing him from entering.

"Let me go to her!"

Ryker doesn't give two shits that Colin's angry at him. Ryker zeros in on the only woman he'll ever love and says, "That's not Beth."

Beth stands over the man he identifies as Dugal, his crumpled body splayed out. She's covered in multiple patterns of blood spatter. She thrusts a bloody screwdriver into his torn neck, then rips it back out with a shaky hand. She's losing steam.

In Dugal's last moments, he claws at his throat and thrashes around on the floor as life pours out of him. He's suffering, and that's all that matters to Ryker. His sister can rest in peace now. *It's over.*

Colin thinks Beth needs saving, but she doesn't. Whatever this asshole did to her, it made her snap. Ryker knows what madness during combat looks like, the brain persistently telling you that you are in danger. He's experienced it himself. *Time to bring her down.*

Ryker stares Colin down. "Stay...here."

Beth draws her arm up to plunge the screwdriver again.

"Beth!" Ryker calls out.

The screwdriver trembles in midair. Her cold-blooded eyes slide up, devoid of rationality, as she draws in bursts of oxygen. He needs her to recognize him and raises his hands. "Hey."

She blinks; recognition ignites as her mind reboots. Her crazed eyes follow Ryker as he approaches with caution.

"Hey," she says, her voice trembling as she lowers the weapon and stumbles.

Tension releases in Ryker as he crosses the divide and devours Beth into his chest. "I'm here now." He relieves her of the screwdriver, tosses it, and drags her away from the filth at her feet.

She nuzzles his arm and clings to his vest like she wants to lose herself in him. "I found my confidence."

"I can see that, my badass girl." *God, I never want her out of my sight again.* Fuck, he'd never have forgiven himself if he'd lost her. His emotions run high at the thought, and he closes his eyes while stroking her back.

"Ryker?"

"Hmm." His vocal cords vibrate as he tilts his head downward.

"Ask me."

His chest pumps as he laughs inwardly, but tears escape as he kisses the top of her head. At first, he struggles to form the words, but then he takes a breath. "Would you like to go on a date with me?"

"Yes," she whispers with an air of finality. "I love you."

His heart zings on those three fucking amazing words. Overwhelmed by the need to connect, he threads his fingers through her messy hair, draws her head back, peers into olive-green eyes, and says, with conviction, "I fucking love you, too." His hungry lips crush hers with an intensity that warms him all over. Her body gravitates into him as their tongues meld with an impatient, unquenchable thirst.

Alex says, "Upstairs is clear. Extracting the packages."

Breaking the connection with her lips but not her body, Ryker takes in the room. The woman from the ground seems to have recovered and helps James to usher the women inside from the roof. He ignores the body of his old enemy and searches out Colin instead. He remains rooted by the doorframe, his love for Beth apparent. At least he followed his order. *You owe him.*

Ryker calls Colin forward with a chin raise and steps away from a confused Beth. Throwing his eyes behind her, he says, "Incoming."

Beth turns to the doorway. "Colin!"

Colin sucks in a relieved breath and even though Colin can see Beth's alright, he reaches out, apparently determined to confirm with his own hands that she's alive, and drags her into his arms. The familiar twitch of jealousy returns, but Ryker stifles it. Colin gazes across to Ryker and thanks him without words. Ryker raises his hand, and Colin greets him with a slap.

***

White glow sticks lie on the table and the ground around Donovan. They emit enough light for Mal to see the man wake up in a groggy state and swat at Liam as he works on Donovan's arm. He recovers his bearings and scours the room in a panic. *Looking for her.*

"You've lost a lot of blood, Donovan. Try not to move too much. The tourniquet will work till we get you to Henry. You lost consciousness. Possible concussion." Liam raises his hand. "How many fingers?"

Donovan flinches, his pain blatant. "Three."

"What year is it?"

"Twenty twenty-seven."

"How you feel?"

Donovan stares up at Liam. "Like I want to see my daughter."

Liam gazes up at Mal. "He's good."

Donovan's probing eyes come to rest on the highly agitated woman in Mal's arms. "Gina?!"

Okay, now you can go. Mal releases her.

"Dad!" She darts to her father, kneels beside him, not caring or not noticing that she's sitting in his blood. From Mal's vantage point, Gina looks painfully slender—delicate, almost—in the glowing light. Her tanned, golden-brown skin matches her messy hair. He quells the longing this inspires.

Having removed his headset earlier, Mal asks Liam, "Ry?"

"Upstairs is clear. They're coming down."

Thank Christ! Mal sheds his stress and breathes it out.

Hoss walks in, lays his sniper rifle against the wall, and wipes fresh blood off his knife with a rag while he takes in the scene before him. "This location isn't secure. We need to vamoose." He inspects Donovan's wound. "Son, he good to move, or do we have to make a stretcher?"

Liam says, "I can't—"

"No fucking way! I'll walk on my own," Donovan declares.

Of course he will. Old man's off his rocker.

"Like hell you will!" Hoss straps his rifle to his back and bends to help Liam get Donovan off the floor. *They're like two old women.*

"Mal, take her," Donovan says through gritted teeth, offering his daughter up.

Me? Mal's not used to being at a loss for words, and he's definitely not sure what to say to that order. On the trek here, he got glimpses of a tall man in uniform when Donovan stood or talked in a certain way. Those were memories Mal had thought he'd lost long ago.

Gina grabs her father's arm. "No. I'm not leaving you!"

He hasn't been with these people long, but even Mal knows Donovan's not fond of being disobeyed.

"Gina, do as I say!"

With sudden strength, Donovan grabs a hold of Mal's shirt with sweaty and bloody hands and stares him down, nose to nose. He has something ready to fire off, but Donovan's intense stare shuts that down. *Maybe not the time to be funny.* "Stay with her. Promise me you won't leave her till I get out."

Out? Mal doesn't want the responsibility, but this is important to the old man, so he placates him. "Do I have to pinkie promise?" Not funny, but Mal loves toying.

Donovan pierces Mal with unbending eyes and growls in warning. "Mal..."

"I'll do what you ask, old man."

Donovan relaxes his hold and suddenly looks pale. Mal has a fleeting moment of uncertainty, but then figures the old man is too ornery to die. Under protest, Hoss and Liam lead Donovan out between them.

Mal can't help but trail back to Gina, her eyes downcast. *Not trusting, yet.*

Her obvious bruises raise his ire; the ones that are visible, anyway. He swallows the murderous rage swirling inside and channels his energy into appearing calm.

Ryker and a bloody Beth help Alex hobble down the stairs, followed by some timid, scared women. One looks utterly spent. *What the hell happened upstairs?* Maybe he doesn't want to— An unwanted memory flares: the shame on his mother's face as she lies on the bathroom floor, her clothes rumpled; his stepfather exits, adjusting his belt buckle. She looks shattered...

Mal closes his eyes, blocks the memory, then opens them again to center back on Gina. She can walk under her own steam, but Mal's urge to protect her is strong. *I need to do this gently or I'll risk scaring her.* "Will you let me carry you, or do you want to walk beside me?"

Brown eyes slide up, cutting him with their raw vulnerability. *Like Mom...* He swallows. Maybe Gina notes the pain reflected in Mal's expression or trusts her father's judgment, but for whatever reason, she says, "I'll walk...if you'll support me."

He offers her his elbow, but Gina pauses. He holds his breath. Her eyes glide up to his and back to his arm. Her touch is soft as her fingers curl around his bicep.

"Hold on tight. I won't let anything happen to you."

CHAPTER 52

The wind dies down as Ryker enters the forest from the open fields with Beth beside him. They follow the others up a slope, then take a sharp left and advance toward an extremely high wall covered in some kind of foliage. Highlighted by heavy lighting in the yard, two towering trees stand guard inside the compound. They pass through a single, open doorway, into a large, grassy area. A limp American flag at half mast hangs, draped around a pole. Further into the dark recesses of the yard, the crisp clang of bells ring out.

The metal door to Haven's yard closes behind them as the last of the group enters. For the amount of people standing or lying on the ground, it is eerily quiet. Now the adrenaline has worn off, he can see everyone is dirty, some bloodier than others, and exhausted. Ryker searches out Beth's hand, desiring her to stay close. The breeze picks up, shaking the leaves into a crescendo of sound.

We are home. Safe. He glances at Beth. *Together.*

He and Liam tried to keep Donovan stable in the zodiac while Hoss navigated the river as best he could with the help of their flashlights. None of the women had adequate protection against the chilly night air, but the residents of Haven seem to have prepared for that with provisions on the other side. Having arrived before Ryker, he can see someone has wrapped the women in blankets and given them mismatching clothes.

A confident-looking man in black-rimmed glasses emerges and addresses the crowd with raised hands. "Hello, everyone, my name's Henry. I'm the doctor here. If you are not injured, go down and surrender any weapons to security. Sylvia and Penny—" He points at the two women standing by an immense piece of steel. "—will assist you in finding the communal area so we can assess your needs."

"I'll go down and help with security." Donovan walks out of Hoss's range, only to stumble after a few steps.

Hoss pulls him in, his voice filled with warmth and amusement as he says, "Slow down there, sparky. You're going to medical like the rest."

"Like hell I will!" Donovan grapples with his friend but his lack of strength makes it impossible for him to escape Hoss's grasp.

"I'll be the judge of where you go, Donovan. Sit down before you pass out." Henry looks at Liam. "Get him a stretcher."

When Liam starts to cross the yard, Donovan holds up his good arm and yells out, "I don't need a stretcher!"

With a pointed finger inches from Donovan's nose, Henry warns, "You give me any more sass, Sergeant, and I'll make you go bye-bye. Copy?"

Donovan relinquishes with a discontented mutter, yet remains stationary as he meticulously surveys the crowd for his daughter.

Gina was by Donovan's side and holding his hand during the ride in the boat. Her battered body and lack of sleep caught up to her though, and when they hit the other side, she couldn't climb out of the zodiac. Mal picked Gina up like a feather. She was so thin, he carried her with ease across the fields.

Ryker finds his brother cradling Gina on a bench, asleep in his arms like a baby. His brother appears detached until Ryker catches him looking down upon Gina with a soft expression. He's only seen Mal this way once, with Barbra Stilton. Does this mean he might stay? It is a long shot, but Ryker needs hope right now.

"Let's take this vest off so I can check you over." Beth glides her hand up Ryker's forearm, distracting him with the shivers.

He's not hurt—well, no more than he was before—but the bruise on his thigh pains him. "I have a few spots you can inspect later." The mischievous smile she graces him with tickles him, and even though the vest is cumbersome, he encircles her shoulders and brings her in for a much-needed kiss. He can't seem to get enough of her again and can't wait until they're alone. He needs to feel her without the vest, to know it's not a dream.

"Beth!"

They turn in unison. Neil dashes across the yard, dodging people to get to them, followed by an overjoyed man who lost the battle to corral the boy. Beth opens her arms to a deliriously happy Neil. They need no words for the love transferring between them...and the dried blood. They'll have to rectify that later.

The man shakes Ryker's hand while he waits his turn. "Parker. Thanks for bringing her home, Ryker."

The sentiment warms him. "My pleasure, sir."

When Beth rises, Parker struggles and lowers his eyes. "I should have rescued you." It is a simple statement, bogged down by guilt.

"That would have been a bad idea and you know it," Beth says, sinking into Parker's chest. His arms close around her like a vise. "Besides, William told me everything happens for a reason. If you came searching for me, I wouldn't have found myself or—" She turns to Ryker and Neil. "—the new men in my life."

Pure joy strikes Ryker when Neil's arms curl around his waist. It hurts, too, but Ryker tolerates the pain. It cuts Ryker deep, knowing the loss these kids have had to deal with. As he vowed to bring happiness to Beth, he pledges to do the same for the boy he's beginning to love like a son.

Parker soothes Beth with light circles up and down her back. *He needs the contact, just like I did.* "Are you hurt?" Parker asks.

Ryker's concern for her deepens as he wonders about the extent of her trauma from this ordeal.

She replies with a simple answer: "My bruises will heal."

Parker brushes his lips across her forehead. "Welcome home, Chickie."

***

With Gina still asleep in his arms, Mal follows the women they rescued and Henry down a set of well-lit stairs to a landing with two doors leading off in opposite directions. The one on the left is closed. He cranes his neck to see inside the other one. Only one word comes to mind: *Cool.*

Alex's twin, Miles, is sitting in front of monitors, similar to the ones at Reed, displaying night-vision images of topside, and is surrounded by communications hardware. Every inch of the walls is lined with rifles and handguns, and the scent of gunpowder lingers in the air. Hardened trunks around the edges of the room keep their contents a secret under closed lids. They mean business here. *Profitable.*

An unfamiliar man greets Mal. His eyes soften at the sight of Gina in his arms. "Name's John Henry," he says in a quiet voice as he strokes her hair. "You have a firearm?"

Mal's wary of the man's affection even after he spots the wedding ring. His jealousy isn't justified, but it remains. But more than that, without the vest, Mal's handgun is his only means of defense in this strange place.

After wrestling with the decision for a moment, he tilts his head in a downward direction, turns his back, and the weapon slides out of his waistband. "Name's Mal. Where's medical?"

John Henry points down the stairs. "Walk straight through the atrium garden, down another short staircase, and straight through the tunnel. Once the ceiling opens up, medical's on your left."

"Thanks," Mal says, resuming his descent into Haven.

John Henry's instructions prove to be accurate as the staircase opens under a sky-high vertical conveyor with rows of tubing and an abundance of flora. It smells like the farm back home, which brings up stale memories. There are dozens of pots filled with citrus fruit trees, rows of hanging strawberries and tomatoes, and barrels full of dirt which, he suspects, contain potatoes.

The ceiling isn't cement, like the walls, but a dome of frosted glass or hard plastic designed to let in enough light for the plants. He checks some of them on the way past and finds different varieties of leafy vegetables floating in water. He wishes he didn't know anything about farming, but if he has to use his knowledge, he'll grin and bear it. Farming isn't a choice anymore, like it was back then; now, it's farm or starve. There are no restaurants or markets or fast-food places to visit anymore. Just the dirt he crossed to get here.

Mal descends another short staircase and enters a white corridor that curves in both directions and is lined with silver lockers, reminding him of a futuristic starship. He gazes from right to left. His shoes squeak on polished floors like they did back at the prison. He ducks as he enters a domed tunnel and guesses not everyone is as tall as he and Donovan are. He files that for future reference. Future? Could he stay here? *Ryker has a reason to stay, but do I?* Mal's eyes slant to the woman in his arms. She has a long road ahead of her.

Mal steps into an enormous room, and his mind is overwhelmed by what he can only describe as an awe-inspiring space. The room must be over ten thousand square feet. The ambient noise of so many people going about their various activities is something he hasn't heard in months. Certainly since the missiles fell, but even his time in prison was never this noisy.

A man with a religious stole on his shoulders walks around pouring water into glasses, comforting the new arrivals with a pat here and there on their tired shoulders. Teenagers mingle and whisper at a nearby table, watching the spectacle of men and women trickling in with the injured. Does anyone sleep down here? He doesn't even know what time it is anymore. Searching for a clock, he spots two gyms with equipment, a room chock full of books, and through a door left ajar, what looks like a classroom.

"Mal, over here," Henry calls out, waving him over. The sign above him says *Medical.*

Turning in that direction, Mal spots Penny with others preparing food in an extensive commercial kitchen. She looks up from the prep counter and smiles as he slips past Henry and into Haven's medical room. His mouth waters at the prospect of eating Penny's cookies. His grumbling stomach reminds him how hungry he is. And he desperately needs a shower.

Spotting Gina in his arms, the women in the room part reverently. Finding this a little unnerving, he cuts through the throng and deposits his charge gently on a hospital bed. Mal's heart deflates as her warmth dissipates from his arms. Should he stay or is this the end of the line for him?

Hoss and Ryker haul a stretcher in, carrying the old man. A young man, a blonde girl, and a teenage boy follow them in. Mal assumes they're Donovan's other children by the looks of them.

"Mal," Donovan calls out, "is she alright?"

"Gina!" the blonde girl says.

"She's in expert hands," Henry says as a nurse draws the curtain closed, cutting them off from everyone else. "Hoss, take them into the surgical room," Henry says from behind the curtain.

"Henry, I want to stay with her," Donovan says. "Mal?"

Don't look at me to save you, old man.

Hoss swiftly moves Donovan's stretcher into the other room. The rest of the gang follow them.

One woman steps forward, her head bandaged, and speaks at the curtain. "Doctor, my name's Melanie. Can I help? I'm... I was a nurse."

Henry's baritone voice says, "Grab some gloves. Evaluate the women for me, and I'll be with you in a moment. We don't have enough beds, so work out who's sharing with whom."

With experienced hands, Melanie plucks out gloves from a nearby box and guides the three women to one of the beds.

Alex hops inside the room, his arm stretched across Liam's shoulders as they enter.

Liam asks, "Henry, where you want Alex?"

"Henry!" Donovan yells from the other room. "Tell me what's going on!"

Henry parts the curtain, exposing his head, eyeballs Alex, and says, "Take him into the surgical room with Donovan. Keep him busy for me."

Liam nods and helps Alex hobble into the other room.

Mal stares at the closed curtain and decides he needs a long, hot shower.

"Don't touch me!" Gina yells from behind the curtain.

"Gina, relax while I—"

"No! Come back!"

"Two milligrams of Ativan! Stat!"

The curtain billows out, and Gina comes crashing through. Brown eyes scour the room and settle on Mal. She rushes at him. Mal's arms tighten around her slight frame as she buries herself into his chest.

"It's okay. Shh, don't worry, I'm right here. I'm right here." As Mal soothes her, he makes the odd observation that she's taller than the other women in the room.

Henry comes up behind her, not wanting to miss the opportunity, and jabs her with a needle. She jerks in surprise. Mal doesn't wait for permission to carry her back to the bed. This time, as the curtain closes, he stays with her. He sees desperation in her terrified eyes and trembling hands. Mal keeps his gaze on her tanned face as he strokes her golden hair.

"Don't leave me," she says, agitated at first, but the drug is already filtering through her system, causing her eyes to flutter closed once more. Her hand goes slack at the same time as Mal's shoulders.

The scratch of Velcro tearing echoes, and Henry wriggles a blood pressure cuff on Gina's arm. "Mal, she's out for a spell. Go get some food, but stay in the communal area. I'll need you to take her to Donovan's apartment once I've cleared her."

Mal nods. Without being able to voice the lost feeling he has from seeing Gina so distraught, he prefers to say nothing at all, lays her hand down on the bed, and turns to re-enter the domed space Henry called the communal area. Mal lets his nose guide him to the kitchen counter.

"Mal, have a seat, and I'll fetch you a meal," Penny says with sympathetic eyes.

He collapses into the closest empty chair, crossing his arms and ankles. The reverberation of so many people conversing bounces off the curved walls as commotion swirls around him. Waving her arms, a short, curvy, older woman with auburn hair shoos reluctant teenagers out. The two children from Reed cry out and rush into the barrel-chested man's arms as his teenage daughter stands silently close by. His eyelids feel heavy, and as Mal tunes out his surroundings, he closes his eyes for what seems like hours, but he realizes, in fact, is mere seconds when a familiar voice sounds.

"Mal, honey, are you okay?"

Alejo might be too much for Mal at this moment, but he opens his eyes to the man's warmhearted smile anyway as he sits down at Mal's table. He's wearing a pink T-shirt, wrapped in an off white, long-sleeved cardigan. The man he guessed was Sean earlier is wearing a clean plaid shirt and sitting down next to his partner. Alejo clings to him and says sweetly, "This is Sean. Thank you for rescuing him."

Mal remains silent but nods.

"You brought Gina in?" Sean asks, sounding concerned.

Mal eyes the medical door. "Yeah."

Sean leans in. "Is she going to be alright? We protested, demanded to see the women, but they wouldn't let us."

"By the look of her, I'd say what she went through is bad. She won't be alone tonight. I'll make sure of it."

Alejo places a hand over Mal's closed forearms. "If you need help, come find us in our apartment. They're all off the outer ring. The name on ours is Turner." He points through the nearest tunnel.

Mal won't need help but he wonders where he'll sleep once he's relieved of his duty.

"Mal." It's Ryker calling to him, but Mal doesn't have the energy to search for his brother. A moment later, Ryker plops down in the seat next to him. "We have a bedroom in Parker's apartment for you. It's through that tunnel and to the left. Name on the door is Livingston." Ryker's too chipper, but he can't blame him.

"Got it," Mal says. He doesn't remember the last time he was this tuckered out.

Ryker bounces back up and walks the way he'd just indicated. *Going to see Beth?* Mal envies his brother at that moment. He has a woman to come home to; someone soft and—

A tray of something that smells divine slides across the table in front of him. He sits up quickly and gazes at a bowl of soup and freshly baked bread. It looks positively heavenly. Then again, with how he's feeling, it could be porridge and he'd still think it the best meal ever. "Thanks, Pen."

She rubs his shoulders, coercing his eyeballs to roll upward in rapture. "I'll grab you some cookies and goat's milk to take back with you." Her hands trail along the top of his shoulders, leaving tingles behind as she heads back to the kitchen. Alejo takes over where Penny left off. Mal's head drops, relishing Alejo's gifted hands. *Damn, I need this.*

"Would you like some of my coffee?" Alejo asks with a purr in his voice.

He's a sweet-tongued devil. That would be the icing on the cake, and Mal might need to stay up, so he says, "I could go for some of that right about now."

The shoulder rub stops. Mal's muscles revolt as he opens his eyes to see Alejo standing over him, hesitating to say something.

"Spit it out," Mal growls, his eyes narrowing with suspicion.

"I'll get you some—" He pauses. "—if you let me trim this mess of hair you have going on."

And there it is, the sales pitch. Alejo is flighty but he's a shrewd entrepreneur underneath all that pink.

Mal doesn't even have the energy to combat that with a snarky remark. "Deal, but the top stays long." A gasp of joy and some clapping follows a draft as Alejo scampers to the kitchen, mumbling something about a bad-boy look. Mal scoffs. *I'm a nice guy.*

Sean grins. "It takes time to get used to Alejo, but he's got a good heart."

Mal glances at the kitchen. Like a boss, Alejo is fiddling with something behind the counter and chatting with everyone around him. Mal doesn't have the gift of easy conversation that Alejo does. He admires that. His eyes trail back to Sean. "You're a lucky man. He was distraught over losing you."

Sean's shoulders rise, and he shoots a loving gaze at Alejo. *Bingo. The right thing to say.* Mal stretches his arms out, feeling good about himself, and then aims his full attention on the food before him, hoping to finish as much as he can before Alejo comes back.

CHAPTER 53

"Donovan will be offline for a while. In the meantime, can you head our security?"

On the couch across from Parker, Ryker gazes at a picture on the living room wall of Beth with her sister, a butterfly in their hands. If someone had told him three weeks ago that he'd be sitting in a compound in the Idaho mountains, he wouldn't have believed them. So much has happened in the last twenty-four hours that Ryker knows he'll need time to adjust to this new life. A life with Beth, a boy who's growing on him, new friends, and brothers-in-arms. He wouldn't trade it for the world. "I can do that."

They have to protect the compound and their people from threats—*his people*—and serving a purpose brings him joy. Miles was right: the farming will be a challenge, but Ryker is up to the task.

"I'm glad Beth found you."

Ryker grins. "I'm lucky she said yes." At last. Only took an apocalypse for her to agree to date him, but he's not looking a gift horse in the mouth.

"Also, glad you didn't give up on her."

He wouldn't give up on her in a million years. Ryker knew, when they met, without a doubt, she was special. He wanted a date but has received so much more.

Neil, hair askew, slides into the living room on his socks. "Am I late?"

Kids bounce back so quickly on the surface. Ryker laughs and gazes up at the wall clock. "No, you have another hour before school."

"There's cereal in the kitchen and goat's milk in the fridge," Parker says.

Neil skips that way. "I can't wait! Henry and Robert will be there."

Parker introduced Neil to his young nephew last night. Since they'll be living in Haven for a while, Parker has enlisted Hoss's daughters-in-law, Lisa and Rita, who were teachers, to open the school. Ryker's happy Neil will bond with boys his age. He'll need friends.

"Beth sleeping?"

"Yeah," Ryker says. "She deserves it after what she's endured." He couldn't get Beth alone fast enough last night. During the ride across the river, Ryker helped secure Donovan but stayed close to Beth. He didn't realize how much the thought of losing her had been weighing on him. He never wanted Beth out of his sight again, and it surprised him how relaxed he felt when they finally entered the compound.

After dropping Donovan at medical and reconnecting with Mal, Ryker practically ran to the apartment he shares with his new family. Parker had steered Neil out of the apartment with the words "You've got an hour. Make it count."

Not wasting time, Ryker carried Beth straight into the bath. The bruises around her throat angered him, but he focused on the fact that she was safe now. He didn't want her lifting a finger and listened to her recount the last twenty-four hours while he spoon-fed her soup. She watched Ryker have a shower, then he gave her everything she wanted in bed. She was hungry, but not for food. A slow smirk graces Ryker's face at the thought.

Neil struggles to reach a bowl in the cupboard. Ryker heads that way, fetches it out, and hands a bowl to him. "Table. I'll get the milk and spoon."

They had come out later to find her friends waiting. Sean thanked Ryker for saving him and hugged Beth, who caressed Sean's new facial scar from a bullet graze. Alejo hugged Beth so tightly, she had to calm him down so she could breathe. He hugged Ryker, too; longer than necessary, but Ryker's learning this is how Alejo hugs. Though, he wouldn't put it past Alejo to use that as an excuse to hug his smokin' hot bod. *I mean, who can resist?*

Ryker slides a drawer open, pulls out a spoon, hauls the bottle of milk out of the fridge, and strolls to the kitchen table.

Everyone had gone quiet when Colin joined them all last night. Alejo unleashed the loudest gasp when Ryker walked over and man-hugged Colin. Neither of them explained it. After, Colin took Beth into his arms for another well-deserved hug. Ryker couldn't deny Colin that. Not now.

That's when Hoss had showed up, saying they had some more "work" to do. Ryker didn't want to leave Beth, but Parker said he'd stay with her. Ryker left Beth with her friends and the promise of "later."

Another smile plays across Ryker's lips as he places the milk next to Neil's bowl and sits down. After washing off the "work" they did, Ryker had stood in the bathroom doorway to their new room. During the night, Neil had climbed into bed with Beth. Ryker enjoyed the moment, knew he wanted more, and was glad he was going to have the chance to make them happen. Ryker enclosed Neil between them and, finally, conked out, but not before noticing the butterfly necklace wasn't around Beth's neck anymore. It was disappointing, but he would far rather have her safe than her necklace.

"Council meeting soon. I'll introduce you before we convene," Parker says.

Ryker ruffles Neil's hair. "Parker will take you to school, so stay here till we come back."

Neil unfolds paper airplanes from a box on the table next to his cereal bowl. "Yup."

As they walk out, Parker slaps Ryker on the back. "Oh, thanks for asking."

"Thanks for putting your trust in me."

***

Mal wakes disoriented in Gina's bedroom to the scent of Old Spice, like his father used, surrounded by bookshelves, stuffed animals, and photos, as well as wood that would impress any woman if he had one. With the dream he just had, he's not surprised. Despite camping out on Gina's bedroom floor, he hasn't slept so well in, hell, months. Prison was rougher this time around. Mal's hands stroke the softness of a blanket that wasn't there when he fell asleep. This tells him Gina didn't sleep well, and it reminds him of his mother. She used to check up on him and his siblings when she couldn't sleep.

Mal sits up, stretches, and eyes her sleeping peacefully on top of the sheets, still in her clothes. The sudden urge to touch her materializes, and he quickly squashes the thought. He slides to the chair instead and reclines against it. *She's been through so much.* Mal's heart tightens, knowing the road she's on. It won't be easy to get back on track.

Last night was a blur of activity after they crossed the river. It felt good carrying Gina, like he was doing something honest for once. She'd fallen asleep in his arms, and he'd swelled, satisfied by it, but not sure why.

Mal scans the room, noting how finished the walls are. *It's hard to believe we're in a cement bunker, hundreds of feet below the surface.* He's impressed by Haven. Mal hasn't seen it all, but Parker has built something remarkable and, considering what happened a few weeks ago, incredibly important.

He crosses the room into Gina's private bathroom. Mal does a double take at his reflection in the mirror, then remembers Alejo negotiated his coffee for a haircut.

Gina moans in her sleep, and the sound goes straight to his groin. Mal needs time and space to shake off this need he's feeling, so he leaves the bedroom in search of his boots.

After Henry brought her out of medical, Mal delivered a groggy Gina to the apartment she'll now share with her family. He figured once she had her siblings around her, his duty would be over. Mal knows a small part of him felt disappointed by this, even though he had no right to be. He spots his boots by the door, grabs them, and heads to the chair to sit down and pull his old socks out.

It was awkward when Gina wanted him to stay. Mal pointed out how they both would benefit from showering, thinking that would free him, but she offered her father's bathroom as an alternative and disappeared, leaving him hanging. Gina's three siblings didn't seem to mind, so he went with it. Not like the old man was coming home soon. The hot water soothed his sore muscles, and the lavish scent of the soap was heavenly. Felt fantastic.

Mal sniffs his socks, withdraws from the stench, and shakes his head. *Nope.* He tosses them in favor of the ones Gina laid out for him the night before.

That was another awkward moment. Mal glances down at the cable-knit sweater he's wearing and rubs the material between his fingers. He doesn't think he's ever worn anything this extravagant before or smelled so good, but when he walked out in them last night, Mal detected the loss in Gina's eyes and knew they were her dead husband's clothes, not the old man's. She looked fragile, alone, twisted in a blanket on the wraparound couch. He wasn't sure where her siblings were, but didn't want to impose himself. And yet, the moment Mal sat down out of reach, she slunk over and curled up into his arms. He'd stiffened, thinking this was the last thing she needed, but he then reasoned why. Gina hadn't mourned her husband yet. She needed Mal, trusted him, somehow, to give this to her.

The truth is, Mal liked the softness of her in his arms. And he couldn't deny her after what she'd gone through. *I can't leave her.* He'd made a promise.

Mal glances at the clock on her bedside table. It's too fucking early is what it says. *I'll search out the communal area for coffee before she wakes.* His stomach grumbles. *And food. She'll be hungry.*

Gina shifts, a contented noise slipping from her lips. The fragrance of her shampoo drifts over to Mal. He likes it too much. She's going to make this hard, being all cute and stuff. He sighs and, like the glutton he is, steals another moment for himself to watch her sleep.

***

"You can't go find Sadie! You don't know where she's at!" Hoss says, exasperated with his oldest child. It's like trying to talk a bull down while wearing red. Stubborn and hotheaded. *Like me.*

Even as a child, Liam was forging a separate path from the others. *Had to do things his way or get out of his way* kinda attitude. Hoss doesn't want his son to learn the hard way. The same attitude didn't serve Hoss well.

Liam looks at the kitchen table like he's lost in despair. On the wall behind him, around an American flag, are dozens of photos in small black frames. Hoss's late wife had arranged them. Among them is a familiar military shadow box with a photo of a younger version of Hoss inside it.

"How can I stay here when she's out there, Dad?"

So far, Hoss has deterred Liam, but this persistent idea of going after her is ludicrous. He loves Sadie, too, and wishes he could do something about it, but it was a mission that would only end in failure. "She can't be that far behind. Trust that Sadie will find her way, son." Hoss might have said that to ease his own fears.

Sadie's not the only one he'd like to rescue. After his conversation with Donovan, thoughts of his ex-wife occupy his mind. Is she safe? He has to trust that she is. *This bites.*

John Henry and his wife stroll into the apartment, hands clasped. They showed up at Reed unscathed with his daughter-in-law, Lisa. *Thank God, she was alright.* She's been distraught every day since, though. Hoss searches her out.

Lisa, with her long, curly, strawberry blonde hair and mournful, downcast eyes leans against the back wall, detached from everyone around her. Hoss's other two sons, Jessie and Steven, Lisa's husband, are grounded in Spain. *I may never lay eyes on my boys again.* He shreds up that depressing thought and refocuses on her. "Lisa, honey, how you doin'?"

She shrugs, preferring to keep her distance. Lisa's never been especially comfortable with how touchy-feely Hoss and his family can be.

"I want you to get over the shyness. You're my daughter, and we're your family."

Lisa breaks down and buries her face in her hands. Penny and Rita both reach out to her and envelop her in their arms.

Lisa grew up an orphan. Broke Hoss's heart when he found that out. *No child should be without love.* Hoss is like a dog with a bone when it comes to making people feel loved; he won't stop loving on her and telling her she's family. *For Steven.*

John Henry steps closer. "I know it's hard to be around me, but I know Steven's okay."

"How do you know?" Lisa wears her grief openly.

"We're twins. I just know."

Physically, Hoss's twins are identical; only those closest to them can tell them apart. As long as John Henry has good vibes, his Steven is safe.

CHAPTER 54

Parker steps into the atrium greenhouse. "Council time, you two."

Ryker and Sylvia both peer up from a discussion over different farming practices. She's a botanist, so between her knowledge and Ryker's farming experience, they should be able to benefit their growing community at Haven immeasurably. Ryker surveys the fifteen hundred square feet of tall vertical trays of seedlings rotating on conveyor belts. He breathes deeply of the smell of fresh dirt and the cool, moist air; a result of the constant watering of the seedlings. *Like the farm in Montana.*

Deep down, he loves farming. The idea of feeding oneself and being self-sufficient appeals to Ryker. The pride he would feel at the end of the harvest was like a drug for him. What he'd hated about farming was his stepfather's controlling nature, choking the fun out of the entire experience. Haven would be different.

"Yes, Parker, we're right behind you," Sylvia says, brushing her hands on her overalls. Two things strike Ryker about her: she's short and curvy in all the right ways, and she's intelligent and knows her mind. *Doc's a lucky man.* Sylvia smiles at him. "Off we go, then."

Colin saunters through in greasy coveralls. He's been working on a farm vehicle in Yard Three all morning. Ryker's not sure where their relationship is going, but he and Colin are currently enjoying a truce at the moment, and keeping the peace will help ease Beth's stress, so it's fine by him.

Sylvia glances up at Colin. "Were you able to find the problem with the combine?"

"Yes, ma'am. It was a simple fix."

"Oh, great," she says with delight.

***

"How are you holding up, Havier?" Beth asks Jose's eighteen-year-old son in an apartment that is very similar to Parker's. She's careful to keep her voice quiet.

He takes a moment and sighs at the table. Sadness hangs on Havier like a well-worn sweater. "I'm not strong enough."

Beth reaches to cover his hand with hers. "Strong enough for what?"

"I promised Mom."

The thought that Sophia didn't die right away pains Beth. "You talked to her?"

"Yeah. She...she thought Father might take his own life. Made me promise I'd take care of him."

Her heart deflates. It must have been quite an effort for Havier to get Jose here, along with his three younger siblings, knowing his father might hurt himself along the way. *Like me.* "Did you help your family get here?"

Havier furrows his brow. "Yeah."

"Did you protect them during the journey?"

"Yeah."

"Then you're strong enough. You'll get through this." *I did.*

"I want my father back." His voice cracks and lips tremble.

"He'll come back. Grief takes time." Beth wishes she didn't know that.

Havier breaks down, not able to stop his tears. "What if he doesn't? What if he—?"

She embraces Havier, not wanting to answer that or entertain the idea of Jose, a practicing Catholic, going against God to do something like that.

"Son."

They draw apart at the sound of Jose's voice from the bedroom door. Havier turns his head away and wipes his tears with his palms. "Yes, Father?"

The man at the door looks a shell of his former self; gaunt, with dark circles under mournful eyes. Beth stands. Recognition flashes in those eyes at the sight of her, then sadness shrouds Jose again.

She steps across the apartment and wraps compassionate arms around him. Jose's familiar smell reminds her of busy days at the diner, as well as staying with him during those first few Thanksgivings and Christmases after her own loss.

"Thank God, you made it, my Little Chickie. I'm afraid I'm a mess right now."

"That's okay. I was a mess once, remember?"

"Yeah, Sophia..." He hitches on her name, not wanting to say the rest, not able to make the leap yet, and wipes a few tears with his sleeve.

Beth understands this grief. "Jose, what did you say to me long ago in that hospital room?"

After she'd tried to end it, her BAMF dads rallied around her in the hospital, each of them saying their peace to her.

Jose doesn't answer. Instead, a small smile appears on his face. Hanging on that gesture, Havier sits up straighter with hope in his eyes.

"You said, 'We'll help you find your way. Family means no one gets left behind.'" She'll help Havier keep his promise to his mother.

"Or forgotten," Jose says, choking up.

***

The council convenes around Parker's kitchen table, and the first item wins a unanimous vote of support: a dinner-dance to raise spirits and help everyone let off some steam.

The last few weeks have been brutal. Parker understands now the fear families go through when their loved ones join the military. The waiting was one of the worst things he's had to experience. It still is. They still don't have everyone accounted for, and the longer they're absent, the more the mind loses hope, and his people need hope now more than ever. A light at the end of this hellish tunnel.

"We can't go around saving everyone or we'll run out of space," Parker says. He can't believe he was excited just a few weeks ago about seeing how Haven held up at half capacity, and now, there's no safety net.

"We could use Reed," Chaplain Isaac Tremblay says.

Isaac immigrated to the states from France as a teenager. "Frenchie" served the Marine Corps well as a military chaplain back in the day. Parker's glad his friend made it, given his frail health. Isaac's been a smoker most of his sixty years and has tried to quit several times over the course of their friendship. He's long been told to stop on account of his worsening cough. Now, with the way things are, Isaac might have to go cold turkey; his meager stockpile of Marlboros won't last long.

"She's our backup plan if we lose this place. No, we need to find another way in case it comes to it." Parker isn't willing to budge on this. Reed is half the capacity of Haven, and they already have fifty-two people here. If anything happened to Haven, and they had to go back to Reed, everyone would go mad with cabin fever if there were too many people.

Hoss locks hands with Penny's on the table. Parker's happy for his friend. He had a good life with Kathryn, but it's about time he moved on. Same for Penny. John was their brother, but she deserves to be happy.

"We should monitor the farmhouse over the river," Hoss says. "More will arrive in the comin' days."

Mal told them about Gideon's brother Wendall and that wherever he was, he would show up eventually with more people. Parker didn't like that this was their new neighbor.

Henry stretches his arm across the back of his wife's chair as Sylvia says to Hoss, "If women are being harmed over there, we have a responsibility to stop them."

Parker nods. He won't attack without just cause but he's not leaving anything to chance, either. Especially if they see any of their family across the river again.

Sylvia's brother, Peter Rush, and his family are still missing, and Parker prays for them. Civilization has to be lost to desperation and chaos by now. But he's equally concerned that any survivors will be traumatized when they arrive, which may create problems.

"Agreed. Ryker, you're setting up guard duty on the farm?" Hoss asks.

"Rotating shifts for now. Everybody who'll be farming is going to learn self-defense so that they can defend themselves while working outside." Ryker glances down the hall, toward the bedrooms.

Ryker has been one of the few pleasant surprises in all this. He knew he would always be wary of whoever Beth fell in love with and had just hoped there was a man good enough for her out there. Parker has to admit, Ryker being a Marine is helping to ease his mind. Plus, his brothers seem to have accepted Ryker, and he trusts their judgment without question.

He wonders if Ryker has had a hard time adjusting to civilian life. Parker thought he'd serve till they brought him home in a box, but it was not to be. His body had different plans, and he'd returned home with an edginess.

Penny turns to Isaac. "How's everyone doing, Father?"

"I've been counseling some of them."

They all need Isaac's counsel in these trying times. "How about the women brought in last night?" Parker asks.

Those men abused the four women in the worst way, and he can't stomach saying the word rape out loud. Parker's frustrated he can't help them personally. Isaac's the closest person they have to a psychologist—the only person qualified to give them guidance—but he's still a man.

"Settling in. Understandably, they're keeping to themselves."

Henry adds his two cents and says, "Melanie's a nurse. We've been discussing setting up a sexual abuse group for the women."

This eases Parker's anxiety somewhat, glad this Melanie is stepping up to help the ladies out. They deserve to feel safe.

"How's Donovan doing?" Penny asks Henry.

"A grumpy patient, but he'll mend."

"And Gina?"

Henry's been tight-lipped about it—doctor-patient confidentiality and such—but he eases their fears. "She's in excellent hands."

***

Gina's eyes flutter open to find she's still in her bedroom in Haven. *Safe?*

The kind man who cared for her comes into focus, standing in front of one of her bookshelves. She takes in his tall frame and notes the pink key chain that dangles out of place from his waist. *Brad was tall, too.* These random thoughts have danced through her head at odd moments since the rescue.

She visualizes Brad on his knees. The way he'd told her he loved her with his gorgeous eyes just before the bullet passed through his... Gina squeezes her eyes shut, willing the memory away. Gorgeous eyes she'll never see again.

She knows she hasn't been herself since. Gina's caged in a silent glass room, looking out at everyone, numb and uncaring, trapped with her last memories. Even when that horrible man touched her, Gina felt like she was having an out-of-body experience. *I should have fought more.*

She broke down in the shower last night as her sister looked on, witnessing Gina's shame. She was too young to help Gina. *I need Sadie.* On their way out of town, they'd spotted a few buses, but her older sister wasn't on any of them. Where Sadie is, she can't say, but she misses her terribly.

She refocuses on the stranger in her husband's clothes. She should be afraid but Gina feels...safe? It's the only way she can describe it. Still numb, but content that she's being protected. Like Brad would protect her.

The smell of food pulls Gina's eyes to the nightstand, where a tray of eggs and bacon perches, and steam curls from a mug. Anticipation flares. *God, I hope that's Alejo's coffee.*

Gina feels guilty for making this man stay. What was she thinking last night? If she could remember his name, Gina could send him on his way. *Starts with an M. Mel?*

***

Mal beholds a picture of the man he buried and the beauty sleeping behind him in happier times. *Handsome guy.* It's going to take time for her to find her footing again.

"Mal?"

"Yes." He tilts his head, liking the sound of his name on those lips, and replaces the photo on a shelf next to a folded, bright pink silk headscarf. It is an odd item to keep on a shelf.

"Where's Dad?" she asks.

Mal gazes into her deep brown eyes. *Arresting.* "Doc's taking care of him. I can take you."

A flicker of hope sparks. Of course she wants to see her dad. Mal wishes that he could see his father again, sometimes.

Gina tracks him to the chair, so he flicks his eyes around, trying to focus on anything but her. *Why am I nervous?* It's best if he stays away from her. Last night felt good. Too good.

As if Gina is reading his thoughts, she says, "You don't need to stay with me. I think I'm safe now."

Mal beholds a vision of her lying on her bed, warm and sensual, which reminds him he was sleeping here with her just a few hours ago. *Whoa boy, settle down.* Mal's eyes dart to the floor so he can focus on other thoughts. "I made a promise."

"A pinkie promise?"

Mal's smile lights up. *She remembers.* He raises his eyes, and life stirs in her brown depths, but guilt lingers there, as well. He should return her dead husband's clothes.

"How did you get here? I mean, who are you exactly?" Gina raises the coffee mug to her lips.

How did he get here? From jail to hiding out, finding his brother to losing a sister, and ending up in the good guys' camp, staring at a heart-stoppingly beautiful woman he shouldn't touch with a ten-foot pole. Life is cruel sometimes. "You know Beth?"

Gina tilts her head. "She's my best friend."

"She's with my brother."

"Hold up, what?" Gina bolts upright with a grin that pushes her cheeks out. "Beth has a guy? Tell me more."

Mal marvels at the love that travels across her face at this news and swallows down his fear. He wouldn't be able to trust anyone who looked at him that way. Love is always conditional, a tool to use and manipulate.

Glad he planted a smile on those gorgeous lips, Mal laughs and leans in, tilting his head.

Chapter 55
June 14, 2027

Beth surveys Haven's communal center as slow music fills the air. The tables have been shoved against the outer walls and decorated with tablecloths and potted plants from the atrium. Some people sit in conversation, while others walk around, mingling with each other and carrying drinks. On the dance floor, in the center, Alejo sways with Sean as Hoss nuzzles Penny. Laughter rings out as John Henry twirls his wife around.

"Hold your horses," Isaac says, queuing up music on the laptop in front of him as younger residents bombard him with requests for songs. Once he fulfills their demands, they run off to join their friends. He yells after them, "You don't know what good music is. The eighties rocked!"

Beth laughs.

"To William!"

She swivels her head to her BAMF dads, their glasses raised high in a toast as they throw back shots and slam them on the table, the sound echoing through the room. They've already managed to bury the table under a chaotic heap of glasses and alcohol. Donovan sports an arm sling and a head bandage and is lounging between Jose, Parker, Henry, and James. They aren't feeling any pain, she's sure.

Donovan wants to resume his duties, but the men have forced him to slow down; Ryker's happy to step in and handle security for the time being. Donovan's beard worries her. She's never seen him with one and fears he's letting himself go because of Sadie's absence.

But Beth's pleased that Jose has improved over the last week. He's cooking again and even whipped up the feast everyone ate tonight. Still dressed in black, though.

Donovan stands up, swiping at his face with his good arm. "I'm turning in, guys."

Parker leans back and stares up at him. "You not sticking around?"

"No. Not really in the mood."

"Sadie?"

"Yeah. Noticed Liam's MIA." Donovan sounds abrasive and cynical. He's been testy around Liam, and she's not sure why. Hoss doesn't take the bait and stays quiet, but Parker nudges Donovan.

She hasn't talked to Liam. He avoids everyone and throws himself into work like he did before the missiles. His discipline is clearly lacking, too, as he now wears a full beard and bears a striking resemblance to his father. Everything seems to be changing, and she's not sure if it's for the better.

Donovan ignores Parker's dressing down and slaps the backs of the men on his way out. Giddy children chase each other around him and through the dancers. The lights flicker for bedtime, and Beth glances around for Neil. Children object and pout loudly as parents either gather or chase after them, but Neil runs into Ryker's arms. She'll need to focus more on Neil and get him in a better head space. There's been so much upheaval in his life in the last month, but Beth's glad he's closer to Ryker. He'll need male role models now more than ever.

Ryker's been her rock since the day they arrived at Haven. He takes the day shift, then at night, they walk to the communal kitchen, where he tells her about his day. Beth has taken a job as the kitchen dishwasher and helps prep the food for everyone with Jose and Penny. She feels the loss of Sophia when she walks into the kitchen, but her memories keep her friend alive.

In the last week, the voice has gone silent. She's not sure if it's permanent, but it's something she wholeheartedly celebrates.

Alejo and Sean walk off the dance floor for a breather, so Beth wedges her way between them excitedly. "Show me, A!"

Alejo presents his hand, showing off a shiny new engagement band. "Alex made it out of a bullet for me. Isn't that amazing?!"

"Congratulations, you guys," she says, leaning into Sean. True to her promise, she cheered Alejo on until he made the move and proposed to Sean. The guys distracted Sean with some farming business up top so they could set everything up below. Alejo wanted it to be the two of them. Penny helped Alejo decorate their apartment with romantic candles and, in the absence of Jose, made them a meal. Alejo deserves to be happy, and she's sure Sean will give it to him in spades.

Beth searches across the expanse of the communal space for her own happiness and spots Ryker rubbing his hands. *Nervous?* It's been an effort for Beth to come down from survival mode and now worry nags her constantly. Colin strolls over to Ryker, leans in, says something, and settles in to check out the couples on the dance floor. Ryker replies, and Colin chuckles before sauntering away.

Something's up with those two. Beth doesn't understand what it is, but Ryker's pretty tight-lipped about it. *At least they're getting along.*

"Elena!" Uncle James yells out as his oldest daughter runs over to Ryker. He takes a knee and greets Elena at her level, which delights Beth. Ryker gets back to his feet as James approaches, and they talk. James takes Elena's hand in his and reprimands her for something.

As James scurries away, Beth approaches Ryker. "What was that about?" Ryker touches his lips to hers, and Beth tastes liquor. *I could go for more of those tasty kisses.*

"I suspect James has a little warrior in his brood."

Beth agrees with his assumption; Elena has always been a rebel. "Hmm." She eyes Neil nearby. "Okay, Little Man, time for bed, too."

"I'll take him."

"Oh, really?"

The rhythm of a tango song begins on the sound system, drawing her eyes back to the dance floor. The familiar tune brings Beth back to the nights she escaped her problems and felt the music flow through her. As if on cue, Colin strides across and holds his hand out to her. *I should say no.* She defers to Ryker, thinking he'll shake his head.

He greets her with an eyebrow wag. "Go for it. I'd love to see you dance," Ryker says, grinning from ear to ear.

What is going on? "What about Neil?" Beth asks, gazing at the boy.

"Oh, I think Neil will be okay for one more song." Ryker turns to Neil. "You want to see her dance?"

"Yes, please," he says, pleading with a toothy grin.

She glances from Neil to Ryker. *Something isn't right.* Across the room, Alejo jumps up and down, distracting her. Sean tries to contain his exuberance, but it's like holding a floaty underwater that keeps coming back up. Beth laughs at them. Alejo always enjoyed watching her dance with Colin. "Are you sure?" she asks Ryker.

A serious expression replaces his nervous smile. "Never been surer in my life."

Okay, now something is seriously wrong. What the heck?

Beth glances back at Colin, who is waiting patiently. She slips her hand into his warm one and lets Colin lead her to the center of the dance floor. People clear the way for them. *Something is afoot. Why is everyone watching?*

Beth falls into the habit of the tango and remembers why she loves dancing with Colin. She smiles at him, loving the ebb and flow. They part. She saunters away, then turns...to see Ryker down on one knee, with Neil beside him, barely containing his giggles behind a tiny hand.

Oh my God! Beth covers her face with her hands. Alejo's questions about Beth's proposal dreams make so much more sense now. No wonder Sean couldn't contain him. Her eyes narrow in Alejo's direction. *I'm going to kiss you later for this.*

The music stops, and the crowd laughs, then settles in anticipation. *Does everyone know but me?*

"Beth—" Her name on Ryker's lips calls her back to him. "—I'm not the romantic type. But this happens when I'm around you." Ryker blows out a nervous breath under the encouragement of the audience.

Beth bites her bottom lip to hold back her smile. *He's so handsome, and he's all mine.* "I owe you a secret. Something I couldn't say till now."

Beth senses his disquiet, but something stirs in the depths of his brown eyes, something solid and unwavering, and she prepares herself.

"I loved you the moment you came out of that kitchen back at the diner, all messy and flustered."

Beth chokes back her surprise. Love at first sight? *Oh, my...*

"My heart seized. On some level, I knew you were the one for me, knew I was in trouble." Ryker dips his head. He struggles with words he wants to say, then he rallies and glances back up at her like she's the only one in the room. It's one thing she loves about him. Tears tickle her eyes. "My love for you is so powerful, it scares me.

"Parker welcomed me to the club."

Beth's watery eyes connect with Parker, the other man in her life who loves her to death. Ryker asked Parker for permission to date her once things had settled down in Haven a little. Cart before the horse, but Beth doesn't care. She is finally happy. Embarrassed, Parker swipes at his face with his sleeve. *My badass softy.*

"Alejo and Sean thought it would be fun if I learned to tango." Ryker's eyes widen with disbelief.

Beth bursts out laughing, along with everyone else. She can't see that happening but would have enjoyed it.

"After that disaster, Colin came up with Plan B."

Beth catches sight of Colin blowing her a kiss through her tears. Her protector and friend whom she loves, just in a different way. One day, he'll find the one, and she'll be so happy for him.

Ryker tugs Neil to his chest. "Beth, will you do me the honor of being my badass girl, the mother of our Neil, and the keeper of our hearts?"

His words chip away at her ability to keep it together. *Could this get any better?*

Ryker and Neil hold out their open palms. Beth smiles down at Neil as he presents her with a bullet ring, like Alejo's, but then she sucks in a sharp breath when she sees the second ring in Ryker's palm; his sister's ring. *I'm going to cry.* "Oh, Neil, Ryker. Yes, yes, and yes!"

Ryker slips Libby's ring on her shaky finger, jumps up, kisses her teary cheeks with nervous lips, and plants a mind-blowing kiss on her. The room and onlookers disappear. Beth tastes spicy liquor, and her toes curl in anticipation of the promise of later.

Neil wiggles in between them with a familiar exclamation. "Ew." He places the bullet ring on her finger. Ryker lifts him up, and they sandwich Neil's cheeks between their lips under his happy protest. Beth realizes the dream she imagined of her man and her enjoying their son between them isn't a dream anymore. *Finally.*

***

Colin watches from the back wall with his hands in his pockets as Hoss joins him. Hoss is an excellent teacher. Not very patient, but knowledgeable. He's growing on Colin.

Hoss is wearing a wicked grin. *Here it comes.* "That was a very sensual dance. Did Ryker lose a bet?" Hoss asks sarcastically.

If you call saving his ass for Beth, then yeah. Dancing with her was both heaven and hell. Colin rubs the smooth surface of her necklace in his pocket. He's been waiting for the right moment to give it back. It hasn't presented itself yet. Until then, he's going to keep this piece of her for himself. It will take time to get over her, if he ever does.

Deflection is best with Hoss, he finds. Hiding his thoughts, Colin grins. "Something like that. You going to tell me why you lost yours?"

Hoss glances down at the floor in thought. "My first wife was in love with another man, but she married me."

Harsh. Colin turns to Hoss in shock.

In a somber tone, he continues. "Married too fast, had children too young; the marriage was over before the honeymoon began. Six years in, I lost my wife and kids to the other man."

He sees himself in me. At a loss for words, Colin says, "I see."

Hoss winks, smiles broadly, and slaps Colin's back. "Don't be discouraged, 'cause I found the girl of my dreams twice more. Got seven more kids to prove it."

Colin must be wearing his thoughts for all to see, because Hoss hands him encouraging words. "You'll find yours. It just won't be the one you thought."

***

A demanding tap pokes Beth's shoulder. "Move over, Superman," Hoss says as he and Penny move in to steal warm hugs. "Congrats, my Chickie."

Beth laughs at Hoss's choice of shirt. He's wearing a black T-shirt with the imprint of a fake tux on it. "Wow, Hoss!"

"Hey, this is my best formal shirt!"

The music starts up, and Penny bends down to Neil. "Okay, Little Man, let's see your moves."

Beth mouths *Thank you* as Penny leads Neil into the throng of the dancers.

Alejo high-fives Ryker and crushes him with a hug. "That was amaze-balls! Told you, you could do it."

Ryker eyes Hoss and pulls Beth back into his arms. "Well, I plan on doing that only once. I can dodge bullets and fight when I'm outnumbered, but that was nerve-racking as all..." He bends in and whispers, "Fuck."

Everyone within earshot laughs heartily.

Parker presents a bottle of Dom Perignon. "I was saving this for a rainy day. Guess this day is as good as any other," he says with a devilish smirk.

Beth laughs at his wisecrack and hugs him. "It's the perfect day!"

FLEE: BOOK TWO OF THE HAVEN SERIES PREVIEW

Prologue

Under the warm sun, Sadie Masters reclines on a lounger, her red bikini top untied, while she indulges in the electronic dance rhythm streaming from the wireless speaker. Today, she aced her Grade-12 English final, so to celebrate, Mark invited her to hang out on his balcony for some downtime.

She's not sure what to classify him as. Friend? Maybe a friend with benefits? She hasn't gone past first base with him, so she's not sure about the benefits part. Does she even want benefits from him? She feels ready, but...

Last week, she and a few friends got their hands on fake IDs and headed out to the clubs for some fun. Mark and his roommates were letting off steam after finishing their college semester and bought the girls drinks. One thing led to another, and they've been having a good time, seeing each other under the radar. Her dad wouldn't approve.

"Shit!" She reaches out and checks her phone. *Five minutes late...* She was supposed to meet him at the playground after she "finished homework at a friend's house."

"Mark, do you see Dad's Silverado out there?"

"No, the coast is clear."

Sadie sits up, clutching her skimpy unlaced top, and scoots over into Mark's lap. "Can you do me up?"

"I'd like to not do you up soon." His hands slide up the curve of her hip before he draws her long auburn hair aside and kisses her shoulder, causing her to shrink and giggle.

"I don't want Dad to kill you," she blurts out, then kicks herself for sounding like Daddy's little girl instead of the independent woman she wants to be.

"Your dad can't be that bad?!"

Sadie stares him down. *He'd eat you alive?* "I brought this guy home once in tenth grade. Let's just say, I'm on the no-fly list at school because of him. He spread around whatever it was Dad said to him, and my social life died there and then."

After that incident, her dad had imposed even more rules, restricting her movements after school until any time with her friends had all but dwindled away. *Sometimes, it sucks being the oldest.*

That's when the arguments started. Her mother said they fought because they were too alike. "Stubborn as mules," she'd said. Sadie thinks someone's stubborn, but it's not her.

A year ago, she disobeyed her father, walked out, and met up with her girlfriends at a nearby house party. Fifteen minutes later, to Sadie's astonishment, her father marched in, grounded her in front of everyone, and dragged her out. The ensuing fight between them has achieved legendary status within the rest of the family. After the yelling match and her mother's intervention, each retreated to their respective corner of the home to the sound of slamming doors.

Sadie later learned her father had found her at the party by tracking her through her phone. The humiliation shook her to the core and fueled her to go underground, but she assumes even her dad realized he'd gone too far. Ever since changing her password and ditching the tracker, he has kept himself at arm's length.

"Can you make it tonight?" Mark's breath skims across her skin, enticing goosebumps to rise.

Sadie closes her eyes and shivers through the sensation. "I'll text you when I can get away." She stands, bends, and kisses him on the cheek, then skips through the balcony's sliding door.

With her ponytail swaying, Sadie hurries out of Mark's apartment building, hoping she is portraying a prim and proper schoolgirl, with a bag slung on her back and a conservative T-shirt and blue jeans hiding her tan lines. She bites the inside of her cheek to keep herself from scowling. She can't wait to graduate, get accepted to a university, and ditch the image to get out from under her father's tyranny.

"You might as well stay here," a deep voice says with a calmness she recognizes.

Caught!

Sadie spins and takes in a young man's lean, athletic body. He is resting against a primer-painted-black Ford Bronco, eyes down, thumbing his cell.

"Liam?" Excitement rushes through her, causing the butterflies to flutter. For a moment, she's frantic, but after peering around, she realizes he's alone. Her shoulders relax. *Where did he come from?* Last she was told, Liam was stationed overseas.

Heated blue eyes connect with hers. Sucked in, she swallows. Nothing's changed; he's still the one for her.

"Glad you noticed me," he says dryly.

She feels the sting, though she doesn't know why. "Sorry. I was looking for Dad's truck."

His golden, shaved head tilts to the truck. "Came in Dad's Bronco." He points his chin in the opposite direction, towards the park. "They're in there, looking for you."

Liam acts disinterested, like he's just along for the ride, but she knows better. He didn't need to come with them, but he did. To prove her theory, she deposits her school bag by the front of the Bronco and saunters closer to him. He shifts uncomfortably, but his eyes don't leave hers.

Theory proven.

Playing coy, she tilts her head, displays her neck, and clasps her hands behind her back. "When did you get here?"

"About fifteen minutes ago," he says, his voice neutral, although his gaze is mischievous.

She throws what she hopes is a cute smile. "No, I mean stateside."

He gazes back down at his cell, driving distance between them. Liam's been serving as an active-duty Navy corpsman, and he's filled out since she last saw him…in delicious ways. *He's certainly not the skinny guy who enlisted three years ago.*

"Yesterday," he says through twisted lips. She's known him long enough to know he's conflicted, hesitating to speak. So, she remains silent. "Who's the guy?"

Sadie's eyes dart towards the building and back. "Just a friend."

With a serious tone, Liam says, "Looks like more than just a friend."

That sounds like a smidgen of jealousy, but she's uncertain. Liam's so guarded around her that she's never really known if he likes her or not.

"Sadie? Thought we were meeting you at the playground?" comes her father's disapproving voice from a short distance away.

She flinches and turns towards the park. She would feel intimidated if she didn't recognize the two men approaching them on the path. At six foot two, muscular and clean-shaven, Donovan Masters walks with purpose while wearing a scowl.

Clocking in at five foot nine, her father's best friend and military brother, Eric "Hoss" Jenkins, swaggers with a devilish smile, holding his arms out. "Hey, Sadie girl. Come in for a squeeze." Hoss scoops her up and twirls her around amid squeals of delight.

She bursts out laughing at his shirt, which says *Cuddle Straps* and displays arrows pointing at his fully rounded biceps. After she gets off the Hoss ride, Sadie points her doe eyes at her father in apology. "Sorry, Dad."

As they called a truce a month ago, she figures her fond look will work on him. Sure enough, he sighs and loses the scowl for an okay-you're-forgiven look. "Next time, text. Get in. Mom's got dinner waiting."

Ever the gentleman, Liam picks Sadie's bag up and gestures for her to get in the truck. Once she's settled in the backseat, he places her bag between them, much to her displeasure. He always hides behind something when she's around, and she's beginning to think he doesn't like her as much as she likes him. A few scars he didn't have before stand out on his strong, tanned hand. What would he do if she laid hers over his? Would he accept the warm gesture, or would it be too weird?

Hoss's Bronco rumbles to life, and he cranks the tunes.

Eyes glued to his phone, Liam leans across the bag, enticing her with his sweet-scented aftershave, and says, "Nice bikini."

Smart. He waited till Dad couldn't hear.

Sadie smirks. "Glad you noticed me."

Liam looks directly at her. "I always notice you, Auburn."

Hearing his personal nickname for her on his lips causes her to clench her legs as a zing of pleasure surges through her. *Maybe there's hope after all.*

Acknowledgements

Creativity truly requires a community to flourish as we navigate life's challenges. There are many to thank for their unwavering support throughout this particular adventure:

The most important is my family—the ones who listened to my adventures, supported my writing journey, and helped to shape my story: my husband, Dave, whom I love dearly; my two sons, Darren and Jack, for landing kisses on my forehead while I typed away; and my parents and extended family for giving me my roots and, in turn, the strength and courage to jump into this arena.

My late mother-in-law, Karen, for recounting stories about her second husband's military career in the British Army during WW1 and the SAS.

My biggest cheerleader is my beautiful cousin, Julia, to whom this book is dedicated, and who has always encouraged me to write. She's been there from the beginning and witnessed my journey through several rewrites, and I know she'll be by my side for the next creative adventure.

My incredible sisterhood of friends, some of whom I've known since kindergarten, has always been there to support and encourage me: Rebecca, Nadia, Sonia, Shawn, Anne, Lisa, Tammy, and Marcy.

Jeffrey, to whom I gave but a few chapters to read. His one complaint: "Where's the rest of it?"

In the writing trenches, I found my tribe: authors and writers in various stages of their careers. They've encouraged me to forge on and write and followed my social media since my first post: Kate and Dayna, we just clicked; Alexa, who runs Women in Publishing, you are a beautiful, giving human being; My BLAB writing group—Shimon, Rebecca, and Leoma; My WIP group—Janelle, Jeanne, Dayna, and Penni; and My Women Authors of Dystopian and Post-Apocalyptic Fiction ladies—Denise, Caitlin, and Christie.

My editor, Dan Cross, for giving me permission to accept that one day this would become a reality. I look forward to continuing our editing adventures in the future.

My designer, Tim Barber, who rocked this cover.

We've zoomed online many times, but Emily, you are my rock star.

Brittany, a writer and the military spouse of a Marine, shines for me with her daily motivations, acronyms, and friendship.

Navy Corpsman Mr. Huckabee for his insights and wealth of knowledge. So many scissors stumped me, and I'm glad I asked the question.

Tom Breeze, a US Army veteran, for his patience in answering all my questions.

And finally, my respect goes out to all those who serve, regardless of country.

About the Author

Tracy embodies the spirit of a modern-day Renaissance woman. As a writer, she weaves enchanting tales that captivate hearts and minds. Her journey began amidst the pages of her local library, where she discovered the magic of storytelling. From those humble beginnings, Tracy's imagination soared as she penned her own medieval fantasy epic.

But Tracy's creativity knows no bounds. Alongside her writing, she explores a kaleidoscope of artistic expressions—painting, drawing, quilting, and photography are all canvases for her boundless imagination.

Beyond her artistic pursuits, Tracy finds solace and joy in uncovering the rich tapestry of her family's history. It's a journey that fuels her passion for storytelling, inspiring her to craft narratives both old and new.

With each passing day, Tracy's excitement for the future grows. She eagerly anticipates the adventures that lie ahead as she steps into her role as an author, ready to share her unique vision with the world. In Tracy's world, every day is an opportunity for creativity, discovery, and boundless joy.

Visit Tracy's website at www.tracymyhre.com.
Or follow her on:

- Instagram: https://www.instagram.com/tmyhrewriter/

- Facebook: https://fb.me/tmyhrewriter

- Pinterest: https://www.pinterest.ca/tracymyhreauthor/

- Tiktok: https://www.tiktok.com/@tmyhrewriter?lang=en